THE
VOTER
FILE

THE VOTER FILE

DAVID PEPPER

DISCARDED

G. P. PUTNAM'S SONS

NEW YORK

PUTNAM
— EST. 1838 —

G. P. PUTNAM'S SONS
Publishers Since 1838
An imprint of Penguin Random House LLC
penguinrandomhouse.com

Hardcover ISBN: 9780593083932
Ebook ISBN: 9780593083949

Printed in the United States of America
10 9 8 7 6 5 4 3 2 1

Book design by Nancy Resnick

To Mom and Dad, my first and most loyal readers

THE
VOTER
FILE

PROLOGUE

Even though the HR director had just fired her, a smile was dangerously close to emerging across Kat's face. So she fixated on the woman's cold eyes.

Problem solved.

"You will get one month's pay if you sign this, but because you were here for such a short time, I'm afraid that's all," the director said, frowning, those eyes narrowing.

"I guess that's better than nothing," Kat said. "It will help me get through this."

The final termination had come quickly, following months of effort. The dour chief operating officer had called Kat into his office after lunch to make clear that this was her last day. He hadn't been nasty about it, but firm. He wasn't going to change his mind.

Good.

She'd cleaned out her desk; sorted through her files; and handed over her work cell phone, office keys, ID badge, and a list of log-in names and passwords. The few personal effects she'd kept in her cubicle lay in the brown Coach purse resting between her legs. And now came the final step: signing the agreement where they'd commit not to disparage one another. This required her to concentrate for a few moments more, not on the words of the HR director, but on leaving the impression that she was upset.

If they only knew. Mere disparagement was the least of their worries.

"I'm so sorry this didn't work out for you, Kat." The HR director leaned over the cheap desk to present Kat with the signature page.

"I'm sorry, too."

She'd never gone by the nickname "Kat" in her life, but it was another way to appear younger and less professional. Ordinary. Just as she'd spent the last seven months hunched over, in flats, hiding her otherwise striking five-foot-ten-inch frame.

"It was the job of my dreams."

Was she overdoing it? Landing the job had been easy, even after she'd dumbed down her résumé. A summa cum laude Princeton grad with an Oxford PhD could pull down a killer salary at her pick of Fortune 500 companies, so why would she want to make peanuts as the party's deputy data director? That would've been a red flag. So her résumé instead touted a North Florida degree with a decent academic record and an impressive history of political activism, enough to land an entry-level post.

She'd mastered the ins and outs in a matter of weeks. Pretty basic stuff—nothing like the jobs she'd held since earning that Oxford diploma. But she'd pretended to catch on slowly, convincing the data director, Emmett, that she needed help. His zealous touching as he man-splained the systems to her reminded her of several handsy professors she'd fended off.

She'd constructed the backdoor in a matter of months. Building it had been the easy part. The tough part had been making sure they could open and close it without a trace, so they'd be able to do their important work from the outside, undetected. Once she'd accomplished that, another month of tests confirmed that it was foolproof.

And that's when she'd first acted up. Showing up late. Alcohol on her breath after lunch. Unprofessional attire. Outbursts on phone calls. Loud crying.

At first the changes led to anxious glances from coworkers. Their faces had said it all: she must be having a rough go of it. Maybe a bad breakup. Cut her some slack. Even Emmett kept his distance.

After a few weeks, the COO, joined by the same HR director who now stared at her, had summoned her to share his displeasure. She explained she was battling personal demons and vowed to do better. But she started up again the next day, arriving late, coming unglued by 11:30, never re-turning after lunch.

That was three weeks ago. And yesterday morning's crying fit had topped them all.

"Well, you have a bright future," the director said as Kat pretended to carefully review the words of the signature page. "Emmett says you're a fast learner. You just need to work out the personal stuff."

She zeroed back in on those miserable, deep-set eyes. *Don't laugh.* Emmett, the data director, calling *her* a fast learner?

"I'm doing my best."

She sniffled, prompting the director to pass her a Kleenex. She dabbed it below the thin square lenses she had grown accustomed to over the past seven months.

"It's . . . just been so hard."

She put the Kleenex down, picked up a blue ballpoint pen from the desk, and signed the last page. Without saying a word, she stood up, care-ful to hunch over.

"Good luck," the director said as Kat walked out of the room. "You need a ride home?"

"I'll take an Uber."

Kat lifted her personal iPhone from her purse and tapped a few keys as if summoning the car service. But she sent a text instead.

Come in 5. Put the logo in the window.

She'd already informed him hours ago that it was her last day. And to bring her bags for the long trip home.

Drizzle fell lightly as Kat waited outside the building's main entrance. The white dome of the Capitol beamed from a few blocks away, making the gray skies around it even more foreboding. A fitting omen.

The black Range Rover pulled up, a spotless "U" sticker in its right rear window. She stepped over a puddle and squeezed her long, thin body into the back seat.

As she closed the door, big brown eyes under dark, bushy eyebrows peered at her through the rearview mirror. He pulled the car into the one-way street, then mumbled something in his native tongue.

"Please," she said. "I'm rusty."

"All good, Katrina?" he said, switching to a thick-accented English. *Oll goot?*

Katrina. Her mood lifted as she heard her full name again. Her real name.

The smile that had been billowing up finally escaped as Katrina took off her glasses and placed them in the tan Birkin bag awaiting her in the other passenger seat. She transferred the contents from the Coach purse into the tan bag, tossing the cheap purse to the floor once it was empty. Reaching back with both hands, she loosened the ponytail she'd worn every day for months, shaking her head side to side so her wavy, sandy-blond hair flowed to its natural length, inches above her waist. Then she kicked off her shoes.

"All good," she said. "You have my bags?"

"Yes."

"All of them?"

"All of them."

"Shoes?"

He reached over to the front passenger seat, then handed back the black three-inch heels she'd stored in the rear of her closet.

She admired the stilettos before sliding them under the high arches of her feet.

"Did Natalie already leave?"

"Two days ago. Same flight. They yelled at her before she left."

Her lips curled in amusement. "Not me. I was just a mess they didn't want to deal with." She was talking more to herself than to the driver.

She sat in silence for the next forty minutes, taking in the last views of a city she hadn't been able to enjoy. The teeming streets of Georgetown. The gray waters of the Potomac, sliced by long white lines as rowing sculls skimmed toward Key Bridge. The glass jungle of downtown Arlington, thousands of windows staring back over the river. It was a long way from the grungy Brooklyn streets and shores of her childhood.

They pulled up along the lengthy curb of Dulles Airport minutes after five, only her second time at the oddly shaped terminal. The first time—her arrival—felt like yesterday. But if the seed she'd planted since then grew according to plan, her third visit would be to a city—and a country—turned upside down.

"Would you like help with your bags?" the driver asked after bringing the SUV to a stop.

"Of course."

She stepped inside the terminal doors with the tan bag in her hand, followed by the driver lugging three calf-leather suitcases behind him. He waved down a baggage handler to take them the rest of the way.

The driver saluted as he stepped back toward the idling car. "Have a pleasant trip. Please give my best to Natal—"

"Where to?" the handler asked from her other side, laying all three bags on his cart.

"Air France. The seven forty flight to Paris."

PART 1

CHAPTER 1

EIGHT MONTHS LATER

PLEASANT PRAIRIE, WISCONSIN

Jack Sharpe? Wait, aren't you like some kind of famous celebrity?"

In this dark cave of a bar, the third Yuengling was definitely taking me where I wanted to go. That, and the sweet simper my auburn-haired bartender flashed as she enunciated my name—she must've seen it on my credit card—whittled away at my weeks of gloom. While this road trip offered me one last opportunity to get off the mat, hours behind the wheel had only meant more time to dwell on how I'd fallen facedown in the first place.

"Well, I'm on television sometimes, if that's what you mean."

I downed the rest of the beer before setting the empty bottle on the sticky mahogany countertop.

She popped the cap off a fourth Yuengling and slid it my way.

"Weather guy?"

"Not that bad. Politics. You ever hear of Republic News?" I took a deep swig from the fresh bottle.

"That's right. I see you on that TV all the time. Up there." She pointed across my shoulder. "With her."

I spun around on the barstool.

Between two mounted flat-screen TVs showing college football, she appeared on a smaller screen—the second-to-last person I wanted to see. Anchor Bridget Turner was interviewing someone about something, words scrolling along the bottom, the Republic News logo beaming in the corner. The sight sunk my mood to where it'd been when I'd stumbled into the place.

"Yep, that's me."

I forced a smile as I turned back to the bar.

"Well, that's cool. So what the heck's a TV big shot like you doin' here?"

"Drinking more than I should, thanks to you," I said, downing another gulp.

"Not here. *Here*, silly," she said, pointing down at the countertop. "Wisconsin."

She topped off two dirty martinis for a couple to my right, then stepped back my way.

"We in the press need to get out to the heartland every once in a while, don't you think?"

Her eye roll made clear that the evasive schtick bored her. So I played it straight.

"I'm actually here for a story."

"What story? Nothing big ever happens around here." She flipped her hand forward. "Did some banker kill his wife or something?"

"You've been watching too much *Dateline*," I said, chuckling, before finishing off the bottle. "No one killed anyone. It's about a recent election. But it didn't happen here. I've still got a few hours to go. This was—"

"The first exit after the state line. Trust me, that's most of our business here. Want another?" She reached into the cooler behind her.

"Sure. But that's the last one. . . . And you should give your town more credit. How could I *not* stop in a place that sounds as nice as Pleasant Prairie?"

But she was right. After a quick trip across northern Ohio and Indiana, the mind-numbing traffic, endless construction, and back-to-back tolls of Chicagoland had slowed my progress. North of Chicago, heading up I-94, I'd hoped Lake Michigan's western shore would liven up the journey. But the only hint of a nearby body of water had been five seagulls pecking at scraps at the Lake Forest rest stop where I'd stopped for coffee. That final blast of caffeine propped me up only temporarily before I dozed off again, forcing me to crank up the radio and slap my cheeks to stay awake. Then came more construction, an endless series of outlets, strip malls, and office parks—still no lakefront—until a big blue sign welcomed me to the Badger State. Although I'd set the outskirts of Milwaukee as my finish line for the day, when a water tower featured the name Pleasant Prairie, I'd exited the highway.

It was time to drop any airs.

"Truth is, I'm from a small town myself. Lived in Ohio most of my life. I feel a lot more at home in a real place like this than in the big city. So, whatever the reason, it's damn nice to be here."

She nodded. "I moved back for the same reason. It's slower going for sure, but I'm good with that. And it's been a much better place to raise my son."

She was getting to me. Her ring finger, I saw, was empty. Like me, she'd likely toiled through the challenge of single parenthood.

"I know the feeling. My son, Scott, is out in California kicking ass, and I'm convinced our days back in Youngstown are the main reason why."

She leaned toward me, brushing her wavy, thick locks away from her olive eyes. "I'm sure his dad had something to do with his success." Her tone had lightened.

"Hardly. I'm impressed he overcame my deeply flawed genes."

"Ha! That's how I always felt. And now my Hank is about to graduate from med school."

"Now, that's impressive. Well done, Mom." I lifted my almost empty bottle in front of me. "Here's to overachieving kids making their parents look good."

We talked a while longer. Turned out Rhonda and I had a lot in common. Varsity athletes in college. Dysfunctional early marriages that had produced messy divorces but impressive sons. If single fatherhood had added speed bumps to my path as a journalist, single motherhood had cut short her sports medicine career. And we'd both endured the doldrums of post-divorce dating life. Of course, I left out a lot, especially my recent career implosion.

"You know something?" Rhonda asked as I closed out my tab.

"What's that?"

"A lot of assholes come through here."

"I bet they do." I'd seen it all as a bouncer in college, but no one got it worse than the women behind the bar. "Must be a daily occurrence."

She nodded, a smile lifting the corner of her lips. "And I figured you'd be the biggest asshole of all."

I feigned a frown but knew enough TV personalities to understand why she'd assume that.

"But you weren't even close!"

I couldn't help but laugh with her. "That's a real ego boost. Thank you."

An awkward silence passed. She smiled again. "I get off in an hour. Any interest in meeting up?"

If I'd stopped at two beers, maybe I would've declined. But I was well past that, enjoying our rapport, feeling liberated. So why not keep it going?

"Can I borrow that pen?"

She tossed a black plastic pen across the bar's worn countertop. I removed a business card from my wallet, crossed out the official email and work number, and scrawled my personal cell phone number on the top. As Rhonda watched out of the corner of her eye, I laid the card back on the bar, next to the unsigned credit card receipt.

As seconds passed, my stomach muscles fluttered. My body tensed.

I stared back down at the card. The Republic News logo, my name, my scrawled number. I lifted the card back up, squeezing it by its edges. I'd purposely left the impression that I still worked there, something she'd probably already seen through. If not, she'd figure it out quickly.

I thought about Alex. Weeks ago I'd been on the verge of proposing. Now here I was, scribbling my number on a business card for a complete stranger.

I put the card back in my wallet. I reached for the black pen again, signed the credit card slip, and walked out of the bar.

The chimes on my iPhone rang for what seemed like an hour. I'd slept for some fraction of the night, but it didn't feel like it now. In fact, this was one of those rough mornings that had prompted me to switch my ringer to chimes to begin with—far easier on hangovers than the blaring truck horn I'd used for years. But the pain would be coming soon.

I opened my eyes.

The light in the room bored into my head like a drill bit. Staring straight up, flat on my back, I squinted to bring into focus the blurry patterns of the stucco ceiling.

Concentrating, I reconstructed my bearings. Days Inn. First stop in Wisconsin. Pleasant Field—no . . . Pleasant Prairie. Two and a half hours from Appleton.

Moments of the night came back to me. The Yuenglings. Bridget Turner. The bar talk. The smile. More Yuenglings. The card.

Using my elbows as crutches, I lifted myself to a seated position, then pivoted to my left, tossing my legs over the side of the bare mattress. Even small movements amped up the throbbing in the front half of my skull, a hammer pounding against my temples from the inside. My mouth was dry, the back of my throat pinched terribly tight. I labored just to swallow. When I did, I tasted stale beer. I nearly gagged, but a quick cough headed it off. Recent practice made perfect.

I must've jumped in bed quickly, because my clothes were strewn across the floor. But it was only when I picked up my phone that I discovered the one other thing I'd done before falling asleep.

I'd texted her at 11:40 p.m.

Alex, you there?

Alex Fischer was still back in Washington. Still at Republic. Seeing Bridget Turner, or the near miss with Rhonda, or both, must've triggered my outreach to the woman whose ring I had sized only eight weeks ago.

Alex, I'd written again at 11:48 p.m. I miss you.

Eleven fifty-four p.m. My final text. No response.

"Way to go, Romeo," I muttered to myself, shaking my head. "Move the hell on."

My temples flared again as I stood up and walked into the small bathroom. I downed a glass of water, chased it with a second, then stepped into the shower for ten ice-cold minutes.

Heading north from Pleasant Prairie, my hopes for a bucolic Wisconsin drive faded fast: Milwaukee-area construction proved as aggravating as Chicago's, mountains of gravel stacked along the highway for miles. Past Milwaukee the road finally opened up, but fireworks, adult stores, and billboards promoting both of those things dotted the route. And despite three Tylenols, two cups of Bob Evans black coffee, and four bottles of water, it wasn't until I hit Fond du Lac, on the southern tip of Lake Winnebago, that my headache eased.

Like the texts to Alex, every mile I traveled provided an unwelcome reminder of how far I'd fallen. A desperate drive—from the cobblestone streets of Georgetown to the tree-lined boulevards of Appleton by way of Youngstown—for a long shot of a story.

But as I passed Oshkosh, I reminded myself that it was my only lead left. And in the news business, once you're out of a job, the leads quickly run dry.

If I was going to claw myself back to professional relevance, this Hail Mary was all I had.

CHAPTER 2

APPLETON, WISCONSIN

Tori Justice groaned through every minute of her shower.

The warm water wasn't able to assuage the fresh bruises forming on her body. Concentric circles of dark purple, blue, and yellow were settling in on her right thigh, right triceps, and left ankle, near where last week's bruises were fading. Although not discolored, the ribs on her right side also ached, making every movement hurt, coughs especially. And the hair-thin green and red scrape marks slicing up and down her knees stung as soapy water streamed across them.

The morning's damage to her tall, wiry body was the usual. Still, the club rugby matches were worth it, her one physical rush of the week. Today she'd burst free for three tries, the last one the clincher, making it her best match of the year.

After rugby, Tori's Saturdays would typically unfold slowly. She'd nurse her sore spots by floating in the fitness complex's Jacuzzi. Donning sweatpants and a sweatshirt, she'd then grab a donut and coffee before spending hours reading for pleasure or for class. When it was nice out, Lawrence University's main green or the banks of the Fox River offered the perfect places to curl up with a book. The brief respite would end at four, when she drove out near the highway to start her evening shift at Cruisers Diner. Serving locals getting off work, Cruisers was a rougher place than the on-campus bars and restaurants, but it paid a good deal more.

This morning, though, she'd skipped her usual routine, limped home, and raced through her shower.

The added pain was worth it. The meeting she'd begged for—begged so many people for—was happening at last. Despite having been told to keep quiet, she'd finally get to tell her story, and to someone who mattered. Someone who could retell it to a far wider audience.

At first she'd had no one to tell. Her lives as student and political aide occupied two separate worlds, so no friends at school would have even gotten it. As for the political side, the small campaign crew had quickly disbanded. And, still gloating from their big win, they wouldn't welcome her skepticism. She'd be a turncoat, recklessly risking their new jobs.

"Let it go, Tori," cautioned her closest friend from the campaign, now working a finance post in Milwaukee. "People are going to think you're nuts. You've got a great job lined up if you leave it alone. Why kill that?"

"Because this is a huge deal," Tori had insisted. "There is no way to explain what happened."

She'd ignored the advice and gone to the press. She'd first called the political beat writer of every major paper in Wisconsin. She'd also tracked down the handful of columnists who still covered politics and reached out to the television reporters who handled campaigns for their stations. Few had returned her repeated calls, and those who had called hadn't bitten. At her only in-person meeting, over coffee, the columnist had worked harder at scoring a date than hearing her theory. The biggest problem was that the election had never felt important to them in the first place. And as a student and part-time campaign worker, she certainly didn't matter.

When the new semester began, she returned to the routine of a full-time, debt-ridden grad student with two part-time jobs. But it continued to nag her. And when her former boss took his oath of office, guilt got the best of her.

And then she'd seen *him* on TV. Took note of his no-bullshit manner. As she did with everything in life, she'd Googled him. A former newspaper reporter with Midwestern sensibilities, he had single-handedly uncovered a plot to rig American congressional elections, digging into details everyone else had overlooked. They'd dismissed him, then attacked him, yet he'd persisted. And he'd ultimately proven them wrong.

He would *get* it.

So she'd called. She'd left him the first message less than two months earlier and had called once a week since. She'd also sent a bunch of emails and dropped some messages over Facebook. But he'd never responded. Not a surprise, given how busy he had to be, but still a disappointment.

And then a week ago he'd called her back. Jack Sharpe.

She hopped out of the shower, wrapped herself in a towel, and scrubbed her hands in the sink with a fresh bar of soap.

In less than an hour she'd finally get to tell her story.

CHAPTER 3

ORVIETO, ITALY

The black Mercedes sedan wound its way up the steep road into Orvieto, a town perched high atop the remnant of an ancient volcanic explosion. Sitting in the passenger seat, lost in thought, Aleksandr Sanadze stared through the tinted window and up at the ornate duomo soaring far above. Each bend of the curved road offered a different view of the magnificent cathedral, from the white pillars stretching into the sky to the three triangular gables glimmering in gold.

Sanadze kept replaying the decision in his mind. And the final conversation confirming it.

"Oleg," he'd said on the phone yesterday afternoon, principal to principal, after days of stewing. "I am honored by your invitation, but I cannot participate. And I will not change my mind."

No argument had followed. Only a dial tone.

He was rejecting an enormous opportunity. A chance to enter the largest market in the world, one he'd been unable to penetrate, and one in desperate need of his cheap copper. It would take a few years, but ultimately the payoff would be there. And the new syndicate's strategy was brilliant: if the politics of America made its marketplace impenetrable, fix the politics and the opportunity would follow.

Declining the offer and pulling out of the long-planned Portofino meeting would cost him dearly. Which was why today he'd driven here instead, to a place that would fortify his decision.

The hill towns of Umbria always brought Sanadze home. The

occasional rocky hilltop jutting up from vast plains below. The gray vestiges of antiquity dotting the landscape. The fortresses and cathedrals, giant sentries keeping watch. As a child, as Sanadze ran the streets of Gori, in central Georgia, a similar fortress had towered over him and his family. He'd always felt secure in its shadow.

He hadn't been back to his hometown in years, and he longed to erase the last visit from his memory. He'd driven in under the cover of darkness only days after a cluster bomb had exploded in the town's central square, creating international news by blowing several journalists and two dozen civilians to bits. One of the bomblets exploded only feet from his seventy-two-year-old mother as she was buying bread and vegetables at the market. He buried her in a closed casket—her fragments no longer recognizable as human flesh. Still, with his wealth, he provided the most ostentatious send-off in Gori since the funeral of its native son Joseph Stalin.

As a kid, Sanadze had never understood the tensions between Russians and Georgians, so he'd ignored them. Yes, Russians made jokes about them: they considered Georgians inferior, his mother had always warned him. But Russians had allowed Stalin to rule over their empire for decades, so things couldn't be that bad. He'd befriended Georgians and Russians alike in his teens and twenties, and those relationships, hard work, and good timing had allowed him to build his copper mining empire. Close contacts with the Russian government had even allowed him to organize Mother's funeral despite the hostilities.

But her murder had changed him. Russian troops had detonated the bomb during a short but brutal occupation of his hometown. Such a pointless battle—nothing but Russia exerting its muscle. And his mother, who'd raised five children alone and wouldn't have harmed a soul unless it was to protect those children, had perished because of it. Looking over her grave at the end of the funeral, Aleksandr Sanadze made a simple vow. He would never work with a Russian again.

He took a deep breath, the tension easing. Seeing Orvieto again, so much like Gori, confirmed he had made the right decision. Yes, what was being offered today at Portofino was lucrative. But it had become clear that taking part meant he'd be beholden to a Russian for the rest of his life. And that he could not do. Not with the vow he'd sworn over his mother's grave.

A sharp jerk and sudden acceleration jolted him back to the hilly climb.

"Mr. Sanadze, I fear that car is following us." His driver sounded uncharacteristically worried as he looked in the rearview mirror. Sanadze's side mirror reflected a large SUV trailing a few feet behind them.

"For how long?"

"He appeared five minutes ago but has come closer in the last minute."

Sanadze gathered his bearings. They were on the steepest portion of the final hill into Orvieto, at their most vulnerable. Worse, he sat only feet from the edge of a high cliff.

The deep growl of a large engine, followed by the high-pitched squealing of tires, affirmed his driver's hunch. Within seconds the SUV shot forward and to their left, pulling even with them.

The unflappable Red Army veteran at the wheel responded coolly, jamming his right foot down. The Mercedes accelerated, pulling a car length ahead of the SUV. But seconds later a loud, metallic crunch drowned out all other sound, and the forceful collision twisted the Mercedes counterclockwise. Sanadze glanced to his left to see the SUV bulldozing into their rear left bumper. Moments later the Mercedes stopped perpendicular to the road, tilted sideways.

As his driver struggled to maneuver the damaged car forward, the SUV's tires squealed once more. The far larger vehicle reversed, then shot forward again, this time smashing into the left front of the Mercedes. The car jolted violently into the air, then back down, spinning clockwise while glass shattered all around them. Sanadze now hung over the cliff's edge; the car still sat partially on the road, but his seat did not.

Blood pouring from his bald head, his driver pounded on the accelerator. The car shook violently as a loud grating sound came from under the hood, but it didn't budge.

"Reverse!" Sanadze yelled out, his heart thumping.

As his driver reached for the transmission, the SUV's engine revved again and its tire treads clawed against the road, nudging the heavy Mercedes farther off the hill's edge. The driver's side of the car rose as Sanadze's side tilted downward. Then the entire car started to slide sideways and down.

The craggy rocks hundreds of feet below portended his fate. His muscles weakened as he glanced up one last time, through a large open-ing in the shattered front windshield. The grand rose window of Orvieto's cathedral stared back, offering him a moment to trace a cross from his forehead to his belly, then from his right shoulder to his left.

Seconds later, with the Mercedes sliding off the cliff completely, he saw only blue sky. While his driver screamed out, Sanadze closed his eyes, a numbness overcoming him as his body spiraled down.

Mother had been right. A Georgian should never trust a Russian.

CHAPTER 4

APPLETON, WISCONSIN

Three hours of air-conditioning had fooled me into thinking I'd recovered. But stepping out into the bright sun, in a parking lot less than a mile from the highway, proved me wrong.

The asphalt parking lot spun wildly, so I grabbed the SUV's roof to steady myself. Standing still gave me a glimpse of my reflection in the window. From bloodshot eyes to bloated cheeks to gray skin, it was not a pretty sight. I raked my fingers through my salt-and-pepper hair, which I'd let grow longer than usual.

The walk to the restaurant's front door took some time as I labored to keep my head still. Oversized yellow script towered over the modest diner: "Bad Apples. Established 1944." A long way from Georgetown, but my kind of place.

The pimply ponytailed teenager working the hostess stand grimaced as if my appearance alone were dragging the place down.

"Can I help you, sir?" she asked, sounding like the few people I'd known from Milwaukee.

"I'm meeting a woman na—"

"Mr. Sharpe! Over here!"

Halfway down the left side of the restaurant, a thin arm shot high in the air as if hailing a Manhattan cab. A wisp of a woman leapt to her feet, her outstretched arm close to the ceiling.

It was definitely her. On the drive from Youngstown, I'd browsed her Facebook page so I'd recognize her. Her long, thin face; small pointed nose; and short black hair with long bangs definitely stood out. In the photo and again here.

What her profile photo didn't capture, but which stuck out even more, was her unusual height. She topped six feet and, as thin as she was, appeared even taller.

"Never mind," I said to the hostess.

I walked toward the booth, but she covered more than half the ground before my third step. She shook my hand with a firm grip while unleashing a wide, toothy smile.

"Victoria?"

Victoria Justice. When she'd mentioned her name in her first message, it had made me think of a superhero.

"Call me Tori, Mr. Sharpe."

"And you can call me Jack, Tori."

We squeezed our long legs into our respective sides of the booth. For a moment I lost my concentration. Head on, Victoria Justice's crystal-blue eyes were startling. Light from the window also revealed elegant streaks of dark blue running through her hair.

"It's nice to mee—"

Her eyes glittered as she burst into a hearty laugh.

"Rough night?"

It was like a hard jab to the nose. "Do you always ask that the first time you meet someone?"

"No, but it's never such an obvious question." She laughed again, gesturing toward the window. "You were taken aback yourself checking your reflection out in the car window. Don't worry, it happens to the best of us."

Outside the window, my Escape sat only yards away. She'd witnessed my entire wobbly arrival.

"You look like you've had a rough morning yourself."

I'd noticed the bruises on her arms when she shook my hand. Since she didn't bother to hide them—as my sister had for years—I assumed they weren't caused by a man. So my snarky retort felt like fair game after her opening barrage.

"Oh, these?" She pointed to a purple spot on her left arm, below the sleeve of her gray T-shirt. "Badges of honor. I got 'em scoring three times in this morning's rugby match."

"You play rugby?"

With her height and build, I would've gone with tennis. Maybe volleyball. Rugby was for squat, muscular types. People shaped like bowling balls, not the pins. No wonder she had all those bruises.

"Oh, yeah. Nothing like a good scrum to start the weekend off right."

"Well, I played football back in the day. So we have that in common."

"Right! You guys wear pads and take long breaks between every play. Not a lot in common there."

I took a deep, steadying breath.

I'd learned the lesson with my young colleagues at Republic. Millennials didn't talk to their elders the way my generation had been brought up to. They just blurted out their thoughts. It wasn't a sign of disrespect, just an intergenerational difference in style. Young Victoria Justice had no idea that every sentence she'd uttered was, at best, confrontational.

Mercifully, another ponytailed teenager came to take our orders. The interruption gave us a chance to start over, and she had the good sense to do so.

"Thank you for coming, Jack," Tori said after our server walked away. "I've been eager to meet."

"No kidding." She'd called incessantly. "So you worked on the recent special? For Justice Beagle?"

I'd checked it out before coming. Justice Beau Beagle had beaten Judge Willie Flannery in the special election for a vacant Wisconsin Supreme Court seat two months back, a week before Tori had first called.

"I did."

"Congratulations. That was a big win. Were you the manager?"

"No. The manager is off running a campaign for Congress. In Madison."

"Good for him. What did you do, then? Field director? Comms? Finance?"

After campaign manager, the three big jobs in a standard campaign were finance director, communications director, and field director. Outside vendors handled much of the remaining work—mainly television ads, mail, and polling. That was where all the money was. Vendors made a mint, hired by staff who worked for peanuts.

"I was actually part-time. But I answered to the field guy and the manager."

Jesus. I'd driven all this way for a part-timer who *answered* to the field guy? Back on my dad's campaigns for state representative, the job title for that was "volunteer."

"So what job were you doing for the campaign?"

"I was the voter file manager," she said.

"The what?"

"You sound like my dad. It's called the voter file manager. You know: I managed the campaign's voter file."

"The voter file?" I'd heard the term in passing. Like all of corporate America, campaigns and parties stored a lot more data on voters than they used to, but I'd never spent a lot of time digging into that side of things.

She scowled as if I'd confused the order of the alphabet.

"Jack, the voter file is how campaigns keep up with every voter they interact with. Everything we do is tabulated and sorted on the voter file. My job was to keep track of all that information."

I nodded. "When I used to knock on doors for Dad's campaigns, I'd bring my walking list back to the campaign headquarters all marked up."

For me, knocking on doors had been the highlight of Dad's campaigns. Dad had served as a state representative in Canton, Ohio, for years. Throughout the summer and fall of every election year, we went door-to-door, listening, talking, then closing with an ask. The conversations were mostly pleasant—a welcome reminder that most people were good-hearted. Nothing felt better than bringing back a precinct sheet with all the *Y*'s circled, meaning they were all going to vote for Dad. A secondary goal was *YS*'s, indicating residents who wanted yard signs. A street dotted with "Re-elect Sharp" yard signs had been the ultimate trophy for my political prowess.

For most of Dad's campaigns, my sister had entered the results of our filled-out precinct sheets into a big spreadsheet. For hours a day, but as a volunteer.

"So," I said, "your job was to input all the data and keep the file on it."

"It's a little more complicated than that, but yes." Her light sarcasm suggested I had just graduated from third grade to fifth grade.

The server reappeared, setting down our drinks and two large plates of scrambled eggs. I took a sip of coffee before digging into the eggs with fervor. Greasy meals had long been my preferred cure for hangovers.

I was halfway through my first bite when Tori pulled a small plastic package from her backpack. She took a moist cleansing wipe from the package and rubbed it between her hands.

I almost waited for her to lift her fork. But after Tori had deposited the used wipe back into her bag, I shoveled a second bite into my mouth.

Still her fork remained on the table. She removed a second wipe and rubbed her hands just as feverishly, in the exact same places, while chewing on her lower lip. Rather than talking or even looking my way, she eyed her own scrubbing as if she were performing surgery.

Now well ahead of her, I stopped eating. She took out a third wipe, scrubbed, put it to the side, then grabbed a fourth. And that's when I noticed that her hands were beet red, chapped on the tips of her fingers and thumbs, and along the sides of her palms.

Apparently my gaze was not subtle.

"I'm a real germophobe," she said without looking up, "so I'll just be a minute. No need to wait."

I dug in again but couldn't avert my eyes. She grabbed a fifth wipe, then a sixth. Only after a final scrub with the seventh did she place the package of wipes back into her bag and lift her fork. With only English muffins left on my plate, she dug into her eggs.

"So are you studying data or statistics?" I asked, trying to save a conversation that kept veering off course.

"Neither. I'm getting my master's in literature."

"Literature? Is that a common focus for voter file managers?" I regretted the words as soon as they came out.

"I know, right? The campaign manager asked the same question when I applied, but the judge actually liked it. The truth is, data work comes so naturally, it bores me. So I chose literature because it's more interesting, and I'm a decent writer but want to get better."

She paused, then batted her long lashes. "It's almost as unheard-of as an injured jock becoming a political reporter."

Only a hard choke stopped a morsel of English muffin from plunging down my windpipe.

"So you do your research."

My path had indeed been a circuitous one. Starred at quarterback in high school and college with not entirely unrealistic NFL dreams. My throwing arm crushed by a sack my senior year at Youngstown State. Stayed in town after graduating to become a sports reporter, then moved over to the political desk. In fact, politics was what I knew best, but it had also stopped interesting me years ago, after Dad lost a nasty primary. But it paid the bills.

"There's nothing that Google can't get to the bottom of." She lifted the last forkful of egg toward her mouth.

"Okay, Madam Voter File Manager with the hygienic hands," I said, cutting to the chase. "I drove hours to get here. So tell me why you called, emailed, and messaged me for weeks about your candidate's big victory."

"Simple." She downed her last bite and grabbed an additional wipe. "There's no conceivable way that Justice Beagle won that election."

CHAPTER 5

PORTOFINO, ITALY

Katrina didn't flinch even as most of the older men who walked past her leered without subtlety or shame.

Natalie, standing on the other side of the ornate double doors, looked nearly identical: heels, black skirt, white blouse, none of it showy but all of it tight. And, like Katrina's, Natalie's dark brown hair fell halfway down her back.

"Good evening, Mr. Xi," Katrina said as a round, graying Asian man approached her, a young stilt of a man at his side. "Welcome to the *Pushkin*. You may sit wherever you like."

The skinny man whispered into his boss's ear, translating her greeting. Mr. Xi bowed his head formally, then entered the large room behind her. As the yacht's stately foyer swayed ever so slightly, Katrina looked down at the iPad in her hand and, touching her finger to the screen, marked off his name.

Katrina had studied all of the guests so she'd recognize them by sight, showing the required respect. But, even more important than their names, she knew their stories. Xi was a steel magnate from southern China. He'd grown up in the countryside, in a family of peasants, but had worked his way up the Communist Party to become one of the country's wealthiest men. He then expanded his business into other parts of Asia until some impolitic moves impeded his progress.

A bald, round-faced man reached the top of the steps and bounded her way. He was exactly Katrina's height and built like an anvil, with thick, tattooed forearms and a barrel chest that narrowed to a trim waist. He might've been attractive but for the crater-like pockmarks and dark skin tags hanging like ticks off his ruddy cheeks and down his neck. Steroids, Katrina guessed, but he should pay to have that mess cleaned up. He certainly could afford it. Curls of charcoal hair billowed up from beneath his patterned shirt, which was open a third of the way down.

Natan Terzian. Armenian, forty-two years old, from the mountains near Yerevan. He'd become a billionaire making rubber and selling it to the former Soviet republics, the Middle East, and China.

"Good morning, Mr. Terzian," Katrina said to him, bracing for a crude reply.

He stopped with exaggerated drama, his steely eyes sweeping her figure up and down. "Good morning, beautiful," he said in a deep, heavily accented English. "You have already made the visit worth my while."

"Thank you."

She nodded politely and cast a professional half grin. Men of this level misread almost any signal from an attractive woman as a sign of interest, usually triggering an unwelcome pursuit. And declining an entreaty later would cause problems.

"This will be a fruitful discussion. Please sit where you like."

His lips twisted. "I can only hope we have fruitful discussions after our meeting as well." His puffy fingers rubbed the small of her back as he finished the sentence.

In any other circumstance, she would've recoiled and scolded the offender. But she neither budged nor breathed. A blowup with a man of his temperament and importance risked sacrificing the entire meeting.

"Let us first have a fruitful discussion with the others," she said, maintaining her forced smile.

He paused as if to speak again, pursed his lips, then walked into the large cabin behind the double doors.

She caught her breath, then placed a checkmark next to his name.

Over the next fifteen minutes, twelve more men and two women stepped onto the rear deck of the 180-foot yacht, walked up the stairs to the main foyer, and strolled past Katrina and Natalie into the grand dining room behind them. Like a UN convention but with an Eastern tilt. A Kyrgyz. A Syrian. Another Kazakh. Two Russians, one from Siberia and one from the Far East, closer to Alaska than Moscow. A Romanian, a Ukrainian, and two Serbians. Three more Chinese, an Albanian, and a giant Afghan.

Katrina glanced at her clipboard. Only two invited guests remained unchecked. She saw the Georgian listed but, certain he would not attend, drew a line through his name. Only one more.

The titans gabbed and gossiped behind her. Some had known each other before the gathering. Terzian, the Armenian, somehow knew them all, yelling out the names of the newcomers, then greeting them each with a bear hug. Global oligarchy was a small club, its members usually subdued about their elite status. But these visitors were more recent entrants, or still pounding on the door to get in, which explained the celebratory buzz in the room. They were hungry, which was why they'd been invited in the first place.

The final guest arrived with one minute to spare. The gentleman of the group, his gaze never strayed from her eyes. In his fifties, the founder of China's largest internet search engine, Zhang Yong sported a buzz cut of jet-black hair and wire-rimmed glasses. He politely grasped her hand.

"Thank you for your hospitality," he said warmly, in British-accented English. "It is good to see you again."

"Thank you for joining us." Katrina rewarded the rare charm with a warmer smile and longer grasp of the hand than she'd offered the others. "We are about to begin."

After he walked through the doors, she made the final checkmark on her list. Out the window, dusk darkened the harbor and the steep Italian hillside towering over it.

"Show time."

She and Natalie each gripped a door handle and pulled the double doors closed as they entered the dining room.

CHAPTER 6

APPLETON, WISCONSIN

Want me to drive?" Tori asked after I paid the Bad Apples bill at the front counter. "You still don't look quite up to it."

"Sounds like a good idea," I conceded, pocketing the change.

We walked past several cars before she stopped in back of a beat-up Dodge pickup truck. Sun-stained red paint speckled about half of the track's surface, the rest a combination of metallic silver and rust.

"Are you sure we're gonna make it?" I asked.

"Hey," she said, giving me the tiniest of shoves to the shoulder. Her jovial push forced me back a step despite her thin frame. Rugby made more sense now.

"This baby spent years hauling everything you can imagine on a working dairy farm. She's earned every scrape she's got."

Unlike its exterior, the truck's cabin was immaculate. The seats looked newly polished, the floors pristine, and the dashboard, center console, and steering wheel were all spotless.

"I see you're waging your war against germs in here, too."

"Definitely. You'll learn that I'm a soldier of sanitation."

We pulled onto College Avenue and headed into town. In the diner, after enticing me by claiming there was no way Justice Beagle won his campaign, she'd offered to show me proof.

"So what changed your mind?" she asked as the street we were on became the tree-lined boulevard of a college town.

"Change my mind about what?" I asked, worried about where this was going. I was here to interview her, not vice versa.

"Returning my call." When I said nothing, she tossed in some refreshing flattery: "Why would a big shot like you call a lowly grad student back?"

Good. She didn't know. So much for Google.

"My best stories have always come from unexpected sources, voices others have ignored."

She threw sidelong glances at me as I laid it on thick.

"The problem with big-time cable news is you have less time to chase them down. So when I had a window of downtime, I was eager to follow up."

She slapped her right hand against the steering wheel.

"Well, Jack Sharpe, that's why I called you."

We entered the heart of Appleton, passing a performing arts center, local banks, eclectic coffee and sandwich shops, and a charming campus. All the authentic amenities a midsized American town would want but that too few enjoyed.

"Why?"

"Your style. Listening to the little guy. Starting from the bottom up. Then never relenting despite roadblocks. That's how you nailed Congressman Stanton and exposed that Abacus scandal."

I nodded. It certainly was, along with some outside help I'd still never revealed. The election-rigging scandal from four years back—when I'd exposed tainted results in swing House districts across the country—had launched my roller-coaster ride to stardom, from a burnt-out Youngstown newspaper reporter to a national cable television talking head. In the process, I'd taken down a presidential front-runner, exposed the illegitimacy of a new House majority, and inspired a year of bipartisan reform on Capitol Hill.

And yet I now romanticized Youngstown as the good old days, when I knew who I worked for and said as I pleased. And the nation's capital had spiraled downward into a partisan mess within days of President Janet Moore's inauguration.

"Yes, keeping my ear to the ground has always worked for me. I appreciate you noticing."

"Speaking of noticing, I also couldn't help but notice the big story in the *Vindicator* the next year as well."

She was good. No one had made this connection before, at least to me directly.

"What do you mean?" I asked as we passed a white-domed stone building at the center of campus.

"The *Vindicator* broke the story that took down Governor Nicholas just as he was about to win the Democratic primary. You know, that awful sex scandal. Janet Moore is president only because that story came out."

Tori took a right onto Water Street and we descended down a hill.

"That's probably true. Great scoop."

"You again, right?"

Of course. Cassie Knowles, my top reporter at Republic, almost quit when I told her we were handing the best story of her career to my old newspaper. But it was the only way we could get the story out safely on the plot to rig the presidential election.

"Nah. I was already at Republic by then. But my old colleagues kicked butt on that one."

"Right," she said, not fooled. "What are the odds of a midsized paper landing two national scoops in two years? And that the second story was written by a new hire and the paper's managing editor?"

"Not good. But that's why they call it the *Vindicator*."

"I'm onto you, Jack Sharpe. And someday you'll learn to trust me." She nudged my shoulder with her right hand. "Still, you're probably the only one who can bring this story home."

"Hey, don't get your hopes up."

If she only knew.

CHAPTER 7

PORTOFINO, ITALY

The full moon above the hillside cast a glow across the historic seaside town, reminding Katrina of June nights in St. Petersburg, when the sun never quite went down.

The centuries-old villas crammed up and down the steep hill looked as alive as the well-lit pizzerias and taverns below, while the ghostlike outlines of old sailboats, sleek luxury yachts, and grungy trawlers bobbed in the harbor. From the shoreline, an intense beam cut across the dark water directly to the edge of the yacht where Katrina and Natalie now sat.

Below them, a Donzi pulled away, the roar of its engine interrupting the din of music, chatter, and laughter. The activity might have been happening onshore, but the water carried the sound so efficiently that it felt like it was happening belowdecks.

The speedboat was carrying away their last guest—Terzian, the Armenian—wasted. His intentions of staying later than the others had been painfully clear. But his final shots of vodka, which Katrina had playfully encouraged, pushed him well beyond the capacity to make a move. His exit finally allowed her to relax.

"Will they all sign on?" Natalie asked as she watched the wake of the Donzi curl in the moonlight.

"I believe they will."

Katrina leaned back, enjoying a martini and the view. In her Brooklyn days, peering out at the ocean from cheesy beaches and the clutches of the few oversexed boys who'd paid her attention, she could never have imagined how beautiful a seaside could be. But with her uncle's success and her own climb, here she was, enjoying the playground of the rich and famous from the ritziest perch in the harbor.

"How can you be sure?"

After she'd ended their presentation and adjourned the meeting, some of the guests had stayed for a round of drinks and conversation. They'd chirped with enthusiasm as she escorted each one down the stairs to be boated back to shore. They were sold on the plan, both the grand strategy and the tactics to get there, and eager to move forward.

"As wealthy as they are, they're outsiders. We're giving them a way in."

"But at such a high price?"

"For the opportunities that will come their way, it's not high at all."

Both women stood up as a second Donzi emerged from the shadow of the shoreline and sped their way.

CHAPTER 8

APPLETON, WISCONSIN

S o, across all of Wisconsin, you know which voters are gun owners and which aren't?"

Through the kitchen window of Tori's tiny apartment, the nearby lock on the Fox River had piqued my interest far more than the voter file she'd logged onto. But that changed once she delved into the personal details of an elderly woman in Milwaukee named Marianne Sanders. Tori pointed to a box on Marianne's page indicating that she was a gun owner with a concealed carry weapon license.

"Oh," Tori answered, "that's the tip of the iceberg."

Now I was interested. "So what's the iceberg look like?"

"Greenland."

"That big?"

She shrugged. "Think about it. Every campaign, every year, adds information on voters into the file. Never subtracting, only adding. So it's gotten huge over time."

"So what kind of information are we talking about?"

She moved the cursor to various personal details available on Marianne Sanders's page.

"Well, first come some basics, over here. Age, birthday, address, some details on her voting history."

Marianne was sixty-eight, born on July 8, Caucasian, a registered Republican, and lived at 848 Humphrey Drive in Milwaukee. No kids at home. She had voted in every presidential election since 1980, most midterm elections, and most primaries in the presidential year.

"Definitely the basics." This stuff had been on the sheets when I knocked on doors for Dad.

"Yes. But—"

She moved the cursor again, revealing private details I hadn't expected. There was Marianne's cell phone number and her email address, along with a link to her Facebook account.

"How'd you get her cell number?"

"Well, the slow way is to collect them over time through interactions between the campaign and voters. The fast way is to buy them from vendors."

"You can *buy* them?"

"Yep. Email addresses, too."

The number $40,000 appeared on the page.

"You have her income? Where do you get that?"

"Oh, that's easy. They get it right out of the census data for her block."

"So it's just an estimate."

"Sure. But America is incredibly segregated by income level. You'd be surprised how accurate census block income data is."

I nodded. Fair point.

"And it looks like she gets a state pension," Tori said, pointing to another part of the screen.

I nodded. That would be a public record. "By the way, who's collecting all this stuff?"

"The party."

"The *state* party?"

"And the national party. It's sort of a mix of the national party, the state party, their vendors, and campaign voter file managers like me."

"That's a lot of people with access to a whole lot of personal information."

"But you only get access to your *part* of the voter file. Not everyone else's."

"Still, all the information is housed in one central place?"

"Yep."

I shook my head. That's one hell of a database.

I leaned closer to the screen. Two groups, Badger Seniors United and the Wisconsin Nurses Association, were listed under the category for memberships.

"Wait—you know what *organizations* people are in?"

"Magazine subscriptions, too."

She pointed to a list on Marianne Sanders's page: *Gun Monthly*, *Pets Galore*, and *Knitting for Life*.

"How do you get *that* stuff?"

She rubbed her thumb against her second and third fingers. "Like cell phones, you can buy this information from whoever sells it—and these days a whole lot of people sell it. So if the party purchased it, it's in here."

"What else can they purchase?"

"More than you want to know."

She clicked a button, opening a new page with a long list of items and products.

"What's that list tell us?"

"Ads she clicked on."

"*Ads?*"

"I'm serious. Digital ads. For products, services, events. If you click on ads from certain locations, that information is captured and they can identify who you are."

"And how does the party get it? Wait—let me guess. That stuff is sold, too?"

"You got it. And mark my words, in the next year or two, vendors will be compiling every voter's Facebook posts, tweets, and likes about everything from hobbies to movies to presidential candidates, and those will also end up on the voter file. Then there are the apps that track your phone location—they're already selling that data to—"

"Okay, okay, you got me. There's a lot of information in the voter file. I'm happy to assure your parents that your job is more important than it sounds, prying into the private lives of sweet old ladies everywhere. But how does any of this prove that your judge didn't win that election?"

"Oh, you'll see. But before we go there, I need you to tell me something first. And you need to be honest about it."

"Okay," I said quietly, staring out the window as four kayaks entered the lock.

"Why are you not on the air anymore?"

My throat clenched. She'd noticed after all.

"What do you mean?"

I could feel moisture building on my forehead.

"Don't play dumb, Jack. Your last appearance on Republic was five weeks ago. Why?"

Before I said another word, she asked an even tougher question.

"And why did you lie about it in the car?"

CHAPTER 9

TRANQUILITY, OHIO

It was the best view on earth—at least compared to the few parts he'd seen.

From the kitchen of Jesse Woods's 1882 farmhouse, through the big bay window they'd added a decade before, the high sun showered light across the wide ocean of soybeans. The stalks stood several feet, the green hues of summer had burnt into brown, and the rows of beans bowed as wind blew across the field. But the telltale sign that the beans were set to burst was that when Jesse Woods squinted, he could make out the yellow dots of the seeds themselves peppering the field, newly exposed in recent days after the leaves protecting them had fallen to the ground.

That yellow color meant this was the big week. A spring, summer, and fall of care, toil, and worry. The stress of every hard rain and dry spell. Except for the worst of years, it all paid off this week.

But as he took in his beloved soybean fields this morning, Jesse Woods twisted his leathery face into a lopsided frown.

Sitting across from him at their white kitchen table, his wife, June, reached over and held Jesse's weathered hands.

"Honey, you held out for as long as you could. You did what you thought was right."

He looked directly into her sunken gray eyes, softly squeezing her delicate left hand with his right. She would never say it. But her eyes, welling up almost daily, gave her away. His decision had crushed her.

"We're dinosaurs and it's time we admitted it," he said, still trying to convince her. "It's time to move on."

But as determined as his words sounded, he felt like a failure. He'd let June and all those who'd come before him down.

Cherry Fork, the Woodses' farm, had been in his family for five generations. Over the years, his forebears had expanded from twenty acres to fifty to one hundred. Then Grandpa Woods had doubled it, and Dad had doubled it again once Jesse and his brothers had grown enough to do much of the heavy lifting. Year after year those acres had churned out a bountiful mix of tobacco, beans, corn, and hay, along with an assortment of fruits and vegetables. Grandpa Woods had once experimented with cattle, but they hadn't been worth the hassle. And tobacco, once their best crop, had cratered decades ago, thanks to the political correctness police.

Through the generations, the Woodses had been damn proud farmers. Farming wasn't a mere profession but a way a life, representing the best of America.

But for more than a century, Cherry Fork's operation had also paid the bills. Like the other farming families of southern Ohio's Adams County, the Woods clan had been upstanding leaders of the community. They not only went to church, they helped keep the church going. They gave generously to the schools and county charities. They hired local boys to do much of the farmwork. When a Woods walked into a room, he walked in tall.

But several decades after Jesse had taken over, their fortunes changed. Not because of the people in Adams County but because of people and institutions worlds away from the county.

The squeeze came from all corners. The collapse of tobacco, unintelligible new government rules, bigger banks less willing to loan to small farms. And with soybeans in particular, more expensive supplies and seeds and much tougher competition from corporate competitors.

All of that hadn't sent the Woodses straight into poverty but had steadily ground them down. Seeing no future here, Jesse's kids had all moved away years ago. They couldn't donate to the church or causes as they used to. Unable to give, they were embarrassed to take part.

This would be the last Woods harvest at Cherry Fork.

"We did our best, honey," he said, shaking his head.

Eyes blinking, June said nothing back. She'd been unusually quiet—not her chatty self—ever since he'd made the decision.

Four months earlier, when the sleek black Audi had driven up their long dirt driveway, June called Jesse in from the barn. They didn't know anyone who drove something like that. On these country roads, they were more likely to see an Amish horse and buggy than a fancy foreign car.

The quick-talking lawyer from Columbus, it soon became clear, had a mission: to buy Cherry Fork. Just like that, offering good money, too. After a few days of negotiating, and long talks trying to convince June, Jesse'd sold.

"The numbers don't work for us," he'd told the lawyer as they walked his fields the day after inking their deal. "How will they work for you?"

"My clients have a plan. With the right scale and support, Cherry Fork can succeed."

"With those seed prices? And fertilizer prices? Both keep going up every year, and there's no negotiating 'em." Jesse was reliving every aspect of his economic nightmare of recent decades. "And our buyer keeps squeezing us on the other end, pushing down our prices. Sure, there's global demand for beans, but someone else is making all the money. We've been getting it from both ends for years."

The lawyer had shrugged. "My client understands."

From the blank look on the lawyer's face, Jesse guessed he didn't know the first thing about farming. But whether his client was a fool or a genius, he definitely wanted farms. Within weeks, that black Audi had wound its way up the driveways of the Canfields, the Pitts, the Groomses, and the Sheakleys, the most prominent soybean families left in the county. And within days of those visits, each family had also sold, securing more money than they'd ever imagined for their struggling properties.

Jesse gazed back toward the field, squeezing June's hand one more time. It would be a good harvest. And selling was the right thing to do.

But he'd sure miss the greatest view on earth.

CHAPTER 10

APPLETON, WISCONSIN

Jack, that's bullshit."

Needing some fresh air, we'd stepped out of her apartment building and were walking along the river, when Tori stopped in her tracks.

"I've been telling you things I shouldn't be telling you. And you can't even fess up about what happened to you?"

Legally, I was barred from saying a word. The nondisclosure agreement I'd signed five weeks ago was airtight. I'd never muzzled myself in my life, but I'd had no choice: signing it got me out of owing Republic thousands of dollars for having violated a clause of my employment agreement I'd never before noticed. But doing so meant I couldn't talk about what had happened or even about the way Republic operated generally. In theory, the agreement was mutual, but since they'd set my career in flames, whether or not they criticized my smoldering ashes was beside the point.

So not only had I gotten screwed, I was barred from talking about how I'd gotten screwed.

"Tori, *you* called me. You *wanted* to tell the story. So please don't act like you're doing me a favor."

She drew a deep, harsh breath before walking again. "I shared it with you out of trust. And out of a belief that you'll do something with it. I have a stake in your ability to get it out there."

"Or what? You'll call someone else? I hate to break it to you, but no one else is going to call you back."

"You never know. I'm persistent."

That didn't matter, but it wasn't worth arguing.

"Tori, let me assure you I can do something meaningful if there's a story here."

"So is that permanent?"

"Is what permanent?"

"Not being on the air at Republic."

"Yes."

"Did they fire you?"

"All I'll say is that we mutually agreed that it was time for me to move on."

Her lips opened, but no sound came out. Then: "Well, how are you going to do this story, then?"

"If it's a story, and it justifies coverage, we can get it out there."

I was holding back again, but not for legal reasons. More like pride.

"*How?*" she asked, her head cocked. Her confidence in me was waning rapidly. "Do you have another television gig lined up?"

"I'm barred from working anywhere else. In television, at least."

I had also signed a brutal noncompete. But even without it, in the incestuous and risk-averse world of cable news, being axed doomed me anyway. There were few places to go, and none would take a chance on a bad apple.

Two large white birds swooped in and landed only yards from us, then stood upright in the river's placid waters.

"Herons?" I asked, impressed by their intense concentration as they stared straight down.

"No, egrets. They'll stand there forever until a fish comes along."

"Ah, patience. What a virtue."

"Patience? More like determination."

"Fair enough," I said, chuckling.

We started walking again.

"So how will you get this story out?"

"Remember the *Youngstown Vindicator*?"

"The *Vindicator*?" She threw her arms in the air.

"Yeah. You know—the newspaper you were so excited about in the car?"

"You're back with them now?"

"Let's just say they'll run any good stories I come up with."

Tori scowled, not buying it. Smart woman.

"What the heck does that mean? Are you on their staff again?"

"I'm not. But we have an understanding. When I generate good stories, they'll run them."

"Sounds like a fancy term for freelance."

The word hit me like a linebacker's helmet to the sternum. I'd been in professional denial since I walked out the doors of the *Vindicator* a week earlier, never categorizing the arrangement in my own mind. To me, "freelance" had always meant unemployed, like people who call themselves consultants even when they have no clients. But I couldn't argue with her terminology.

"You can call it what you want, Tori. Good stories will be rewarded lucratively."

She stopped again, so I did as well. Her blue eyes stared right at me. She was studying me. Figuring me out. Then, for the first time since I'd met her, Tori frowned.

"And *that's* why you returned my call," she said, more quietly than her previous sentences. Not a question but a declaration. More to herself than to me.

Without any heads-up, she took off briskly back for her apartment, forcing me to jog to catch her.

"What do you mean by that?" I asked once I drew even.

She kept walking in silence.

"Tori?"

She trudged quickly forward but answered. "You *need* a story. Just to make money. And you have no others. So after you ignored me, I became your only option."

We walked past the egrets, their eyes still fixed downward, their long legs planted exactly as they'd been before.

"Spare me the 'listening to the common folk' reporting approach, Jack. You ignored me when you were a big shot and only called me now because you're desperate."

I tried to respond, but no words came to mind.

She'd figured it out.

Figured *me* out.

CHAPTER 11

WASHINGTON, D.C.

Y ou're on in ten . . . nine . . . eight . . . seven . . ."
Even as her producer counted down in her ear, the concentric circles of the camera lens merging as her photog zoomed in, Cassie Knowles struggled to focus.

Jack Sharpe's departure may have given her more airtime and a hefty raise, but working at Republic hadn't been the same. Yes, Cassie got to cover politics at the White House and Capitol Hill, the dream assignment of most journalists. But that day-to-day tussling took away from the investigatory work that was her life's purpose. Even worse, without Jack, the mission of the place had changed. The passion was gone, hers included.

Plus, her new beat placed her on the front lines of partisan rancor. Ever since Janet Moore had been elected president—ending a twelve-year span of Republicans in the White House—a handful of extremist groups rallied against her every move. And the narrow Republican majority in Congress—backed by big money, they'd hung on to the House and Senate despite Moore's big win—caved to that right-wing grassroots fervor, blocking the new president's agenda. When Moore had pushed laws reforming immigration and battling discrimination, the opposition scuttled them all. And her populist economic agenda was buried in committee, going nowhere.

Cassie's job was to cover every scene of this drama. Not at all what she'd signed up for when Jack coaxed her to leave the *Boston Globe* for Republic's new investigative unit.

So here she was, a prop in front of the Capitol, covering a looming government shutdown. For the second time in a month.

"Four . . . three . . . two . . . one . . . You're on."

"Thanks, Chuck," Cassie said, forcing the smile she'd spent weeks practicing after management told her to perk up both her expression and her wardrobe. "The story is the same today as it's been for months. No progress. No compromise. Lots of name-calling. And very little sense of how they're going to avoid a shutdown this time."

The wind had gusted all day, so she'd pulled her hair back to keep it from blowing around. But the breeze also drowned out Chuck Massa's next question.

"Say that again, Chuck?" she said, jamming the earpiece deeper into her ear.

"Do you know if the president called any of the congressional leaders today? Is she willing to compromise to keep the shutdown from happening?"

Her head flinched at the odd take.

"Chuck, the president would say she's compromised a lot already, cutting things she wouldn't have dreamed of cutting on Inauguration Day. But to answer your question, no. I don't think she called them today."

"Doesn't a shutdown risk her whole presidency? She promised to work across party lines to fix problems. But that's the opposite of what she's doing."

Cassie balled her fist, smiling through clenched teeth. The aggressors in the shutdown fight were clearly the new Republican leaders on Capitol Hill, led by Speaker Elmore Paxton of Michigan's Upper Peninsula. When he'd taken the job, diplomacy exited the building, replaced by an eagerness to go to war over everything. He didn't care if the government shut down. As he'd told her off the record days ago, it would prove his point that government didn't do all that much anyway. People wouldn't miss it, so he could starve it.

But here Chuck Massa was blaming the president, picking a side in a way that Jack never would've. But she didn't want to openly disagree with the anchor on air.

"It's not clear who the blowback will hit hardest," she said, opting for the most tepid response possible. "It's not good for the president *or* the

Republicans on the Hill. But of course she can't be happy about any of this. At this point her agenda is dead."

"It sure is." Chuck sounded a little too pleased.

"But this new leadership team has hardly let her out of the gate. I guess the American people will have to sor—"

"That's all the time we've got, friends. Back after a break."

"You're clear," the producer said.

She reached up to remove the earpiece, when a steely voice bellowed through.

"Don't you ever fucking do that again," Chuck Massa said, dropping his cheesy broadcaster baritone for his more gravelly alto.

"Do *what*?"

"Undermine me live, on-air. Never again."

"Okay."

She removed the earpiece so he couldn't get another word in.

Her heart skipped a beat. But as she stepped away from the camera and put her white opal stud back into her nose, a grin flickered across her lips.

She'd never been chided like that before—by Chuck or anyone at Republic. But if her pushback had added balance to his one-sided bullshit, it was well worth the tongue-lashing.

CHAPTER 12

APPLETON, WISCONSIN

Tori and I reached a truce.

I wouldn't tell her a thing about my departure from Republic as long as I spilled the details on my *Vindicator* deal. And I learned quickly that this literature major and data geek would've made one hell of a reporter.

"Why didn't they hire you back?" she asked as she unlocked the door to her apartment.

"If it'd been up to my old boss, I'm sure they would have."

"Is Mary Andres not there anymore?"

She even knew my old editor's name.

"Oh, she's there all right, but on a very short leash."

"Why's that?"

"Surprised your Googling didn't discover this," I said, feigning disappointment.

The *Vindicator* had been bought out eight months before by a private company that was gobbling up midsized papers all over the country and chopping them up into pieces. In and around Ohio, they'd bought papers in Akron, Canton, Wheeling, and Erie, and more recently Youngstown and Columbus. Their cookie-cutter model squeezed profits out of the dying business, cutting the length of the papers and printing them on tabloid-sized paper. They centralized much of the content and many key functions, laying out all newspapers at company headquarters in Philadelphia, miles from anyone who knew anything about each town.

I explained this all to Tori. "You can kiss goodbye real investigations as well as most editorial boards, cartoonists, and columnists—so the personalities of these papers are basically gone."

"That's terrible."

"And an invitation for corrupt local government. But all that cost cutting also means no money for reporters with actual experience, like yours truly."

"So they wouldn't hire you back despite your national profile?"

"Mary argued that I was worth it, but I don't fit their model. Too costly when they can hire kids out of college."

"Rough."

"Humiliating. Here I've generated the best two scoops in the paper's recent history and I can't even get my old job back."

"Two scoops. I knew it!"

She didn't miss a beat.

"See how much I trust you?"

"Yeah," she said dismissively. "So how'd the freelance gig come up?"

"Mary and I brainstormed about it, then she went to bat for me. Told them that if anyone had the chops to deliver major, moneymaking scoops, it was me. And ultimately they bought it."

"And what are the terms?"

I leaned back, defensively.

"Tori, I'm not going to get into—"

"Jack, this was our agreement. Nothing on Republic but the details on the *Vindicator.*"

I reconsidered. Confiding in her was somehow putting me at ease.

"They told me I could eat what I killed. 'Get big stories. We'll pay you for them.' And there are bonuses based on clicks and any increase in paper sales."

Her face twisted as if she'd swallowed sour milk. "Is that even ethical? It sounds like a recipe for sensationalism and bullshit reporting."

"Young Tori, that horse left the barn years ago. Everything's about clickbait these days."

"Right, but not where the reporter gets a bonus. That's a really perverse incentive."

My initial reaction as well. But a man's got to survive.

CHAPTER 13

PRICE, UTAH

'm not sold yet. Tell me more."

Thea Pappas was a stubborn woman, so she'd uttered those sentences many times over the years. According to her parents, long since passed, Thea's stubborn side had first emerged in her early years of competitive riding. No matter how many times she'd been thrown off Thumper, her chocolate-brown Hanoverian, she'd climbed back on. Thea and Thumper went on to win the Utah girls' jumping championship three straight years.

But Mom and Dad had always reminded her that her stubborn streak hadn't started with her. It came from a long line of sturdy Pappas stock who'd shipped out from Greece in the late 1800s to mine coal deep in eastern Utah's Wasatch Mountains. Many had settled in Carbon County.

Eating bagels and sipping coffee, Thea and the bearded dark-eyed man studied each other—only miles from those now-shuttered mines. The man maintained a neutral expression, but Thea assumed he was not accustomed to rejection. Not with the amount of money he was offering. He spoke fluent English, but with an accent she didn't recognize.

He replied confidently, as if she'd just agreed to a deal. "We think you're a strong bank with a robust brand, so we don't want to change what you do or who you are. Athenia will still exist but would benefit from the heft of our national infrastructure."

It was her pint-sized *papou*, her granddad, who'd decided there was no future, at least for him, in mining. But he did perceive opportunity in the emerging diaspora of Greek families, who lived separately from the Mormon culture that otherwise dominated rural Utah. So with a small loan and a cadre of initial customers comprising family and friends, he'd founded the Athenia Bank of Utah. The first branch, in Price, had prospered from the outset. The family business grew steadily into a medium-sized regional bank with twelve branches across eastern and central Utah and an intensely loyal customer base.

"And who are you?" Thea asked.

"We're new to America. But our investors have utilized an ambitious model in eastern Europe to great success and want to import it here."

Eastern Europe? Not what she expected.

"So you'd keep my employees and the current branches intact?"

"Absolutely. And we hope to get back into markets you had to leave after 2008. You still have a strong brand in those communities. Then we go bigger."

"And how are you going to do that? I got crushed in those places. BankUS and FirstAmerica are too strong."

When she'd taken over the business fifteen years back, things were already going south. At its peak, Athenia was the largest bank in Price, Park City, Ogden, and other Utah towns. But starting with Ogden, branches of the nation's biggest banks had moved in, marketing aggressively for new customers and adding ATMs everywhere. Then those same large banks had bought up other community banks, transforming friendly rivalries with like-minded locals into fierce competition against out-of-town behemoths.

Of course, those same national banks had sought Athenia as well. But that's where the Pappas genes had kicked in. Papou and her parents had worked too hard to build Athenia up to let it become another cookie-cutter branch of a national bank with no connection back to the community. And as she watched other community banks get acquired, that's exactly what they had become, with half their hometown workforces let go.

But, over the long run, the business wasn't working. Twelve branches had decreased to eight, and after the 2008 crisis they'd shrunk all the way to four, confined to Price and Ogden. And while the big banks adjusted to the new regulations that had followed that crisis, the burdens were heavier on smaller banks like Athenia.

Like her grandfather, Thea was stubborn but not stupid. So when a broker from Manhattan had called with an especially rich proposition, she'd agreed to take the meeting. At least to hear him out.

The bearded man put down his coffee cup and leaned forward.

"Our investors are willing to lose money at first. This is a long-term plan. They want to get in the market, build a base across the country with strong regional and local banks like yours, and position themselves for steady growth."

Thea crossed her arms. It sounded nice—but naïve.

"I admire the vision. But I've got to tell you: the big banks are so dominant, something major would have to change for that strategy to work."

"We understand the challenges. It is a risk the buyer is willing to take."

She remembered Thumper. Getting knocked off. Climbing back on. She could do it back then, young and full of energy. But things were different now. Other people were relying on her. Her employees would fare better within a robust national structure as opposed to a small family bank's dwindling footprint. And her family would profit as well, particularly with college around the corner for her kids.

"Like I said, I'm skeptical. But have your lawyers call my lawyers and let's talk specifics."

CHAPTER 14

APPLETON, WISCONSIN

I s the colonoscopy over?"

I'd never shared so many private details with a stranger in my life. Tori had skillfully extracted every piece of information she wanted.

"That'll do for now." Her wily grin returned. "So where were we?"

"You were about to tell me how, from that treasure trove of voter data, you're so certain that Justice Beagle did not actually win that election."

"Right."

She leaned over and double-clicked on the mouse, moving to a new page. The bruise on her left arm had swelled since breakfast; it was now deep purple and the size of a fist.

"So every data point we collect from a voter gets entered into their file, right?" she said.

"Right."

"Well, as all the data comes in, every voter is assigned a score based on their likelihood of voting for your candidate."

"Based on what?"

"Well, ideally, they say who they're voting for, either to a volunteer at their door or over the phone. And these days that can happen on social media as well."

I eyed Mrs. Sanders's voter score.

"So our gun-wielding knitter was a 'five'?"

"Yes, and a 'five' means she was definitely *not* voting for Justice

Beagle. Looks like she told a volunteer that on June 23, the last time the campaign contacted her."

I remembered those hard "Nos" from my days helping Dad. Never fun—testy arguments, slammed doors, torn-up literature. I'd joke with some voters—"So I'll put you down as undecided"—but I didn't. I'd circle the N on the sheet.

"Okay. So if you're definitely voting for Justice Beagle, that's a 'one'?"

"Yep. And 'twos' lean in your direction, and 'fours' lean against you."

I paused, doing the math in my head.

"There are millions of registered voters in Wisconsin. How could you possibly get enough voter responses to make a difference?"

She grinned as if she'd been awaiting my question. "Well, you talk to as many as you can, but you're right. That's where the modeling comes in."

"What modeling?"

"Statistical analysis. Based on the profiles of the voters—all those details on Mrs. Sanders—and comparing those voters to others we've identified as 'ones' and 'fives,' we can project who else will be 'ones' and 'fives' across the state."

"Or 'twos,' 'threes,' and 'fours'?"

"Right." She paused again. "If you have enough data on each voter, you can construct algorithms that predict voting patterns based on similar voter profiles that you've directly talked to. We call them 'look-alike' voters."

I nodded.

"So my entire job over the course of that campaign was to create the most accurate and updated voter profiles possible. That data then shapes every action the campaign takes, especially late in the game. My universe of 'ones' became the people we contacted repeatedly to turn out to vote, because we knew if they showed up to vote, they'd vote for us. The 'twos' needed mild persuasion, then a push to come out. 'Threes' needed more persuasion. And then we hoped to hell that the 'fours' and 'fives' didn't show up."

"So the file is the playbook of the campaign, broken down for every single voter."

"You got it."

"Like polling."

"Better than polling. Far more precise. But—"

"So how do you—"

She placed her hand over mine and squeezed. "*But . . . only if the file is accurate and up-to-date. Bad data can kill a campaign.*"

"Of course. But back to my original question: How do you know Justice Beagle didn't win?"

She leaned forward and double-clicked on a separate chart. A bar graph with five thick vertical bars. The bar on the left and the middle bar rose a third of the way up the page. The second bar was slightly lower. The fourth line was also about the same as the first line, a third of the way up. And the fifth line was the highest, much higher than the first line.

"See this chart?" she asked. "I made this the weekend before the election."

She pointed to the fifth bar, the tallest one. "Those were the 'fives.'"

"Supporters of your opponent. Flannery."

"Right."

Then she pointed to the first, much shorter bar. "Those were the 'ones.'"

"Beagle supporters."

"You got it."

The graph spoke for itself—lopsided in Flannery's favor—but she summarized it anyway.

"Well, the data wasn't even close. Beagle was cooked."

CHAPTER 15

PORTOFINO, ITALY

Katrina's guest was still in bed next to her, asleep and facing the other way, so she inched to her side of the bed gingerly.

She'd been out only a few hours, but because her phone vibrated in response to several high-priority senders, she couldn't ignore it. She grabbed it from beneath the stateroom's large oval window, then lay on her side, facing the window.

She opened the app they'd specially designed for internal communications, which both encrypted their messages and deleted them fifteen seconds after they were read.

The new message came from the senior member of her tech team. He hailed from Transylvania, so they all called him Drac—a menacing moniker he liked, since he was five-foot-two and weighed 120 pounds only after a big meal.

His message hit her like ice water.

> Someone exported data from the Wisconsin
> race.

Wisconsin. One of their test cases. In fact, such a pristine example that they'd featured it for the visiting delegation hours before.

The Wisconsin race had taken place months before. No fanfare at the time, and no activity since. Drac had confirmed that, as was typical for low-budget elections, one of the campaigns had shut down their account within days of victory. And the other had checked back in only twice.

Drac's message disappeared from the screen.

Do you know who? Katrina wrote back. The DNC or RNC? The national parties still had access, so party officials poked around in the file whenever they wanted.

A hand lightly touched her shoulder, jolting her as a soft breath warmed her neck.

She quickly flipped her phone over.

"Beautiful, why so tense? The time for work is over." Zhang's smooth British accent had soothed her a few hours ago, when his boat returned to the *Pushkin*, and did so again now as his lips whispered only inches from her ear.

She kissed his cheek. "Unfortunately, this project never rests. Please excuse me."

Again the gentleman, he rolled back to his side.

She swung back toward the window and flipped her phone over just as words disappeared from the app.

Missed your answer. Please send again.

A few seconds passed.

Am I interrupting something:)

Just my sleep. What did you send?

It was not the national parties. Or the state parties. Someone else. But don't know who.

Who would have access now? Katrina texted back.

Zhang stirred again. She peeked his way, but he still faced the other wall.

Nobody . . . in theory. But someone named
RUGBYDEM opened the file and exported
data.

And who is RUGBYDEM?

We can't find any more information on him. He
is accessing the account from the outside.

She shook her head. Someone who knew what they were doing.

And what data did they export?

All of the 5's and 1's in the city called
Appleton.

Katrina gazed out the oval window, facing the well-lit sea. Months after an election victory, someone might enter the voter file for any number of reasons. To update it. To clean it up. But that would likely be someone from the party.

Downloading all the voters who were expected to vote for or against the winning candidate in a particular town? That was not a task one would routinely take. Unless . . .

Concerning, she wrote back, clenching her jaw.

Very, Drac wrote. Should we tell the boss?

She typed back: Not yet.

PART 2

CHAPTER 16

Cassie's legs shivered beneath her as President Janet Moore grasped her hand.

"Welcome to the White House, young lady," the president said.

She looked far more striking in person—thinner and younger, too. Wearing a conservative blue pantsuit, the president took her seat, flashing another smile Cassie's way.

Her friendly greeting only made Cassie more nervous, knowing she was about to punch the leader of the free world in the nose.

They were in the small but stately Vermeil Room, on the first floor of the White House. Cassie had never heard of it until they told her to set up there. Sitting in ornate white chairs feet away from a marble fireplace, a photo of a buttoned-up and grim Mary Todd Lincoln watching over them, it felt as if they'd gone back in time—at least if she ignored the jungle of modern equipment, lights, wires, and cameras that surrounded them.

The White House communications director must have enjoyed Cassie's live confrontation with her anchor, because he'd called hours later. Now here she was, conducting the first one-on-one interview with the president in months.

It was a coup for her and Republic, although their agendas diverged after that. Cassie's bosses had handed her a pointed and confrontational script—but after the cameras were rolling, she would do what she wanted.

"Thank you, Madam President."

Cassie took a quick sip of water. As she did, the numerals tattooed along her left wrist buoyed her—the time and day that her parents were killed, and the constant reminder of why she did what she did. Mom and Dad would be proud.

"Let's get started," the president said.

She opened with the hardball her bosses had insisted on.

"Your central campaign promise was to end the partisan food fight in Washington, Madam President. How do you explain to the American people how partisan things have become since Inauguration Day? Isn't that your failure?"

The president shook her head, her mouth tensing.

"I'm as frustrated as anyone, Cassie. In Colorado we were always able to cross party lines to get things done. And as a candidate, I won both Republican and Democratic votes and have run this country in a bipartisan fashion since. But this is not a town that wants that. Too many people prefer the bickering."

Knowing her bosses would want a tough follow-up, Cassie dug in harder.

"That may be, but you knew that going in. You promised the American people you were up for the challenge and that you'd bridge the divide. How can you—"

"Cassie," the president said impatiently, "it takes two. I have compromised again and again, just as I did less than forty-eight hours ago to end the latest shutdown. But Speaker Paxton prefers fighting over governing and keeps moving the goalposts. At some point enough is enough."

"But, respectfully, will blaming and finger-pointing from you *or* the Speaker get the country anywhere? Will you ever find a way to rise above it?"

The president took a deep breath, smiled wistfully, then answered. "Cassie, I have worked to rise above it every day of my presidency."

After three uppercuts, it was time to divert from the script.

"So what's next?"

The president's face relaxed. "What's next?"

"Yes, what's next on your agenda? Now that this deal is done." The president hadn't been able to set the public agenda in a year, so this was her chance.

Media-savvy, the most powerful woman on the planet didn't miss the opportunity. Leaning forward in her chair, her prosecutor's eyes narrowing with intensity, she pounced.

"Whether or not the Speaker and his henchmen will admit it, our economy is slowing. And that's not due to taxes or regulations. It's because the American marketplace is broken. Our rigged political system has allowed a small number of major corporations to control too much, stifling growth and innovation in so many sectors and crushing the small businesses and family farms that are the backbone of the American economy. The competitive market which has always made ours the most dynamic economy in the world is fading. As a result, consumers suffer and workers suffer. And at some point innovation stops."

Cassie nodded, but Chuck Massa was still in her head.

"That sounds like Governor Moore the candidate. But can you really make progress on that agenda now? You can barely get basic budgets done. And don't those same corporations invest in the politicians to keep things from changing?"

The president's blue eyes sparkled on hearing the question.

"Oh, yes, we know these big corporations will invest heavily to keep the Speaker in office for as long as possible, along with all sorts of other secretive efforts to keep the status quo in place."

Smart: harkening back to the scandal that had sealed her victory in the first place.

"If that's the case, what can you do about it?"

"Keep the issue on the national radar. Keep laying out solutions. And when the American people give me the opportunity, I'll be ready to do something about it."

"And if that opportunity never comes?"

"Then we're stuck where we are today, where a small number of people horde for themselves most of the benefits of the American economy. But, Cassie, I will do all I can to make sure things *do* change."

Cassie hoped the goose bumps forming on her arm wouldn't be visible in the camera shot. It was the most on-message the president had been in months. She meant every word.

CHAPTER 17

APPLETON, WISCONSIN

M rs. Block?"

"Who wants to know?" Even as she asked that, short and gray-haired Erma Block offered a cordial smile as she peered past the open front door. Her small ranch house anchored one end of a cul-de-sac on the outskirts of Appleton.

"I'm a news reporter. Jack Sharpe. Could I talk to you for five minutes?"

"Wait—aren't you from Republic News?"

"Well, I was. We went our separate ways." My shoulders sagged slightly, but admitting it was getting easier.

"What's the matter? You too liberal for them?"

I didn't consider myself liberal, but that wasn't worth explaining. "It wasn't really ab—"

"Never mind. I was hoping you'd say yes."

This squared with her voter profile, which tagged her as a loyal Democrat. She'd voted in every presidential election for forty-eight years, both general and primary, but skipped most midterm elections.

"So I take it you're a Democrat."

"Absolutely. To my core. . . . C'mon in. I can't stand for too long at a time."

Framed photos of Presidents Kennedy and Franklin Roosevelt adorned the hallway we walked through, followed by several pictures of a smiling Hubert Humphrey. One was autographed.

"That's from the county fair." She pointed at a photo of Humphrey in front of a giant hog. "He came by every year. Wonderful man. I volunteered on his presidential campaign."

"He really was a great man." Although I grew up a moderate Republican, I'd always admired Humphrey. Old-school and a champion for civil rights, like Dad.

She offered me a chair at her small kitchen table. I declined her offer of coffee, but she fixed herself a cup. And her slow-motion pour forewarned that I'd be there for far longer than I'd hoped.

"Actually, I'll have one, too."

"Now, how can I help you, Jack?" She leaned forward to pour my cup. "I've been passionate about politics my entire life. When I was a little girl, my parents took me to see Harry Truman in Madison."

She recounted the Truman tale for at least ten minutes, walking through everything from his dapper attire to the warm and windy weather that day. I listened patiently, waiting for a pause to interrupt with my short set of questions.

My goal for the next few days was to learn what voters like Mrs. Block had experienced in the election. Did their "treatment" by the campaigns line up with how voters slotted as "ones" and "fives" would typically be engaged?

Mrs. Block was designated a "one" on Justice Beagle's voter file: every data point on her profile indicated that she would vote Democrat, including having signed recent petitions to end the electoral college and increase the minimum wage. But, given her poor history of voting outside of presidential years, the campaign's goal would have been to make sure she showed up to vote.

". . . and then the train carrying him pulled away. It was incredible. The next ti—"

"Mrs. Block, what a wonderful story," I said over her, cutting off her next tale before it was too late. "I actually wanted to hear your views on a more recent election. I'm curious who you voted for in the supreme court election a few months back."

She sat up higher. "Well, I voted for Justice Beagle, of course."

"And why's that?"

"Oh, it was a very important race here." Her expression hardened and she folded her arms. "So much was at stake."

"Like what?"

"Just about everything we Democrats care about. Workers' rights. Schools. Health care. Did you know that our workers here in Wisconsin have been under attack for years? I was a teacher for decades, so I went to a rally the other day and . . ."

The rally story consumed another ten minutes. I jumped back in as soon as she wrapped it up.

"Good for you for being part of that," I said, then pivoted back. "Can I ask how you got your information on the campaign? How you came to know that so much was at stake?"

"Which campaign?"

"The supreme court campaign. The one Justice Beagle won."

"Oh, yes. By the end, everyone knew."

"Who's everyone?"

"Everyone in our Democratic club. We were so passionate about that election."

"And do you remember, specifically, how you were all informed about the need to vote in it? When I researched it, Judge Beagle didn't have much money to run television ads."

"It wasn't television ads. No. I don't care about those anyway," she said, waving her wrinkled hand forward, echoing every voter's belief that television ads didn't influence them. "It was the phone calls. They called to make sure I knew when the election was. Then a nice young woman came to my door, and we must've talked for hours. She was lovely. From Kenosha. And we agreed that my plan was to vote on Election Day like I always do. I also got some flyers in the mail, too. So I guess, to answer your question, you couldn't miss it. We were all talking about how important it was."

"I see. Anything else?" I clipped my comments, hoping she'd do the same.

"Yes. The campaign was nice enough to remind me to vote the day of the election."

"How'd they do that?" In addition to her high rate of opening party emails, the voter file indicated she had replied to several campaign texts she'd received.

"Well, someone called here and left a message on my answering machine, but I didn't get that until after Election Day. But a text message also came on the new phone."

She held up an old mobile phone with a small digital screen similar to one I'd owned five phones ago.

"They think of everything, don't they? I don't think I would've forgotten to vote, but that text came through and I voted an hour later. I used to vote down at the middle school, but the text reminded me that I had a new poll location."

"How good of them to do that. Did you get any other communications telling you to vote?"

She narrowed her eyes and took a sip of coffee the way a cat lapped water from a bowl. I'd never witnessed a single cup of coffee survive so long.

"I can't say I remember anything else."

"How about any internet ads?"

A smile crinkled her mouth. "Oh, no, Jack. I'm not an internet person. Heck, I only discovered text messaging two years ago. You know how they used to do it, don't you? Back in the day, they used to . . ."

Thirty minutes later I walked back to my car.

It took Mrs. Block the longest to say it, but the six other "ones" I talked to described similar treatment. Phone calls and mailers reminding them what was at stake and when to vote. Two had had volunteers knock on their door; three had not. Several recalled seeing some digital ads. All received Election Day text messages.

Bottom line: at least in Appleton, if you were tagged as a "one" for Justice Beagle, you couldn't have missed the fact that a crucial election was taking place.

CHAPTER 18

LONDON

D rac stormed into Katrina's corner office only minutes after she'd returned from her flight home.

"They were back in the file yesterday," he said, his hands gripping her desk's sides as he leaned over it. "For hours."

"Again?" she asked, powering up the twin flat-screen monitors on her glass-top desk. Three beeps sounded as the screens lit up. "Did they export more data?"

"Not this time. But they updated the file."

She double-clicked on the mouse, opening a new window. "WISCONSIN" appeared at the top of the page.

"With what?"

"The final data from the most recent election."

Katrina clicked again and leaned toward the monitor on the right. "I see that now. So they're examining who voted?"

"It appears so."

"And what will they learn from the current state of the Wisconsin file?"

"That their best voters showed up in very strong numbers, and that the voters most against them did not."

Katrina stood up and parted the blinds at the windows behind her desk. The day had a dreary cast to it.

"Should we manipulate the data so the differential is less clear?" Doing so would be technically simple, she knew. They'd done it before.

"I think not. If they notice the change, that would be more suspicious than what they will find now."

"Especially since they were on the winning side."

Drac was one of the few who didn't need an explanation for what she meant. To achieve the desired outcome in Wisconsin and elsewhere, they had to actively manipulate the losing campaign's data. While accessing and understanding the winning campaign's data was important, nothing needed to be altered.

"Yes. There should be no discrepancies from anything they've seen before."

Katrina sat back down and eyed her screen. "You're right: no exports. So all they will see is that their tactics and targeting proved highly effective, correct?"

"Exactly. We can only hope they don't talk to their opponents."

Katrina smirked while standing up again. "This is American politics. That won't happen."

CHAPTER 19

The small celebration of Cassie's coup ended quickly.

Having eaten dinner quickly and put their one-year-old son, Aiden, to bed early, she and her wife, Rachel, were lying on opposite sides of their old couch by 8:00 p.m., white-socked feet resting in one another's laps.

Bridget Turner led off the program, recapping months of deadlock. She reminded her viewers that President Moore had promised to clean up the partisan mess. "Let's see how she responds to being directly confronted about her failure to do so."

The opening footage captured President Moore entering the Vermeil Room, looking around awkwardly before being mic'd up, then sitting down across from Cassie. Their pleasant handshake and the president's friendly greeting hadn't survived the editing room. And whether it was the lights or the camera angles, none of the warmth of the moment emanated through the television screen. Instead, the shadowy lighting made the president appear dour. Unfriendly.

On the screen, Cassie stiffened as she asked her first question, coming across far more harshly than it had felt at the time. The president's answer—sharing the frustration about the partisan stalemate and touting her efforts to work across party lines—sounded as strong as it had in person.

Bridget Turner didn't agree. "That's stunning, don't you think?" she asked as the camera cut to her immediately after the president's answer.

Sitting across from her, a bald, bow-tied guest sneered. "It sure is. She takes no responsibility whatsoever but blames it on Washington as opposed to her own failings. No wonder nothing is getting done around here."

Bridget cast a cynical smile at the camera. "Let's see what she says next."

Cassie looked equally stern as she began her follow-up question. But after her initial words, the show aired an intense, unattractive close-up of the president. Impatience—pursed lips, narrowed eyes, creased forehead—engulfed her face before she jumped in to address Cassie's point.

"Cassie, it takes two . . ."

The tight shot on the president made the interruption appear aggressive, as if she'd snapped in anger.

Turner reappeared, her chin up and blue eyes protruding. "The president didn't even let Cassie finish her question. And now she directly attacks Speaker Paxton? The one person she needs to work with? We're seeing the problem tonight, folks."

"You're pretty rough on the president," Rachel said softly to Cassie from the other side of the couch.

"*They're* making it look a lot rougher than it was." Cassie boiled inside at the way they had butchered her big moment. "But wait: I give her a chance now."

The shot captured Cassie asking what would come next, then panned back to the president: "Whether or not the Speaker and his henchmen want to admit it, our economy is losing momentum. And that's not due to taxes or regulations. It's because the American marketplace is broken."

Bridget Turner reappeared. "Henchmen? Now she's calling top leaders of the House of Representatives names, too? What is this, third grade?"

"And, Bridget," the bald man chimed in, "what is she talking about? The stock market is soaring. Business is booming. The marketplace is 'broken'? Who knew?"

The show cut directly to Cassie's next question.

"Wait!" Cassie cried out. "They didn't run her full answer. She explained what she meant!"

"Shhh," Rachel urged. "Let me listen."

The president talked directly into the camera. "Whether or not they block me, I will always push this agenda. And I'm prepared, when the American people give me the opportunity, to do something about—"

"They cut out a bunch more." Cassie's face reddened as she yelled at the TV. "There was a lot more in there."

Turner came back on-screen. "Well, there you have it. The president is going to keep pushing her agenda attacking our strong economy no matter what anyone says. And somehow it's up to the American people to bail her out."

The guest laughed out loud. "I see now why Speaker Paxton is so frustrated. Kudos to your reporter for providing such an eye-opening glimpse of the problem."

"Yes. Good for Cassie Knowles for holding the president accountable."

CHAPTER 20

You didn't have to wait, Jack."

As Tori put down her final wipe, I squeezed the sourdough buns together and lifted the Bad Apples half-pounder to eye level.

"I'll enjoy this more now that you're done. Your routine stresses me out."

"Honestly, it's not something I can control."

I'd seen it before. My sophomore-year college roommate followed a precise routine each night. For ten minutes he'd twist the knob furiously, pull the door to confirm it wouldn't open, untwist, then twist and pull again. "It's locked," I'd always say. Didn't matter. Before and after, he was the most normal guy in the world and one of the smartest in my class. But for those ten minutes, nothing stopped him from twisting that doorknob, as firmly locked as it was.

"I get it. I figure the only reason you got me here is because of it." Who else would call a reporter days on end to raise questions about an election they'd *won*?

"True enough. Well, along those lines, I spent the afternoon scrutinizing the election turnout."

"Find anything?"

She pulled a single sheet of paper out of her bag, then laid it down to my right.

"You recognize this bar chart, right?"

It was the graph from the other day: five vertical bars representing the voter scores from the supreme court election, skewing in Flannery's favor. But now a handwritten percentage number appeared above each bar.

"What are those percentages?" I asked, pointing at the figure "62%."

"They're the voter turnout for each voter category. I spent today updating the file and putting this together."

"Wow. No wonder Justice Beagle won."

The graph told a simple story. Sixty-two percent of Justice Beagle's "ones" and 50 percent of the "twos" had voted. Only 35 percent of the "fives" and 25 percent of the "fours" had. The middle bar—the "threes"—came in at 45 percent.

She leaned forward, placing her chin on her fist.

"Exactly."

"From the people I talked to all day, I'm not surprised the 'ones' showed up like that. They were keyed into the election, thanks to your phone calls, text messages, you name it."

"Maybe so, but that's a freakish difference between the two sides. It's not like the other campaign wasn't doing the same stuff we were. We had about the same amount of money."

"Maybe you did it far more effectively."

"I can't imagine they would do such a poor job. Once you have the voters categorized, it's not like this is rocket science."

I savored the final three bites of my burger while keeping my thoughts to myself. Maybe the Beagle campaign had simply outhustled and outperformed his opponent. Sometimes one side just wanted it more.

But that would also mean that my breakthrough scoop was not a story at all.

CHAPTER 21

SAN FRANCISCO

Bernie Cho was convinced the framed Stanford Business School diploma on his wall was a curse. A depressing reminder, looming over him every day, that his career had failed to live up to its once-great promise. If so, the good news was that today would be one of its final days up there.

"So are you ready to do this?" asked his longtime lawyer, Manny Shepard, looking across Bernie's paper-strewn desk with a forced grin.

Bernie kept his empty stare directed at the diploma. He'd stopped going to reunions after the fifth. Too humiliating. So many of his classmates had already made it big and found no greater joy than yammering on about it. Those who had joined the tech giants after graduating were now rocketing up those corporate ladders, gobbling up stock options on every rung. The venture capital and private equity guys were doing equally well. And while some of the start-up guys were struggling just as he was, many had already struck it rich: within a few years of that first reunion, a number would either sell or go public, pocketing millions. They'd either retired or returned to pioneer a second start-up.

But Bernie remained stuck on his first. In fact, at his five-year reunion, he was already up to his ears in angry investors. And while he and his team had continued to hone their world-class technology since then, the business never blossomed. His latest setback was that board-demanded cost cutting had forced him to move from the rarefied air of Palo Alto to the cramped loft and grungy streets of the Tenderloin, in the heart of San Francisco.

What made it all worse was that Bernie Cho had been the star of his Stanford class, voted most likely to succeed. Back then, the technology at the heart of his start-up, named Sherlock, had run circles around the competition. He and several Caltech engineers had developed it even before Bernie graduated, which was why he'd rejected job offers that less talented classmates had seized, choosing to venture out on his own instead.

But in hindsight he'd made one fatal mistake. He'd chosen the wrong product category: internet searches.

He turned back to Manny, impeccably dressed, now a partner at the top tech law firm in the Bay Area. How their fortunes had changed. As a young lawyer, Manny had begged to sign Sherlock on as a client, eager to get in on the ground floor before the company soared to titan status.

"Earth to Bernie." Manny waved his hand in the air. "Are you ready?"

Bernie sighed, rubbing the back of his neck. Of course not. Selling now, at this price, meant that he'd failed, even if Manny couldn't hide how eager he was to close the deal.

"I get that we can't compete," Bernie said. "But is this really the best offer we can get?"

It was the only offer they'd received since the early days, and a pittance compared to those. But his largest funder, a Menlo Park venture capital firm, was hammering on him to cut their losses.

"We've talked about this. I can't imagine anything better is going to come along." Manny stole a quick glance at his watch. His charity work was evidently taking time away from clients who paid full freight.

"Yeah," Bernie said, stalling, "but has their lawyer ever revealed how they plan to make the company work?"

Manny crossed his arms. "She says they're confident in your technology and engineering talent. She kept calling it a long-term investment, building off the strong position they've built in Asia."

Bernie chuckled as he scratched his head again. "She's as dumb as I've been all these years."

An awkward silence hovered over the small office. They'd been a lot closer in the early years, Bernie a high-flying entrepreneur and Manny a hungry associate. But their weekends in Sonoma sipping wine with their wives had ended once Sherlock stagnated, while Manny emerged as one of Silicon Valley's most successful lawyers. Until this deal arose out of the blue a few months back, they hadn't seen each other in more than a year.

Manny glanced at his phone before breaking the silence. "You gotta give yourself a break, Bernie."

"It's hard to do that after wasting millions of other people's money. And now I'm dumping Sherlock for so little. I let so many people down. And what am I supposed to tell my kids?"

"That you and your team designed the best search engine on the internet. You can be proud of that."

Bernie gestured up at the diploma on the wall. "I'd be proud if I'd turned it into a successful business."

Manny removed several pages from a manila folder.

"I'm afraid the lesson of your efforts is that in the search engine space, no one can build a successful business. No one can compete."

Bernie smiled grimly. "That's the truth. But I win the award for being the last person to figure that out."

Manny cast a lopsided grin as he passed the documents across Bernie's desk.

"Given this sale, I'd say you're the second-to-last person."

CHAPTER 22

APPLETON, WISCONSIN

The voter file ranked Maple Avenue's Ernest Stiglitz as a "five"—a strong "No" on Judge Beagle. But his red Dodge pickup made a strong case for a new category entirely, at least a "ten."

The yellow "Don't Tread on Me" sticker covered the top left corner of the truck cabin's back window, with an "I Carry" sticker below it, followed by the impressively subtle "Deport Illegals (Future Democrats)" below that. And in case the second sticker left any doubt, a rifle rack hung inside the truck's back window. The window's right corner displayed an American flag, a Green Bay Packers sticker, and a diagnosis Mr. Stiglitz apparently agreed with: "Liberalism Is a Mental Disorder." The rusty bumper below boasted more jarring messages: "Politically Incorrect and Proud of It," "Can't Feed 'Em, Don't Breed 'Em," and, showing spirited local flavor and keen historical insight, "McCarthy Was Right."

I double-checked my clipboard to confirm it. Despite his mobile billboard of right-wing views, Mr. Stiglitz—who hadn't missed a presidential general election or primary in decades—had skipped the special election.

"Who is it?" a husky voice asked a minute later, after I'd knocked on the door three times.

"My name's Jack Sharpe. I used to work at Republic News." Conservatives generally liked the station.

"Yeah? So?"

"You're Ernest, right? I wanted to talk about the most recent election."

The door cracked open six inches and a thick round head appeared on the other side. A week's growth of beard on the man's jowls, chin, and neck was only slightly shorter than the buzz cut on top.

"What about it? Frickin' disaster as far as I'm concerned."

"And why's that?"

The door opened a few inches more.

"President Moore?" He scowled, the veins in his lower neck lifting his dry skin like thin wires. "She's taking this country straight to hell."

"I'm sorry. I meant the special election a few months back. For the Wisconsin Supreme Court."

The tension left his face. "Oh, that one."

"Yeah. Can I ask you who you voted for?"

His eyelids sagged. "To tell you the truth, I didn't end up voting in that one."

He didn't widen the door, so our conversation was going to stay at the doorstep.

"Not with all that was at stake?"

His chin wrinkled as he tilted his head back. "Hey, buddy, why're you asking me this stuff?"

"I'm looking into that election. It was a surprising result."

"Not really. No one was paying attention. I didn't hear much either way."

Odd. As a Flannery "one," he should've received a surge of information imploring him to vote.

"You're a passionate Republican." I gestured back to his pickup truck. "Didn't they remind you to vote?"

"I might've gotten a phone call or two. Told them I supported whoever that Republican was. But I didn't hear much after that."

"Well, when—"

"But I also saw some things that made me not too excited about the Republican, either."

"Like what?"

"On the internet. You know, those annoying ads that pop up when you're trying to read stuff. This guy was squeamish. A RINO for sure." RINO: Republican in name only—the same accusation they'd used to take out my dad.

"You didn't receive any mail?"

"I don't remember any. But the ads online—I remember those. Mealy-mouthed crap. We don't need weak-kneed Republicans in office, for cripes sakes. Either way, I basically forgot about the election till it was over."

He started to close the door.

"So you didn't get any late calls, texts, or mail urging you to vote?"

"I didn't. It's like they didn't want my vote. Well, they got what they deserved if that's the case. RINOs don't respect us true conservatives."

I made five other home visits the rest of the day. Two senior couples, a forty-five-year-old homemaker, a junior partner at a law firm, and another whose pickup truck rivaled Stiglitz's. They all told the same story: little contact from the campaign and no turnout push at the end. And two others complained that the digital ads had made Flannery seem unacceptably moderate.

I filled Tori in as I drove back to my motel, summarizing the day's conversations.

"They didn't even text at the end to remind them to vote? Or call?" she asked.

"Nope."

"Strange. That's the bare minimum you'd do for your 'ones.' And were the digital ads they didn't like run *by* Flannery?"

"Sounded like it. They were positive, but centrist, scaring off the conservatives."

"That's what you'd send to 'threes.' Not 'ones.' I can't imagine my counterparts on that campaign committing malpractice like that."

"Do you actually know them? The manager? The voter file manager?"

"Not personally, but I know they've been around enough to know what they were doing."

"How about we track them down and find out?"

CHAPTER 23

TULSA, OKLAHOMA

Y ou're gonna win this thing, Angelique," the twenty-four-year-old
campaign manager said as they drove up to their first poll on Election Day, minutes before seven. "You're gonna make history."

"Well, what's new?" Angelique asked with an indulgent laugh. The kid
didn't get the joke, but Angelique Robbins had spent her life breaking
barriers.

In her neighborhood. At school. Even at family reunions. As the daughter of a white Oklahoman dad and a Vietnamese mom—they'd met during
his second tour, she was born twelve months later, then Dad had tracked
mother and daughter down after the war and brought them home to
Tulsa—she'd always stood out growing up. With her dark olive skin, round
eyes, and black hair, no one else in her world looked anything like her.

Reactions had evolved as she grew up. In elementary school they either looked at her funny or ignored her. In middle school they bullied her,
so she focused on her studies. Once she hit her teenage years, the boys
fancied her, lifting her confidence. Angelique graduated as both class
valedictorian and homecoming queen—the first ever to do so.

Decades later she was hours away from becoming the first Asian
American member of the Oklahoma State Legislature.

After her manager's morning pep talk, Angelique spent the next two
hours chasing down voters in the parking lot of a north Tulsa voting location. Turnout was light, so she shook the hand of every person who
walked in. Car-to-car as opposed to door-to-door.

"You definitely got my vote," one elder gentleman said as their hands parted.

"Thank you. You honor me with your confidence."

After voting in her home precinct, which two cameras filmed live, she stopped by two more polling locations that morning. Light turnout, even over the lunch hour. But still a generally friendly response.

"How is it out there?" Angelique asked her manager when he rejoined her shortly after one.

"Looks fine," he said, his brow wrinkled as he said it.

"What's wrong?"

"Nothing's wrong."

"Tell me. I can hear it in your voice."

"Nothing to be alarmed about. Turnout's a little light."

"Well, of course it is. It's a special for a statehouse seat."

"I know, but it's light in places where we expected better."

"Oh."

Her skin suddenly prickled. Her chest tightened. Both new sensations. She'd led from the campaign's first day—fawned over as the favorite, including a glowing profile in the *World* touting her as a rising star and a future congresswoman. It had never dawned on her that she might lose. Until now. Even that sliver of doubt made her nervous as hell.

"But we have hours to go and we're blowing up the phones now," he said through a strained smile. "We have a lot of time left."

"Okay. Good."

But the feeling in the pit in her stomach remained. Hundreds of friends and family members had stepped up to help, expecting a win. So many had given money. Held parties. Bragged about her to their friends. Many were standing at polls right now. How would she ever explain losing?

She greeted voters at a church, a school, and an American Legion hall over the next four hours, grabbing a late lunch in between. Turnout was still light. And she was also learning how to read voters. Those who planned on voting for her would say without hesitation, "I got you," "I'm voting for you," and "You got my vote!" Those who'd just voted for her were equally explicit as they walked out. A thumbs-up and "I got you."

Those who didn't vote for her? They were polite. They usually said hello. But they didn't say the words. They didn't commit. And they didn't look her in the eye even as they wished her luck. With her manager's update echoing in her head, every voter who walked by and didn't commit juiced her nerves a little more.

She was standing outside an elementary school when her manager rejoined her.

"Any news?" she asked, with an hour to go.

"It's going to be close, Angelique." A trace of perspiration shone on his brow.

They'd never once talked about it being close.

"Is it? Did things not pick up?"

"A little."

"Where we needed them to?"

"We hope."

"I don't understand. What happened to this morning's confidence?"

He jammed his hands in his pockets.

"We're going back over the file now. The modeling might have been off. Or something."

"'Or something'? What does that mean?"

"We're checking."

Forty minutes later a large crowd of volunteers, staff, and friends cheered as Angelique walked into Molly's Pub for her victory party, a smile frozen on her face. They were all expecting a win.

The polls closed at 7:30 p.m. and the first returns—the early and absentee mail-in votes—came in minutes after. Tied, as expected.

But the crowd quieted once the day's returns started coming in. Angelique was down from the start and lost ground quickly. A few cheers erupted after several highly partisan areas came in in her favor, but those spurts reversed quickly.

By 8:40 it was over.

By 9:00 the pub had cleared out.

Angelique Robbins had begun her day excited to make history. She lost, 54 to 46 percent.

CHAPTER 24

Drac always called at the worst times.

From the back of a black limousine, Katrina was admiring the verdant banks of the Dnieper as it cut through Kiev. The drive back to the airport followed a productive meeting with the soybean king of Ukraine, who was scooping up farms across the American Midwest at a breakneck pace.

"The Oklahoma operation was our most effective to date," Drac said.

"How so?"

"Several new techniques are proving to be incredibly powerful."

The limousine veered left to cross a Soviet-style bridge. An old cruise ship was docked on the riverbank below, similar to the type she'd seen in Brooklyn as a girl.

"Good. Even better than Wisconsin and Florida?"

"We have fine-tuned our approach since those elections."

"So that means our work is harder to trace?"

"They will not detect it," Drac said. "The losing campaign will be confused—blamed as incompetent. They will never know that their data was actually quite accurate. The irony is that the better the campaign, the more effective our work will be."

Halfway across the bridge, Katrina gazed back at the Dnieper's right bank, dominated by an immense statue of a robed woman lifting both a sword and a shield. Amid the promising updates, the robust figure reminded her of her greatest concern.

"Any further activity in Appleton?"

"Nothing."

"Good. Let's hope that's the end of it."

CHAPTER 25

NEAR MADISON, WISCONSIN

It was like a Cold War summit. Two sides who'd worked against each other for months now eyeing each other face-to-face.

And I was the UN.

"Strange circumstances," Johnny Yost, Flannery's campaign manager, mumbled when we first sat down at the greasy spoon just off the highway. Next to Johnny was a mousy guy with glasses named Ned, the voter file manager.

With Tori sitting to my left, we all mostly just stared at each other in between ordering and sipping orange juice. They clammed up at most of my questions, while Tori's hand wipe process only heightened the awkwardness.

I finally dissected the problem. Both Ned's and Johnny's eyes were glued on Tori even when I was speaking. Her presence—the opponent's data guru—was putting them on edge.

"Tori, why don't you tell them why you called me?"

As Tori told her story from Election Day onward—no bullshit, friendly, sincere—they eased up. My guess was that, while they were intrigued by both her appearance and what she was saying, what won them over was that she was willing to say it to the enemy. I didn't know another person in politics who would do such a thing.

"So you suspect foul play?" Yost asked.

"Let's just say I'm here to dig into it," I said.

"And what have you found so far?"

"Something fishy took place. But we won't know unless we also under-stand what happened on your end."

. Their shoulders sagged simultaneously. The topic triggered painful memories.

"The end of the campaign was a complete nightmare," Yost said.

"How so?"

"We felt good most of the way through." His right hand tightened into a fist. "We had a good sense of what we needed to tell the undecideds. We'd built a robust model about which voters needed to turn out for us, we knew who your voters were, and it was clear that we way outnum-bered you."

"That's how I saw it, too," Tori said.

Yost looked down at the table.

"And then our turnout cratered. There were warning signs in the early vote period—a lot of committed voters flaking—but we hoped Election Day would make up for it. Halfway through the day, we knew something was wrong. Our best voters weren't turning out, nor were our leaners— and so many of the numbers we were calling were bad." He looked at Tori. "Your voters showed up in big numbers, and then the swing voters went largely your way, which also surprised us."

Ned spoke up again. "I spent the rest of the week reviewing the initial numbers and couldn't figure it out. After the official vote came in, I cross-checked our file with the final results, and it was even more bizarre."

"Did you tell anyone?" I asked.

"Tell them what? That we didn't know what happened? That the data was screwed up?" Ned's face turned a bright pink. "Judge Flannery and the entire Republican Party already blamed us for the loss. They said our modeling was way off. Some even accused us of having misled them in-tentionally. So whining that something was wrong with the data would've only made us look worse."

It must have been rough. When a campaign went down in flames, the scapegoating broke out before the night ended, with managers and staff the first ones thrown under the bus. No doubt this sad pair remained unemployed because of it.

"Would it surprise you to know that when I talked to your best voters, most hadn't heard from you in the final weeks?"

Ned leaned forward. "That's bullshit. We hit our 'ones' hard."

"Some of them also complained that your digital communications made Flannery appear moderate."

Yost arched his back. "That's also BS. Those would've only gone to swing voters and independents. Our core voters got the hard-core stuff. Flannery's a big gun guy and a strict constitutionalist. That's what we hit our 'ones' with."

Stiglitz's bumper stickers flashed in my mind. Those would've been the perfect message to get him to vote.

"Well, the ones I talked to hadn't seen those ads."

Ned pushed back again, glaring at me. "You talked to the wrong people, then."

Tori the peacemaker jumped in. "You guys bring your computer like we said?"

"Of course."

"Let's trade notes."

I sat back and let the computer folks do their thing. An information swap—peering into the other side's data—clearly excited them more than arguing across the table. They logged on to their respective voter files.

Tori kicked off. "We had Ernest Stiglitz, on Maple Street in Appleton, as a 'five'—hard-core conservative."

"Oh, yeah, total hard-core. Big Second Amendment guy. Has both a state hunting license and a concealed carry permit." He pointed at his screen. "See, he's a perfect example. We hit him hard, he said he was going to vote, but he never did. We have no idea why."

"I know why. He told me he barely heard from you guys lately, and that Flannery was a RINO. Said your own digital ads turned him off."

"That's not right." Ned pointed at his screen. "He confirmed that he was for us early, then confirmed he was voting through both a late phone call and a text. And I have no idea how he would've gotten moderate messaging."

"I hate to break it to you, Ned, but that *is* right. The man told me this to my face. Your data must be off."

He blinked at me repeatedly in disbelief as if I'd told a preacher his Bible was wrong.

"It's the truth, Ned," Tori said. "Jack talked to him for fifteen minutes."

"Well, then how in the hell—"

"Either you had a major problem with your own team inputting data," Tori said, "or someone was messing with your file."

Ned didn't like either conclusion. "Let's check out some others."

They swapped information on other Appleton voters for the next twenty-five minutes, discovering the same disconnect. As with Stiglitz, Ned's voter file was wildly inconsistent with the conversations I'd had.

"Guys, your eggs are gonna go cold," I said as they completed the list.

While Tori's and my plates were spotless, they hadn't touched a thing since taking out their computer.

"I can't eat," Ned said, swallowing hard. "I'm going to be sick."

CHAPTER 26

LONDON

The door swung open and Drac burst into Katrina's office.

Just back from her Ukraine meeting, she looked up from her monitor, where a map displayed all their target states in blue.

"The Republican campaign in Wisconsin accessed their database," Drac said. "For the first time in weeks—"

"And what are they searching for?" She hated wasting time on information she already knew.

"It's worse. They accessed their database at the same moment that RUGBYDEM accessed his database."

He didn't have to say another word.

"Were they examining the same voters?"

"Yes. They were clearly comparing notes, one voter at a time."

She folded her arms as her pulse sped up. Drac should never have been so sloppy in Wisconsin in the first place.

"Then we have no choice. We need to spike the files."

"But that will only draw their suspi—"

"Their suspicion is already drawn. We can't afford to have them dig deeper."

"But once we spike them, won't they . . . ?"

She picked up her phone and dialed. "*They* won't be around to tell anyone."

CHAPTER 27

APPLETON, WISCONSIN

W hat's wrong, Cassie?"
    I was sitting on the bed in my Hampton Inn room when I got
a call from the one person at Republic who'd never let me down.
"You can tell?" she asked.
"I can tell."
"It's about work. Things are—"
"Are you on your work cell?"
"I am."
"Well, call me back from a landline or Rachel's phone."

I'd never told her any details. And she was the one I'd been most tempted to tell, for her own sake. Because I'd recruited her there, I was protective of her career. Then again, my departure opened much more opportunity for her.

The phone rang again. An unfamiliar 202 number.

"Jack, this place is scaring me."

"Cassie, I had to sign a nondisclosure agreement. I can't say much."

I cringed, realizing how unhelpful that was. Then again, the nondisclosure didn't prohibit me from listening to her complaints. "Let's try this: What are they doing that scares you?"

"The coverage against the president is over-the-top. Every day, I'm supposed to parrot some anti–Janet Moore script they spoon-feed me, but then I don't feel like a reporter at all."

"All I can tell you is be careful with how you handle it. And read your contract closely."

"My employment contract?"

Reporters didn't usually think about their contracts until it was time to negotiate a new one. And even then they focused only on how much they were paid and for how long.

"Yes. The fine print." That was as far as I could go down that path. "What have you been trying to cover?"

"Honestly, I've just been aiming for balance. Between her and Paxton."

"How can you balance out those two?" I asked. Since he'd taken over the House, Elmore Paxton had pinned Moore down. As far as I could tell, the guy was well paid by big business to crush the president's agenda.

"Every time I try to be neutral, give her perspective—anything—they shut me down. I had an exclusive interview with her the other day, but they cut out all the parts where she stated her case."

"Let me guess: her economic agenda."

"Exactly. They butchered it to make her come across terribly. And it turned me into their hatchet man."

"And what did you do in response?" This was the moment when I'd screwed up, and Cassie was at least as hotheaded as I was.

"Nothing yet. I've been stewing for a day. That's why I called you."

Good.

"Cassie, go read your employment agreement. For now, I wouldn't say anything. Play the long game."

"But it feels so wrong."

"I understand. But trust me: Tread carefully. That's all I can say."

The call ended, but before I put my phone down, a new message arrived. From Tori.

> Jack. Call me right away. Someone nuked their voter file.

Tori picked up on the first ring.

"What do you mean the file got nuked?" I asked.

"It's wiped out. Flannery's data is now a mishmash of nonsense."

"So it's only *their* data?"

"Yes. That guy Ned called and told me about it. Our file is fine."

I sat down on the bed.

"Jack, this is really weird."

"The timing is definitely strange."

"It's the timing and it's specifically what happened. Ned and I talked through it. We've seen system screw-ups in our voter files in the past. Bugs come up all the time. But nothing where an entire file is wiped clean of any useful data."

"Could he tell if other candidate files were impacted?"

"He checked with the state party and no one else in Wisconsin had any problems."

I stewed for a second. About the timing.

"Can people see when you guys log on to the voter files?"

"Yes. Each state party has data people who manage the state's voter files. National parties have the same. A few people have a high enough level of access that they can access every candidate's file."

"And what can they see you doing?"

"When we log in, when we export data, when we run reports. You name it, they see it all."

I cringed. Someone might've watched everything Tori had done since I arrived. But her work alone had not spurred any repercussions.

"Well, either it's a sheer coincidence, or the fact that you and he logged on at the same time triggered his data being wiped."

"Sounds right to me. But, Jack, think about it. Someone in the Democratic Party can see when I'm logging in. And someone from the Republican Party can see when they're logging in. But who—"

I finished the sentence for her.

"Who in the hell saw that you both logged in at the same time?"

CHAPTER 28

AIR FORCE ONE

The Washington Monument shrunk, then disappeared, as Air Force One ascended before banking west into the setting sun.

Every few weeks the president traveled to her small ranch near Aspen, Colorado. In the summer, in between meetings, she'd get in a few hours of horseback riding or hiking. In the winter she'd ski for a day or two on Ajax Mountain, Snowmass, or a smaller resort nearby. The spectacle of Secret Service agents trying to keep up with the president, a former competitive skier, as she bounced between moguls was creating a public relations nightmare for the White House. And Cassie's bosses at Republic made sure to highlight the overall cost of each trip. But the president insisted it kept her head straight amid all the pressures of Washington. Plus, she'd made a deal with her husband when she decided to run.

For the press that accompanied her, the Air Force One flight to Denver was a luxury—the cuisine especially—but the jaunt to Aspen from Denver could be a bear. Either they loaded onto a small charter plane and rode the roller coaster of mountain breezes into Aspen Airport, or they took a van or bus and drove for more than three hours. In bad weather, neither was a good option.

Cassie was in the small pool of D.C. reporters assigned to this weekend's trip. Once the 747 hit cruising altitude, she removed a manila folder from her laptop bag.

She hadn't looked at her employment contract since signing the final page a couple years back. And even then she'd counted on her agent to review the fine print. But, heeding Jack's warning, she now scrutinized every word.

Three sections stuck out.

The first was the section on news content. "Republic News has the exclusive right to determine the content of every communication by EM-PLOYEE while on air, and owns the exclusive right over the appearances and images of EMPLOYEE. Refusal to communicate news content accordingly shall be deemed a violation of this agreement."

Cassie stared at the back of the seat in front of her, contemplating the words. She had always assumed that the company had the ultimate right to dictate what she said and how she appeared. But seeing it written in legalese was jarring.

"Hey, Cassie, your contract up soon or something?" The mocking voice came from the seat behind her. Brady Jones was a young NBC White House correspondent who always nosed around her business. The skills that made for a good reporter often were the recipe for an annoying colleague.

"Not at all, Brady." Gossip spread so quickly in the business, she wouldn't want that rumor out there. "Is yours?"

Brady's shock of blond hair appeared in the gap between the seats. "So you're just checking out your contract in your free time? Sure, I buy that!"

She waved off his nosiness, but he kept pushing. "My agent says that Republic has the most onerous contract in the business. So you better read every word closely."

"Hey, Brady, I know this is your first. Why don't you sit back and enjoy the flight?" She moved over in the seat, obstructing his view.

She dove back into the agreement.

A section on the second-to-last page was labeled "Liquidated Damages." While she didn't recognize the term, the description spoke for itself. "If EMPLOYEE quits Republic News prior to the contract term, or is terminated for violation of this agreement prior to this contract term, EMPLOYEE will owe Republican News 40% of EMPLOYEE'S annual compensation."

Cassie drew in a long breath as she twisted her wedding ring. That was serious money. Paying that out would devastate her young family. She'd worked too hard, mostly alone, to climb out of poverty and crushing debt to tumble all the way back down.

"That bad, huh?" Brady now stood in the aisle, smirking at Cassie.

"Brady! I've got work to do. By any chance, do *you*?"

He shrugged and walked away.

She examined the contract one more time, rereading its noncompete provision, which kept her from working with any of Republic's competitors for twelve months. Her agent had assured her that was standard and that any new employer would pay the penalty incurred for violating the noncompete. But Jack's situation gave her pause. There were only a handful of employers in the industry to begin with. And if she was fired in controversy, as Jack had been, none of the others would pick her up, let alone take on such a penalty.

"Ma'am?"

"What?" she asked before lifting her head, tired of the interruptions.

"Hello, ma'am. Chicken Parmesan or steak?" A man in a crew cut and sharp blue suit stood above her, a presidential pin on his lapel.

"I'll take the chicken. And can I have a glass of wine? Rosé?"

"Of course, ma'am."

She placed the contract back into the folder.

The man laid a full plate on her tray, but Cassie went for the rosé first. She sipped it slowly, staring out the window as towering gray thunderheads fired up to the south. Storms that ominous would normally make her stomach churn, but she ignored them. Her stomach was already fluttering.

Jack was right. She was trapped. She had to do what Republic said—to appear as they commanded her to appear and say what they told her to say. They could fire her if she acted otherwise, and then she'd owe them tens of thousands of dollars and be jobless for the ensuing year.

Trapped. Controlled.

She emptied the glass.

CHAPTER 29

APPLETON, WISCONSIN

Caked in mud, Tori hobbled back from the rugby field, too stressed from the last twenty-four hours to enjoy her usual Jacuzzi recovery. She'd been distracted, and it had been her worst match in months: no tries for her, and they'd lost badly. Being distracted in rugby also meant you got hurt, and pain was now shooting through her right ankle as though she'd done some severe damage. But she wasn't focused on the loss, her ankle, or the fact that the Republican voter file had been wiped out.

Worse than all that, Ned had gone dark.

They had been texting back and forth late afternoon about the destroyed data. She'd updated Jack, grabbed a bite to eat, then texted Ned another question right before her shift started.

He'd never responded. She'd texted him an hour later during a break. Still nothing.

He'd been responsive all day, so the sudden silence was odd. But she didn't know him well enough to pester him. Plus, having OCD always made her skeptical of her own reaction to things. Was she being paranoid?

He'd definitely be awake now. So as she walked home she took out her phone.

> Live it up last night? Let's reconnect as soon
> as you can.

She winced through her shower, discovering every new pain point pounded into her during the morning's match. At least the throbbing in her ankle was ebbing.

After stepping out of the shower, she checked her phone again. Twenty minutes since her text, and still nothing.

She dialed Ned's number. Four rings, then voice mail.

She hadn't talked to Jonny Yost, the campaign manager, since their meeting. But she now worried enough to call him.

He picked up on the first ring.

"Hi. It's Tori Justice calling. We met the other day."

"Um, yeah. You're not easy to forget."

She enjoyed being tall, but towering over men meant enduring comments about her height daily since she'd turned fourteen. Sometimes they came as compliments, other times as if reactions to a strange mutation. Her general approach was to ignore them all.

"I'm worried about Ned. We'd been texting about your data being destroyed, and then he stopped respon—"

"What do you mean our data was destroyed?"

"He didn't tell you?"

"*That our data was destroyed?* No!"

"He texted me yesterday afternoon. I figured he would've also told you."

"He'd reached out to meet for a drink last night. Maybe he was going to tell me then."

"And he didn't?"

"He never followed up. But Ned can be flaky like that. So I spent the evening on Tinder."

She also preferred to ignore unnecessary details.

"Well, he didn't respond to me last night, either. And I've texted and called him all morning. Is that normal for him?"

"No. He doesn't show up at things sometimes, but he's quick to respond to texts."

A pause followed Johnny's last comment, the implications of Ned's silence sinking in.

"Tell me more about what happened to our data."

She explained the details.

"You know, this all happened after we met with you," Johnny said.

She brushed aside his insinuation. "Which means someone may be watching us."

"Watching you guys?"

"You too. And when I say 'watching,' I mean monitoring our voter files. If they saw that we logged on at the same time, they know we were sharing intel about the election results. Which might have triggered the data wipe and—"

"You really think someone took Ned because of our meeting?"

"Let's call it the worst-case scenario."

"And who is 'they'? Who in the world would be able to see us *both* logging on at the same time?"

He was finally catching on.

"We have no idea. That's what I wanted to brainstorm with Ned about. Can you can check on him?"

"I can get to his place in less than an hour. I'll drop by and let you know what I find."

The call ended and Tori got dressed. After lacing up her sneakers, her phone beeped once, indicating a text had come through.

Ned.

Finally.

Sorry. I misplaced my phone.

CHAPTER 30

Lute Justice had said no, gruffly, to the first offer. And to the second offer. On the third, he declined again, but more politely. He really didn't want to give up his dairy farm.

Now they were offering nearly double the initial amount.

"I've gotta give you points for persistence," he said to Sal Pavano, the New York lawyer who'd visited his small dairy farm in western Wisconsin four times over the past eight weeks. "But this farm and my daughter are all I have."

Lute towered over his guest as the two ambled between the barn and the modest farmhouse he'd called home most of his life. Looking down at the mud caked on Sal's polished black shoes, Lute chuckled. Sal had to be a real big shot back in New York City. But on a farm he'd be useless. The lawyer looked fit, so he'd be strong enough. But he insisted on wearing a dark suit and those fancy shoes on each visit. The man glared at Lute's cows as if they were rats, and the one time Lute had showed him the milking process, the city slicker squirmed like he was witnessing open-heart surgery.

"We know that, Mr. Justice. That's why we're trying to make this worth your while." He paused. "And hers."

Having grown up a rabid Knicks fan, Sal had recognized Lute Justice at their first meeting. If Lute's career had come a decade later, he'd have reaped millions for his skills, something Sal brought up again and again.

But it had never been about the money—and playing a game for a living had always struck Lute as strange. So coming home and working the farm had been the natural thing to do. His wife passing away at a young age had forced him to raise two kids himself, and the dairy business had grown next to impossible for family farms like his. But he'd never regretted coming home.

"This little operation ain't what it once was, and your offer is generous. But what's an ol' man like me gonna do to pass the days?"

"Besides squeezing those cows' nipples?" Sal asked. "Geez, maybe basketball?"

"That's all in the past," Lute said, although given his run as a Badger—his Wisconsin rebounding record still stood—maybe he could be a commentator of some sort. Other than that, he was just a sixty-eight-year-old giant with shredded knees and an aching back.

If he sold, his main worry was what to tell Tori. She knew about the offers, but he'd downplayed them, insisting he'd never sell. Ironically, a major reason he was considering the deal was to help her. Watching her work two shifts while piling up student debt made him feel that he'd failed her. The cash from selling would let him help her like a good dad should. But this was the part she'd hate the most.

They walked past Lute's blue Ford tractor before reaching Sal's silver Mercedes. Sal opened the door and sat down.

"You're a good man, Mr. Justice," he said, his perfect white teeth gleaming up at him through the open window. "I'll overnight you the paperwork. You'll be able to replace that old tractor as soon as we process the payment."

Lute smiled wryly. After four visits, Sal still didn't get it. That tractor was perfect the way it was, old and reliable. He wouldn't exchange it for anything. Still, the man's client was offering a boatload of money.

"Send it along and I'll check it out."

As Sal drove away, Lute texted Tori from his cell.

Hey honey. We need to talk.

CHAPTER 31

ASPEN, COLORADO

Covering presidential escapes to Aspen turned out to be more grime than glamour.

After enduring a stomach-churning landing at the Aspen airport and too little sleep at a nearby Days Inn, Cassie and five others boarded a bus at dawn and rode for thirty minutes to a parking lot at the edge of Wingspread, the president's sprawling ranch. From the parking lot, holed up in a small news van, Cassie sat bored the rest of the morning.

The high point came when three identical caravans of dark SUVs entered the large double-gated entrance and disappeared down the long gravel driveway, kicking up dust behind them. The problem was, there was no way to know who was riding inside them.

The interior secretary and EPA administrator were on the official schedule, as were four governors of Western states, so Cassie did her best to make out their faces through the SUV's tinted windows as she ducked the spraying dirt. At one point four people on horseback trotted through the fields behind the ranch house, the president atop her gray mare, Eleanor. And for an hour a small group of antigovernment protesters lined up in front of the ranch's gates demanding the president leave their guns and land alone. Thankfully, the mustached bruisers with colorful home-made signs also made for good background footage, as the conservative nonprofits bankrolling the protest knew.

"Here at her ranch near Aspen, in the house far behind me, the president is finalizing her long-awaited public lands expansion plan," Cassie reported in her live shot, the ranch and mountains in the background.

"It sounds like some who don't like those plans showed up to leave her a message," a youthful voice said in her ear. Cassie had already forgotten the name of the new weekend anchor.

"They sure did. A small group protested for about an hour, although I'm not sure the president even knew they were there."

"Right," the young whippersnapper said back through her earpiece. "She was off riding horses in the other direction."

Even this newbie was already reciting Republic spin on the president. Cassie recalled the three contract clauses but couldn't help herself.

"Actually, she was meeting with four Western state governors about the plan when the protests were taking place. She's trying to build some consensus, at least among those who will meet with her."

"Well, how do we know who she's meeting with when she refuses to make the Aspen guest logs public?"

"Those governors were on her official schedule today. But you're right, we're not sure who else might be there. Unfortunately, that's a practice going back through a number of presidencies. The difference is that this president skis and rides horses, while the others golfed."

It was an unseemly tradition. Every White House presidential visitor was listed, but vacation visitors were shrouded in secrecy. Cassie had been equally troubled by the prior president's regular, secret getaways to Maryland's eastern shore. But D.C., including the press corps, accepted it.

"Still, it makes you wonder," the anchor said, pressing further.

"Always has. We'll check back in tomorrow with any other news from Aspen."

The red light of the camera shut off, and she handed the microphone back to her cameraman. As she took out her earpiece, the gates opened slowly. Seconds later another caravan—this one with two SUVs and a sedan—sped by.

Turning away from another dust cloud, she didn't even bother to look in those tinted windows. There was no way to know who was inside.

CHAPTER 32

LONDON

Katrina sat at the head of the table, Drac to her right, Natalie to her left. But the most important place at the conference room table was a small circular speaker at its center.

"How are your treatments proceeding, Dyadya?" Katrina asked.

Even as an adult, she'd never called him anything but Dyadya. Uncle. But he'd played a role far larger than that in her life. Indeed, he'd made the life she now led possible.

Drunk most of the time, her father had been unable to hold on to a job for more than six months at a time, while her mother had earned minimum wage sweating away in a local textile mill. So she and her little brother, Mikhail, had grown up dirt-poor in Brooklyn. Katrina still recalled the constant squeeze in her lower abdomen—a mix of a bad cramp and an upset stomach—after days in a row of only bread and beans at dinner. Pictures from those days, of her drawn face, spindly arms, and thin legs, still grieved her. Her hair had even looked thin and patchy.

It was around her seventh birthday that Mother's younger brother had first visited. When he'd walked through their front door, his sharp, angular features startled her; he looked like a ghoul from one of her storybooks. But she quickly discovered that, apart from her mother, he was the kindest person she'd ever met, a sharp contrast to the hardscrabble community around her. For two weeks Dyadya had chaperoned Katrina and Mikhail far beyond the rough streets of Brighton Beach—to Coney Island, to the top of the World Trade Center, to FAO Schwarz, to Central

Park, to Broadway—places she'd never seen and trips she'd never forget. But the highlight of each day were the feasts she'd gorged on for breakfast, lunch, and dinner. Croissants, cheeses, fresh fruits, and vegetables, succulent meats. Foods she had stared at through windows but never smelled or tasted.

According to Mother, Katrina almost never cried as a kid, and even then only from the sharpest physical pain. But the day Dyadya left, she bawled for hours.

Yet his impact on her life was only beginning. Within weeks of the visit, Father left and Mother stopped working at the mill, a combination that instantly buoyed the spirit of their small home. Even without Mother working, more food appeared on their table as new clothes replaced tattered Goodwill donations, and a shiny new station wagon allowed Mother to drive them places.

The most important of those destinations were the homes of two tutors—one to perfect their English, the other their math—and new schools where Katrina and Mikhail found themselves surrounded by the sons and daughters of financiers, lawyers, and bankers. Mother never explained how she provided these new bounties, but Katrina sensed even then that Dyadya was watching out for her.

"Never mind my treatments," a raspy voice said back through the speaker. "Please fill me in on everything."

She winced on hearing his frail voice. This was a man who had started out with as little as her mother, in a country roiled by danger, but had conquered as much as any one person could. She'd spent her teenage years and twenties convinced he was invincible. Yet here he was, exhausted and weak, cancer ravaging his insides.

"Dyadya, you need to get well. We have things in good order, awaiting your return."

"It does not sound in good order, Katrina," he said in a cold tone. "Please fill me in."

He was a man who did not ask for things more than once, so she straightened her back and provided a detailed update.

"And you have dispatched security to Wisconsin?" he asked when she was done, instantly focused on the greatest risk to their operation.

"Yes, and we will control it quickly."

"And how can you ensure others will not discover our work as they did?"

"I don't believe they know what they've found—"

"Katrina, they know something is not right. How will we avoid this in the future?"

She shot a fierce glare at Drac, still blaming him for the Wisconsin problem.

"With each test case, we have fine-tuned our tactics," she said. "Our three interventions since Wisconsin were far more precise and therefore better masked. And there are no more test cases needed. We are ready."

"And no more defectors?" Dyadya asked.

"None. The Orvieto accident made clear that there is no walking away. And no one has expressed anything but enthusiasm to stay involved. They are acquiring American assets at a rapid pace across the country."

The silence that followed gave her the chance to ask her question.

"Have you been able to advance your conversation?"

A round of staccato coughs burst through the speaker. Five in a row, then a pause, then five more. Quick and high-pitched, wheezing as each ended, the raw coughs of a deeply sick man.

"I have. Very productive. It helps that I am here for treatment."

Dyadya was in America undergoing the experimental regimen that gave him the best chance of beating the long odds.

"What a blessing that you are sick."

Both Drac and Natalie gawked at their boss, but she knew her uncle's dark sense of humor.

Faint snorts of laughter sounded through the phone, interrupted quickly by another round of coughs.

"Katrina, laughing is the most painful of all."

He coughed a dozen or so more times, then returned to her question.

"We are close to alignment on what must happen. If you eliminate the obstacles and accomplish your tasks, the rest will follow."

CHAPTER 33

MADISON, WISCONSIN

Who are you, James Bond or something?"

Tori asked the question as the white granite dome of Wisconsin's statehouse came into view.

I'd insisted on joining her for the rendezvous that Ned had suggested after his phone mishap. Renting a car, we'd left at seven for her ten o'clock meet-up, leaving an hour to spare. And at a gas station along the way, I'd picked up a baseball cap and cheap sunglasses, which I'd just put on.

"Tori, we need to approach this carefully."

"Why's that? Between the two of us, we can handle little Ned."

She chuckled as she said it, but I glared back. She needed a wake-up call.

"It's not Ned I'm worried about," I said. "I've dealt with this stuff before. Maybe Ned misplaced his phone like he said. But on the off chance that's not the case, this will get dangerous quickly."

"Dangerous?"

"Think about it. When people are willing to rig the outcome of an election, then wipe out entire data files, they are playing for keeps. They'll fight to protect what they're after."

I parked the blue, Youngstown-made Chevy Cruze five blocks from campus, leaving Tori in the passenger seat while I walked to the McDonald's where they'd agreed to rendezvous. I ran through the list of possibilities.

The most likely scenario was that Ned had told the truth—he'd misplaced his phone and it had died—which meant he would saunter into this meeting and grab a seat. And that would be that.

The less likely scenario, but the one to prepare for, was that Ned had gone dark because someone had nabbed him. His phone going missing had been an excuse he'd been forced to text, or that someone else had texted. Either way, this meant that the McDonald's meeting would be an ambush.

But even an ambush could play out in several ways: Ned could be the bait, dangled to draw Tori in, or he might not show up at all. If Ned was the bait, he'd arrive early to get a booth they would've preselected, and he'd appear nervous as hell. And whether or not Ned was coming, if this was an ambush, someone else would case the place. Two people, probably, and they would arrive early.

Hence my insistence on arriving even earlier.

There was no good place to watch from outside, so I walked into the McDonald's, ordered an Egg McMuffin, a hash brown, and a Diet Coke, and grabbed a back corner booth that offered a view of both the dining room and the parking lot.

For forty minutes all shapes and sizes strolled through the glass doors. Four families showed up to eat breakfast, the parents and older kids wolfing down oatmeal, McMuffins, and hash browns while the toddlers climbed all over the booth, playing with Happy Meal toys. A crew of workers stormed the place a few minutes after I sat down, jamming up the line and tracking mud along the floor while chattering loudly. The din they created was matched by three separate groups of college kids who stumbled in, dousing their morning hangovers with greasy fast food while burying their heads in their phones. And a number of customers walked in alone, waited in line quietly, and left with carry-out bags.

But amid this revolving door, it was the twosomes that most drew my attention.

Two couples wore wedding rings and looked happily married, so I dismissed them along with the two pint-sized women who ordered only drinks. One pair of men ate their oatmeal quickly, downed their coffee like shots, and left only minutes after sitting down.

At ten minutes before ten, only two booths concerned me. In one, an attractive olive-skinned woman with long black hair sat across from a heavy-set, broad-shouldered man. His thick mop of straight brown hair looked stapled to the top of his oversized head, and his bulbous nose and large pores rounded out the Hollywood caricature of a henchman. They were an odd pair: he wasn't old enough to be her dad, but the mismatch in appearance and age ruled them out as a couple. They barely talked to each other and only nibbled their food, lacking the fervor of the other customers. On the plus side, they weren't looking around the place with any curiosity.

The second duo worried me because of their size. Two guys who could've played linebacker at Wisconsin. Even from twenty feet away, their muscles bulged from forearm to calf. And they kept peering out the window at arriving cars, neither taking a bite from his meal.

As Ned's arrival time grew close, I ate steadily to blend into the scene. At five minutes to ten I finished the McMuffin. At three minutes to ten I swallowed the last bite of the now-cold hash brown. At ten o'clock I sipped the Diet Coke down to its ice.

Still no Ned.

At three minutes after ten he first appeared across the street—alone. In jeans and a fleece jacket, he was even smaller than I remembered. He looked both ways before jaywalking, then sauntered across the parking lot and into the restaurant. Relieved, I slurped at the Diet Coke residue. The fact that he was late was a good sign.

Once inside, he scanned the restaurant for Tori. Not seeing her, he stepped to the back of the food line. If he was concerned about what booth to sit in, he was hiding it masterfully.

Suddenly the two muscleheads stood up, even more menacing at full height. But then two attractive women, similar in age to the guys, entered the restaurant and walked toward them. The four greeted one another and sat back down in the booth. The Mickey D's double date left only one couple to watch.

Ned reached the front of the line and ordered. A minute later he picked up his tray, walked to a table in the middle of the dining room, and sat down. The odd couple in the booth didn't look at him once.

I texted Tori.

He's here. All looks fine. C'mon down.

Leaving now, she wrote back.

Ned waited politely, not touching his food. At twelve after, he took out his phone and typed for a few seconds.

He just asked me where I was, Tori wrote in a new text.

And where is that?

Three blocks away.

So tell him that.

Okay.

And that's when I noticed it. A tiny movement, but at the critical moment.

The dark-haired woman glimpsed down to the left of her tray, then back up again at the big guy. It was a quick peek, but she hadn't done it once since sitting down. I couldn't see what she'd looked at, but it wasn't her food.

Text him again.

What?

Text Ned again.

What should I say?

Anything. But make it harmless. Like you're looking forward to meeting.

Okay.

The woman again glanced down to the left of her tray.

The hair on the back of my neck lifted as a new scenario dawned on me.

Stop. Walk back.

Why?

They've hacked his phone. They're reading your texts.

My pulse was now racing. Ned was the bait without knowing it.

And text him that you're almost at the parking lot.

Okay.

The woman peeked down a third time. Again, only a split second. If I hadn't been focused on her, I would never have noticed.

Get in the car and drive this way.

Thirty seconds later I texted again.

Tell him you left your computer and that you'll be right back.

The woman looked down again. This time her raven eyes widened as her dark eyebrows drew together. Worried their plan was going awry, no doubt.

Ned finally broke down and nibbled at his food.

The odd couple sat frozen, not yet giving up on their siege.

Let me know when you're a block away.

A minute later she texted back. Here. Across the street, at the light.

Tell him something's come up, and you'll meet
with him later this afternoon. Three o'clock.

?!?!?! He's going to think I'm the biggest flake.

Just do it.

Seconds passed before Ned and the woman looked down at the same time. Ned shook his head and downed the rest of his McMuffin. The woman glared at her booth mate, shaking her head twice, signaling that the meeting was off.

A minute later, drink in hand, Ned stood up and left, walking back across the street.

The odd couple waited for him to reach the sidewalk on the other side before standing up and walking out the door and alongside the restaurant window. Above the man's left hip, a squarish bulge creased the bottom of his sweater—no doubt a gun. The two climbed into a black Range Rover, the woman assuming driving duties.

I called Tori.

"What the hell's going on, Jack?"

"Ned was hacked. They were reading all his texts. A big man and an attractive woman are in a Range Rover that's about to pass you. Get the plate number if you can."

The Range Rover drove past the parked Cruze.

"Got it. I'm going to follow them—"

"The hell you are."

The Cruze pulled out seconds after the Range Rover passed it.

CHAPTER 34

MADISON, WISCONSIN

N ow who's the secret agent?" Jack asked.

"You still are. I'm just using common sense."

Tori had followed the Range Rover for twenty minutes, keeping her distance through Madison while running through two yellow lights and a red, then tailing it a few miles up I-90. She was now idling in a Motel 6 parking lot, a block over from the Holiday Inn where the couple had parked.

"So what's next, Ms. Common Sense?"

"I'm going to check out the hotel real quick."

"Tori, I don't know why you don't like my advice, but do not set foot in there."

"Maybe it's because you keep talking to me like you're my dad. Now that we know where they are, why would we walk away?"

"Tori, don't go in there. He's got a gun. Do you?"

"Mine's back at Dad's farm, but I'm actually a darn good shot." She paused a beat. "Okay, I won't go in. I've got a better idea."

She took a key chain out of her jacket pocket. On it hung her truck keys, a key to the farmhouse, keys to her apartment building and the apartment itself, a locker room key, and a key to her bike lock. But there was also a small, black, circular disk—the size of a half-dollar—which she removed from the chain. She'd recently bought the device to keep from losing her keys.

"I've got a way to track these guys."

"You do?"

"Yeah."

"Tori—"

The fatherly tone in his voice meant another objection was on its way.

"Jack, I can handle this."

She got out of the car, traversed a no-man's-land of weeds and trash, and entered the Holiday Inn lot. Then she approached the Range Rover while keeping her eye on the motel's lobby doors and windows. No one was watching.

A black Chevy Malibu was parked to the right of the Range Rover. She walked in between the two as if she were the Malibu's driver, took her wallet out of her backpack, then dropped it on the ground. As she bent down to pick it up, she took out the small disk and tore off the tape that covered an adhesive patch. She slipped her left arm under the Range Rover's passenger door and pushed the disk against the sideboard. She picked up the wallet in her left hand, fumbled around in her bag as if she were searching for the car keys, and cursed as if she couldn't find them.

Five minutes later she was back on I-90.

CHAPTER 35

MADISON, WISCONSIN

You're as stubborn as I am, Jack Sharpe!"

Cassie was practically yelling through the phone as I sat in the McDonald's booth, waiting for Tori to pick me up while drinking my third Diet Coke.

"Now, that's a low blow," I said. "What makes you say that?"

"Jack, I went back and watched the tapes of your final appearances. Your body language gave you away. They ordered you to stop bringing up the president's anti-monopoly push, but you couldn't help yourself."

"What are you talking about?" I asked, playing dumb even though she'd described my final week perfectly.

"They told you not to bring up the monopoly stuff, and they canned you when you ignored them. You violated the same agreement you told me to read."

When I'd stressed that she review her agreement, I knew she would. But not this fast.

"You know I can't talk about that, Cassie."

"You don't have to. And you're not denying it, are you?"

I stayed silent.

"See. You're not denying it."

I took another sip, again saying nothing, although my stomach knotted as every detail came back. The week before the July Fourth holiday, during a Bridget Turner interview, I'd described the president's anti-monopoly agenda on the air. But Corporate had sent word that they didn't want me discussing it again. In my next several appearances I'd complied.

But censoring my analysis to kowtow to Corporate's wishes had felt so dirty it became a character test. So in a show days later I'd decided on the spot: Screw 'em. I brought it up again, live on the air. The producer squawked in my ear like a dying seagull before I pulled the earpiece out and kept talking.

"Did you enjoy my last hurrah?"

"It was bold, I'll give you that. Bridget looked like she was going to puke."

I laughed. Bridget's face had indeed turned as pale as the oxford shirt I had on.

"Jack, that monopoly stuff is what they cut from my interview with President Moore."

"Well, give me credit, then. I at least got it on air a few times."

"You did the right thing. I'm tempted to do the same."

Tori pulled into the lot in the blue Chevy Cruze and parked near the window. I stood up to go.

"Yeah, well, look at me now, Cassie. I wouldn't recommend going through this at this stage of your career. You can do far more good employed. Keep digging."

Within an hour of walking off the set, sitting in the Republic HR director's office, the company's chief counsel recited every word of the clause I had violated. They told me I was being terminated and owed them hundreds of thousands of dollars unless I signed the nondisparagement agreement. I caved quickly and walked out of Republic for good by midnight, out of a job and lips sealed. Alex Fischer dumped me by text a week later, explaining that she needed to maintain her standing in the industry.

A day after that brutal ax had fallen, with her perfectly sized ring in my glove compartment, I'd picked up and driven home to Youngstown.

The flimsy apartment door flew open a few seconds after we'd knocked, a red-faced Ned appearing behind it.

"How the hell did you guys end up here?" he asked, far more animated than he'd been at our first meeting. "And what happened to our McDonald's meeting?"

"Johnny told us where you live," I said in a stern enough tone that he stepped out of the way. "We need to talk."

Tori and I sat down on a tan futon as Ned slumped into a chair. To his credit, the place was clean for a kid his age who hadn't expected visitors. But the cramped one-bedroom apartment underscored how little campaign staff were paid for all their hard work.

"So what happened?" he asked.

"Ned," I said, "things have gotten a lot more serious. And dangerous."

He waved his hand at me. "You're joking, right?"

"I'm not. When you lost your phone the other night, it was hacked."

"That's impossible." He leaned forward in the chair, clasping his hands together. "I was here the whole time, and so was my phone."

"Trust me, it happened. Pros could get in and out of here no problem." The apartment was on the ground floor, and the latch over his window wasn't locked.

"What pros?"

I explained what I'd observed at McDonald's and how the two had glimpsed down at their phone every time Tori and Ned had texted.

Ned's face blanched from red to ashen as the full scope of the predicament sunk in.

"Okay, so what do we do now? I'm not going to any three o'clock meeting back there, that's for sure."

"That was a delay tactic. We're not going to let them get anywhere near you. My guess is they're trying to mop things up so they can move forward."

"Move forward how? On what?"

"Well, that's the million-dollar question. But my guess is this goes beyond Wisconsin."

"What makes you say that?" Ned asked.

"This election wasn't big enough to justify all this."

Both Ned and Tori looked at each other, then at me, as if I'd insulted them.

"Not big enough?" Tori asked.

"Not even close. If someone's meddling in an election, it's because they're aiming for an outcome worth the risk and the investment. As far as I can tell, Beagle's win didn't alter a thing. I mean, the court was split five to two before the election, and it's still split five to two, right?"

They both nodded, still glaring.

Tori leaned back and crossed her long arms. "Okay, Sherlock Holmes, then why did they do it?"

"The truth is, if someone has access to both voter files—let's say at the national level—and they're able to alter results, they could—"

"Manipulate any election they wanted to," Ned said, interrupting. "So why our race? Just some sort of test run?"

"That's my best guess," I said. "To pull something off on a wider scale, you'd need to hone the tactics of meddling so you could change outcomes without being noticed. In your election, they got a little too greedy, which is why Tori noticed."

"So you think they've done it in other special elections, too?" Tori asked.

"There's one almost every week somewhere. And turnouts are low and unpredictable, so it's not like people will question the results. Those specials would give them a lot of opportunities to perfect their work."

"Perfect?" Ned asked. "For when? This November?"

"That's my assumption."

"That's less than one hundred days away. Shouldn't we be alerting the national parties about the breach?" Tori asked.

"We need a lot more details first or we'll look like kooks," I said. "In the meantime, we have two advantages over these guys. One, *they* don't know that *we* know they've hacked Ned. And two, we can now track them."

"You can?" Ned asked.

"We sure can," Tori said, glimpsing at her phone. "And they're still at the hotel."

I leaned forward on the futon, then stood up.

"Good. It's time to go on offense."

CHAPTER 36

ASPEN, COLORADO

D o you make a lot of airport runs?" Cassie asked as the cab pulled out of downtown Aspen.

"Ya. Sure do," the driver said in a California surfer's accent. A lumberjack of a man with a deep tan, muttonchops, and two armfuls of tattoos, he looked, sounded, and smelled like a guy who'd moved out here decades ago to party and ski. A laminated ID card on the dashboard indicated his name was Axel.

"In the daytime that's most of what I do when I'm not on the mountain. Nighttime, it's all bar runs. Why d'ya ask?"

"I'm curious about how the rich and famous get to Aspen."

"That's why I do the airport runs. Good tippers," he said. "It's flying or nothing for those with enough dough to own a private jet."

He'd confirmed her assumption. No one with money would put up with the long, mountainous drive most people endured from Denver.

She sat quietly as they sped down a single-lane highway, cutting between two high ridges before the small control tower appeared in the distance, off to the left. Minutes later, as they drew even to the tower, the cab slowed, took a left, and pulled to a stop in front of the same airport terminal where Cassie had deplaned.

"Do you mind showing me where the private planes land? The guys with the dough?"

"Sure, that's further down the way."

He exited the terminal driveway, turning left, back onto the narrow highway. A minute later they took another left and stopped in front of a building that looked like a ritzy ski lodge you'd expect to see halfway up Ajax.

"Nice digs, huh?" Axel asked.

"Not your typical airport terminal."

"No, ma'am. And not your typical airplane passengers."

"So when you pick up folks who fly in privately, is this where you get them?"

"Sure is. There are a couple separate corporate hangars for people who are based here, but they have their own transportation. The rich and famous? This is where they all come in."

Sleek jets of various sizes and colors were lined up to the side and behind the terminal, close enough to the driveway that their tail numbers were visible.

"Axel, do you ever see the president's guests land here?"

"All the time. Governors, millionaires, celebrities, foreign leaders, you name it. They shuttle in and out all weekend when she's here. Sometimes they hang out in town after, or go skiing, but most go straight to her ranch and straight back, all business."

"Do you ever take any to the ranch?"

"You kiddin'? Those fancy big shots don't use cabbies like me. They're all high-end car service companies and dark SUVs."

"I've seen a few of those myself."

"You can't miss 'em." He paused for a beat, then stared in the rearview mirror, one eyebrow lifted. "You getting out?"

The question threw her for a loop. Then she realized they'd been sitting there for minutes.

"I'll head back to the hotel, please."

"Um, okay." He shrugged and pulled back out of the driveway.

Then: "Hey, there's one of those caravans right there," Axel said as three dark SUVs whisked by them in the other direction, left turn signals on. "Some political bigwig just kissed the ring."

Cassie grinned, but said nothing as she tapped both feet against the floor mat. The president preferred to keep her meetings at Wingspread a secret. But unlike most destinations in America, this one had only one entrance—and it was in the wide-open.

Finally, a story her bosses would be excited about.

CHAPTER 37

MADISON, WISCONSIN

I can't meet until 4:00.

Reclining on the futon, Tori typed the words we'd agreed on.
"That works," I said before she pushed "send."
Ned, sitting right across from us in his closet of an apartment, waited a few seconds before writing back.

Okay. Where's good?

We needed to find out more about Beauty and the Beast, our nickname for the duo who'd spied on Ned at McDonald's. Who were they? Where were they from? And, most important, who were they working for?
Without sharing too many details, I'd called an old source and friend, Youngstown police chief Bill Santini. If we sent him photos, the chief offered to run them through the national facial recognition database. So Ned, Tori, and I concocted a plan to get the best shots possible.
Tori waited a few more seconds before responding.

Let's do Jordan's. It's always a blast.

A chaotic environment would give Beauty and the Beast the least control possible, and Ned had vouched for Jordan's Big Ten Pub as the wildest place in town. That day's Packers preseason game would only add to the mayhem.

Fun!

See you then.

At 2:20 the three of us drove back to campus, stopping in a sports apparel store. Ned had donned his Packers jersey back at his apartment, but Tori and I each needed one as well. The XXL fit nicely, even if green and yellow didn't feel right on this lifelong Browns fan.

Jordan's lived up to Ned's prediction of ear-shattering chaos. Wall-to-wall TVs blared out the whistles, grunts, and commentary of the game, so—like everyone else around us—we had to yell to hear one another. After walking in at 3:05, we squeezed past every size of jersey, whether Packers green or Wisconsin red. Tori led the way, guys stepping back to check out her striking stature and blue-streaked black hair. After twenty minutes we sat down in a booth before ordering three beers to fit in and three waters to drink. A week on the wagon was worth building on.

Tori took out her phone. "They're still at the hotel."

"Good," Ned said. "What's the plan now?"

"We need to grab our photos and get out of here. And, Ned, we can't let them see you."

"It looks like they're leaving the—"

An explosion of cheers cut Tori off, fans leaping to their feet all around us, throwing their arms straight up into the air. The Green Bay quarterback sprinted twenty yards for a touchdown.

"So they left?" I asked Tori when things died down.

"Yes. It'll take them about thirty minutes."

Minutes later, Tori sent Ned another text. I'll be there at 4:10.

He waited a few seconds, then texted back.

Great. I grabbed a booth towards the back. Close to the restrooms.

There was a line of booths along one wall, chock-full of Packers fans. Forcing Beauty and the Beast to head all the way back there would give us time to snap photos.

Perfect. I'm in my Wisconsin jersey. See you in
a few.

"Where should I go?" Ned's face was paler now than it had been in his apartment.

"There was a Subway a couple doors down. Wait there and stay away from the windows."

"Okay."

As Ned took a step toward the exit, a tall, skinny guy seated just beyond us leapt to his feet. Already jittery, Ned ducked the other way. But it was just a Packers interception, and when the defensive back ran it in for a touchdown, the place boomed.

"He's a nervous little guy, isn't he?" Tori asked as Ned recovered and walked out the front door.

"Yeah. But he's also the only one they've seen."

She glanced at her phone again. "They're a few miles out. Where should we be when they get here?"

"Are you sure they didn't get a good look at you as you drove?"

"I'm pretty sure."

"Remember, they're pros."

She glared at me. "I'm sure."

"Then stand near the main door when they walk in." I scanned the room. Half the people were texting, especially women as their boyfriends watched the game. "Text me when they come in. I'll take a photo before they get too close."

"And what if they see you taking it?"

"They'll be past you at that point, so run for it. Keep yourself safe."

"But you'd be trapped back there," she said, gesturing toward the bathroom.

She was right. There would definitely be no way out.

Groans erupted across the bar as the Green Bay running back absorbed a monster hit.

Tori chimed in seconds later. "They're parking. Three blocks away."

"Go time."

She got up from the booth and walked toward the door, guys clearing the way like before. I pushed the other way, along the row of booths, guys not giving an inch. I stopped just before the men's bathroom.

I think I see the Beast . . . Yes, here he comes.

Beauty?

Don't see her.

Shit. We needed photos of them both.

The Beast walked in. Even in a crowd, his awful hair and large, round nose stuck out. I lifted my phone, lined up the shot, and zoomed in.

As I touched the button to snap the photo, a red object exploded across the phone's screen. I looked up to see the biggest guy in the place, at least three hundred pounds, six-foot-six, and wearing a Wisconsin jersey, lumbering toward me, blocking the view.

I leaned to my left and opened a new line of sight, again capturing the Beast in the screen. I zoomed in further, and—*wham!* The pain shot through my left wrist as my phone flew to my right, bouncing hard off the wall before hitting the ground.

"Why the fuck are you taking a picture of me?" the giant yelled, the stench of beer and spicy wings exploding from his breath. The hand that had smacked my phone was now only inches from my face.

"I wasn't tak—"

"Fucking pervert." He shoved me into the wall, my left shoulder taking the brunt of the collision into the brick surface.

Typically, I would have pushed back. But neither this guy nor the timing was typical, so I didn't say a word as he barreled past me to go to the bathroom. I leaned down and fumbled for my phone, clawing it off the ground on the third try. Fortunately, it wasn't broken.

By the time I stood back up, the Beast was only yards from me, sending a tremor through my body. Taking a photo would give me away, so I stepped along the wall while holding my breath. We passed within inches of one another, then he ambled along the row of booths, glancing at the people seated in each. His right hand hovered around his waist, shooting my heart into overdrive.

My mind raced to revive our plan. Where could I go to grab the photo? Where was the woman? Should we abandon ship?

Out of the corner of my eye, a playful young couple on barstools answered my questions with the most common of modern activities.

I walked briskly to Tori, her alarmed eyes signaling that things weren't going well.

"I didn't get a photo yet. . . . What's he doing?"

"Still checking out booths. He's pissed. . . . Wait. He's heading back this way."

"Step to the left and look the other way, up at the TV. Same direction I'm looking."

"Okay."

My phone was still in camera mode. I held it out with my left hand, my arm fully outstretched. A television monitor appeared in the phone's screen.

"What are you doing?" Tori asked.

"Hold on." I hit the icon with the circular arrows, and we were now staring at ourselves, along with all the people within ten feet of our backs.

"Smile." I snapped photos as fast I could.

Her quivering lips curled into a wide smile.

I kept snapping until the Beast appeared in the corner of the phone's screen.

"Go, Packers," I said in the drunkest tone I could muster. He stepped a few feet closer, and I tilted the camera to point it right at his face, between Tori's and mine. I held the button down and it snapped a dozen rapid-fire photos before he wandered toward the center of the restaurant.

"Got him. Let's get out of here."

Tori raced for the door, then stopped short, blocking me.

"Keep go—"

"Jack. Look up."

The dark-haired Beauty was darting into the bar.

Our expressions must have given us away, because she fixed her flinty eyes on us.

Then she reached down.

Tori lunged forward, her shoulder crashing into the underside of the woman's jaw. The jarring crunch of bone hitting bone, and teeth likely shattering in the process, pierced the air as the woman's head whipped straight back and the rest of her body careened, ass-first, onto the wet sidewalk—a rougher hit than any televised inside.

We sprinted past as she screamed in pain, hands grabbing at her mouth.

"Go left," I yelled.

Tori raced down the sidewalk as I struggled to keep up.

As we veered around the corner two blocks from the sports bar, the woman shouted orders to her companion.

"Should we get Ned?" Tori asked without even a hitch in her breath.

"No time," I said, huffing. "We'll circle back in a few minutes."

The Cruze came into view a block away, on the other side of the street. We ran diagonally toward it, dodging a pickup truck heading in our direction as we crossed the street. I unlocked it remotely and we jumped in and drove off.

"See if they've left yet."

Tori looked down at her phone. But instead of typing, she glanced over at me, her lower lip quivering.

"Ned messaged me. . . . I mean, *they* did."

"They? What do you mean?"

She lifted her hand over her mouth.

"They got him. Somehow they got him. And they sent a photo to prove it."

Tori's eyes were glued to her phone. "They entered the highway, heading north. They must be heading back to the hotel."

On the eastern edge of Madison, my huffing from the run finally easing, I took a right and headed for I-90.

"How in the world did they find him?" she asked.

There was no way they'd just spotted him at Subway.

"When they hacked his phone, they could have added malware to track it. So when Ned left for Subway, she followed the phone. He would've been safer staying near us."

"Terrible. So what do we do now?"

The photo alone said it all: Ned strapped tightly into the back seat with rope, blindfolded, blood flowing from a gash in his forehead.

If we were going to save him, we had to do it fast. I had the accelerator floored.

"They texted again." We had not yet responded to the photo. "'Do you want your friend back?' What do we say?"

"Tori, you gotta play hard to get."

"Jack, we shouldn't play at all. We need to help him. We should do what they want."

"I've got some bad news for you. What they *want* is to clean up the mess as quickly as possible. They had their hands on their guns back there. They were ready to kill all of us, even in a crowd of kids. Your little move saved our lives. Any meeting we have . . . you, Ned, and I . . . we don't walk out of it alive."

Tori stared straight ahead, absorbing my words without moving.

"Tell them he's not our friend."

I hated even saying the words, but we had no choice. I'd learned painfully in recent years that the best way to avoid bloodshed was to stand strong and leverage whatever cards you held.

"Awful." She typed on her phone for a few seconds, chewing on her lower lip.

"They say if that's true, he won't live much longer."

"Tell them we're fine with that."

"Jack!"

"Tori, their goal is to find *us*. Killing Ned means they never will. We have to make this hard for them."

My mind raced for a solution. I desperately wanted Ned back, but his captors were armed and we weren't. Our best opportunity existed while they were on the move. Once in that hotel room, he'd be trapped, probably for good.

We passed a state patrol car, sirens on, sitting behind a car pulled over in the right berm. And that's when the best solution became clear. So damn simple.

I picked up my phone and dialed three digits.

"Dane County 911," a low-pitched woman's voice said. "What is your emergency?"

"I'd like to report a kidnapping."

After getting my name, location, and phone number—I made up a name—the dispatcher ran through a series of questions, after which I described the Range Rover, heading north on I-90, along with the license plate and basic descriptions of Beauty, the Beast, and Ned.

"Do you know any of the three?"

I hesitated.

"I do not. They dragged this little guy out of a Subway shop as we were leaving a sports bar. We followed as long as we could but they lost us. Oh, and the man was holding a gun to the victim's back." I didn't want the cops to show up unprepared.

"Thank you. We'll dispatch officers right away." The line went dead.

Within minutes, a highway patrol car and sheriff's car flew past us, sirens blaring. Then a local squad car entered the highway in front of us, sirens also lit up, followed a minute later by a highway patrol car speeding south, doing a 180 in an emergency lane, and disappearing the other way.

"Wow. The cavalry is on its way. How far ahead are they?"

Tori was still tracking them on her phone. "A couple miles. And they are absolutely flying. They're already past the ho— Hold on, I'm getting a text."

She waited a few seconds.

"Jack, they say we've made a big mistake. That they will kill Ned before they ever stop the car."

They were losing their cool. "Ignore it. They won't do it." I couldn't afford a rattled Tori.

"Hold on. Now they've stopped. But they're still on the highway. The cops must've pulled them over."

No way these two would simply pull over. "How far ahead?"

"I'd say three miles. They're definitely no longer moving."

A mile later, brake lights flashed in front of us as cars slowed. A minute after that, we came to a complete stop.

"Maybe another mile," Tori said.

Another set of sirens blared from behind. But these were the longer, more gradual wails of fire engines as opposed to the patrol cars from before. In the coming minutes, three firetrucks and two ambulances flew past us, straddling the left lane and the left berm.

"Shit," Tori said. "Do you think they crashed?"

A chill ran the length of my spine, but I said nothing.

We merged into the right lane and drove slowly forward, no more than fifty yards a minute. Tori kept waiting for another text from Ned's number. Nothing.

Minutes later a plume of black smoke appeared in the distance, towering above the highway and answering her question.

Tori gasped. "Oh, God."

The initial smoke didn't capture the intensity of the fire up close. Underneath the high, vertical shafts of black smoke, thick gray vapors billowed across the center and left lanes of the highway, orange and red flames sparking and dancing throughout. Amid it all, the contours of an overturned semi stretched diagonally across two lanes of highway, its cab smashed into the berm dividing the north and south lanes of I-90.

And somewhere within that sickly gray and orange cloud was a Range Rover.

Well past the accident, three cars idled on the side of the road, their drivers gawking as the firefighters battled the blaze. After passing them, I pulled over and walked back to the car closest to the accident, the heat growing more stifling with every step.

"You see what happened?" I asked the driver, yelling over the roar of the fire and the low, whirring groan of the fire pumps.

"Yeah. I've never seen anything like it. A bunch of cops were chasing a Range Rover. He took off like a fighter jet—at least a hundred—almost collided with me, then tried to pass that semi. He hit the divider, bounced hard to the right and into the semi's trailer, and that was that. Ran right into him. Total idiot."

"Anyone make it out?"

He wiped sweat from his brow with his shirtsleeve.

"The truck driver did, right before the rig blew. But the Range Rover hit the truck so hard, the entire top half of the car disintegrated. Then it flipped. My guess is they were dead before the explosion."

"So no one's gotten out?"

"No, sir." He wiped his brow again. "No one's getting out."

CHAPTER 38

ALMATY, KAZAKHSTAN

"Adnan was an oaf."

Katrina shook her head as she spoke, walking through the airport terminal at her usual brisk pace. Natalie trailed a few feet behind.

"I have no doubt he was driving. What a waste."

Katrina had always been skeptical of the Albanian contribution to the syndicate's joint security apparatus—more muscle than brains. Fatima, on the other hand, had impressed her, especially during her time in Washington. The Syrian beauty never made mistakes. So Drac's news that both had died in a high-speed chase on a Wisconsin highway darkened her mood.

"So their target was killed with them?" Natalie asked.

"Only one. There are others. And now we're left with no knowledge of who they are."

"Can we still find them?"

"Drac is working on that now. Someone called the police, so he's starting there."

They descended a flight of stairs to the lower floor of the terminal, which housed the airport's lone baggage carousel. A nation's baggage claims opened a window into its economy. So here in the capital of Kazakhstan, where a fortunate few ruled over legions in poverty, only a handful of Western-style suitcases circulated, far outnumbered by ratty duffel bags, overstuffed burlap sacks, and clear plastic bags stuffed with clothes and food.

Having flown privately, bags in hand, Katrina and Natalie kept walking until reaching a short man holding a white placard with Katrina's name on it. Pulling their small travel bags behind him, the man led them to a black limousine parked in its own reserved space directly outside the terminal.

Ever since her first visit, she'd considered Almaty one the world's great mountain metropolises. Its central city was an eclectic hodgepodge of Soviet-era buildings and palaces, mosques and cathedrals, mixed in with modern skyscrapers and needlelike towers piercing the sky. Framing that dynamic skyline on three sides were lush green foothills and snowcapped mountains.

After traversing the city, the limousine powered up those foothills before navigating a series of steeper switchbacks that ended at a thick iron gate. The limo driver waved at a small guardhouse to the left. Seconds later the gate whisked open.

"Welcome to the most spectacular home in Kazakhstan," Katrina whispered to Natalie as they drove up the private road that offered the smoothest part of the entire ride.

Minutes later Katrina and Natalie found themselves in a dark library as ornate as Dyadya's, sitting on opposite ends of an antique Victorian couch. Red velvet cushions pushed them each to the edge of the couch, forcing them to lean forward uncomfortably. Across from them, in a small chair made of the same dark hand-carved maple as the couch, sat a pint-sized and frail man, made to appear even smaller by the floor-to-ceiling bookshelves and wood-framed paintings surrounding him.

But his physical stature was misleading. The man they were meeting, Nazer Aliyev, was an economic giant.

A giant who needed to be tamed.

Like much of the former Soviet Union, Kazakhstan's economy was dominated by energy, particularly uranium, oil, and gas. The country's agricultural sector was smaller, with the exception of one product: Kazakhstan remained one of the planet's leading producers and exporters of wheat. And diminutive Nazer Aliyev had seized the lion's share of state wheat production when Soviet communism collapsed several decades back. From that initial perch in Central Asia, Aliyev had forged inroads into China, then built a global wheat empire. The only place Aliyev hadn't penetrated was the second-largest wheat market in the world, the United States. Their plan, already under way, was to enter in force.

"My uncle is eager to learn of your progress in America," Katrina said.

Which was her polite way of demanding a lot more information than Aliyev had provided. Full sharing of data was the central tenet underpinning the syndicate; after all, each partner would owe a fraction of every dollar their American enterprise generated. But Aliyev had thus far been the least forthcoming of the group. Her trip's purpose was to re-set expectations, before the dollars flowed.

"Oh, you may tell him we have had great success."

As Natalie typed notes on her small tablet, Aliyev eyed her hands with suspicion. Like any oligarch, his instinct was to shield the details of his operations. In countries with rampant corruption, not to mention staggering tax levels, that instinct was the only way to stay in business. Plus, he'd not likely had to report to a woman half his age at any point in his life.

"Farmers across America are giving up," he continued. "They are squeezed by major conglomerates on all sides. Most have been eager to accept our offers."

"We have experienced the same thing with dairy, beef, and soybeans," Katrina said. "What have you been able to acquire?"

The small man lowered his head, studying her. "We have built strong positions in North Dakota, Kansas, Washington, and Montana."

"The leading wheat states in America," Katrina said, smiling, making it clear she understood his business.

"Yes."

He grinned, then crossed his legs, hiding behind his generalities.

This would not do. Katrina leaned farther forward.

"My uncle wishes to know how many acres you control," she said, her emerald eyes boring into him.

His pleasant expression slipped away as he looked down at his feet. "Approximately four million."

"And your target for the year?"

"We should reach six million by next year."

Natalie typed the figures into her tablet.

"And how much wheat will that produce?"

He slumped farther into his chair.

"We estimate more than two hundred million bushels of wheat per year once we have modernized the operations."

"And how many total bushels are produced in America?" Katrina asked.

"Over two billion."

She smiled, laying her elbow on the couch's armrest. "Is two hundred million enough?"

"It is *more* than enough. Any higher, and we will invite the same scrutiny that we are advocating be applied to others."

Katrina nodded. This was a strong foray into the market, and he was right to pace himself. Too large, and it might cross the threshold of what would be permitted in the coming years.

Katrina stood up, scanning the room.

"This is a beautiful library you have. So much like my uncle's. This country is fortunate to have such a knowledgeable figure like you to help guide it."

A gracious host, Aliyev ushered them around the grounds for the next hour. As he walked them back to the limo, she delivered her final order with a smile.

"We look forward to hearing more details of your success."

CHAPTER 39

WATERLOO, WISCONSIN

Wait, your dad's 'Big Lute'?"

From his height, jutted chin, and hawk nose alone, I recognized Lute Justice immediately, even though his signature crew cut was hidden under a white Stetson. As we parked at the end of the dirt driveway, next to a pickup truck as beat up as Tori's, he'd hobbled out from the side door of an old farmhouse. He was at least six feet, ten inches, although he was hunched over in a way that he'd never been in his prime.

"You've heard of him?" Tori asked, a gleam in her eye.

"If you grew up watching Big Ten basketball, you don't forget 'Big Lute.' No wonder you're so damn tall."

The lineage also put in context the brutal hit she'd put on the woman as we ran out of the bar. "Big Lute" had been a physical force long before the far bulkier forwards and centers of today's game, scooping up every rebound in sight with his long arms, thick shoulders, and sharp elbows.

Tori jumped out of the car and squeezed her dad tight. The intensity of the hug made it clear Ned's death was still weighing on her. Her eyes were bloodshot after having cried for much of the drive.

"Now, what the heck brings you here, Tori?" Lute asked, fixing a cold gaze my way. "And who's this fella?"

His scowl signaled an understandable concern that his twenty-something daughter was dating a much older guy.

"Daddy, let me introduce you to Jack Sharpe. Remember that story I told you about that no one would listen to? He's a famous reporter who's helping me look into it."

I walked around the back of my car and extended my hand.

"Mr. Justice, it's an honor—"

I grunted as he clutched my hand with a crushing grip, cracking at least three of my knuckles.

"Media, huh?" he asked, speaking over me. "No offense, but that's one thing I've never missed since retiring."

"Daddy, be nice. He's helping when no one else would."

"What's yer name again?"

"Jack Sharpe."

"Never heard of you. Why don't you guys come on in?"

Waterloo added a few hours to the trip back to Chicago. But our detour wasn't for a father-daughter reunion. After a quick stop in Appleton to get some clothes, Tori had insisted on getting her gun at her dad's farm.

We entered a side door and walked into a small kitchen that felt more like a museum of artifacts from the 1950s. Against one wall sat a squat GE refrigerator with rounded corners and the same vertical metal handle my parents' fridge had had back in the day. Along a tile counter ran a sink that looked like a mini-tub, with separate hot- and cold-water faucets. A rusty metal teakettle on the stovetop appeared older than Lute himself. A banged-up microwave, with dials instead of a keypad, was the only sign that Lute has added anything new to the kitchen in the last twenty-five years.

Still, the most conspicuous site in the kitchen were the stacks of cardboard boxes along the walls.

"Daddy, what's going on?" Tori asked, stopping a few feet past the door and glaring at the boxes, then at him. "Where is everything?"

"Have a seat, Tori."

I recognized his tempered voice immediately, having used that tone many times myself. The divorce. My sister and parents dying. When I'd gotten canned a few weeks back. No matter how old your kids got, the tone you used to deliver bad news to them didn't change.

Tori sat in one of the kitchen chairs before Lute continued. "I wanted to tell you in person, so I guess that's now."

"Guys, I can step out," I said.

Lute looked my way. "Probably a good idea."

I walked back out to the dusty driveway. The soothing breeze and the lowing of cows in a nearby pasture provided an unexpected window of quiet relaxation. Finally, a real Wisconsin dairy farm.

Then the phone rang. Having already ignored two calls from the Dane County Sheriff's Office, I picked this one up.

"Sir, we need you to come in," the somber voice said.

"Come in where?"

"To Dane County headquarters."

"I'm almost in Illinois. How can I help you?"

"The kidnapping you reported? It ended in a fatal crash." He described the accident in a bloodless monotone.

"Did you find out who they—"

"Sir, we need you to come in."

"Okay."

Stalling further wasn't going to work, so we scheduled my visit for the next morning. I'd be far from Wisconsin by then.

The call reminded me to return one from Chief Santini.

"Jack, that's a bad guy you're messing with," the chief said right as he picked up.

"How bad?" I paced back and forth in the dirt driveway, kicking pebbles.

"Mobster. Out of Queens. A long rap sheet in his twenties—narcotics, assaults. Nothing huge, but enough to get him in and out of Rikers into his thirties. Then he became a lot more deadly. A hit man and security goon of some sort, suspected of multiple murders and assaults."

"What mob?"

"The Albanians. Or at least its American-based affiliate. Really nasty bunch."

"So why would he be in Wisconsin, tailing me?" This wasn't the time to tell him he was dead.

"Wisconsin? Beats the hell out of me. Maybe he was just a hired gun for this assignment. But when I say gun, I'm talking howitzer, so be careful."

"Understood. Thanks, Chief."

Seconds after we hung up, the kitchen door opened and Lute invited me back in. Tori remained seated at the wooden kitchen table, her eyes moist once more.

"Daddy, I'm going to go pack some clothes for the drive. Can you keep Jack company?"

"Sure."

She disappeared down a long hallway, leaving us to gin up small talk. I sat in one of the chairs at the kitchen table while he remained standing.

"So you guys think someone's stealing elections around here." Lute stepped toward the tile countertop, still narrow-eyed with skepticism.

"That's what we're trying to find out." The less he knew, the better. "It's not at all clear at this point."

"So why're ya taking her to Ohio to do it?" He picked up a red apple out of a bowl and bit into it, crunching loudly. His jaw looked as fierce as his grip.

"It's a precaution. On the off chance that people did do something wrong, we're safer looking into it from somewhere else."

He eyed me again, sizing me up.

"Maybe she'd be safer here."

"Whatever she wants to do," I said.

We were silent for an awkward minute.

"So you're moving?" I asked, gesturing toward the boxes.

"Yep," he said, chunks of apple visible in his mouth as he spoke. "Running a dairy farm ain't what it used to be, so I took the best offer I could get."

More silence.

"Who'd you sell to?"

"Huh?"

"Your farm. Who'd you sell it to?"

"Some fancy lawyer from New York approached me out of the blue. Gotta imagine it was someone big, buying up a lot of smaller farms, because what I got here definitely doesn't stick out."

I shook my head, having written about the struggles of family farms in Ohio. "You're a small farm holding your own against the big boys. You stick out like a sore thumb."

He chuckled. "More like a relic. And I wasn't holding my own lately, which is why I sold."

"All set!" Tori burst back into the kitchen, a large backpack slung over her shoulder.

Ten minutes and another punishing handshake later, I steered back onto the narrow gravel road that led to the highway.

"I thought you were getting the gun?"

"I did. While you were talking, I circled around and loaded them in the trunk."

"'Them'?"

"Yep. I got two rifles. Thought you might want one as well."

CHAPTER 40

N ow, *that* is a great story," Bridget Turner said, her blue eyes gleaming just the way they did on air.

The square-jawed Chuck Massa hummed as he and Cassie left Turner's corner office together, a bounce in his step. The plan was for Cassie to identify the flights in and out of Aspen the next time the president visited her ranch, exposing her secret meetings once and for all.

As she got back to her small office, Cassie dedicated the rest of the afternoon to a topic they wouldn't be so pleased about: trying to figure out why the bosses at Republic were so insistent on keeping the president's anti-monopoly agenda off the air. She used her personal laptop so they couldn't monitor her work.

In article after article, economists decried the problem. From airlines to banking, a small group of corporations had come to dominate a broad swath of the American economy. The trend had exploded in recent years, squeezing out new entrants, especially medium-sized and small businesses, and cramping innovation. Cassie had not appreciated the scale of the problem or the uniformity of opinion among economists that the trend was holding back America's economy in countless ways while driving an ever-widening gap between the ultra-rich and everyone else. No wonder the president was so passionate about addressing it. And with the big money sloshing around Capitol Hill, it was clear why Speaker Paxton stood in the way.

But one article in particular stopped Cassie cold. It hadn't run in a mainstream newspaper or magazine. It was an academic paper that only a narrow group of elite academics read. But an article in the *Economist* had cited it, and an op-ed by a liberal senator had referenced it as well. So Cassie dug it up.

Crunching a wide variety of data, a Princeton economics professor named Miguel Mercurio had created a formula to measure monopolies in the United States. Some of the industries he listed had routinely come up in other articles. Google, for searching the internet, led the list. First-America and BankUS in banking. The airlines. And others.

But listed at number seven was the cable industry. And number fourteen was the increasingly monopolized local media. And under both categories, Professor Mercurio highlighted one fast-growing media and cable company whose business model—a national cable network scooping up local television stations—was particularly problematic.

Republic News.

Clenching her jaw, Cassie stared at the tattoo on her wrist, the daily reminder of the injustices she was meant to right.

She'd entered the profession to take on the Man.

Now she worked for him.

Cassie dialed the Princeton economics department, pressed the extension for Professor Mercurio, and waited through five rings and his voice mail greeting.

Cassie left a message, saying only her name.

CHAPTER 41

GENEVA-ON-THE-LAKE, OHIO

All the tension evaporated away.

Tori and I were both lying back on wooden chairs, on the deck of my cottage, peering out over Lake Erie. She nursed a glass of Riesling we'd bought at a gas station while I grabbed my first Yuengling in a week. I'd promised myself only one drink, so I was savoring every sip.

Heavy afternoon gusts had quieted to a comfortable, cool breeze, easing the usual Lake Erie chop. And now the sun inched down over the water, first a tight, blinding yellow ball, then an orange semicircle, widening into a long crescent along the horizon, a kaleidoscope of orange, red, and yellow exploding outward into the thin wisp of clouds above it. Then all of it fading completely, and with it my worries.

For a few minutes, at least.

"What's next, Jack?" Tori asked as dusk turned to dark, a dim half-moon appearing to our far right.

"Bedtime."

"I mean, what are we going to do next about what's going on?"

I'd spent the car ride pondering the question. And I had some basic answers: to keep us safe while getting to the bottom of what was happening.

"First thing we're going to do is phone a friend."

With that, I took out my iPhone.

"Hey there!" Cassie answered calls faster than anyone I knew. "I'm home. I'll call you back from Rachel's line."

My phone rang a few seconds later.

"You solve the riddle of Republic yet?" I asked, confident she had.

"I did. They hate the president's anti-monopoly plan because they're building one themselves."

I stayed silent.

"Tell me I'm wrong."

That was better. "Wish I could."

"I knew it. But I assume that's not why you're calling."

"Cassie, we need your help."

"Who's 'we'?"

I put the phone on speaker.

"I'm here with a young woman named Victoria Justice."

"Victoria Justice? Is that really her name?"

Tori spoke up from her chair. "Yes. But call me Tori."

"Tori's the one who called about the odd election in Wisconsin I mentioned."

"Don't tell me it was really rigged," Cassie said.

"We're pretty convinced it was. And it looks like some dangerous people are behind it." I walked her through everything, ending with the crash.

"Jesus, that's awful. What are they after? And why Wisconsin?"

"It's a lot bigger than Wisconsin. Both voter files were penetrated, and there's at least one Albanian mobster involved. It's gotta be national or bigger. Which is why we're calling you."

"What can I do?"

"This must have gone through the national parties. They're the ones with the voter files."

"Even for state races?"

Tori spoke up. "Yep. For all races. The national parties and their vendors are the ones who house their voter files."

"Jesus, so hacking them means you control any elections you want."

"If you know what you're doing," Tori said.

Cassie went quiet, the gravity of the plot sinking in.

"So you want me to just walk in and tell them they've been hacked?"

"Not exactly."

CHAPTER 42

YOUNGSTOWN, OHIO

've got a problem, Chief."

The soles of Chief Santini's polished black shoes stared at me from the top of his desk as he leaned back in his swivel chair.

"You always have problems, my friend."

"True, but this one's a law enforcement problem."

His knees creaked as he lowered his feet to the floor and sat up straight. The grave expression of a twenty-four-year beat cop replaced the troublemaking smirk that had crossed his face only seconds before.

Despite the soothing sunset, I'd tossed and turned for hours before falling asleep at the cottage. And that's because I could see what was coming. After I'd bailed on my scheduled interview with the Dane County Sheriff's Office, they'd soon go to a judge and secure the warrant they needed to trace my cell phone's location. They would then reach out to nearby police forces to have me apprehended. No doubt, that broad call would generate the type of chatter that a capable mob operation would detect, meaning whoever hired the Albanian would soon know exactly where Tori and I were holed up.

So, rather than waiting for the inevitable, I preferred jumping the gun.

"I need you to call the police in Madison, Wisconsin, and tell them you've arrested me."

He jerked his head back.

"What the hell, Jack? For what?"

"You pick the crime. But it has to happen right away. You know that

Albanian guy we talked about? If we don't act quickly, his buddies are going to figure out exactly where I am."

"His buddies? What about *him*?"

"He's dead."

A vein popped up on the chief's forehead. "Jack, what the hell's going on?"

We went back years. He'd helped me out of a few prior jams, Youngstown-style. So I trusted him enough to explain it all and ask for this inappropriate favor.

"All you and the girl did was call 911 and report a kidnapping, right?"

"Right."

"Just tell them that. You shouldn't have run, but they're not gonna do anything to you."

"The minute we go down that road, I'm back in Madison, right where the bad guys will be waiting. Chief, you're the one who called the guy a howitzer. They want to bury me and the girl right alongside that poor kid."

He nodded, getting it.

"How much time do you typically hold people in your jail for other jurisdictions?"

"Anywhere from hours to weeks. It all depends on what crime they committed here and what they're wanted for in the other place. And how bad the other place wants them back."

"So if I did something really serious here, or you said I did, you could keep me here?"

He tossed his right hand forward. "Jack, that's totally inappro—"

"Chief, I'm not bullshitting. Something big is going on and I need a week to figure it out. I either have a couple hours if you don't help me, or you can get me that week."

He raised both hands in the air. "Okay, okay. But even if you're here, those Madison cops are going to want to talk to you."

"Can't you ask their questions for them?"

He gave an ambivalent shrug. "I can see if they'll go for that. *I* wouldn't."

He stared past me for a few seconds, chewing his lower lip, then looked directly at me. He'd made up his mind.

"I'll try to buy you a week. But I may be getting myself in more trouble than you."

"Thank you, Chief."

He laughed out loud. "You *never* thank me."

"What do you mean—"

"Jack, just tell me what else you need."

He knew me too well.

"Those cops will be tracking down the identity of that other kidnapper. The attractive brunette."

"With an accident that bad, it may take a few days. They'll need to hunt down her dental records."

"Well, when you talk to them, see if they've made any progress there."

"Jesus, Jack. Do I at least get a byline this time?"

CHAPTER 43

GENEVA-ON-THE-LAKE, OHIO

Sporadic drops of rain pelted the paper-thin roof above.

"Let's think this through," I said, leaning back in Dad's old rocking chair as Tori and I huddled in the main room of the cottage. "What's at stake on the ballot that would justify what we're seeing?"

Tori, seated at our old cedar kitchen table, shrugged. "Maybe it's not about this year at all. Maybe it's about the president's reelection in two years. A bigger prize."

Definitely possible. Lots of powerful forces wanted Moore gone. If she ever had the votes on Capitol Hill, she'd cost some of them a whole lot of money. But if this was about the president's reelection, we had all the time in the world to solve it.

"Let's assume this is about *this* November," I said. "Why would you need access to both national voter files?"

"Because you're doing something nationwide."

"Right. So what's at stake nationwide?"

"The House is the big fight right now, right?"

"It definitely is," I said. "But that would be a stretch. Speaker Paxton is in good shape."

The party *not* in the White House always fared well in the midterms, so that alone bode well for Republicans to pick up seats. Plus, the big-money forces were all in for the Speaker, thanks to his willingness to stand up to the president. Super PACs and other dark-money groups were already blitzing the Democrats' strongest challengers and weakest incumbents while Paxton flooded the campaign accounts of his priority candidates with lobbyist money. Because of the acrimony, no one anticipated a wave election. But in the targeted swing districts, Republicans were rightfully optimistic.

"True. You couldn't alter the House results without it being so blatant, everyone would see it."

"And the truth is," I added, "the Senate isn't all that different."

Although the Senate was split 52 to 48 in the Democrats' favor, Democrats were stuck defending a number of vulnerable seats. Republicans were again expecting a decent year: maybe two or three pickups if things went right, and the states in play were so big it would be hard to meddle with them. It was in two years, when Moore was up again, that the Republicans risked losing seats.

My phone buzzed from the kitchen table. I stood up to grab it, the wooden chair rocking back and forth in my absence.

"Chief! What's the word?"

"I talked to Dane County. You were driving drunk, ran over a little old lady, and drove away."

"Did she die?"

Tori looked over at me, her blue eyes widening.

"Unfortunately, she did," the chief said. "We brought you in, and then you fessed up to running from the cops in Madison."

"Perfect. And what'd they say?"

"They get why we're keeping you but definitely want to talk to you."

"Will they let you do it?"

"I'll see what I can do."

"Anything on the brunette?"

"Not yet."

"She's key, Chief."

"I get it, Jack. I get it. I'll see what I can find."

I put the phone down. "We have a few days,"

The rainfall picked up, drops now bouncing off the roof more steadily, each hitting with a dull thud. Up from Dad's chair, I started pacing.

"So neither the Senate nor House makes sense. Obviously a whole lot of governorships are up, along with other state offices."

"Doesn't each state have completely different issues at stake?" Tori asked. "Outside of the parties themselves, who would care about winning thirty governor seats?"

"There might be a few issues that stick out. Around energy. Different types of regulations. Worker and wage issues. Taxes. Someone might take a shot. Those governors together control a hell of a lot."

"But even if you elected them all, could you get them all to move in the same direction?"

"Wouldn't be as easy as Congress, but maybe on some issues."

Tori had good instincts. Thinking back to the governors of Ohio I'd covered, each had assumed he was on the path to the presidency, considering other governors his prime competition. Rigging nationwide gubernatorial elections in the hopes that they'd follow some uniform direction would be a shaky plan.

Sounding like a train passing by, the roof suddenly roared under a heavier downpour.

"You sure this cottage can take this?" Tori asked, glancing up at the ceiling while speaking more loudly.

"Oh, we've been through worse than this."

Outside, curtains of rain raced from left to right across the lake. Small bursts of white exploded on every square inch of the dark, waveless water. Not far from shore, a small boat sped westward, its driver and passenger huddling forward, no doubt seeking shelter at the docks on the other side of the nearby state lodge.

"Jack, how about state legislatures?" Tori asked. "They're up across the country."

I stopped pacing to consider it as the boat disappeared to the west. I knew state legislators best of all.

"Yeah, but they're the messiest by far. Thousands of elections. A bunch of minor-league politicians. And talk about herding cats: Who the hell knows what they'll do after you elect them?"

"But can't that be a good thing?"

"Can't what be a good thing?"

"That there're so many. And so messy."

"Why's that?"

"Because, unlike congressional, or senatorial, or even gubernatorial races, not a lot of people are sitting around watching these elections.

There's not even polling for ninety percent of them when there are far bigger races on the ballot."

She had a point.

"So interference would be less noticed," I said.

"And there'd be no basis to challenge the outcomes. Just like our Wisconsin court race. Who the hell knows why someone wins or loses a close race for the Oshkosh statehouse seat?"

"Or Chillicothe."

"Exactly. So it may be easier to steal statehouse seats than any other positions," she said, sitting up straight. "But that again begs the question: What do you get out of statehouses that's so important nationally?"

Her question took me back to Columbus, Ohio, the state capital that I knew best, both as a reporter and as a son. Even when Dad had served there, the sausage making hadn't been pretty. But it was worse now than ever. Gerrymandering had long ago meant that few of the pols walking the halls of the statehouse had had to win a general election to get there; they'd simply emerged successfully from their primary. And all they had to do to stay in office was stave off any challenge in their next primary.

Then came term limits. As popular as they were, they'd changed the place, and not for the better. With politicians cycling in and out of Columbus rapidly, lobbyists now ran the place. They understood the levers of power and how and when to pull them. They had the money. And they lingered a lot longer than any of those elected by the people. So Columbus was their town now. The politicians were short-term guests hoping to gain from their short stays, often by becoming lobbyists themselves.

So the typical statehouse session involved two tasks: enact a steady stream of extreme legislation designed to fend off primary challenges, and usher through lobbyist-backed legislation to cater to the special interests and donors. Then repeat the drill, year after year.

The only drama of the place involved personal scandal. On the one hand, the misbehavior was predictable, inevitably rooted in money or sex. The politicians—mostly from small towns, miles from home, suddenly seated at the center of power—couldn't help themselves. But the drama each term was: Who fell, and how far? In the last year, three members had resigned, including the Speaker, and two more were under investigation.

That summed up Columbus, but from Albany to Sacramento, Ohio's dysfunction was pretty standard.

I grabbed a can of Diet Coke out of the fridge and opened it.

"The lobbyists already control most statehouses. So what would you get by rigging the outcomes that you couldn't already get through those lobbyists?" I asked the question out loud but was asking myself more than Tori.

She shrugged.

I glanced at the cedar walls of the kitchen. Framed, fading photos of Dad, friends, and family captured him doing what he loved: holding up a string of walleye, steering his sailboat, playing tennis. His hearty, open-mouthed laugh centered every picture.

In all his career, through all our hard work to get him elected, was there a moment when any decision he'd made had gone beyond Ohio, impacting the whole nation? He certainly had been showered with attention every presidential primary, when his endorsement might have moved the needle for the candidate begging for it. And during general elections for the president, he'd stumped hard for the nominee—which mattered, since Ohio was a swing state and he was a big name in it. He even had spoken at two conventions, the highlights of his career.

But as a state representative, had he ever played a national role? Had his official votes ever carried a national impact? The sad answer was that, for all his hard work, for all he'd given to the party and to the statehouse and to the people of his Canton, Ohio, district, not one issue of national importance came to mind.

"Maybe it's about the presidency after all," I said. "In two years." The tension in my shoulders eased. We had a lot more time.

Then I glimpsed back at Dad's rocking chair. My dominant memories of it were his long, loud naps. While the rest of us played board games or read books on a rainy day like today, Dad would ignore the noise, tilt back, and snore away, his mouth open even wider than when he laughed.

But those had been the later years. The day's rain took me further back. When he was a leader in the state legislature, that old chair had served as his northern headquarters, a hub of activity. He'd always hated working from here, but sometimes duty had called, and if it was raining, he couldn't sail or play tennis anyway. So he'd rocked in the chair as he read reports, made phone calls, and dictated long notes to colleagues and constituents.

One particular memory flashed in my mind. One week, during one summer, when that duty had called more than usual. When Dad had been planted in that chair for days, including through perfect weather.

I remembered it well because he had stopped rocking altogether; planting his feet, he'd sit tall as he talked in the low tone that signaled something important was taking place. The calls had come not only from his fellow Ohio legislators but from national leaders. Washington. The House minority leader and he talked two or three times. Names I recognized from the Sunday news shows reached out. I had answered one of the calls myself—the House minority whip with his deep Texas twang—before nervously passing the phone to Dad. At one point we all had to step out of the cottage, dragging our dog with us, because Dad got a call from President Reagan himself only a few months into his first term. Dad didn't want any distractions.

And why all the calls? As we huddled in our car during the presidential call, Mom explained that Dad faced a big decision. That the president and those congressional leaders needed Dad's help.

And she'd been right.

As I later came to understand, with one vote Dad would be able to make their lives a lot easier. He would be able to help his party immensely, not just in Ohio but across the country—and for years to come. But I also remember Dad being unusually tense about the decision, snapping at us uncharacteristically as dark circles shadowed his eyes. He wasn't comfortable with what the callers were imploring him to do.

I sat back down in the chair, curling my palms and fingers over and around the hand-carved handles. I rocked back and forth. The rain let up, the lake's surface stilling to glass. The thunder on the roof faded, replaced by the rush of water streaming from its corners onto the deck.

Years later, in this very room, from this very chair, Dad had told me it was a vote he'd regretted. One of the few. That single vote was perhaps the most consequential of his career. But he'd come to believe it had made politics worse in Ohio. And in the country.

Seated where Tori was sitting now, I'd wholeheartedly agreed with his assessment. Then, and even more so now.

But that was beside the point.

Far more relevant was that that same vote, on the same issue, came around every ten years. And it was coming around again. After November, anyone who happened to be in Dad's position—state representative—would face the same decision he had faced all those years ago. Not just in Ohio, but in statehouses across the country.

I placed my feet on the ground and stopped rocking. I should've seen it long before. Every muscle tightened as the implications raced through my mind.

"This isn't about the presidency."

"It isn't?"

"No. It's bigger."

CHAPTER 44

s it true that the Democrats are running circles around you guys?"

It was the question that had landed Cassie the interview in the first place. Details on technology and data were generally not something party leaders would discuss with the media. But those same leaders also were maniacally competitive and eager to publicize how much better prepared they were than the other side. So when Cassie informed each party comms director that she was exploring who had the more cutting-edge operation, they couldn't say no.

"That's utter nonsense," said Emmett Lanning, the RNC's data director, as they sat in the party's cramped Robert Dole Conference Room. The ends of his mustache quivered as he cast a confident grin. "We've leapt way beyond the Democrats when it comes to our technology and digital work."

Off the record, with the party's comms director looking on, he described in detail the party's many tools and technologies as Cassie took notes, oohing and aahing a bit to egg him on.

When he got to the voter file, Cassie played dumb.

"Wait—so you guys have some kind of profile on every voter across the country?" she asked.

"You could describe it that way. We've built an incredibly rich database, and we work to enhance it every day. Come election time, we unleash all that data to target everything we do down to each voter. It's a science at this point."

"Do the Democrats have the same thing?"

Emmett leaned forward. "They've got a file, but not nearly as good as ours."

He walked through all the enhancements they'd made in the past two years. The cell phone numbers they'd purchased so they could text voters. Consumer and membership data they'd overlaid onto the file. Location data. How they scraped personal data from Facebook and other social media apps. Then he described the complex modeling that allowed them to predict every voter's behavior in every race.

"And the national party houses all this information for candidates and campaigns across the country?"

"We're the mother ship."

"And you're the captain?"

He nodded proudly, the beam from the ceiling light reflecting off his wire-rim glasses.

Time to pivot.

"It's all so impressive. I had no idea things had gotten so sophisticated. Thanks again for your time." She put the pen and steno pad into her purse as if the interview was over.

Then, in a softer, more casual tone, she broached a new topic, dressing it up as an afterthought. "That's so much private information in one place. Do you ever worry someone might hack into the file?"

Emmett stiffened, remaining anchored in his chair. This was clearly a question he took seriously. "Oh, that could never happen."

She shrugged. "I'm sure people might try."

"Oh, they *try*," he said, chuckling. "But we're better than Fort Knox."

"But haven't people hacked party emails and other things? Why not the voter file, if it's so much more valuable?"

The comms director eyed her colleague, uncomfortable with the conversation's shift. But Lanning leaned further forward, eager to defend his handiwork.

"That's mostly the Democrats, but, yes, it's happened a few times. Emails are harder to protect but have a lot less valuable information.

Because the voter file is the holy grail, we've built multiple impenetrable walls around it. We test them all the time. People try to break in, but no one's ever come close—and every time they try, we learn more about how to make it stronger."

The comms director eyed Cassie impatiently. "You got everything you need?"

Cassie ignored her, focusing on Emmett. "What exactly have you learned?"

"Where they try to get in," he said, also ignoring the press flack's interruption. "The perceived weak spots that attract them. The techniques they use. And what stops them. When sophisticated hackers try, it allows us to strengthen our defenses. And I'm telling you, they've never come close."

If he had any worries, Cassie believed she would have sensed it: reading bullshit was one of her strengths. But he wasn't bluffing. The guy was absolutely confident in what they'd built.

"Okay, that's the thirty minutes we agreed to," the flack said, standing. "Send me any quotes you want us to consider and I'll get back to you."

Cassie stood up. But as she stepped toward the door, a new angle dawned on her. Everything he'd talked about involved attacks on the voter file from the outside. But there was still the old-fashioned way in.

She turned back toward Emmett, who remained seated, and asked one more question.

"Could *you* hack in?"

"What?" He leaned back in his chair and put his hands behind his head, the damp armpits of his shirt on full display.

"Could *you* hack the voter file?"

"Why would I hack my own—"

"You know the system cold," she said, buttering him up again. "So if anyone knew how to hack into the voter file, *you* would."

He lowered his arms and rolled forward, knowing what she was getting at. An inside job. If the system was truly impenetrable to outsiders, the only way into the voter file was through an insider—someone like Emmett Lanning himself. The weak link would be a person, not the technology. Someone who'd designed it or worked on it every day.

"No one from here is going to hack our own system." His pupils flared as he spoke. "That's nuts."

"Okay, time to go." The comms woman lightly brushed Cassie's back, making it clear they were done.

They walked toward the elevators, leaving Emmett Lanning sitting by himself in the Dole Room.

CHAPTER 45

GENEVA-ON-THE-LAKE, OHIO

Reapportionment?"

As much of a wonk as Tori was, she didn't know the term. Almost no one did.

"Yeah," I said. "After each census, the Constitution requires that the 435 House of Representative seats be apportioned among all 50 states, based on the new population counts."

She rubbed her forehead. "I thought that was called redistricting. Where they draw all those crazy-looking maps."

The clouds had cleared out to the east and the sun now beamed out on a perfect fall afternoon. Water occasionally dripped onto the soaked deck.

"First they apportion the number of seats to each state based on the national census. Then each state draws those crazy districts."

"And it's the state legislators who draw those districts, right?"

"Sort of. It's the party power brokers in the state and in Washington who actually draw the maps, using the latest and greatest computer programming to rig them perfectly. Then they tell the legislators to vote for what they've drawn. But, yes, it's the legislators who vote. And they do what they're told."

"Don't any of them object? The maps are so ridiculous."

"It's become the ultimate test of party loyalty. You're allowed to stray from your party on some things, but not this."

I'd watched it firsthand.

All those calls that summer, from back rooms in D.C. to our little cottage, cajoling Dad to vote for a map he knew was absurd. The map split cities and counties across multiple districts. Crammed African Americans into a few districts. Stretched districts across hundreds of communities that had nothing in common. All to guarantee that Ohio would have thirteen Republicans in the House, leaving only five seats for Democrats to fight over. He knew it was wrong, and that the districts didn't represent the Ohio he knew so well. But he ultimately caved. Who could say no to Ronald Reagan? And if Dad—who had more of an independent streak than most—couldn't say no, it meant everyone went along.

Tori opened her laptop and typed away.

"Yep. Ohio, Wisconsin, Pennsylvania, North Carolina."

She paused again, taking in whatever website she'd called up.

"Looks like more than forty states total. Legislatures will draw the new lines next year in all of them." She read further. "But some states have moved to other methods to do it."

"A few," I said. "California, Arizona, and some others have changed the process so that the politicians aren't involved. But most are still drawn by the legislatures."

She kept her gaze on the laptop screen. "Pretty much." Then she looked up. "So, by interfering in state legislative races around the country, you can determine which party runs Congress for the next decade?"

"Exactly. If you're going to interfere in this year's elections, that's the biggest prize."

I paused, considering the plausible plot. "You wouldn't have to interfere in all of the legislative races. Pick five in some states, ten in others. Maybe a few more. Just so you get a majority. The overwhelming number of districts wouldn't need to be touched. Multiply that by a bunch of states, and you get the majority for a decade."

Tori shook her head. "All by meddling in a bunch of local races no one's watching."

I stood up and slid the porch door open, letting the cool breeze blow in.

"The question is, who's doing it?"

CHAPTER 46

LONDON

Obsessed by the one loose end that wouldn't go away, Katrina eyed Wisconsin even as the large monitor in the conference room displayed all fifty states. With only weeks before early voting began in some states, Drac was walking through their final plans.

"We have narrowed the universe down to fifteen states that have large numbers of congressional districts and whose legislatures we don't now control but reasonably might attain."

The fifteen states he referred to were colored light blue.

"So how many additional House seats can we gain if we win in all these places?"

Drac pushed a button.

On each light blue state, a number appeared with a plus sign in front of it. Ohio, Pennsylvania, Florida, and North Carolina each had a "+3" over them. Wisconsin and Michigan, "+2." Most of the other states had a "+1."

"Even with very conservative estimates, we would secure twenty House seats at a minimum and up to as many as thirty. Permanently."

Katrina said nothing as she wrote down the numbers.

"Have you gotten any more information on the situation in Wisconsin?"

"We've picked up nothing from the sheriff's department that handled the acci—"

"Accident?" she asked angrily. "Listen to the tape of that 911 call. The man who called was calm, lied, and let the boy die. That entire rendez-vous was a setup, an attempt to identify us. It was no accident."

"I understand. Well, we assumed the police would aggressively track down the caller, but, strangely, they have gone quiet."

"Forget the caller. How about finding out who the direct contact from the campaign is? The one who called the boy. There must be a way to do so."

"Nothing yet."

Her temples ached with rage. He wasn't working hard enough on this. He was too busy playing with his maps.

"This is too important now. I have sent the Butcher to find them."

CHAPTER 47

E mmett Lanning had impressed Cassie all the way up to the end of their interview.

But then he'd stumbled.

Unlike every other question, he hadn't answered her final one. And then he'd been defensive, even whiny, in evading it. Emmett was a tech guy, and in that realm he was a ninja. But Cassie's question had been about people. And on that ground, he was shaky. So if there was a soft spot at the parties, it would more likely be with the people than the technology.

With three empty Diet Coke cans and a half-eaten salad sitting on the corner of her desk, Cassie now huddled over her laptop researching the tech staffs of the Republican and Democratic Parties. But since the parties would not simply release their staff rosters, she'd have to reverse engineer it all.

For two hours she deployed every online tool available. LinkedIn and Facebook profiles, a variety of political websites, party conference agendas and rosters, job postings and other announcements. She then dug up several long articles where—as in her interview—party leaders and staff couldn't help but tout their digital prowess, including bragging about their growing tech teams.

Not surprisingly, both parties had undergone significant turnover after the presidential election. Then they'd ramped up steadily for the current election cycle.

According to his LinkedIn account, Emmett Lanning had become the party's chief technology officer the January after Janet Moore's election. Several mid-level staff had stayed with him, but within months of the election, far more had moved to the private sector or signed on with elected officials and candidates. Over the following year, Lanning rebuilt the department with sixteen new hires. A few stars from Silicon Valley joined, while several more came from state-level Republican parties and campaigns. And they hired four junior staff out of college.

Same story on the Democratic side. Most of the tech staff had left after President Moore's win to take roles in the new administration. The number three in the department, a Boston native named Dan Druffel, moved up to the CTO spot. As with the GOP, his new hires combined private sector and campaign experience. The party added three newbies, who'd recently earned bachelor's or master's degrees.

Cassie created a spreadsheet of all the names that had passed through the parties' tech departments over the past two years. Then she compiled a short dossier on each individual: their personal and professional background, when they'd arrived, and the specific job they did for the party. She underlined anything that stood out.

And for those who'd been added in the past two years but had left since, she tracked down where they'd gone. The bad news was that they were harder to trace after leaving their party. The good news was that only six people had turned over that quickly.

CHAPTER 48

CHICAGO

The jagged, raised scar that curled from Arman Kasabian's right ear down to the sharp jut of his chin drew more gawks here than in any other country he had visited.

One more thing that made him hate America. And Americans. They pompously strutted their military before the world but displayed their softness by ogling wartime injuries so common in countries like his.

Restless after twelve hours on two planes, Kasabian moved briskly through Chicago's O'Hare Airport. Having packed lightly, he walked past the baggage claim and breezed through customs, where the young border agent examined his perfectly forged British papers before letting him through.

"Enjoy your visit, Mr. Kozar," he said, leering at the side of his face.

With the road trip ahead, he would've preferred a faster car than the black Jeep Compass, but he already stood out enough in the American Midwest.

Although it was the longer route, Kasabian chose to head north to Milwaukee before cutting west across Wisconsin. He'd read a lot about America's Great Lakes and hoped to see Lake Michigan as he drove. But as he proceeded through stop-and-start traffic for the next hour, there wasn't a boat or beach to be seen—only mega-stores, office parks, and fast-food restaurants, the same gray commercialization destroying the culture of so many cities thousands of miles to the east. America. He was eager to complete his mission and return home.

An hour west of Milwaukee, he pulled off the highway and parked at a large sporting goods store. Fifteen minutes later, he walked out with a Glock 19, fifty rounds of hollow-point 9-millimeter bullets, and a serrated ten-inch-long hunting knife. He shook his head as he got back in the Jeep. One of the world's most high-priced assassins could walk into America's most common retailer and fully arm himself in minutes.

Back on the highway, the first sign he passed confirmed he was close.

Madison
16 Miles

CHAPTER 49

WASHINGTON, D.C.

S o funny, Dan," Cassie said, laughing out loud. "I was all Red Sox all the time, too."

If Dan Druffel, the DNC's chief technology officer, was a typical Boston native, Red Sox Nation would provide the best way into his good graces. Sure enough, ten minutes into drinks, they had already bonded.

The redheaded, freckled Druffel was accompanied by the party's press secretary at an Irish pub in Dupont Circle. Cassie preferred the pub's informality to the RNC's Dole Room, hoping it might loosen lips.

"So you want to know how much we kick the Republicans' ass on data?" Druffel asked after his second beer arrived.

The perfect entrée. His competitive spirit was what she was banking on.

"Actually, they told me they were kicking *your* ass. Better technology, better people."

He waved his hand dismissively, his smile fading. "That's ridiculous. One reason Janet Moore is president is because of how much more advanced we are. And we've only gotten better since."

"Well, they told me six of your best eight are now either in the White House or helping a cabinet secretary, and that you've been unable to replace them with people as talented."

He was a big man with a round face, and his ruddy cheeks jostled as he shook his head. "Yeah, well, what the hell do they know?"

"A lot, according to them. They say they've surpassed you."

Druffel fiddled with the silverware.

"I can assure you they haven't."

His chubby fingers lifted the oversized stein in front of him.

Cassie cut to the chase. "So you've improved upon the voter file and modeling from two years ago?"

After a long swig of the dark beer, he put the stein down. "In this business, you either keep improving or you lose. There is no richer database in any industry than the DNC's voter file. It's amazing how much we know."

Like Emmett Lanning, he talked through the details of their file. The two parties appeared to be on par with how deeply they pried into millions of lives.

When he was done, she homed in.

"And how have you filled in the vacancies left by the exodus? Emmett Lanning said you were only number three until after the election."

Druffel's cheeks reddened again. "I run circles around that hack. And because we have the White House, believe me, we're able to get great talent in all these positions."

"Any examples?"

"Oh, we've brought in a great group of people. Top to bottom."

He walked through a number of their new hires: the former digital director of the Florida Democratic Party, two from winning Senate campaigns, and three from President Moore's campaign.

Cassie listened intently, recognizing every person from her research even if he didn't name them.

"Impressive. I read that you've been able to swipe some talent out of Silicon Valley as well."

"We grabbed two from Google and three from other start-ups." He walked through their backgrounds.

"Were they able to transition to the political world?"

"Seamlessly. They're bringing new innovation to our work, in addition to building partnerships with their former employers. And are really shoring up our security infrastructure."

He was bringing her where she wanted to go.

"Speaking of security, do you worry about security risks when you're bringing on so many new people?"

He leaned into the table and stared right at her. Like his counterpart, he took this issue seriously.

"We do an extensive background check on everyone we hire. Plus, it's a small digital team: we're in each other's faces all day every day, so I see everything."

"You ever flag anyone?"

"We've rejected a few people after some bad references. And one foreign national didn't check out."

"How do you do background checks on people right out of school? With such thin résumés and work histories."

"We do the best we can. But they're lower-risk. First, they're the least skilled, so they wouldn't be able to do much damage even if they wanted to. Second, like I said, I can see everything everyone does anyway. Plus, these new hires are actually the most eager to impress. They've been great."

"All of them?"

For the first time he hesitated, looking at his near-empty stein. "Not all. You always make hiring mistakes. Or sometimes things don't work out."

Cassie's research had found that three Democratic tech staff had left in the prior nine months.

"A guy named Pierre Porter left after about a year. What happened there?"

He didn't miss a beat.

"Pierre was a rock star—one of the Silicon Valley guys. But his wife wanted to move back to the Bay Area. He landed a good job and we stay in touch. His company may actually do some work for us if they don't get bought out first."

"What about John Sebring?"

"Super guy. He got recruited to run one of our main vendors, but we still work with him every day." He laughed. "Sebring now makes twice as much as I do."

"How about this woman, Natalie Hawke? She was here for about eight months and then left."

Druffel shifted in his chair. "Oh, Natalie. I almost forgot about her."

He looked over at his press person. She shrugged, apparently unconcerned.

"Natalie was young, green. A really sweet person. But she had some personal issues that made it tough for her. So we had to part ways. I'm sure that happens in your business, too."

He tipped the stein vertically and finished his second beer.

Cassie waited for him to put the glass down. "What were the issues?"

"I really can't get into that. Personal stuff. We sign agreements when people leave. But we wish her well."

"She landed some data job at a New York think tank."

"Did she?" His orange eyebrows lifted in genuine surprise. "Good for her."

"Yes. Some institute that researches politics and economics."

Cassie paused to observe his response. No reaction at all.

"Does it worry you that people who had full access to your voter file are now working elsewhere?"

"We shut down all their access right away. There's no way they can get back in. And if you're referring to Natalie, she was as junior as it gets here, and struggling with even that. It's good she's somewhere with a slower pace."

"But wouldn't she, or anyone, have learned your systems after months here?"

"Sure, the basics. Actually, in her case I'm not even sure if she learned those. Either way, we cut you off when you leave. The key is ongoing access, and when you leave, you lose that."

CHAPTER 50

MADISON, WISCONSIN

S treaks of red spiraled down the sink's basin and curled into the drain.

Plastic gloves had kept Arman Kasabian's hands spotless, but the knife needed a good cleaning. He let the water run after the last speck of blood dropped from the serrated teeth, rinsing the sink's enamel surface back to an ivory white.

He was outside Madison, at the first rest stop on the way out of town.

He looked up from the sink and stared straight ahead, studying his face in the mirror. His frown twisted the lower half of his scar.

His mother had always implored him to choose an occupation he enjoyed. But he'd ignored her. Not practical advice in the third-world poverty he'd grown up in. Although at moments like this, when his mood darkened, her words rang true.

Instead of listening, he'd pursued an occupation he was good at. Using the skills he'd spent years honing—not because he'd chosen to but because he'd been forced to—it was the only vocation that would take him anywhere.

His first love had been soccer, the sport he and his brothers had grown up playing because it required nothing but an old ball. Back in his small mountain village, they didn't even have a goal; they'd just draw lines in the dirt and rule out any shot higher than the tallest player. They'd play until dark, sleep, then start up again the next morning. In between games, they'd talk about someday competing in a World Cup together. Given the turmoil of their region, they just didn't know for what country.

But all that fun and banter ceased in their early teenage years, when the older men of the town ripped away the frayed ball and replaced it with their first rifles. They started killing not long after that, as they'd been trained to do. And they killed all sorts of people. Men, women, old people, children. "As long as they are Azerbaijanis, kill them," they'd been instructed.

Of all his friends, he'd killed the most. He didn't enjoy it. But he was good at it. The best aim. The fastest. The most methodical.

And he'd benefited from another skill. He was a survivor, good at anticipating danger and escaping death, unlike too many of his friends, including his own two brothers. He still remembered crying as their limp bodies were lowered into shallow holes he'd helped dig, months apart. But after those two burials, and those of his other soccer mates, he had never cried again. He'd grown harder.

As he came of age—transitioning from conscripted warrior to hired gun—the younger the person he killed, the darker his mood afterward. At least the elderly had had the chance to live a full life. To love. To raise children. To understand joy. And while it was not his place to judge his prey, he at least found solace knowing the older ones must have done something to spur his assignment. Somehow they had sealed their own fate.

But young people? Like his brothers? They hadn't yet lived. And they'd done nothing to deserve it.

Which was why he now saw such a deep scowl in the mirror.

Looking up from a couch in his small apartment, the former campaign manager of the new Wisconsin Supreme Court justice had a far younger face than he had expected. No older than his mid-twenties. Certainly not a child, but young. And the rounded eyes of surprise had made him appear more youthful.

The target had known nothing about the plot. Or the recent activity in the campaign's voter file. But he did possess the one piece of information Kasabian needed: the identity of the digital manager of the campaign.

Once Kasabian had entered the apartment and demanded that name, the young manager's fate was sealed. But his refusal to answer only made things worse, forcing Kasabian to use the knife's serrated edge. The young man had never endured true physical pain before—so *soft*, these Americans—so he'd given up the name and other information quickly. Then Kasabian had ended his pain. Mercifully.

Kasabian cupped his hands under the faucet, lowered his head, and splashed cold water onto his face. Turning away from the mirror, he walked out of the bathroom, out of the building that housed it, and back to the Jeep. The tension within him eased as he moved to his next assignment—at the least, someone older.

After closing the Jeep door, he took out his phone and opened the app he'd been instructed to use to communicate his progress.

The name is Victoria Justice.

He pulled out of the rest area, heading for his new destination. Thankfully, the town called Waterloo was also in Wisconsin, less than an hour away.

CHAPTER 51

WASHINGTON, D.C.

Where to, honey?" the driver asked as Cassie shut the door behind her.

It had started drizzling at the end of her discussion with Dan Druffel, so Cassie had grabbed an Uber home.

"Not far. P and Connecticut."

"Sounds good, sweetie."

"Honey" had sparked a head shake. But now "sweetie," too? Her teeth clenched in anger. At what age would this garbage from older men end? One more comment, she vowed, and she'd get out.

Long ago, way before Republic, she'd committed to do her part to end the verbal injustices young women faced daily. As a young reporter at the *Boston Globe*, the indignities had come hourly. "Sweetie." "Young lady." "Darlin'." Always accompanied by a big, awful smirk. As if they had been talking to their teenage granddaughter, not a professional journalist. And back then, it wasn't only the Uber drivers but her editors, fellow reporters, sources—and the big shots she was assigned to cover.

Three months in, she decided to correct her bosses. "Unless you'd call Bob your honey, too," she'd say, gesturing at a male colleague, "please stop calling me that." One comment at a time, she'd respond. Some would roll their eyes, but few would say it again. And if they did, she'd repeat her line, wearing down even the worst offenders. Especially after she'd landed a few front-page scoops, establishing herself as a journalist to be reckoned with, they'd heeded. In the newsroom, at least, the comments died.

But she did *not* correct her sources or the big shots she interviewed. Because she'd learned early on that enduring their comments often delivered a payoff in the form of interviews with older men who avoided her more senior, male colleagues. When these men observed her youth and her gender, they saw sweetness. Weakness. They detected no threat. So they'd agree to interviews and pollute the conversation with every patronizing put-down imaginable. But she went along with their outdated notions, playing the naïf they'd pegged her for while taping and writing down every word they uttered. She smiled, listened, and politely nudged them along through her questions as they talked and talked and talked.

By the time they were done talking, and she had published her stories, they'd learned a tough lesson. About her. About the unleashed power of a young woman. But for some, the lesson came far too late. A governor in jail. Three top officials resigning, cutting deals, testifying against their old boss. Then two state senators and a city councilman falling, along with a long line of other lower-profile officials. They'd all honeyed and sweetied their way right out of office and behind bars.

Fortunately for the Uber driver, he didn't say another word.

But the memory made her relive her chat with Dan Druffel.

He'd treated her with respect. Like an equal. But of course he'd known who she was going into the interview. Her round hazel eyes and short hair still made her look youthful, but her role at Republic gave her a stature that minimized the patronizing talk.

But the way Dan Druffel had described the last woman she'd brought up, the young one who'd left after less than a year, sounded all too familiar.

She reviewed her notes, studying the words he'd used to describe Natalie Hawke. Sweet. Green. Young. He hinted that she'd had emotional problems—that it was good she'd gone somewhere with a slower pace. Having placed her in that frame, he'd clearly dismissed her as any type of threat.

Just like those Boston big shots Cassie had taken down.

Druffel wasn't stupid, but neither were those men from her *Globe* days. On the contrary, they were whip smart and appropriately paranoid, on guard against any political enemy. They suspected the worst of everyone and protected themselves accordingly. But when it came to young women, they had a blind spot. They hadn't seen Cassie coming, and she'd taken advantage of that.

The car came to a quick stop in front of her building.

"We're here, sweetie," the driver said, Cassie's right foot already planted on the curb.

Despite her vow, she said nothing back to him as she shut the door.

He'd been too helpful.

CHAPTER 52

WATERLOO, WISCONSIN

A cloud of dust kicked up at the end of Lute Justice's long driveway, interrupting the otherwise perfect view of the sun's slow descent.

With only two months to go, Lute was committed to enjoying every sunset left. The sun would still go down after he moved, of course, but not over his own fields. So sunsets would never be the same.

Sitting on his old wooden bench outside his back door, Lute trained his gaze away from the sun and onto the visiting vehicle.

It was a black SUV. No, a Jeep. A clean one. Which definitely meant it was no one he knew.

But that didn't trouble him.

The last time a strange car had arrived unannounced, clean and polished like this one, it was that fancy New York lawyer whose client would keep Lute living well the rest of his life.

Plus, he hadn't talked to a soul since Cassie and that old reporter had left, unless talking to heifers counted. So company, even mysterious company, provided a nice break.

He stayed glued to the bench as the Jeep made its way up the long hill, dust and dirt billowing behind it like a rooster's tail. It proceeded more slowly than most visitors, even the New York lawyer. The driver was probably taking in the fields. Or perhaps the jostling of a true dirt road was getting to him. City slickers weren't used to that.

When the car reached the flat part of his driveway, which he'd once measured as twenty-one yards away from the house, Lute stood up, his knees cracking like knuckles. When someone approached your home in Waterloo, especially a stranger, that was the polite thing to do.

Standing up also provided his first look at the driver. Through the lightly tinted window, he couldn't make out much but jet-black hair, a wide, square jaw, and dark sunglasses. Lute didn't trust people who wore sunglasses when they weren't needed. The only way you could size up men was eye to eye, and the dark shades got in the way.

The Jeep came to a stop earlier than Lute expected. Several car lengths away. Earlier than made sense. The engine was shut off. Then nothing. No movement. No sound. The driver simply remained seated in the vehicle, facing forward. He appeared to be looking at Lute, but even that wasn't clear. Damn sunglasses.

Lute took a cautious step toward the car.

That's when the car door opened.

A polished black dress shoe was planted on the ground under the door, followed by the other shoe. A thick head then rose above the open door, same dark hair, same sunglasses, same broad jawbone atop a narrow neck. But most prominent of all was a newly visible feature, a thick purplish scar running from the man's right ear down to his chin, jagged and thick like a crevice. This was a violent wound, a wound of battle, which meant the man was not just another lawyer.

Clasping his hands together, Lute took a step back.

The visitor's left hand appeared around the side of the Jeep's door, slamming it shut and revealing a full view. He was no more than six feet tall, and his large head now looked oversized on an otherwise slight build. He dressed as slick as the car, reminding Lute of a cop from the old show *Miami Vice*: dark blue jeans and a gray tweed sport coat over a black, collarless shirt.

Unfortunately, he shared another trait with *Miami Vice*. Resting in his elevated right hand, a black Glock was pointed right at Lute. Even more ominously, a cylinder extension doubled the length of the gun. A silencer.

"Now, wait a second, mister," Lute said, taking another step back while raising his hands in the air.

Lute had been around guns his whole life. So as soon as the man lifted his left hand to join his right, pushing the gun up and extending his arms forward, he knew.

Three rapid puffs of smoke burst from the front of the silencer.

CHAPTER 53

"Are you really going to keep working?" Rachel asked impatiently, standing over Cassie's right shoulder in her sweatpants and long-sleeved T-shirt. "You've been going nonstop."

After putting Aiden to bed, Cassie sat back down at the kitchen table and opened her laptop, a Diet Coke at her side.

"This won't take long. I promise."

"Right." Rachel headed into their bedroom.

Cassie reopened the document she'd created earlier in the day.

Natalie Hawke. Young woman. New hire at the Democratic Party. Left early after having convinced the bosses that she was harmless.

If Cassie's hunch was right, there'd be a similar narrative on the Republican side.

Cassie scrolled down through her spreadsheet. Three people had been hired by the Republicans since President Moore's election and had departed since. Two women and a man.

She skipped over the man, a thirty-four-year old who'd jumped ship to work on a governor's campaign.

The first woman also didn't fit the bill. In her late thirties, she'd worked for a variety of candidates and state parties. She jumped to the national party two months after the last election, but then left a year later to join a conservative advocacy group needing digital help. Advocacy groups now did as much campaigning as parties, so the jobs would be similar. But she'd probably earned a big raise with the move, along with a better title. Not at all like the departure of Natalie Hawke.

Cassie examined the final name on the list.

Kat Simmons. Hired right out of North Florida. Very junior, appearing on only two lists of employees, a couple political websites, and presenting at one party conference. Lasted seven months. Now enrolled in a master's program at the University of Washington.

That was more like it.

She went back to Kat Simmons's LinkedIn and Facebook pages. The Facebook page didn't provide access to private information, although the photos showed a professional-looking young woman. Glasses, sandy-blond hair in a bun. Professional. The LinkedIn account, which documented the basics of her education and career path, displayed a similarly meek photo.

Appearances aside, Natalie Hawke and Kat Simmons had similar profiles, had served short tenures at their respective parties, and had left around the same time.

This was no smoking gun. But if two people had simultaneously hacked the two national party voter files, they were the leading candidates.

CHAPTER 54

I-80, YOUNGSTOWN TO NEW YORK

It was the most shameless of false advertising.

A sign on I-80 East near Youngstown touted New York as a destination. Although four hundred miles away, the mere listing of the Big Apple on an Ohio highway had always made me feel connected to the East Coast. But the long trek across Pennsylvania quickly shattered any sense of proximity.

It didn't help that we'd woken up at four in the morning or that Tori had slept most of the way, but the drive east proved painfully long and deadly dull. Brookville, Clearfield, Danville. Who would've thought New Jersey could be the highlight of anything? But the western entrance along I-80 was the most scenic part of the drive.

We crossed the George Washington Bridge into Manhattan just before 2:00. I'd been to New York's Republic studio often in recent years, but Tori's wide-eyed gaze at the skyline made it clear this was her first visit to the city.

We were in New York to track down a young woman named Natalie Hawke. The night before, Cassie had filled us in on the two women she suspected of infiltrating the political parties' voter files. We'd agreed to find Natalie, while Cassie checked out the other woman.

"Are we just going to walk in and ask for her?" Tori asked once we'd entered the heart of Manhattan, heading south on Broadway.

I chuckled. "We'll need to be more conniving than that."

We'd done the basic research along the way. The Atlantic Center for Public Policy, the think tank where Natalie Hawke claimed to work, was based in Lower Manhattan, not far from Union Square. Its website touted its progressive research on issues such as wages, health care, and family leave. And it housed a small staff of academics along with support staff, one of whom was Natalie Hawke.

But one thing stuck out: I'd never heard of it. And given my job in Washington, that was odd.

These think tanks hustled to get their experts on the air. In response to every major news item and political fight in Washington, they'd bombard us with their studies, reports, and research projects while offering up their experts to speak on camera. Those interviews were how they proved to their donors that their investment was paying off and that their agenda was being advanced. So, in my years at Republic, my in-box had been filled daily with pitches from the most established D.C. think tanks to the smallest policy centers across the nation.

So the fact that I couldn't recall receiving a single item from something called the Atlantic Center for Public Policy meant they were either really bad at what they did or this was a phony group.

With Tori waiting in the car, I entered the ground floor of a building right off Broadway. After waiting for two people in front of me to get through, I stepped up to the security desk.

A heavyset bald man glared up at me. "Where ya headed?" he asked.

"The Atlantic Policy Center."

No reaction.

"Do you have an appointment?"

"I don't."

"What's your name?"

"Bill Sharpe."

He suddenly waved his hand high in the air, a wide smile breaking out. "Chuck! How's it going?"

A tall guy in a gray suit waved back as he walked toward the building's exit.

The guard looked back at me.

"Name again?"

"Bill Sharpe."

"From?"

"Channel 8 TV, Atlanta."

I'd done a quick search of men named Sharpe involved in media. Several Bills popped up.

"Got ID?"

I placed my Ohio driver's license on the counter. He held it a few inches from his face and squinted. Suddenly he lifted it high in the air.

"Heidi, almost quitting time! You're going the wrong way."

A mousy young woman in a pantsuit waved back before walking through a turnstile and stepping into the elevator.

He looked again at my license, then glowered back.

"You said Bill Sharpe. But this says Jack Sharpe on it. What's that about?"

"See the *W*?"

The license read Jack W. Sharpe. Jack Wallace Sharpe.

"Sure do."

"That's for William. People call me Bill."

"I see. And what channel was it again?"

"Eight."

"In Ohio?" he asked, gesturing toward my Ohio license.

"I'm from Ohio. But moved to Atlanta."

"I see." He lifted a pen from the desk. On a sign-in sheet, he wrote in the name "Bill Sharpe, Channel 8 Atlanta." Then he wrote, "Atlantic Center" and "2:04," the time.

He glanced to his right at a list of numbers, then picked up the phone and dialed five digits. An older man lugging a large carry-on suitcase lined up behind me.

"Dottie, how goes it?" He paused to hear the answer. "I got a Bill Sharpe here to see you. From Atlanta."

He listened for a few seconds, twiddling the pen in his fingers.

"Who are you visiting there?"

"Tad Craven."

A Dr. Tad Craven, sporting a beard and pince-nez glasses, was described as an economics analyst on the think tank's website, which also included a long list of papers and articles he'd published.

"He's visiting Tad Craven," the guard said back into the phone. Another pause.

"Mr. Craven isn't in today." He leaned his head to the right as a younger woman lined up behind the older man.

"Okay. How about Maggie Gerard?" The website described Dr. Gerard as a respected labor economist.

He repeated the name into the phone. Another pause.

"She's not in, either." He glared at me. "I need to help these other people, Bill. Maybe you should come back another day."

Four people now waited behind me.

"Hold on. I need to talk to one of their analysts. It's for a major story we're working on down in Atlanta."

He repeated my words verbatim into the phone, then scratched the top of his head as he listened.

"You're out of luck, mister. Apparently no one's in today that can talk to you." He peered at the man behind me. "Sir, sorry for your wait. Can I help—"

"Well, can I at least go up there to make an appointment?"

He sighed heavily before repeating my request into the phone.

"I'm sorry. They say you'll have to do that by phone. Not in person."

He hung up the phone. "Next up?"

The man behind me struggled to pick up his suitcase, giving me one more shot.

"Gee, you'd think they'd want to get some free publicity."

The edges of his thin lips angled down sharply. "Sir, to tell you the truth, since moving in nine months ago, they don't appear to want any attention at all."

"Is that right?"

"Yeah. I can't remember the last time anyone came to visit them."

I cocked my head. "But you seem to know everyone. You must see Dr. Craven and Dr. Gerard? They're very respected economists."

"It's part of my job to know the people in this building by name. But I couldn't pick Drs.—" He stopped talking.

"Craven and Gerard."

"Yeah, whoever. I couldn't pick any people by those names out of a lineup." On cue, he waved to an older woman as she stepped out of the elevator.

As he was talking, I'd pulled up the photo of Dr. Craven, the more distinctive looking of the two, on my phone. I held it in front of him.

"Wait a sec, you're telling me you don't remember this nerdy guy?" I asked in the most lighthearted tone I could muster.

The man behind me coughed, reminding us he was still there.

"Hold on," the guard said to him, now intrigued. He studied the photo seriously. "Honestly, I've never seen that guy before. And I'd remember that guy. He looks like a chipmunk!" He laughed at his own joke.

"How about anyone else from the Atlantic Center? You must see someone."

"Dottie, the lady I was talking to. She comes in every day at eight thirty. Leaves at five. Like clockwork since they moved here. But she's the only one I see. I always wonder what the hell she's doing up there all day by herself."

He was really gabbing now, so I held up the photo of Natalie Hawke from the website.

"She works there, too. You ever see her?"

He shrugged, his mouth twitching.

"Cute girl. But she's never set foot in this place."

CHAPTER 55

WATERLOO, WISCONSIN

Who the hell are you?"

The old man's gruff voice was muffled as he yelled through the rag wrapped tightly around his head and mouth.

Displays of great courage, and a high tolerance for pain, always impressed Kasabian. Most men, no matter how strong in appearance, caved quickly. Agonizing pain, and the fear of more, usually ensured it. But this old man, bound to a wooden chair in his kitchen, impressed him. He had endured much already.

Shooting someone without even a greeting was not his usual approach—too uncivil. But the old basketball player's extreme height and long wingspan posed a unique threat. Kasabian had had no intention of killing him, but he'd needed to disable him. He'd targeted the three bullets precisely—one ankle and both shoulders—to do exactly that without risking vital organs or arteries. After cutting down the giant, he sedated him with a needle and dragged him inside.

Shaking the chair violently, the old man yelled again.

"I'll be six feet under before I tell you a damn thing about my daughter."

His face already looked decades older than the day before—his skin a grayish hue, his eyes as crimson as the blood below. The large plastic sheet beneath the chair was caked with crusts of dried blood from the night before and wet blood from this morning.

Kasabian had learned long ago that knives inspired more terror than any other weapon. So he'd learned to master their use. He found it ironic that his last name meant butcher in his native Armenian.

Over the past twenty-four hours, he'd use his preferred tool to carve in places and in ways that inflicted the maximum amount of pain. And the man had screamed loudly. He'd cursed. He'd shaken the chair violently and torn at the ropes that shackled him.

But through it all, Lute Justice hadn't given in.

"My holes are shallower than six feet," Kasabian said, smiling. He held the knife up in the air, eyeing it as he twisted his wrist back and forth.

His tour of the grounds had made clear that the daughter had visited in recent days. The tire tracks in the space next to the old man's pickup were fresh. Shoe prints in the dirt indicated both a driver and passenger had entered the house. The daughter had entered her room, the empty gun case suggesting that at least one rifle had been taken. At one point her companion had paced alone outside, near the fence that separated the driveway from the fields.

Even with all that evidence, the old man had endured hours of pain before even confirming that Victoria had been there.

"I will ask you again: Where was she going?"

"I have no idea, mister. No goddamn idea."

"And who was the man she was with?"

The old man had yet to admit that anyone had been with her.

"You can cut me up all you like. I'm not talking."

Kasabian glared at the old man's weathered face. Studied the ferocity of his gunmetal eyes. He wasn't bluffing.

With valuable time slipping away, he faced an important decision. The cleanest path to eliminating Victoria Justice was a surprise ambush and kill. But that required her father giving up her location. If he refused, the alternative path—drawing the young woman to him—would be more challenging. And the path would be far more painful for the old man.

He swallowed hard. In the end, there was no choice.

Kasabian stopped pacing back and forth several meters in front of the chair. He studied the old man's head.

When it came to motivation, only a few options did the trick. The bait needed to be easily recognized by eyes unaccustomed to horrific sights and threatening enough to spur action. But it also needed to be measured so as not to cause death.

Staring at the man's bloody face, Kasabian looked slightly left, then slightly right.

Which ear would it be?

CHAPTER 56

SEATTLE

The view was just as stunning the third time Cassie walked by.

Mount Rainier's white-tipped summit loomed like a ghost behind the large, majestic fountain that served as the centerpiece of the University of Washington's campus. The panorama of lush trees and green forests that framed the fountain even obscured the construction equipment in the foreground.

Cassie studied her campus map one more time, trying to figure out why she kept ending up back at the fountain. Somehow she'd walked past sleek new buildings named after benefactors like Bill Gates and Paul Allen two and three times but couldn't find the old brick edifice she was looking for.

On her fourth try, she figured it out.

Minutes later she sat down in the humble third-floor office of Sue Schwartz, a tiny woman with shoulder-length blond hair whose job it was to earn the Daniel J. Evans School of Public Policy and Governance as much free and glowing publicity as possible.

"What a treat to have you visit us," Sue said, her brown eyes sparkling as she leaned forward over her desk. Landing a Republic story about the school would be a huge feather in her cap.

"Glad to be in *this* Washington and out of the chaos of the other one, at least for a day," Cassie said. "As I said on my message, my bosses and I were wondering how public policy schools like this handle the political realities of the day. Are you even relevant anymore when everything is driven by partisan poli—"

"Oh, we're more relevant than ever," Sue said, jolting up in her seat.

"Of course, your job is to say that, but how can that be true?"

Sue did a double take. "And I'm sure you're paid to ask tough questions. But our mission is making sure the next generation of public leaders is grounded in good policy, not just politics. Given the partisan chaos you described, there's no more important time to do this work than now."

Cassie pursed her lips and nodded.

"You make a good point, Sue. But count my bosses skeptical, especially with the tuition these kids are paying."

Sue's eyes bulged, panic setting in that her PR opportunity was imploding into a disaster.

"We'd love to hear from your students, especially those with political experience. Some D.C. sources mentioned that a couple of their former employees are here."

"Who do you have in mind?"

"You've got one student who worked for Congressman Swallow." Cassie peeked down at her notebook. "His name is Jay Dillon."

Sue jotted the name down on a pad on the desk. "The congressman has always been an advocate of ours. And Jay's a real star. Who else?"

"Another, Kat Simmons, worked at the Republican Party before coming here. Her old bosses there said she was impressed by the place."

"Great." Sue let out a breath, then wrote Kat's down as well. "Any others?"

"Those two would be fine. We're talking to a number of schools. The feedback's been all over the map."

Facing her desktop computer, Sue double-clicked to open a page that featured "Evans School for Public Policy & Governance" across the top, with a photo of the large fountain prominently displayed below.

Cassie's eyes fixed on the image. The angle looked familiar. Not from fifteen minutes ago, but previously.

"Let's see where they are," Sue said quietly, then typed on the keyboard. "Jay's in the middle of Advanced Public Finance, on the second floor. He gets out in fifteen minutes. I can message the professor."

"Perfect. And Kat Simmons?"

She typed again. Paused. Then hit some more keys.

"Funny." She tilted her head but didn't elaborate.

Cassie maintained a casual pose, legs crossed and leaning back. She knew what was coming.

Sue typed for a few more seconds.

"Oh, I see now. Darn."

"What? Is something wrong?"

"Nothing's wrong. But you're not going to be able to interview Kat Simmons."

As she expected.

"Shoot. Why not?"

"Because she's one of our remote students. It's a program we started two years ago."

"Remote?"

"Yeah. Students take all their classes online. Tests, too. It's really helped us expand enrollment and is more accommodating to students with families."

Genius, Cassie thought. Escape the scene of the crime, enroll in a school two thousand miles away, and then attend remotely so you're even further off the grid.

"So how can I get in touch with her? Is she in another part of the state?"

For the first time, Sue Schwartz looked at Cassie askance. "They can do it from anywhere. But we can't give out that kind of private information. You're going to have to interview someone else."

"Too bad. Sounded like she would've given good feedback for you guys."

"That *is* too bad. But we've got rules here. Let me see if I can find any others."

Two hours later Cassie walked out of the old building and back past the Gates and Allen Centers, stewing.

The students lavished praise on the school and were eager to make a difference in the world. To their credit, they believed that politics could once again be about policy. Cassie hoped they were right.

But guilt dampened her mood. Each student had skipped his next class to talk to her, and she'd scheduled times later in the week when they'd connect up via satellite to do the actual interviews. "You guys are perfect," she'd assured them, a relieved Sue Schwartz beaming next to them. But in a few days she'd call to inform them that the story had been canned. The story that never was.

Before heading back to the airport, Cassie had one more stop to make. After a short walk, she grabbed a seat on a wooden bench near the fountain, close enough that tiny droplets of water kissed her face as a light breeze blew through. From her seat, Mount Rainier towered in the background, a dense green forest beneath it. The yellow and gray construction equipment remained in the foreground, along with even more trees and bushes encircling much of the fountain.

This was the view she'd seen on Sue Schwartz's computer, the one she'd seen once before.

She took out her phone and called up Kat Simmons's profile once again on Facebook. Because they weren't friends, she could only see what Kat had chosen for the whole world to see. But what Kat displayed told Cassie everything she needed to know.

First, the location listed on Kat Simmons's page was Seattle, not some remote town far from UW.

Second, the third-most-recent photo displayed was a selfie. In it, Kat looked every bit the grad student, wearing a ponytail, glasses, and a UW Huskies sweatshirt. But it was where she was standing that mattered even more: within yards of where Cassie now sat, the cascading water of that fountain in the foreground, Mount Rainier rising behind it, trees all around. But, as in the picture on Sue Schwartz's computer, one element was missing. There was no construction equipment anywhere in the shot.

Cassie cast a knowing smile.

It was absolutely perfect. A postcard-worthy image placing Kat Simmons in the Pacific Northwest studiously pursuing her master's degree. Holed up and off the radar.

Unless someone was enterprising enough to fly thousands of miles for a site visit, there would be no way to know it was Photoshopped from the campus's website.

CHAPTER 57

Oh my God!"

Tori's words began as a shriek and ended as a wail. She twisted her head toward her window and pushed the phone away with her left hand.

"What? What is it?"

We were forty minutes outside of New York, driving west amid the placid waters and rolling, wooded hills of the Delaware Water Gap, when her phone vibrated.

"It's my campaign manager!"

"What about him? What did he say?"

"He didn't say anything. His face is cut to pieces."

Shaking, she angled the phone in my direction.

I swallowed hard, smothering the nausea building in my throat.

I'd visited morgues. I'd covered deadly accidents. I'd paced murder scenes. All had provided stomach-churning glimpses of lives that ended horribly. But nothing like the mangled, bloody mess on her screen. The kid's cheeks were gone, what was left of them a combination of wet, pink flesh and skull. His nose was no longer there, the center of his face now flat with two oozy, oversized holes not far below his eyes. In contrast, the eyes were fully intact—both buggy and glassy—freezing into place the sheer horror that must have marked this kid's final seconds alive. And it looked like his ears were gone, too. With his lips removed, both rows of teeth were fully visible in a haunting grimace. And a deep gash stretched across his neck, opening an inch-high window into the purple flesh inside.

Beyond the gore, each wound was so intentional, the slices symmetrical. Like a turkey after Dad had finished carving.

I grabbed the phone and placed it facedown on my lap.

"Are you sure that's him?"

"I'm sure."

The phone vibrated again. Tori recoiled as if it might bite.

I picked it up, my heart pounding.

It wasn't another photo but a text message. Thankfully, the photo had scrolled up so that the chin and neck were the only parts still visible.

> Greetings Victoria.

An ellipsis appeared as new words were being typed. I alternated between watching the road and the screen.

> After losing his ears, he told me who you are.

"What is it?" she asked, shaking. "Another photo?"

More words appeared.

> But he wouldn't tell me where you are.

Another pause.

> So I had no choice.

"Just some texts."

"From who? What do they say?"

"It's sort of cryptic."

> Regrettable.

"I'm not a child, Jack. What do they say?"

My skin prickled with alarm as I contemplated the messages. The violence was bad enough, even if the tone was oddly polite. The monster knew her phone number. He knew her name.

Before I could react, she snatched the phone out of my hand.

"Oh, no." Her voice steadied, her initial horror swelling into anger. "They killed him to find me."

She leaned forward in the seat, gripping the phone with both hands. Her thumbs lifted as she prepared to type a message back.

"Stop! Don't type a thing."

"Why not?"

"This was sent to spark a reaction. *Your* reaction. We can't write back."

"Jack, two people have died because of me," she said, practically yelling. "What are we supposed to do? Keep letting it happen?"

I paused, choosing my words carefully.

"This person is clearly a professional. And he gave up the element of surprise. He wouldn't have sent this if he had another way of finding you. This is desperation."

"Desperation?" She glared at me like I was nuts. "Aren't *we* the ones who are desperate?"

"It may feel that way, but no. They are desperate to find you, and now he's trying to smoke us out. Let's keep him guessing."

She handed me the phone. "I don't want to think about it."

We drove another ten minutes in silence, crossing the Pennsylvania line. The combination of dusk and low clouds dimmed everything around us to a stormy gray.

The phone buzzed again, and I picked it up.

The first image that came through looked like an odd-shaped piece of undercooked meat. A pinkish-tan oval with a circular chunk missing from one side.

Normally, I wouldn't have guessed that it was a human body part. But because of the prior texts, seconds of studying the image made clear what it was. A human ear, removed from its head. Disgust turned to anger. The sender had already shown us the dead kid's butchered face, so why a separate image of his removed ear?

The next image, seconds later, chilled me.

The photo was a profile shot, but not of the campaign manager. The person in it was very much alive. And the hawk nose, the buzz cut, the protruding chin, gave him away immediately. But below where his buzz cut ended, a semicircle of ooze appeared, a hole in its center—where his ear used to be.

"What now?" Tori asked, clearly reading the alarm on my face.

"Tori, you do not want to see this." I shifted the phone to my left hand so she couldn't grab it again.

"What is it?"

"They have your dad."

No daughter was going to sit idly by as her own dad was tortured to death, so I gave in. We would respond.

I pulled into a rest area near a town called Stroudsburg, navigating a maze of snoozing semis and RVs to find a parking spot.

What do you want? I texted, somehow feeling better if I served as the middleman.

Is this Victoria?

No.

Who is this?

Her boyfriend.

A pause. Tori wiped her red eyes, then leaned over to watch the conversation.

If you lie to me again he will lose his other
ear . . . Who is this?

A friend trying to keep her safe.

He didn't care about me. What he wanted was to find Tori and eliminate her.

What do you want?

I want her father to live. He agrees. But only
she can make that happen.

"Jack, we need to do what he says."
And how can she do that? I typed.

She must come home.

Then what?

Then we will talk.

Tori shook my left shoulder. My guess is she meant it to be gentle. It wasn't.

"Jack, tell him we're coming. Please. We can't do this to him. My God, he already lost an ear. *That monster cut off my dad's ear.*"

"Your dad would not want you to go home, Tori."

"Of course he wouldn't. But I don't care. *We have to help him.*"

"Help? Look at what he's already done. This guy is out to kill you and will kill me and your dad as soon as he gets rid of you."

"*I don't care, Jack,*" Tori said, almost yelling again, shaking even more than before. "*We're not leaving my dad alone any longer.*"

I couldn't say no.

We will drive back to the farm.

When?

Now.

CHAPTER 58

CLEVELAND

Through large glasses balanced on the tip of her nose, the gray-haired nurse zeroed in on her target. She thrust the needle into his spindly arm, below his armpit, creating the lifesaving conduit between the gray bag hanging above his head and the quarter-sized port implanted under his pale, loose skin.

The needle's pinch was hardly noticeable. What he dreaded was what would come next.

"Are you comfortable?" the nurse asked, walking toward the door of the palatial private room at the Cleveland Clinic.

"I am."

But Oleg Kazarov wasn't comfortable. Nothing about the circumstances—the treatment, the room, the old city on the lake—comforted him. Even worse was the weakness. The lethargy. The grogginess had already set in after the previous day's chemotherapy and would surely intensify along with the nausea. And it was on the second day that sudden jolts of pain would flare up throughout his body like earthquakes along fault lines in his bones, in his joints, in the blood vessels just below the skin. The permanent low-grade headaches would also kick in soon.

But worse than even those side effects was the distance.

From his earliest days, he had seized full and direct control of every enterprise he ever led. The initial takeover of a Soviet-era energy concern in the nineties. His successful expansion into Siberia and eastern Europe. The development of fracking technology. The foray into the United States'

Midwest and the perfectly timed acquisition of a dying election equipment company to secure his American operation's success. Step by step, he'd risen from his humble Leningrad beginnings to unimaginable riches by exercising fanatical oversight of all aspects of his operations. Of course, he delegated tasks, but all the big decisions came to him.

But because of the port lodged in his arm and the chemicals about to flow through it, he'd been forced to loosen that iron grip. And, most frustrating, this was all occurring amid the most audacious enterprise he'd ever pursued.

As the nurse closed the door behind her, drops of fluid fell from the bag, one every few seconds, worming their way down to the bottom of the translucent tube. Kazarov watched each trickle impatiently. With voracious cancer cells eating away at him from within, these meandering droplets presented such a timid response. So unnecessarily slow when the cancer was so aggressive and he had such important work to do.

He trusted Katrina more than anyone in his life. She was family and the only person alive who understood him. On his first visit to Brooklyn, he could already see the nascent genius within his young niece, smothered by her deplorable circumstances, waiting to be unleashed. So he'd arranged for the best schools and private tutoring along with the sudden exit of her drunk, derelict father. Apart from his corporate conquests, Katrina's success had become his most important mission. And, elevated by his intervention, she'd surpassed every expectation he'd had.

The liquid amassed at the tube's curved bottom until the pressure pushed it up the other side, through the port, and into his arm. He eased back in the leather chair. Comforted that the cocktail of poison was about to renew the months-long battle inside him, he closed his eyes.

After attaining her PhD and leaving several unsatisfying posts in corporate America, Katrina had flown to London and lobbied that they work together. And he'd agreed, having always assumed that she'd someday take the reins of his empire.

He hadn't expected it to be so soon.

He cursed himself for his obstinance, having endured months of burning pain in his lower abdomen before finally consulting his London physician. Days later the doctor delivered the bleak news: an aggressive cancer was ravaging his bladder and nearby lymph nodes, giving him only a 30 percent chance to live. To beat those odds, his doctor insisted on an immediate trip to America for intensive treatment. He flew to Cleveland three days later for testing and, a few weeks after that, relocated to the Ohio city to receive the best care on the planet.

That was five months ago.

"All flowing well?" a woman's voice asked.

He opened his eyes to see a young nurse strolling through the door, a bright smile beaming across her intensely tan face.

"I believe so."

He scowled as he cast her a glassy stare. It happened each round. Every fifteen or twenty minutes, just as he'd escape to faraway thoughts and places, an intrusion would pull him back into this cold room.

The bronzed nurse inspected his arm, then examined the bag, which still was full.

"All looks nice and clean," she said before walking out as quickly as she'd appeared.

Kazarov said nothing as the door closed behind her. He closed his eyes again.

The original idea had been all Katrina's: he'd been too narrowly focused to notice. She'd been an idealist since childhood, so it hadn't surprised him. Not long after joining him in London, she explained that a small number of corporate giants—including the two she had worked for—were squeezing the life out of the American economy. After he requested a deeper analysis, she delivered binders of articles and a short academic book that he spent a week absorbing.

And she was right.

Banking, agriculture, natural resources, new technology, airlines, media—a few behemoths dominated sector after sector of the world's largest marketplace. It reminded him of the calcified economic structure that was impeding progress in the countries of the former Soviet Union.

"If the system ever changes as proposed here," she predicted, holding up a copy of the book she'd given him, "there will be vast riches to be gained in a liberated American marketplace."

He initially dismissed it as academic theory. But as she talked about it again and again, they brainstormed a plan to take advantage of this structural weakness in the American economy. Which industries presented the greatest opportunities? Which partners should they bring in? How to structure it all?

But the biggest obstacle involved the politics of Washington. Since initiating his American operation, Kazarov had seen it all up close. The wheels were greased by large corporate dollars. No doubt, a primary goal of those corporate dollars was to ensure that the top-heavy system remained in place. Getting around the stranglehold of that money to topple the American system was a necessary step, but his experience told him it posed an almost insurmountable obstacle. He'd pulled it off once, but on a much smaller scale.

For a time they were stumped, especially since Congress had clamped down on voting machine security since his last endeavor. Then came two more breakthrough observations that, along with good timing, illuminated the path forward.

It finally hit.

Like a thick blanket pushing down every inch of his body, a paralyzing languor fell over him, clouding all his senses. His head suddenly weighed as much as a boulder, too much for his emaciated neck to bare, so he leaned back farther in the chair, placing his head against its cushion.

Their plan had moved forward smoothly, even after his treatments started. The creation of the syndicate of oligarchs who had eagerly embraced the idea. Katrina's masterful infiltration of the political parties and their voter files. The dry runs in special elections, allowing them to fine-tune their work. Even the high-level conversation he'd forged while in the States had gone well, ensuring that after November they'd get all the policy results they were seeking.

And then Wisconsin had flared up. A small sore that, if allowed to fester, could destroy the entire enterprise. Katrina had not managed the problem as cleanly as he'd hoped, a reminder that she was still young. A reminder that he needed to be back in charge.

Thankfully, this was his second-to-last day of chemo, and it appeared to be working. Then would come one more meeting, a final CAT scan, followed by surgery. If all went well, he'd return to London to reassert full control by Election Day.

Just in time.

That hopeful prospect eased Kazarov into a deep sleep.

CHAPTER 59

I-80, OHIO TO ILLINOIS

We arrived at the lake house at two in the morning. We slept for a few hours, showered, packed, then headed west again.

Past Toledo and across rural western Ohio and northern Indiana, extreme exhaustion set in. I wasn't simply tired in the way that, after a long day, your mind and eyelids politely request some rest. This exhaustion was sapping my whole body, wrenching my already empty stomach, wearing down the muscles of my arms and legs, playing tricks on my senses. Tori slept on and off, which kept me from unleashing my most proven tactics for staying awake on long drives: loud music, louder singing, and slapping my own face. So I plodded on, squeezing in a few short naps at rest stops and downing a constant flow of coffee and Diet Coke in between. Each cup or can of caffeine bought me a few minutes of relief, but the steady dosage also sparked a splitting headache.

I fought through the fog of sleep deprivation to think through a plan. And one thing was clear: simply driving up Big Lute's driveway was *not* the way to go. We would be dead within minutes of a front-door arrival.

I first texted Chief Santini at 6:45, not long after we'd crossed into Indiana.

Chief, we're heading back to Wisconsin.

He wrote back two minutes later.

When?

Now.

Why?

We've got a problem.

Tori stirred, so I placed the phone on my right knee. She maneuvered herself in her seat, yawned, and rested her head back against her window. She began lightly snoring five minutes later.

I picked the phone back up and finished my conversation.

"Jack, I'm sorry you've had to do all the driving."

We were thirty minutes past Chicago, and the rising sun awoke Tori from hours of sleep. Her crackly voice startled me but, after my night of driving hell, it was good to hear.

"You needed the rest. And I've always been a road warrior." The droopy-eyed zombie staring back in the rearview mirror looked like anything but a warrior. "Want any breakfast?"

Forty minutes later, an Egg McMuffin in each of our hands, we continued north amid the gray concrete of I-41. Even though the commute south was a parking lot, traffic was flowing smoothly in our direction.

"So what are we going to do?" Tori asked.

I finished my bite.

"About what?"

"When we get to my dad's farm."

"I'm not sure. This guy's clearly dangerous. But he won't do anything until he has you. So maybe I'll drop you off nearby and drive to the farm myself."

"Doesn't that scare you?"

"Not as much as letting you get near him. That's when we all die and he leaves the country on the next flight."

"So what are you going to do once you get there?"

"Try to negotiate something. Size him up in the process."

We passed the last exit in Illinois. My GPS indicated we would enter Wisconsin in about a mile. I checked my watch. Seven forty-six in the morning. Not far off my prediction.

I enjoyed the last morsel of the McMuffin and tossed the wrapper into the empty McDonald's bag. I picked up the McDonald's cup and took a sip, grimacing as the still piping-hot coffee singed my tongue.

"Then what?" Tori asked.

"Then we call some audibles depending on wha—"

We blew past the large "Welcome to Wisconsin" billboard.

"Hey, we're home!" Tori said in mock celebration.

"Getting there."

We passed the first median in Wisconsin. Nothing there.

Moments later we passed the large Pleasant Prairie water tower. My tired mind wandered back to Rhonda in that bar. Our talk weeks ago felt like months back. Next time I'd drink a lot less and enjoy it more.

"Jack, maybe we should try and draw him out. Tell him to meet us somewhere. That'll make it harder for him to control things."

I looked her way. Definitely better than the nonsense I'd been throwing out.

"Good point. You know the town. Where would you have him meet us?"

"We have one main diner in town. Maybe that'd work."

A sign in the distance indicated we were approaching another median.

"I'd hate to endanger other people. Anywhere else that wouldn't put others at risk?"

"Let me think for a sec."

I blew on the top of the coffee before taking a few more sips.

As we neared the median, two gray patrol cars, one pointing in each direction, sat with their lights and engines on.

We zoomed past.

"There's a local dive a few towns over," Tori said. "It's open twenty-four hours and crowded at night, but no one would be in there this time of day."

"Now, that might work."

My side mirror reflected both patrol cars pulling out a few hundred yards behind me. Moments later, sirens wailed behind us.

Tori craned her head to look back. "Oh, no. Jack, were you speeding?"

The speedometer showed only sixty-eight miles per hour. "Not me."

"They must be going after someone else."

I veered from the fast lane into the middle lane to let them pass. But one of the patrol cars maneuvered right behind me, and the other, still in the left lane, pulled up to our side.

"Damn. They must've run our plates or something. Traced us back to the 911 call."

"But . . . my dad. We'll have to explain it all to them."

I pulled into the right lane, then maneuvered into the narrow berm, coming to a complete stop as cars and trucks whizzed by only feet from my door. The two cars, sirens still blaring, pulled up behind me.

"Tori, they're not going to buy any of that right now. These guys think we're on the lam after being involved in a kidnapping that ended in three deaths. Until we're in the station, we should sit tight and not say a thing."

"But—"

"Trust me."

I put my hands high on the wheel where they could see them.

"Jesus, they have their guns out," Tori said, observing the same thing in her mirror I had just noticed in mine.

Two patrolmen were approaching the car, one from each side, guns drawn but pointed downward. Tori placed her hands up against the glove compartment.

"Both of you," the patrolman from my side yelled from a few yards behind me, "get out of the car and put your hands on the roof!"

CHAPTER 60

WASHINGTON, D.C.

Kat Simmons.

Natalie Hawke.

Cassie sipped her Starbucks iced latte, stared at her keyboard, and mouthed both names.

Kat Simmons.

Natalie Hawke.

The only names she knew, if those were even their real names. They'd infiltrated each party, disappeared, then covered their tracks with an elaborate trail of social media footprints.

Find Kat Simmons and Natalie Hawke and find who's behind the entire scheme.

She spent the next hour on her laptop digging. And, like a house of cards caving in when a single card is removed, every element of the two online profiles collapsed as pure fabrication.

North Florida and Tufts, the colleges Kat and Natalie attended? Cassie's deeper dive found that women with the same names had graduated from each school the same years as Kat and Natalie. But the photos of the actual grads looked nothing like the Kat and Natalie she was researching. And each had stayed in Florida and Massachusetts; one was now a paralegal and the other a med student.

None of the other professional stints from their LinkedIn profiles checked out. The institutions were legit, but there was no trace that they'd ever employed two women by those names.

As for their broader Facebook profiles, both teemed with life and spirited interaction. Back-and-forth chatter, good-natured ribbing, and birthday wishes, along with tagged photos and goofy emojis. Standard stuff.

But a closer look revealed that most of the intense activity occurred in the past eighteen months, involving colleagues they had met while burrowing into the respective national parties. Fellow party staffers, Hill staffers, partisans from around the country, and the like.

Prior to those jobs, their pages changed.

Cassie had once done a story on "catfishing"—people, usually men, creating false online profiles to lure in women. The earlier years of Natalie's and Kat's profiles bore all the telltale signs, although they were sophisticated. Each woman had hundreds of Facebook friends, but that was misleading. Two attractive women could run up their roster of Facebook friends quickly, mostly with eager men, and that was who made up most of their friends. Those men did the majority of commenting and "liking" of everything Kat and Natalie posted. There was a lot less back-and-forth, less "tagging" of photos, and few comments indicating that the men actually knew Kat or Natalie at all. A small group of other "friends" interacted more regularly, but it still felt stilted. And no family members were listed on either Facebook page.

Cassie took a final sip through the straw, slurping up the melted ice with a weak coffee taste. Discovering the twin trails of lies was equally unsatisfying. It confirmed what Cassie had suspected but left her with nowhere to go to find the two women.

Was there anything about these women that she knew for certain? Amid their fabricated profiles and false friends, was there any trait or element that set them apart? Something they couldn't hide?

With nothing coming to mind, she shut her laptop and dialed Jack, grinning as the phone rang. It didn't really matter whether he was the boss at Republic or a starving freelancer: the guy knew how to get to the bottom of a story. He always knew where to turn.

His phone rang five more times, then went to voice mail.

"Jack, I need your help. Call me back."

She put her phone down.

Then it hit her.

Kat and Natalie. They were just like Jack.

There was one quality each possessed—an asset they shared—that none of their social media bullshit and fake names and job titles could conceal.

She reached to the edge of her desk, where a bunch of reporter's notebooks were stacked up. She grabbed the one on top and leafed back through its crumpled pages, searching for her notes from a few days back.

There they were.

She found the name she was searching for and picked up her phone.

CHAPTER 61

MADISON, WISCONSIN

A cocktail of noxious smells wafted over the holding cell—body odor, alcohol, cigarette smoke, and weed—but the stench of rotten feet overwhelmed them all.

Among a crowd of drunks and derelicts and druggies of all ages, I weighed who to keep the most distance from. The two who were talking to themselves topped the competition, edging out the beefy guy who kept pacing back and forth. The least threatening was a wiry albino huddled on the floor, shaking feverishly from what had to be opioid withdrawal. I sidled over to the corner next to him and waited.

After cuffing us on the side of the highway, the two patrolmen had put us each in our own car. If the stiff-jawed patrolman who'd driven me in was privy to the plan that Chief Santini and I had concocted, he was one hell of an actor. Or maybe the chief hadn't gotten through to the authorities after all, and this was a true arrest.

Once at the Dane County jail, with cameras staring down at us from every corner, they'd processed me as gruffly as the others in line. Again, if this was an act, the corrections officers were a damn fine cast.

The plan was to keep us detained as common prisoners until Lute Justice's torturer left the farm. Then they'd nab him and pull us out immediately.

But in addition to fretting that no one here knew the plan, I had a bigger worry.

I'd been in this hellhole for four hours.

Something was wrong.

Every few minutes the echo of hard-soled shoes approached the cell, followed by the click-clack of the steel lock opening. And each time I'd sit up straight. Maybe, finally, the next visit would be my exit.

But instead, repeatedly, that hope was dashed.

First, a guard came for the albino. Then they dragged out one of the self-talkers. Then the other. Then the beefy guy coldcocked an inmate who'd gotten into his personal space, so four guards dragged both out screaming.

I was quickly becoming the senior member of the cell.

The parade of new inmates into the cell was as motley as those leaving. There was the giant whose heavy wheezing sounded like an unending asthma attack. Then came a man whose blond hair was so matted and filthy, it looked and smelled like an old, shabby rug. He was followed by a guy who barely topped five feet but whose every inch was filled with sadistic tattoos.

Each time it became clear the visit was not for me, I'd slump back down, my mind racing through the possibilities. Had the hit man not left the farm? Why not? Even if he knew I'd orchestrated the arrest, I presumed he'd still come. He couldn't get to Tori from fifty miles away. Had he somehow escaped, or killed Chief Santini and his small crew?

Ten minutes after the short guy entered, two sets of hard-soled shoes echoed down the hallway, heading our way. One set of shoes paced steadily, as the guards always sounded. The other set shuffled unevenly, in shorter intervals, followed at times by the squeak of rubber dragging. This new inmate was struggling to walk.

The lock clicked and the door slid open.

Dark eyes half-open, head tilted back, leaning heavily against the guard, he was the drunkest one to enter yet. The guard shepherded him across the cell to the one vacancy left on the concrete bench. Short and trim, with close-cropped black hair and thick, dark eyebrows, he was the most normal-looking guy in the cell besides me. Good-looking, even. But his face and arms were caked with bruises and welts, several fresh with blood. He teetered gingerly, leaning against the guard to keep from falling.

As the guard deposited him on the bench, the new inmate slumped down while whirling back toward the cell door. The new angle gave me the first glimpse at the right side of his face and its one prominent feature: a long scar curling down from his ear to his jaw, clearly a war wound. This poor guy was probably a veteran, fighting the demons so many faced when returning home.

I slowly shook my head. Someone who'd fought for our country deserved better than being stuck in a place like this.

CHAPTER 62

WASHINGTON, D.C.

There's no freaking way!"

Not a single hair budged even as Emmett Lanning jerked his head. He probably hadn't taken a shower since their last meeting.

It was the response Cassie expected to hear from the RNC's data director. For the same reason ego-driven men got fooled in the first place, they were equally stubborn about recognizing it later.

"How can you be so sure?" she asked, sipping on another iced coffee.

They were huddled in a corner of a Starbucks near Chinatown, halfway between Lanning's Capitol Hill office and Republic News. Cassie had explained her theory that Kat Simmons had infiltrated the Republican Party's voter file.

"I told you the last time. First, we have foolproof security and we're always upgrading it. Second, we do security checks daily and we fend off hack attempts of every kind almost hourly. We would know if anything is amiss. And nothing is. Third—"

"But she had months to set this up from the inside. Couldn't she have—"

"—*third*, there is no way Kat Simmons could ever pull something like this off."

"You sure about that? She faked her whole online identity. She went to real lengths—"

"Listen, she was a misfit here. We're talking serious problems. What do they call it? Borderline personality? Chemical imbalance? Something like that. So it wouldn't surprise me if she was making stuff up about herself, her boyfriend, you name it."

"But you kept her on board for some time, right?"

"We're humane that way. We gave her every chance, and things only got worse."

His tone was so defensive, so emphatic, that Cassie sensed Lanning had been attracted to Kat Simmons. Maybe kept her on longer for that reason. So she decided to pick at that scab.

"But if she enticed you into hiring her, and keeping her that long, maybe—"

His cheeks turned bright red.

"Listen, anyone can fake a résumé or make up an online profile. But not anyone can pull off the type of operation you're talking about. That would be a world-class hack. Kat Simmons is anything but world-class."

Cassie took another sip. It was actually better if he remained in denial.

"So how does someone become world-class?" she asked calmly.

"What do you mean?" He leaned backward, a beam from the ceiling light reflecting off his thick glasses.

"You said it would take a world-class hacker to pull off something like I described undetected. Who could do that?"

"Undetected? Almost no one."

"But if anyone, who? Where would they come from?"

He fumbled his cup, spilling latte onto the small table.

Cassie prodded further. "If you wanted to hire the best of the best to do something like this, where would you go?"

He laughed, swatting his hand forward. "We can't afford the best of the best. We're a political party."

"Fair enough. But if you could afford them, where would you get them?"

He paused again, stroking his mustache.

"You're talking the best in the world?"

He took a sip, some foam ending up on his chin. "Well, militaries and intel agencies around the world are a great training ground. Ours as well as other countries'. Russia, China, Israel."

"Yeah, I'd assumed that as well."

She motioned to her chin, and he wiped away the foam with his sleeve.

"Thanks. But I can assure you Kat Simmons was not military."

Although she shared his hunch, Cassie held up her hand, annoyed with his obsession with the young woman.

"Stop worrying about her. Just tell me where I'd find the world's best. *Outside* of the military."

"Well, the best of the best can make a boatload of money in the private sector."

"So who hires them?"

"Major companies, the ones with massive amounts of data that need protection. Online giants like Facebook and Google. Banks and credit card companies. Insurance companies. If data security is central to their existence, paying top dollar for the top talent in the world is worth it."

Made sense. "And where do they hire these people?"

"From each other. It's a seller's market."

"*Before* that."

He bobbed his head, following her train of thought.

"Well, I guess the best of the best are coming out of top PhD programs. Computer science. Engineering. Places like MIT, Stanford, a few others. A small crop comes out every year, and some get nabbed even before they graduate."

"Could you make me a list of the best schools?"

A cynical smile twisted his lips as he slapped the table's edge. "So crazy Kat Simmons got a PhD from Stanford? Good luck with that."

Cassie ignored the after-the-bell jab at his ex-employee.

"Can you make me that list?"

"Sure. Let me talk to a few tech buddies and see what we come up with."

CHAPTER 63

MADISON, WISCONSIN

Unintelligible arguing erupted into angry yelling. Then, like a wave flowing across the room, the mass of bodies started tumbling and shoving, grunts and shouts filling the cell amid the smacks, cracks, and thuds of wildly thrown punches.

Before I saw it, a haymaker slammed into the left side of my jaw, knocking me to the floor.

With my head pounding, I huddled in the corner, hands and arms shielding my face. But the brawl spilled over into every corner of the confined space. As bodies lunged my way, I had no choice but to fend them off—a push here, a kick there, desperate to keep a safe distance. It helped that I was one of the largest people in the cell and likely the only one in full possession of my faculties.

The stakes of the brawl changed when a high-pitched shriek pierced through the more muffled sounds of the fracas, followed by cries of agonizing pain. Pain far greater than even the hardest punch could cause. A second inmate screamed out with equal intensity. My heart pumped faster.

Someone in the cell had a weapon—and was using it.

The cell door's lock clicked. Like an army of robots storming a spaceship, guards charged in wearing brown helmets and full body armor and wielding long black sticks.

"Break it up!" the first one through the open gate yelled. "Everyone down on the ground!"

A staticky crackle of high voltage sparked more yelps of pain. To my right, near the open gate, a guard jammed the end of his black stick against a prisoner's abdomen, triggering tiny flashes of white light and another burst of crackling. The inmate doubled over and crashed onto the cement floor.

Not wanting to be shocked—I'd been tased once for a police training story and didn't need to endure that again—I threw myself to the ground, facedown, and put my hands over my head.

It first struck like a hard punch, square into the back of my left thigh, a few inches above the knee. Not as bad as the fist to the face. But then came a searing heat, burning narrowly at first before enflaming my entire lower thigh. An intense pressure shot through my leg from deep within, so paralyzing I couldn't find the air to even scream out.

I reached down to the site of the pain, finding a narrow rip in my jeans surrounded by a sticky ooze.

"Put that hand back over your head!" A guard was standing directly over me, wielding the studded end of his black stick only inches from my neck.

"Hold on!" I yelled back between short breaths, hoping my words came out clearly through the pain. "What did you do to my leg?"

As I pulled my hand back over my head, my palm and fingers were coated in the watery crimson of fresh blood.

The guard glanced down.

"I didn't touch you. You got knifed." He sounded amused. "We'll get you help as soon as we clean this mess up."

After another five minutes of yells and commands, interrupted by the occasional zap, the room settled down. Inmates lay on the floor in a mishmash of positions, many of us moaning in pain, while a dozen guards stood over us, sticks poised to shock anyone who moved.

Five minutes later, two other inmates and I were hauled out on stretchers.

"How the hell did someone get a knife into that cell?"

Lying on a cheap cot in the jail's medical unit, I'd woken up to find Tori and a barrel-chested, bearded guy staring at me. He wasn't in full uniform, but a silver star on the man's black shirt indicated he was the sheriff. Then I noticed the salt-and-pepper hair of Chief Santini a few feet behind them, prompting my second question.

"And, Chief, why the hell did you leave me in there for so long?"

By the time we'd arrived at the medical unit, my left thigh blazed like it was roasting over an open flame. As I wailed in agony, they'd laid me down on the cot and shot me up with some type of painkiller, sending me in and out of consciousness ever since. My left leg was now wrapped in a large bandage, no longer on fire but numb and tingly. The only pain I felt now was a tight pinching on my right calf.

The sheriff spoke first. "I'm Sheriff Tucker. And it wasn't a knife, it was a rudimentary shiv, and we have no idea how someone got it in there. But we're damn glad he didn't get you a few inches higher on that leg or you might've bled out on the spot. Doc?"

A short bald guy in light blue doctor's garb stepped around the sheriff.

"We've now cleaned, stitched, and bandaged it up, so beyond some throbbing for a few days, you should be good to go. But keep your weight off it. Like the sheriff said, that was a close call."

The details of the fight replayed in my mind.

"Two others were also stabbed. How are they doing?"

The doctor answered. "In and out quick. They should be fine. Your leg wound was the worst by far."

"That's good, I guess." I looked back at the sheriff. "Did you catch who did it?"

"Not yet. We found the shiv after we cleared the room, and there were no prints on it. And we couldn't see what happened from any of our cameras. That was as much mayhem as we've had around here for a while. Any idea what started it?"

"None at all. It exploded from argument to all-out brawl in about five seconds. Too many wastoids in one place."

"Yeah, that's our customer base." The sheriff's smile faded as he got down to business. "Mr. Sharpe, most of the guys in there are regulars, and we know the violent ones. So we'll push 'em hard to see who knows what."

I lifted myself to a seated position, cringing as my right calf throbbed with pain. "What happened to my other leg?"

The doctor responded. "It also had a gash in it, but not as serious as the leg. And not caused by a knife. You might've cut it up when you fell. We bandaged it and it should heal quick."

Satisfied that I was not on my deathbed, I looked past the sheriff.

"Chief, why'd you leave me in there so long?"

Chief Santini stepped forward.

"Because we never saw him leave the farm."

My head pulsed with pain. "I'm confused."

"We got there early like we'd agreed and sat at the end of that driveway for hours. His car was still there and never left. We assumed he was waiting you out, seeing if you guys blinked. So we were stuck waiting there, unable to pull you out."

"So why are you here now?"

"Well, we finally stormed the place, right around the time of your little knife fight. He had abandoned the place hours before."

"Really? He was gone the whole time?"

"Yep."

Scary. He'd left before we'd even feigned the arrest and left his car in the driveway to fool us. This guy was way ahead of us.

"So he left on foot?" I asked.

"Must've."

The pictures of old Lute flashed in my mind.

"And your dad?"

"Beaten up badly," Tori said. "But alive. And free."

The chief spoke up. "Jack, this asshole pounded the hell out of him. We thought he was dead when we first got in that kitchen. But he was breathing, and we got him off to the hospital before heading up here. He's going to recover."

"And he's safe?"

"Surrounded by four cops as we speak."

"Good. Did he say anything? Describe the guy?"

"He wasn't in any condition to pump for information. And now they've got him under heavy sedation."

Tori wiped tears from both eyes.

"You okay?" I asked.

She nodded. "And don't worry, I know why you did it. You probably saved all of us, including Dad, with that crazy plan. I'm just glad he's free of that monster."

Chief Santini cleared his throat. "Hey, Jack, I meant to tell you one other thing."

"What's that?"

"Those dental records came back on the girl. Ya know, the one with the Albanian?"

"And?" I asked.

"She was Syrian. Even more dangerous than your Albanian friend. Interpol listed her as one of the top assassins in the world, but no one could ever nab her."

"Right," I said, taking that information in. "Until her jaw met Tori's right shoulder."

CHAPTER 64

WASHINGTON, D.C.

Subject line: Wild-Kat Chase

While Cassie rolled her eyes at Emmett Lanning's attempt at humor, the email itself provided an unsurprising list of elite schools.

MIT
CIT
Stanford
Berkeley
Princeton
Carnegie Mellon
Cornell
Harvard
Duke
Georgia
Good luck!

With the list in hand, Cassie got back to work.

LinkedIn offered the easiest way to search people based on their alma mater. By typing in each school's computer science department, she created a spreadsheet of students who'd attended any of the ten schools' computer science programs over the prior decade. Her goal was to find at least five to ten students for each class, and after an hour she'd surpassed that number for all ten schools.

She then switched over to Facebook. If experience was any guide, a number of these students would allow strangers to see photos they'd posted, along with photos in which they'd been tagged by others. And odds were also good that many of these students would've posted photos of their time at these graduate schools. Some of the students would've posted a formal class photo of some sort: orientation, graduation, or something similar.

Those class photos were the gold she was digging for.

Helpfully, a number of the graduates behaved exactly as she'd hoped. Over the next hour, Cassie tracked down a photo for each class of each school, going back ten years.

The classes were typically small, usually a dozen, two dozen at most. The men outnumbered the women, often overwhelmingly. And the students were a kaleidoscope of ethnicities.

These patterns made it easy to scrutinize the handful of Caucasian women photographed. Cassie flipped back and forth between the photos she'd collected of Kat Simmons and Natalie Hawke and the women from the class photos. Several women four years back at Duke warranted a close look, as did women from a few years back at Stanford, Harvard, Princeton, and MIT. From chins to eyes to hairlines, she scrutinized every attribute, knowing that plastic surgery and hair dye could mask even the most distinct features of a human face.

In the end, only two women were even close, but they ultimately weren't a match. Disappointing, but this had always felt like a long shot anyway.

As Cassie shut her laptop, her phone rang.

"Hi. This is Professor Miguel Mercurio, from Princeton. I'm replying to the voice mail you left for me a few days ago."

Holding her phone up to her ear, she was stumped.

"I'm the one who writes about monopolies. You called about that study I did a few years ago."

Now she remembered—and she again felt the thrill of possibility. "Of course. You're the anti-monopoly expert."

CHAPTER 65

NEAR WATERLOO, WISCONSIN

All who'd come into contact with the hit man had ended up dead. Save one.

Clearly not a coincidence.

This brutal reality set me on edge as we drove to visit the one survivor: Lute Justice, recovering in a small rural hospital near Waterloo.

"He's out there, probably lying in wait near your dad's hospital," I said to Tori as we sat in the back seat of Chief Santini's unmarked Chevy Suburban.

Marked sheriff's vehicles drove ahead of and behind us.

"Jack, I'm not going to let my dad recover all by himself. He needs me. Plus, he's surrounded by cops, and so are we. Toughen up."

I sat in silence for a few minutes. In addition to the danger of it, this detour led us further away from the story. Every day we wasted driving around rural Wisconsin was one day closer to an election someone was trying to rig.

So I focused on what we could do in the meantime.

"Tori, early voting starts soon in a lot of states, right?" I knew the answer but wanted to pivot gingerly.

"It's right around the corner. Why?"

"So if you were going to mess around in elections these days, you'd start with early voting, right?"

"As much as possible. In most states, the early vote has become a huge chunk of the total. Which makes the voter file more important than ever."

"Why?"

"Because that's when you're pushing your sporadic 'ones' and 'twos' out."

I rolled my eyes at more voter file manager lingo. "Sorry. Slower."

"A smart campaign uses the early-vote window to expand their total number of voters. A not-so-smart campaign only pushes their most loyal voters out early without actually netting any new votes."

A woman's voice crackled through the chief's radio. "Chief, Deputy Conklin here. The same car's been behind me for a few miles now. Solo driver. Keeping real close."

Tori and I both looked out the back window, but the deputy's car blocked out everything behind it.

The chief stared in his side mirror. "Okay. Keep an eye out. And don't let him pass."

"Ten-four."

The chief looked our way through the rearview mirror. "No worries, guys."

I downed most of the bottle of water the chief had bought for us.

"So what exactly is the smart campaign doing to expand their total number of voters?"

"In a year like this? You're banging away at your sporadic voters—the ones who vote regularly in a presidential year but rarely in a midterm. You use the early-vote window to bank as many votes from those sporadic voters as possible—at least the ones you've identified as likely to support you—"

"Because," I interrupted, catching on, "the most regular midterm voters are going to show up either way."

"Exactly. If someone votes in every midterm no matter what, getting them to vote early doesn't gain you a thing."

"But if you get a whole lot of sporadic voters to cast their vote early, you're expanding your total."

"Right. That's why—"

The radio crackled again.

"Sir, he tried to get around me." The deputy's voice had an edge to it this time.

I whirled around. The deputy's car now straddled both lanes of the highway.

The chief replied sternly. "Deputy, do *not* let him pass you. Stay right where you are. Call to get someone else to pull him over."

"Ten-four."

Unfazed, Tori was still facing me. "They got this, Jack," she said, patting my right leg. "Like I was saying, the early vote is all about your sporadic 'ones' and 'twos.'"

I took another sip of water.

"So," I said, "if you were going to mess with a campaign's voter file in a midterm, you'd be pushing hard for as many of those sporadic votes to come early as possible."

"Definitely, for the candidate you want to win," she answered. "And once you have access to that voter file data, you'd know exactly who to go after."

"And for the campaign you want to lose?"

"Do everything you can to keep them from showing up."

The radio crackled again. The deputy's words were inaudible, but the Jeep was accelerating around her.

"Say that again, Deputy," the chief said, his voice firm. "You didn't come through."

"Is this better?"

"Yes, it is."

"Problem solved, sir. The guy's wife is in labor, lying in the back seat. They're going to the same hospital we are."

"Jesus," the chief said. "Let 'em through."

CHAPTER 66

CLEVELAND

O leg Kazarov lay in his bed, core functions of his body in full melt-down. As his doctors had warned, the final round of chemo hit him the hardest.

From the first day of treatment months ago, he'd grown accustomed to the fatigue, the coughing, the pinprick pains bursting all over his body.

But this round, a host of other side effects flared up for the first time, or far more intensely than before. His dry throat burned whenever he swallowed; his skin had dried so much, it became flaky; and his ears rang constantly, making it hard to fall asleep. His muscles, numb by day two, grew deeply sore by the morning of day three, as did his jaw. By the end of day two, the nonstop nausea had exploded into vomiting so intense that even the nurses were alarmed.

Worst of all, he couldn't think straight. He and Katrina had attempted three business calls, but he was unable to concentrate. She was patient each time, but they ultimately had hung up, agreeing to talk later. He left the impression that he'd been too tired to comprehend it all, but the truth was he'd been wide-awake each time. He just couldn't *focus* on what she was saying, or how to respond.

The morning after the latest round, the worst of the symptoms had subsided enough to try Katrina again.

"How are you, Dyadya?"

"Healing," he said curtly, never comfortable showing weakness, even to her. "Where do things stand?"

"Voting starts soon in a number of our targeted areas, and we are prepared to execute in all of them."

Kazarov nodded. The day's *Cleveland Plain Dealer* lay on the desk in front of him, a headline touting that voting would kick off the next Monday. Of course, the story focused on races for Congress and governor in Ohio, not on the lower-level offices around the state that he and Katrina were targeting.

"And have you solved your Wisconsin problem?"

"We are close, Dyadya. Our man made direct contact with one of the two, and when they are next together and in the open, we will have—"

"So you have not yet solved it."

"Soon, Dyadya."

He let seconds pass in silence. She would know what that meant.

"Will you be feeling well enough to make your trip?" Katrina asked.

Because of his weakness, he could not imagine walking down the hospital hallway, let alone flying to another state. But this meeting was critical, the last opportunity prior to Election Day.

"I will make the trip. It is too important."

CHAPTER 67

NEAR WATERLOO, WISCONSIN

You've done all you can do for him, Tori."

Sitting alone in the hospital's small cafeteria, we each dug into bowls of fruit that might have been fresh once. A sheriff's deputy was posted at the cafeteria door, two more sat outside Lute Justice's hospital room, and two were at the hospital's main entrance.

"He needs rest, and he's safer if we keep our distance."

It'd been a long night. We'd arrived to learn that, fearing fatal brain swelling, the doctors had placed Lute in a medically induced coma. Like a scene from an old war movie, his head was wrapped in a thick white bandage, fully covered except for his swollen eyelids and a breathing tube that emerged from his nose. For almost twelve hours Tori had huddled at his side, holding his hand or caressing his forearm. I'd spelled her several times so she could nap in the room next door, but she came back after less than thirty minutes each time.

I remained on edge, knowing the hit man was not far away. But I used the time to catch up on my own rest, touch base with Cassie on her progress, and assure the *Vindicator* that there was still a story coming. A nurse had also been kind enough to clean and rewrap my leg wounds.

"What's next, Jack?" Tori asked, her voice weak from exhaustion. "Can we still do something about all this?"

For the first time since I'd met her, she sounded defeated.

"Of course. And we will." Our conversation from the day before had actually provided the path forward. "You have your laptop with you, right?"

Chief Santini was set to arrive in ten minutes, gas tank filled and ready to take us back to Ohio. So we had time for a quick research project.

Tori took her computer out of her backpack and powered it up. "What do you need?"

"Go ahead and look up the statehouse districts in Ohio."

She tapped a few keys, waited a few seconds, then tapped some more. "Okay."

"What's the current breakdown of the districts?"

"Fifty-seven to forty-two, Republicans."

"So if you wanted to flip that to a Democratic majority, what districts would you target?"

"It'd be tough. That's a lot to flip."

"Of course it's tough. That's why they're hacking the voter files to do it. But what districts would make the most sense to target?"

She typed a few more words, then stared at her monitor for a good minute, her pupils dancing as she absorbed the information.

"There are about eleven worth going after."

"Where are they?"

"Mostly suburbs. Two near Columbus. Two outside Cleveland. A few near Dayton, Akron, Youngstown, and Toledo. Then several in Cincinnati. They all lean Republican, some strongly, but none are out of reach for a good challenger."

"Okay. If you had to pick two—the ones easiest to flip, especially if you were to interfere with the voter file—which ones would you pick?"

She studied the screen again, going quiet as she considered my question.

Then she pointed at the lower-left corner of her screen, as if I could see it. "Cincinnati. That one in suburban Cincinnati."

"And number two?"

She pointed to the top of the screen, slightly left of center. "I'd say up there, by the lake."

"Toledo?"

"Sort of. But east of there. More like the Sandusky area. Port Clinton."

"Great. Cincinnati and Sandusky. That's where we're going next."

CHAPTER 68

PRINCETON, NEW JERSEY

t was like a campus full of Celeste Lodges, the fanciest girl in Cassie's high school class.

The pristine greens, ivy-covered walls, and Gothic buildings set the Princeton campus apart aesthetically from any other college she'd visited. But the khakis, striped oxfords, patterned skirts, and pearl necklaces also distinguished it as the single most preppy place she'd ever seen. Cassie took it all in as she strolled toward and then into the stately gray building that housed Princeton's famed economics department.

"Professor Mercurio?" she asked, stepping through the doorway one minute ahead of their scheduled 10:00 a.m. meeting.

"Ah, Ms. Knowles. Welcome to Princeton."

A pixie of a man stood up behind a flimsy wooden desk. With short brown hair dusted with specks of gray, a pointy nose, and a goatee that looked out of place without an accompanying mustache, he fit her image of a French artist, short only the beret and handheld palate. He circled the desk to shake her hand with a grip as wobbly as Jell-O.

His office was dark, cramped, and cluttered, unimpressive for one of the world's leading economic minds. Then again, the school's benefactors were likely not fans of his work, so VIP visits must've been rare.

"Thank you for meeting so quickly," Cassie said as he returned to the chair behind his desk.

"It's my pleasure." He gestured toward a wooden chair that faced him and waited in silence as she took her seat. "Usually we academics spend our lives pontificating in a small echo chamber. So it's a treat that some-one from beyond the ivory tower is intrigued by my work."

Given his first name, Miguel, she'd expected him to speak with an accent. But the only trace of one was British.

"Ivory tower? If your research is right, it's highly relevant to the real world."

His thin lips curved upward into a closemouthed, confident grin. "Ms. Knowles, have no doubt about its correctness. It is as sound as scientists' consensus on climate change."

"But then, why no progress along the lines you suggest?"

"For the same reason we see none on our climate."

Cassie understood his point but preferred to draw it out of him.

"And why is that?"

"Our present circumstances generate great riches for a small number of people, who wisely invest a portion of those riches to preserve our pres-ent circumstances."

She chuckled. "I think they call that corruption, Professor. But at least the president appreciates your work."

He beamed. "Most definitely. She is sincerely dedicated to acting on my recommendations."

He cleared his throat.

"Forgive me, Ms. Knowles, but I am intrigued that your employer would task you with this visit. The only times my name has appeared on your airwaves have been amid scathing critiques of the president. Your bosses hold me in the same low regard as they do her."

Cassie shifted in her chair, not ready to fess up that this was a rogue visit.

"I'm not surprised, given that you suggest Republic's entire business structure should be illegal."

He leaned forward over his desk, which creaked from the added weight.

"To be clear, I believe it already *is* illegal under the law. But as with so many other industries, no one is willing to enforce that law."

The professor looked her directly in the eye, projecting a calm, formi-dable confidence. He was a missionary who'd dedicated an entire lifetime to a singular, righteous cause, burning with passion yet patient enough to play the long game.

"So what can be done?"

"You mean what *must* be done? It's not complicated. We must refine the law and revive the Teddy Roosevelt spirit of trustbusting before it's too late. And it is perilously close to being too late."

"The necessary laws are not in place today?"

He leaned back, placing his hand on his chin.

"The old antitrust laws were both clear and broad, but the courts weakened them over time. And in a system awash in corporate money, that weakness has allowed the monopolies to run roughshod over politicians, regulators, and today's courts. So the law is dead, along with enforcement."

He spent the next thirty minutes walking her through how monopolies controlled most major industries in the United States. Although she'd read all those articles, his in-person lecture painted a far more dire picture.

"And the ultimate risk," he concluded, "is to democracy itself."

"How is that?"

"Because the corporations that dominate our country's economy also are coming to dominate its politics. Not the people themselves."

"And having the president of the United States in your corner is not enough to change all this?"

"You tell me, Ms. Knowles. Does it appear to be?"

"No, it doesn't." She felt like a student in his classroom.

"She has some enforcement powers, but what she needs—what *America* needs—is a far more stringent antitrust law that dismantles the monopolies. And because enforcement takes time, this requires a Congress in support for long enough to see it through."

"And what would happen if such a law passed?"

"If enforced?" He sat up in his chair, eyes sparkling at the thought. "You would see an explosion of economic activity across this country. Small businesses and entrepreneurs stifled for a generation would thrive. New entrants and investors would come from within and abroad, and technologies unimagined today would sprout and blossom. Think about the revolution after the breakup of the telephone monopoly—voice mail and home modems and the entire information revolution that followed. That would all happen again—"

"You sound like the president."

His chin lifted.

"With respect, she sounds like me."

"Have you spoken with her?"

"Several times during the campaign, including when she came to campus. She asked me to join a small group of economists advising her on economic policy. We only had a few meetings, but she was highly engaged in my work."

"And as president?"

"Once." He hesitated. "In Aspen."

"Of course. So no one would know."

"That was not the intention. I was there for a conference, and she invited me to the ranch afterward."

Cassie smirked. That's what the dark SUVs whisking into the president's ranch were all about.

"And how was the meeting?"

"Energizing. She has absorbed all I have written."

Cassie nodded, having witnessed the same thing up close.

The professor circled back around to Republic. "Ms. Knowles, I'm enjoying our conversation, but may I ask again why you called? Are you doing a story on my work?"

The meeting was near an end, so Cassie opted for honesty. She walked through her interview with the president, the editing of it, and what had happened to Jack Sharpe.

He listened carefully but without expression until she wrapped up.

"I'm not surprised. A media monopoly with your breadth and depth carries great risk, both financial and informational. In many ways, it's the most dangerous of all to democracy, and it's one reason I single you out as a problem. Monopolies in other informational platforms present equal risk."

"You continue to say 'you,' Professor. I'm also troubled by Republic's behavior. That's why I'm here."

He quietly stroked his goatee, not knowing what to make of her.

Cassie stood up to leave, then remembered one other thing she'd hoped to gain from the visit: homework.

"Professor, do have any publications that summarize your work?"

He bounced out of his chair. "Why, of course!"

He stepped over to the far corner of the office, next to several cardboard boxes stacked on top of one another. He pulled out four copies of a small hardcover book and handed them to her.

She read the title out loud. *"Breaking Them Up: How to Unleash the Next American Revolution."*

"This little book covers it all—the problems and the solution."

"Thank you, but I don't need four."

"Take them. Give them away. I'm not going to start my economic revolution by keeping books in boxes."

CHAPTER 69

CINCINNATI

D o you know how to use the voter file?" Chet, the young campaign organizer, asked.

"I learned the basics in the last campaign I worked on," Tori said, forcing back a smile.

Clipboard in hand, she felt right at home in the campaign headquarters of Evan Walker, the upstart Democratic challenger to longtime statehouse incumbent Buddy Seitz. She had just completed three hours of knocking on doors in Hyde Park, a high-end neighborhood on Cincinnati's east side.

Chet's question about the voter file meant those three hours had paid off. Now all she needed was to secure a password to get in whenever she wanted.

"Good. So you're okay entering the data yourself?" Chet asked. "With early voting starting tomorrow, we'd love to get your results in ASAP."

"I should be fine. As long as I can ask you questions when I get confused."

"Yep, that's why I'm here." Chet stood tall as he said it, brimming with confidence.

He led her over to a desk where three elderly women were busy making phone calls to voters, clipboards lying in front of them. The fourth chair at the table was empty, a laptop laying on the desk.

"Here you go. You can enter your data here." The computer was already logged onto the file. "And I'll be right in the next room if you have questions."

Tori sat down, the small table jostling as her knees bumped against it. Still, none of the three women looked up from their phone calls. Tori relished the familiar sight. Whether through calls, door knocks, or data entry, women like these had served as the infantry in every campaign she'd been part of.

She pushed the campaign laptop to the side and opened her own instead. Chet remained behind her.

"What's the password?" she asked casually.

"I'm really not supposed to—"

"I'm so much faster on my own computer. That's how I always did it on that other campaign."

"Okay. Just this once." He leaned over and placed a small notecard in front of her. On it he wrote two words: "Walkervol" and "GoEvanGo!"

"There you go."

"Gotcha. Thanks."

She logged in.

CHAPTER 70

MARBLEHEAD, OHIO

Marblehead was like no town I'd ever visited.

On one end was an old white lighthouse rising above a rocky point of limestone, grass, and evergreens, and peering out over a blustery Lake Erie. From the lighthouse, a two-lane road curled around the edge of the thumb-shaped peninsula, then ran uninterrupted—no traffic light, no stop sign—past several blocks of restaurants, inns, and tourist-oriented shops nestled up against Lake Erie's south shore. Past the buildings, a narrow conveyer belt towered high above the road, hauling chunks of limestone the length of several football fields out to awaiting barges and freighters.

Amid all of this, in between an old tavern and an even older hardware store, sat my destination for the afternoon: a small storefront whose windows were plastered with red, white, and blue "Reelect Ted Kovak" signs. While Tori was covering the Cincinnati district she had identified as the most likely to be meddled with, my assignment was covering the district along Lake Erie that she'd ranked number two.

After checking into an old inn across the street, I limped to Kovak headquarters; the stab wound in my left thigh ached more, but the smaller gash in my right calf still stung. As I stepped in the doorway, a young man introduced himself as Daniel, the campaign's volunteer coordinator.

"Just the man I'm looking for!" Tori had assured me that I would get in faster by laying it on thick. "I'm here to make sure we send Ted the Tiger back to the statehouse!"

The kid looked more alarmed than excited about my ebullient introduction.

"Well, that's great. What's your name?"

"Bill Sharpe." I clapped him on the shoulder.

"Are you from around here?"

"No. Youngstown area. All Democrats there. So I want to help Ted win here."

"Why'd you pick here?"

"Lots of friends spend their summers here. So I've seen Ted the Tiger up close. Awesome guy—wish we had more like him!"

"Well, I agree with that, sir."

"I sure hope so. His fate is in your hands."

Republican Ted Kovak's headquarters comprised two small rooms, each as tidy as any campaign office I'd ever set foot in. A number of volunteers—mostly guys like me but a little grayer—huddled in the back room, picking up packets of paper.

"We're about to send a group out to hit some doors."

"Awesome, Daniel. That's what I'm here to do."

"Great. Please sign in here. And here's a packet to start with." The kid handed me a clipboard with about a dozen pages clipped to it. "Since this is your first time, we're going to pair you up with Jimmy here. He does this all the time and knows the area."

A stout guy wearing a Browns cap stepped toward me and introduced himself. I didn't want the company, but objecting would've drawn attention. Five minutes later, with Jimmy at the wheel of his Dodge minivan, we drove under the conveyor belt and off to our first precinct.

Jimmy couldn't have been a nicer guy. He operated a crusher at the quarry on the other end of that conveyor belt, and spent our short drive describing the mining operation that had kept the town employed, year in and year out, for a century.

My barrage of follow-up questions reflected sincere interest in Jimmy's work. But they also kept him from noticing the SUV that trailed us the entire way.

CHAPTER 71

NEW JERSEY

The *Acela Express* was pulling away as Cassie walked into the station. But she didn't mind. The regular Amtrak back to D.C. was scheduled to depart twenty minutes later, and its slower pace would give her more time to get through Mercurio's short book.

She stood for one stop before grabbing an open seat in the dining car and opening the book. It took only minutes to see why Mercurio and the president were so passionate about their cause.

Mattresses and washing machines. Beer. Pet food. Cell phones and smartphone operating systems. All were controlled by a few players. The book walked through how retail was overwhelmed by monopoly power—from home improvement stores, where two companies controlled 80 percent of the market, to drugstores, to home craft stores. And from corn seed to candy, from meat to mayonnaise, from peanut butter to jelly, two or three companies now controlled huge shares of key food sectors. Mercurio even observed that Americans faced monopolies from birth to death: baby formula and diapers to pacemakers and coffins.

The book devoted a separate chapter to the new monopolies in the digital world. "Along with the growing concentration of national and local media," he wrote, "monopolies over our access to information raise a whole new threat to the American way of life." Several pages explained his deep concerns about the Republic business model.

The closing chapter proposed the economic revolution he'd referenced in his office. Its opening pages presented complex equations for his fellow economists to absorb, so she skipped those. But then came his two proposed solutions. First, the book called for far more strict reviews of mergers and acquisitions. Second, he advocated for what he called "control caps"—a hard limit, up to a certain percentage, on how much one or several corporations could control each industry. He didn't present a single cap but a formula establishing a "control cap" for each industry.

For any industry where those caps were surpassed, the book advocated breaking up the corporations involved. The largest banks, airlines, and drug companies would be split up. From soybeans to dairy, major food industry groups would need to be broken up. Technology giants like Google and Facebook would face especially onerous limits, selling off recent acquisitions and opening themselves up to real competition. And media companies like Republic would have to decide whether to continue as national cable stations or operate a limited number of local stations— but could no longer do both. Same rules for print journalism and local newspapers.

"Baltimore!" a male conductor yelled out in a heavy New England accent, one Cassie had spent years watering down. "Next station stop is Baltimore, Maryland."

The train slowed as Baltimore's skyline emerged in the distance, an eclectic mix of old and modern. Cassie shook her head as she realized that many of the corporate names on the sides of the buildings were the same names listed in the book.

As they came to a stop, people lined up to get off the train. But Cassie went the other way. She put the book down on her seat and stepped to the dining car's kiosk, buying a bag of pretzels and a can of Diet Coke. As she sat down again, she placed the book, cover down, in the now-empty seat next to her.

And that's when they caught her eye. Three words, in small print, in the lower corner of the back cover.

The book's publisher.

Cambridge University Press.

CHAPTER 72

MARBLEHEAD, OHIO

You sure?" I asked. "I'm as persuasive as you're going to find."

Daniel, the volunteer coordinator, looked even more worried about me than before. "There's no reason to have you hobbling around in pain when we need data entry as much as we need door knocking."

After I'd limped from one door to the next for an hour, Jimmy politely suggested we head back to headquarters early. The fact that I'd argued loudly with four separate voters on their Stone Street doorsteps might've spurred him to action. Twenty minutes after that, Daniel had set me up at a computer in the back room of headquarters.

"Okay. Whatever it takes!"

He walked me through how to enter data into the campaign's voter file, and I spent the next forty-five minutes inputting the details from our curtailed walk, along with data from other volunteers' walks and phone calls. While it was mind-numbing work, it also reflected the brief history of Marblehead that Jimmy had shared with me. A century ago, large numbers of Slovaks, Hungarians, and Austrians had traveled to this region to mine limestone. As I entered names like Mazurik, Mizla, Hudak, and Simchak, it was clear their grandkids still lived here.

When the room cleared out, I snuck a text to Tori.

I'm in the voter file, entering data, but didn't get the password. It was already logged on.

Log off. Then ask for help.

How?

She walked me through it.

"Um, Daniel?" I called out seconds later. "I need your help."

He walked in from the next room over. "How goes it?"

"Great. I entered all these sheets"—I pointed to the large stack to my right—"but then something happened; I can't get back in." I gestured at the screen, which was asking for a name and password.

"That's weird. That shouldn't happen. Are you sure?"

"Yeah, all of a sudden this damn screen showed up. I was on a roll, too."

"Okay, okay. I'll log you back in."

He leaned in from my right, reaching for the keyboard. I stared at the two blank boxes on the screen, ready to consume whatever he typed.

Next to "name" he typed in *DanielH.*

Fortunately, the letters remained onscreen. Less fortunately, he was a quick typist, which meant the next box, *PASSWORD*, would be tougher to follow.

C

He typed too quickly for me to catch the next letter. But I caught the one after that that.

**d

Missed a few more.

*******o

Missed another.

*********n

Missed another.

Then he typed the number *1* before the main voter file screen popped up again.

"There you go," Daniel said. "You're back in."

"Thanks so much. I'll get through the rest of these."

As soon as he stepped back into the other room, I grabbed a pen and piece of paper and jotted down the letters I'd seen, along with my best recollection of what spots I'd missed.

C _ d _ _ o _ n _ 1

I stared at the paper for a few seconds. No obvious names or words jumped out, so I played with different letter combinations to fill in the blanks.

Cade
Cadre
Code
Cede
Cid

Did you get in? Tori asked.

        I'm in. Used his sign-in name. But didn't get
        the password. He typed too fast.

You get any of it? Send my way.

        Not enough. I'll have to watch him enter it
        again.

Will be weird. Go ahead and send.

        Too few letters to figure it out.

Just send!

Okay!

I typed in the letters: C _ d _ _ o _ n _ 1
She wrote back.

Easy.

What's easy? I wrote.

The password.

Oh, really? What is it?

CedarPoint1

. . .

or Cedarpoint1

I chuckled, forehead in hand. That was it.

Cedar Point, America's top-rated amusement park, was only a few miles down the road.

CHAPTER 73

BALTIMORE

Caffeine and adrenaline rushing through her, Cassie couldn't wait.

Using her phone as a hot spot, she connected her laptop to the internet as the train pulled out of Baltimore.

The back cover of Professor Mercurio's book reminded her of his impressive pedigree. Just like he'd published his book through Cambridge University Press, after having graduated summa cum laude from Harvard, the professor had earned his PhD from the renowned British university.

And he wasn't the only one. High-flying American college grads had for generations sought prestigious graduate degrees at Cambridge and its ancient competitor, Oxford.

Which jogged her memory.

In response to her request, Emmett Lanning had sent over the who's who of premier research universities. But he'd included only American schools. Cambridge and Oxford, absent from his list, now gave Cassie two more places to search for Kat Simmons and Natalie Hawke. And she had forty minutes left on this train to do so.

As before, she combed through ten years of Cambridge computer science graduate students. It was a far more international crew than the American schools and included more women. But none who looked like either Natalie or Kat. With Cambridge out, it was Oxford or bust.

"Baltimore/Washington International," the Bostonian conductor yelled out. "Next station, BWI."

The train slowed to a stop. While a few riders departed, far more piled on, lugging their airline baggage and filling every vacant seat and most of the train's aisles. Cassie's seat rattled as a man plopped down in the empty spot beside her. He angled his elbow well over the armrest, forcing her to squeeze close to the window.

From that uncomfortable corner, she was signing back onto LinkedIn when her neighbor leaned in her direction, eyeing her computer screen through his thick glasses.

"Can I help you?" she asked, trying to sound friendly while shifting her laptop to her left.

"It's almost quitting time, young lady. Why ya working so hard?"

"Oh, I'm not working." She grinned to hide her irritation. "Just catching up with old friends."

"I've never really gotten much out of LinkedIn." He was eager to start a longer conversation. "I don't get it at all."

"I'm just learning it myself."

Dreading more small talk, she pivoted toward the window and focused on the scene beyond the dirt-stained glass. A blur of trees, homes, parking lots, and gray buildings whizzed past as low clouds passed overhead. Her seatmate said nothing else for minutes, so she ran through her search process one last time.

She examined the pictures from Oxford from two years ago. No one looked anything like either Kat or Natalie, so she crossed that class off the list.

She was scanning the class from three years back when the train slowed again.

"New Carrolton. Next station stop, New Carrolton. Last stop before Washington."

Her neighbor wriggled in his seat, then leaned forward. Their shared armrest creaked as he pushed against it to stand up.

"Want anything to drink?"

"Um, no. Thank you."

He shrugged. "Your call."

She turned back to her laptop.

The Oxford alumni from three years back displayed two large group photos. One was a graduation photo where the entire class, in robes and caps, posed in front of a round yellow building she recognized as a storied Oxford theater. The other captured the students inside an arena-style lecture hall, each student seated behind a dark wooden desk, each semicircular row of desks elevated above the one before it. Without caps and gowns obscuring the students, the lecture hall photo was the easier to scrutinize.

"I'm back, little lady." Her seat shook again as he flopped backward into his, a beer bottle and bag of potato chips in his hands. "Now, what's that tattoo on your arm all about?"

Ignoring the guy wasn't getting the job done. "Sir, I'm sorry, but I've really got to concentrate on this right now."

He raised his hands in the air, still holding his purchases. "Fine," he said, scowling. "Fine."

She focused back on the lecture hall.

At first, no one stood out. Then one woman drew Cassie's attention. She was sitting in the back row, off to the left, as if hoping to avoid being in the frame entirely. Pale, thin, no makeup, she kept her black hair in a short, straggly bob while large round glasses magnified her almond-shaped brown eyes. While most of the students smiled, even if awkwardly, this woman, her thin lips pursed, appeared somber. Sad.

But none of these features, most of them mutable, mattered to Cassie. What caught her eye was an aspect of the young woman's face that would be much more difficult to alter: its physical shape. Cassie was used to seeing faces structured like ovals, squares, and circles. Long faces and round, heart-shaped faces. But this young woman's face was none of those. Below a narrow forehead, her high, sharp cheekbones and ears spanned wide. Then the lower half of her cheeks and jaw narrowed sharply again, back to a thin, understated chin. It was a long face, but more angled than oval. It resembled a diamond.

And that stuck out. First, it was so distinct. Second, the first time she'd found pictures of Natalie Hawke, Cassie had observed the same thing.

She jumped back to Natalie's Facebook photos, leaning into the screen. Her basic appearance had hardly changed over three years. Long brown hair. Blue eyes shaped like almonds. Heavy eyeliner—always. Lips invariably a bright red. An altogether different appearance from the Oxford student. More attractive, and exuding confidence.

But those differences aside, Natalie's face shared the basic structure as the student's. The same diamond shape: narrow forehead, high, wide cheekbones, narrow jaw and chin.

Cassie zoomed in on the photos even more closely, hopping back and forth to compare each feature at a time. Other similarities emerged. With or without makeup or glasses, the almond-shaped eyes were the same. They shared the pixie nose. Thin lips and wide mouths.

Cassie sat back, her heart pounding. Despite a spirited makeover, the woman claiming to be Natalie Hawke had graduated from Oxford three years earlier.

"Final stop coming up," the conductor yelled out. "Washington, D.C." Cassie peered out her window. Through streaks of rain streaming across the window from left to right, the Capitol lit up the sky in the distance.

She had time.

Kat Simmons and Natalie Hawke were around the same age. They presumably had similar digital skills. Natalie was an Oxford grad, while Kat had not shown up at any other school. Yet.

What were the odds?

Cassie reexamined Natalie's class. No one in the lecture hall resembled the meek, bespectacled, ponytailed Kat Simmons.

She scanned the Oxford class from the year before. Again nothing.

The train car darkened as they entered the last tunnel leading into Washington's Union Station. Then came a rumbling below, accompanied by repeated vibrations as the train traversed a series of switches.

Her neighbor grabbed the seat in front of him and pulled himself up, huffing heavily. Small remnants of potato chips fell from his sweater to the floor.

"Have a good day, young lady," he said, a smirk twisting his thin lips. "Good luck finding whoever you're searching for."

"Thank you." Although creeped out, she didn't say another word.

She jumped back one more year. Oxford, five years ago.

The photo shared by the most graduates was of the class posing on a narrow street, standing below an ornate yellow archway and enclosed footbridge that connected two buildings. Most of the men and women in the archway photo looked the way Cassie pictured computer programmers. Frumpy hairstyles atop glasses of various shapes and sizes. And most were buttoned up in dark, drab sweaters and ill-fitting pants and jackets, standing in uncomfortable poses while casting halfhearted grins.

But there was one glaring exception.

A woman at the photo's center looked like a runway model crashing the scene. Tall and thin, she stood above all but one of the men, and with her right hand pressed against her hip, elbow out, she brimmed with confidence. Straight chocolate-brown hair flowed around her long face, which was touched up with just the right amount of makeup to add color to her cheeks and life to her full lips. A streak of dark eyeliner curled expertly up and away from the outer corners of her emerald eyes, creating a feline look. And she was dressed to the nines, from black heels and leather gloves to the Gucci purse that hung from her shoulder.

She not only stood out from her own class, she was unlike any student in five years of Oxford graduating classes.

As with Natalie, Cassie homed in on the student's individual features.

The differences from Kat Simmons were plain. Kat's hair was lighter, a sandy blond as opposed to a dark brunette, and always tied back in ponytails. Kat's eyes were an aqua blue, always behind small, squarish glasses. Her skin appeared wan overall but flushed in the cheeks.

But the immutable features aligned, and too well. It started with her height: while Kat Simmons was always hunched or leaning over, it was clear she was a tall woman. The Oxford woman stood tall as well, accentuated further by her upright posture. Consistent with their figures, each had long faces. And both had dimpled chins, small noses, and narrow eyes that arced slightly down at the outer corners.

As the train slowed to a stop, the passengers around Cassie lined up for the exit, lugging their bags behind them. But Cassie didn't move, her eyes darting back and forth between photos.

The Oxford student.

Kat Simmons.

She leaned her head forward, then drew a deep breath.

If a drab Natalie had undertaken a dramatic makeover to glam up to the present day, Kat had done everything in her power to bury her natural beauty. But, like Natalie, she'd failed.

"Uh, ma'am?"

A tall figure emerged above Cassie. The train's conductor, with that perfect Boston accent.

"Thank you, sir," she said, hopping up from her seat. "Everything's great."

CHAPTER 74

MARBLEHEAD, OHIO

Y ou're late."

My watch indicated 9:35 in the morning, five minutes after I'd told Daniel I'd arrive. But the short, curly-haired elderly woman glowered at me as if I'd shown up at Kovak headquarters two hours late.

"My leg is in—"

"Doesn't matter. Here are last night's walk shifts." She handed me a manila folder stuffed with sheets of paper. "Daniel said to go ahead and enter them. Here's the volunteer log-in info for you." A small note with a new name and password was stuck to the folder.

I logged on in the back room where I'd worked the day before. My greeter sat down only feet away to make phone calls, eyeballing me every few minutes.

I texted Tori.

> I'm in. But someone is right next to me.

I laid the first walk sheet to the right of the laptop and began entering data.

She wrote back.

> Okay. Do the best you can.

Consistent with Tori's explanation back in Wisconsin, the sheets were made up entirely of "ones" and "twos" who voted in most presidential elections but often skipped midterm elections. These were the sporadic voters who were so crucial to the election.

The notes on the walk sheets also reflected what I'd experienced the day before: most people weren't home or didn't answer. Still, I recorded each attempted knock on the voter file. Those voters would remain on the list to be called or visited during future volunteer shifts.

Thirty minutes in, someone knocked on the front door in the next room.

"I'll get it," the elderly woman said, leaping to her feet. "You keep typing."

Her absence gave me my chance. I took out my phone and snapped photos of sheets I'd already typed in. I was halfway through the stack when she returned.

"What were you doing with that phone?" she asked, scowling.

A bead of sweat fell from my forehead onto the keyboard.

"Just catching up on the news."

"Son, early voting is under way and we have work to do. As we tell the high schoolers, you can play later."

"Understood." I put my phone down and entered more data as she resumed her calls.

Outside of those who weren't home, the second-largest group of voters were those who'd told a volunteer they planned to vote early for Kovak. Next to each such voter, a date appeared. Tori had also predicted this, explaining that modern campaigns asked voters what their "plan" to vote was: what date they planned to vote, and how. Doing so carried two benefits. First, studies showed that thinking through a plan to vote made people more likely to vote. Second, knowing each plan gave the campaign an individualized timeline for each voter. If a voter missed her planned date to vote, a campaign volunteer would follow up.

I entered each of these.

Then there were the handful of voters who'd told the volunteers that they no longer supported Kovak, news that led the volunteer to mark down a new score for that voter. A "three" if they appeared undecided or, worse, a "four" or a "five." On these sheets, Kovak wasn't losing much support.

In all, I spent two hours entering information for 154 Marblehead voters, interrupted only by two visits to the campaign fridge for Diet Cokes, one bathroom break, and the occasional need to scratch the scab on my right calf, which was itching more than ever.

Fortunately, my watchdog also used the bathroom several times, freeing up precious minutes for me to snap photos of all the sheets I'd entered.

When I handed her my completed stack of sheets, she flashed me a sweet smile. "Great job, sweetie. Come back soon."

Once down the block and out of sight, I sent Tori all the photos I'd taken.

CHAPTER 75

CINCINNATI

They would move quickly, Tori guessed. Because that's what she would do. The less time the original data sat on the file, the less time the campaign had to detect any meddling.

So as soon as Jack's photos came through, she stepped out of campaign headquarters for a late lunch and some privacy at Zip's Cafe, which locals had touted as serving Cincinnati's best burger. The small, wood-paneled restaurant was quiet except for an electric train chugging around the dining room's perimeter on a platform a foot below the ceiling.

After ordering a Zip's burger and wiping her hands and the wooden table clean, she opened her laptop and leaned her phone against the right side of the screen. She then logged in to Ted Kovak's voter file under the username Jack had snagged the day before, entering *CedarPoint1* as the password. The file opened.

One street at a time, she compared the original data—captured in Jack's photos—with the data as it appeared in the Kovak voter file.

She started with the five voters at the top of Jack's first photo, who lived on a street called Lifeboat Station Drive. Named Molnar, Nagy, Smith, Peterson, and Horvath, they were solid Republicans—all categorized as "ones." But they were hit-and-miss when it came to voting every year, which made them exactly the type of sporadic voters a well-run campaign would urge to vote early.

According to Jack's photos, last night's attempt to talk to them hadn't been fruitful. A volunteer had made contact with Smith, who'd indicated he'd vote by mail for Kovak in two days. But the other four hadn't been home.

She scanned the profiles of the five Lifeboat Station voters as they now appeared in the voter file. The first three names squared with Jack's photos, reflecting the unsuccessful attempts to contact them.

Then came Horvath's profile. Tori scanned it closely, then looked back at Jack's photo. Then back at the voter file.

Two key data points had changed.

Jack's photo indicated that Horvath, like the first three, hadn't been home. But the voter file reflected not only a successful voter contact but that Horvath had committed to vote for Kovak in person in two weeks.

Tori's heart skipped a beat, knowing that this change triggered an important consequence. Rather than trying to contact Horvath again in the coming days, the campaign would not contact him for at least two weeks.

Then she checked the final targeted voter on the street, Smith.

According to Jack's photo, Smith had told the volunteer he planned on voting for Kovak in two days. While the voter file accurately showed that a conversation had taken place, Smith's profile now categorized him as a "four," meaning he no longer supported Kovak. This change also brought a major consequence: Smith would never again hear from the Kovak campaign.

Tori looked away from the laptop, her eyes drawn by the train as it motored in front of her and to her right. Her stomach churned, but not because the burger was taking too long to arrive. To a layman, converting a "one" to a "four" or falsely documenting a conversation that never took place might feel trivial. To a data guru, who understood how important every piece of information was, it was like watching a mugging in plain sight. Two strong pro-Kovak voters—and two ideal targets for early voting—had been wiped off the campaign's active list.

She spent the next hour comparing the data from Jack's photos with what appeared on the Kovak voter file. One street at a time—Lake Shore Drive, Blue Water Road, Hidden Beach Road—the pattern from Lifeboat Station repeated itself.

Usually the voter file accurately reflected the data Jack had entered. Which made sense. Altering every interaction would be too noticeable and wasn't necessary.

But on every street she examined, critical components of some voters' profiles had changed.

The most common alteration involved voters who, according to Jack's photos, hadn't been home. But the file indicated that many had been spoken to and were now tagged as "fours" or "fives." For others, the file indicated that they had committed to vote on a date several weeks away. Either way, this meant that voters who supported Kovak—but who needed strong encouragement to vote—would not hear from the campaign again for weeks, if at all.

Then there were the voters who, per Jack's photos, had committed to vote early for Kovak. For some, like Smith, their updated profile indicated that they had become "fours" or "fives," never to be talked to again.

Next were the voters who had expressed a change of heart—prior "ones" and "twos" who'd moved to "fours" and "fives" in Jack's photos. Many of these voter interactions were recorded as unsuccessful contacts and remained "ones" and "twos." Even more alarming, others not only remained as "ones" and "twos" but were also recorded as having committed to vote early *for* Kovak, with their planned dates specified.

"Unreal," Tori muttered to herself. The Kovak campaign would be proactively calling "fours" and "fives," voters who opposed them, to ensure they voted.

Then there were the "threes": voters who'd informed volunteers they were now undecided. In a close election, late in a campaign, the bloc of "threes" became *the* pivotal group, often determining the election's outcome. Identifying these swing voters and then engaging them with the right message constituted a critical part of a strong campaign's late communications effort. Whoever did so best usually won.

In the voter file, a number of voters who Jack's photos labeled as "threes" were now categorized as "fours" and "fives." So these critical voters would not hear from the campaign again, while they no doubt would hear regularly from the other side.

Finally came the outright deletions. A handful of "ones," "twos," and "threes" were simply purged from the file completely. In an era of highly targeted campaigning, these voters would now be second-class citizens, never to hear from a campaign again.

"Ma'am, do you want me to warm up your burger and fries?"

A young, freckle-faced woman in a blue Zip's shirt stared down at her. As hungry as she was, Tori had forgotten about the food that sat on the other side of her open laptop.

"That'd be great. Thank you."

The girl walked away with her plate.

Tori walked back through her notes to understand the scale of what she was seeing. From a single night of voter engagement, 28 percent of strong but sporadic Kovak voters were now recategorized or purged outright so that they would not hear from the campaign, for weeks or at all. Almost 40 percent of the newly identified swing voters were mischaracterized as something else, guaranteeing they wouldn't receive the campaign's tailored message. And 25 percent of voters who were now opposed to Kovak would still be reminded to vote—meaning the Kovak campaign would be pushing out voters who actually opposed their candidate.

She scribbled some quick calculations on her napkin. Each Ohio district represented about 115,000 residents, 80,000 of whom were registered voters. In a good year, about half would vote, which meant that a shift of only several thousand votes was enough to flip a seat from one party to the other. The rate of meddling in Marblehead was well above that.

Tori picked up her phone.

Jack, you there? she texted.

Jack responded seconds later. Was what I sent helpful?

Yes, she wrote back.

You figure anything out?

Yes, she wrote back. They're stealing the district.

Tori asked Jack to send another round of Kovak entries. This time he sent her his photos of the voter contact sheets in advance, then he entered the data from a phone bank from the night before.

As he typed, she watched the Kovak voter file live.

Thirty minutes in, he texted her. Just entered Holloway, on Stone Street. Anything happen?

Everything reflected what he'd entered. Nope. Everything good so far.

Fifteen minutes later he checked in again.

All good, she responded.

Ten minutes after that, he wrote again. All done.

Great, she wrote back. Go ahead and log out.

As she reexamined the profiles she had been watching, what she saw sent her stomach roiling.

She wrote Jack.

It's a program.

What do you mean?

As soon as you logged out, it all changed.
Even altered phone numbers. Too fast for
manual changes. They've got this thing wired.

CHAPTER 76

WASHINGTON, D.C.

The smartest woman Cassie knew had started reading the *New York Times* in fourth grade. She'd been the spelling bee champ of Boston, the high school debate champ of Massachusetts, valedictorian of her Tufts class, an honors graduate of Harvard Law School, and a clerk for the U.S. Supreme Court. Now she taught law at Duke, and Cassie met her once a year for coffee.

There was only one blemish on her friend's lifelong winning streak. Her senior year at Tufts, she'd applied for the Marshall Scholarship. But after advancing a few rounds through the brutal interview process, she didn't make the cut.

Ever since, the rejection had left Cassie with one question: Who the heck won a Marshall Scholarship?

Within hours of her Oxford breakthrough, she found her answer: Katrina Rivers.

Tracking down Kat Simmons's and Natalie Hawke's real last names hadn't been difficult. Several of the Oxford alumni who'd posted photos had been nice enough to list their classmates by name, including Katrina Rivers and Natalie DesJardins.

They had hidden their tracks well. An initial search of both names, paired with the name Oxford, uncovered no other information since they had graduated. And nothing showed up at any points of Natalie DesJardins's life.

But true superstars couldn't whitewash their entire past. High achievement earned public attention. And in Katrina Rivers's case, a ten-page newspaper with a print circulation of just two thousand outed her.

On page three, days before Thanksgiving a dozen years ago, the *Daily Princetonian* announced the school's three Marshall Scholarship winners, the most from any school in the nation that year.

One of the winners was a senior named Katrina Rivers.

The brief article provided interesting insight into Katrina Rivers's past and her ambitions at the time. She was a computer science major and economics minor who wanted to use both fields to accomplish big things.

"Growing up in poverty, I was disconnected from the world even as I lived in the shadow of its greatest city," Katrina told the newspaper, which also mentioned that she originally hailed from Brooklyn and was a member of the Charter Club, one of Princeton's eating clubs. "I want to use my time at Oxford to study how technology can connect the economically disadvantaged to economic opportunity, as it has for me."

A photo of a young Katrina Rivers appeared alongside the article. In a boyish blue button-down, her cheeks flushed, strands of black hair straggling from her pulled-back ponytail, she looked far more like the Kat Simmons Facebook photos than the glamour shot at Oxford.

Cassie's phone rang. A 970 area code. Colorado.

She eagerly picked up.

"Thanks for calling me back, Axel. She gets in late tomorrow night. Are you still able to help me?"

"Sure am. I have the next three days blocked out. Hell, I'll make more with you than rides anyway."

"Great. Just send me the info we talked about as you get it."

"Will do. Thanks."

Putting her phone down, Cassie looked back at the *Daily Princetonian* article.

She reread the quote. "Growing up in poverty . . . economic opportunity . . . as it has for me."

Cassie quickly Googled Princeton's eating clubs. Nothing symbolized Princeton's elitist character more than these. And online descriptions and campus chat boards made clear that the fanciest, most elite clubs were named Ivy, Cottage, and Tiger Inn. Charter, where Katrina was a member, was described as the most down-to-earth of the clubs, dominated by engineers.

Cassie clicked back to the Oxford photo. The Gucci purse. The heels. She had money and wasn't afraid to show it, looking a lot more like Ivy or Cottage than Charter.

Then Cassie dug up details on the Marshall Scholarship. A prestigious honor, of course. But the scholarship paid for only two years of graduate school, not the seven years Katrina had spent there. And she'd gone right to Oxford, meaning she hadn't worked a real job between Princeton and those Oxford photos. Maybe she'd been paid for summer gigs. But no summer jobs or graduate student teaching salary would've paid her way through the rest of the program, with enough money to spare to afford the highbrow clothes and accessories she'd so proudly displayed in the photo.

From poverty to opportunity.

From Charter to Gucci.

Where had the money come from?

More precisely, *who* had it come from?

CHAPTER 77

CINCINNATI

If Ted Kovak was getting his knees cut out from under him along the shore of Lake Erie, Evan Walker was off and running on the banks of the Ohio River.

Tori hesitated to read too much into the first two days of early voting. And on the surface, Walker and Seitz, his opponent, were running about even in early votes; by party ID, Seitz was slightly ahead.

But as she'd explained to Jack, even if that was all the media focused on, that wasn't the number that mattered. For the measure that counted, there was a stark difference developing in who was voting early.

Only about a fifth of the Seitz early voters were sporadic voters. The rest were voters who showed up every midterm. So the incumbent wasn't moving the needle.

In contrast, almost two-thirds of the early Walker voters were sporadic voters—a strong performance.

Curious, Tori perused the voter file to see how the Walker campaign had been engaging the sporadic voters who'd already voted. Were they doing something special to stimulate this surge of early voting?

Not really. They had them all targeted for early voting but had only begun reaching out to them. So while a few of those voters had received a recent door knock or phone call encouraging them to vote, most had not.

According to the voter file, they were just showing up and voting. Unprompted. In huge numbers.

CHAPTER 78

BRYAN, OHIO

Where'd you get that scar, sweetie?"

From a slight distance, American women were drawn to the Butcher. To his svelte, wiry build. To his olive skin and coffee-brown eyes. To his confident vibe. But when they got close, when they spotted the scar, they'd turn away.

But not her.

Even after sitting next to him, on the scar side of his face, the young redhead didn't gawk. She leaned in and posed her question.

"I'm a veteran," the Butcher said somberly, eyeing his martini. "I was injured in the war."

Her smile broadened her already cherubic face. Out of the corner of his eye, he saw her green eyes sparkle. She reached out and ran her fingers along the side of his chin.

He usually would've flinched at a stranger's touch, but he didn't move as his leathery skin tingled.

"Thank you for your service. My dad served in Iraq. He lost his right eye and right arm. I spent a lot of time taking care of him as I grew up."

He drew in a long breath as his shoulders relaxed. Although successful, it had been a tedious four days.

His instinct at the farm—to walk away after having sent the old man's photo—had proven right. He'd guessed that they'd come to Wisconsin, but they were not going to simply drive up to the house. So, better to hunt them down at the hospital where the old man would recover. He'd killed at hospitals before—so many opportunities, and easy to escape.

When Drac had informed him about his targets' arrest, he changed plans again. He'd already stolen another pickup truck, making the drive to the jail simple. But the added delay from the brawl and resulting investigation scuttled the hospital plan. Still, he'd accomplished his mission, and now was only hours from his destination.

But since he never initiated an operation in the dark, he'd stopped at the first motel over the state line. He'd been nursing a martini at the motel bar—an evening drink helped him sleep—when the young woman sidled up next to him from a few seats over.

He stared straight ahead. "Please thank *him* for his service."

"Oh, he's no longer with us. But thank you."

Occasionally, when he was on the road, a woman, sufficiently drunk, would ignore the scar. Or tolerate it. Small talk at a bar would escalate into flirting, then touching, then sex back in the motel room. The woman would never leave the room alive. He had a job to do. And that job required eliminating any trace.

Tonight was different. This young lady wasn't drunk. She'd seen his scar and moved in closer, then spoken to him gently. Touched him, sent his pulse racing. His injury wasn't an obstacle this time but a connection he now yearned to explore.

But the clock was ticking. A countdown on her life. Even a few more minutes together meant it would be her last night on earth.

"You're welcome," he said, never turning her way even as his heart ticked. Sparing her.

The man in him wanted to look at her, wanted her to stay in that seat and stroke his worn face again. To tell him more about her father.

The assassin in him understood what that would mean.

CHAPTER 79

MARBLEHEAD, OHIO

You couldn't tell by looking at it, but the quarry took up most of the peninsula where Marblehead was located.

"The town hugs the lake because there's no other room," Jimmy explained as we each nursed a beer at the Veterans of Foreign Wars hall, his recommendation for the best lake view within walking distance. With two large freighters hovering offshore, bright deck lights against the darkening sky, the old hall lived up to his hype.

"That's why there's no stoplight in town, or even cross streets. There's nowhere to go in that direction unless you want to plunge eighty feet into the quarry."

"I never realized it was so deep," I said. "Where does it start?"

"Not far beyond the road. In fact, that little inn you're staying at?" The old brick inn, formerly a schoolhouse, was on the non-lake side of the road, down the street from campaign headquarters. "It's not far be-hind that."

"You mean past those woods?"

He laughed. "Don't let those big cottonwoods fool you. Take too many steps into them and it'll be the last step you ever take."

"Guess I'll jog along the lake, then," I joked.

Halfway through my response, a dull whir started droning through the restaurant, as if a quiet train were passing by. No other VFW patron budged, including Jimmy.

"It's the conveyor," he said.

"What is?" I asked.

"You were looking around for that noise. It's the conveyor. Outside. Hauling limestone to those boats out there. Runs about once a day." He paused, eyeing me. "I thought you said you've spent a lot of time here."

My phone rang at just the right time.

"Excuse me." I pivoted away from Jimmy as I picked up.

"Good news, Jack!" Tori hadn't sounded this excited since waving me down at Bad Apples.

"What's that?"

"It's Dad. He woke up."

Jimmy stared at me as I spoke. Ever since the drive back from door knocking, he'd watched me closely. My conveyor slip-up had only made it worse.

"Hold on." I stood up and took a few steps away from the table. "Did he? Great news. And how's his health?"

"He's weak but coherent. He remembers some of what happened, even though he's still in shock. The doctors were stunned he's able to remember anything after all that damage."

"He's a world-class athlete, Tori. That's got to count for something."

My leg still aching, I limped toward the VFW hall's patio, which opened onto the lake.

"Guess so," she said.

I took a deep, steadying breath before asking the question that mattered most.

"Tori, was he able to describe the guy who did it?"

"He struggled. They've got an artist in there trying to walk him through it, so we may know in a few hours. But the doctor said it's sapping him of energy."

Damn. The sooner we knew what the guy looked like, the safer we'd be. And maybe the queasy feeling gnawing my stomach would finally go away.

"Well, getting his rest is most important."

"Dad'll do his best."

I hobbled back to the table and sat down.

"Man, you've got a lot going on," Jimmy said, his squinting eyes sweeping me up and down.

"Always! But none of it's more important than reelecting Ted Kovak."

"And how'd you hurt that leg, anyway?"

"Bike wreck." I laughed out loud while patting my leg. "You should see the truck I ran into!"

Jimmy crossed his arms.

"Forget about my shit. Tell me how you crush limestone."

CHAPTER 80

J ack, can you check your email?"

Nestled in the inn's blue-walled library, surrounded by navigational charts and books, I'd started my morning drafting the opening paragraphs of the story for the *Vindicator*. Then Tori had called.

"Of course. What's up?"

"Dad refused to sleep. He insisted on staying up until they had a final drawing."

"Did they make progress?"

"More than that. They're done. That's what I want to email you."

I gave her my email address.

"Okay. Coming right up."

"Thanks. I'll share it with my undercover guy so we can be on the lookout." Never far away, Santini's guy was asleep in a small room next to mine.

"I already did the same."

I logged into my Gmail account. As I waited for Tori's email to arrive, I sent one of my own to Mary Andres, my editor at the *Vindicator*, attaching the opening paragraphs of my story.

Seconds later, the email from Tori arrived, forwarding an email from a sergeant in the Wisconsin State Patrol. A PDF was attached.

I double-clicked to open it, curious to see what someone who cuts off a man's ear looked like. I pictured someone like the Beast, the ugly hulk from the McDonald's who'd driven himself, the Syrian, and Ned to their fiery deaths.

My muscles tensed and mouth opened wide as the penciled image filled the screen. I recognized the guy instantly. His hair. His eyes. And one unmistakable feature.

I dialed the chief and rambled quickly after he answered.

"Slow down, Jack. Half the people we lock up have an ungodly scar carved somewhere on their body."

I took a deep breath.

"It's him, Chief. He was ten feet away from me. Ten damn feet."

CHAPTER 81

BALTIMORE

"Come on in!"

Unlike most politicians Cassie had interviewed over the years, Councilman Razi Dallas opened the door to his office the very minute they were scheduled to meet: 8:00 a.m. sharp.

As she stepped through the door, preparing to say something, the boyish council member spoke again, as loudly as the first time. "Welcome to Baltimore! How'd you like entering this incredible building?"

"It's beautiful."

And it was. With its green lawn, fountains, gray edifice, and white dome, Baltimore's City Hall was a stunning site.

Even after Cassie took her seat, he remained upright behind a standing desk. As awkward as it was to be planted in a chair, staring up at him, it was too late to get back up.

In two minutes Razi Dallas was living up to the hype she'd read about. His hazel eyes, light brown skin, and short, curly hair made a striking first impression despite his average height and weight. Throw in his outsized personality and palpable energy, and she could see why he'd become an overnight star in Maryland politics.

That combination propelled him to win a district that hadn't elected a Republican in decades. And as the only Republican on the council, the former assistant city prosecutor gained national attention by walking the most dangerous streets of his district side by side with his residents—mostly elderly and African American—to reclaim those streets from drug dealers. Then he spent weeks at a time sleeping in vacant apartments of public housing projects, forcing the police and building owners to clean them up. He did it all with a severe hearing impairment that required him to wear hearing aids and watch the lips of whomever he was talking to—which he claimed made him a better listener. And he captured it all on FaceTime live, where he now had almost a million loyal followers.

"I'm honored you're here, Cassie. How can I help you?"

The chatter in Maryland was about what office he would run for next: mayor, attorney general, or even a long-shot bid for senator. And that was probably why he'd agreed to an off-the-record interview so quickly.

But she wasn't here to talk about his future.

"You were quite the star at Princeton."

He'd graduated summa cum laude and earned the award for the school's top political science student. Not just a member of Ivy Club, he'd been its first African American president.

"I muddled through, yes." His expression sobered. "What I lack in intelligence I make up through hard work."

"I'll say. You apparently worked hard enough to win a Marshall Scholarship."

"I'm still not sure how I made it against such amazing competition. But it led to experiences and friendships that I will cherish for a lifetime. I'm a blessed man."

His humility struck her as genuine. No wonder he'd won a council seat no one thought was winnable.

"Those friendships are why I'm here," Cassie said. "One in particular. I'm curious if you remember Katrina Rivers; she was your year at Princeton."

The *Daily Princetonian* article announcing Katrina's selection as a Marshall Scholar had mentioned two other winners that year. One now taught philosophy in California. The other was a young Razi Dallas, the son of two Baltimore teachers—an African American father from Upton and a white Jewish mother from Pikesville—who told the paper he planned to study political philosophy at Cambridge.

The councilman's round face froze.

"I do remember her, but not well. Why do you ask?"

One good thing about new politicians: they will lie or dodge as much as their more experienced colleagues, but before they have mastered the art of hiding it. For the first time Razi didn't look at Cassie as he answered, flashing a strained smile.

"You sure you didn't know her well?"

He swallowed.

"Why are you asking? Is she in trouble or something?"

"Why would you say that?"

"Cassie, if I'm known for my loud voice, you're famous for kick-ass investigations," he said. "So the first thing anyone's gonna think when you call is 'Am I in trouble'?"

"Really?" she asked with dramatic flair, proud of herself. "But you still agreed to talk to me."

"Of course. Because I'm damn sure I'm not in trouble. I'm honored to talk to you."

She laughed out loud. Despite the lie, he was good.

"Then why are you hiding something when it comes to Katrina Rivers?"

"I'm not hiding anything. Just hoping she's not in trouble."

"But you said you don't remember her well—" She stopped her sentence abruptly. An honest guy like this wouldn't be comfortable letting a lie hang out there in silence.

He stared back for a few seconds, glanced down, then back up. The uncomfortable grin returned.

"Okay, let me revise my statement. She and I spent a good amount of time together for a few months."

"Were you guys romantic?"

When they'd spoken last night, the California professor—the other Marshall winner—had speculated that Razi and Katrina had been an item.

"This is all off the record, right?"

"Every word."

He gazed up toward the ceiling, answering quietly. "I didn't know her at Princeton until we hit it off during the interview process. Then, after we won, and in our early months in England, we spent a lot of time together. There was chemistry between us, maybe even some temptation, but we never became more than friends."

"Were you—"

"We were never intimate, no."

"You look a little wistful right now, I have to say."

"Like I said, we spent a lot of time together, then life happened. Your questions are bringing back memories, that's all. She was a special person."

He was on the psychiatrist's couch now, Cassie providing the therapy.

"Tell me more about her."

The council member peeked at his watch, uncomfortable. "I believe we only set aside half an hour for this."

"I don't need every detail. Just the basics."

His eyes brightened.

"I've never met a sharper person in my life. She ran circles around the rest of us, even if she hid it most of the time."

"How so?"

"She had an encyclopedic mind and a photographic memory. But nimble, too. She could talk and debate any topic, from science to the arts. I told her it was a waste of her brainpower to go into coding and programming."

"Why did you say that?"

"She was passionate about making the world a better place. And I didn't see how immersing herself in coding would let her do that. But if anyone could figure that out, it was Katrina."

Cassie smirked. She was on her way to changing the world all right.

"Do you know why she wanted to make the world a better place?"

"Well, doesn't everyone?"

"Unfortunately, no. What drove that?"

"Oh. I think it was her past."

"What about her past?"

"She didn't talk much about it, but my impression was she grew up with almost nothing. Not middle-class like some of us, but poor. To the point of being hungry."

"But she didn't talk about it?"

He shook his head. "But it was the way she talked about the wealthy kids she'd been surrounded by, going back to prep school. She wasn't rude about it, but she would comment that they had no idea how lucky they were. That they didn't know what poverty or hunger were. And when she talked about those things, her eyes got . . . It seemed clear she was speaking from personal experience."

There was so much Cassie wanted to ask, but time was short. "You mentioned a prep school. Do you know which one she went to?"

"Roosevelt School for Girls."

Cassie wrote the name down.

"Is that a fancy one?"

His teeth glinted white as he flashed a friendly smile. "The fanciest. Imagine the daughters of New York's rich and famous, with a few scholarships thrown in the mix. More than half end up at Princeton or the other Ivies."

Three knocks rapped on the councilman's door.

"Come in, Iris."

A young Asian American woman, her black hair tied back in a ponytail, poked her head through the doorway. "Your next appointment is here."

"Okay. Tell him two minutes." He returned to Cassie. "You might've noticed, I like to stay on schedule."

"It's interesting you say she was poor. I found some later photos of her at Oxford. She was dressed in expensive clothes, tall heels, a Gucci purse and—"

"Katrina was?"

"Oh, yeah. She looked like a supermodel when she graduated."

"At Princeton, she was as down-to-earth as you can imagine. It was one reason I liked her."

As he mentioned Princeton again, Cassie recalled her own college days. Her parents' accident when she was fourteen had forced her to spend her teenage years almost penniless. To get through Boston University, she loaded up on loans that still soaked up a big part of her paycheck. But beyond the loans, Cassie had always worked one or two jobs—in the dining hall, an off-campus waitressing gig, research for a professor. She remembered watching with envy all the kids who only had to worry about getting their reading and problem sets done. She used to pull her cap low over her eyes, trying to avoid the gawks that inevitably came when privileged classmates discovered her serving them food or clearing their trays.

No doubt Princeton financial aid kids had to endure the same thing.

"Do you remember if she worked to get through Princeton?"

"You mean besides schoolwork?"

"Yeah. To get through Princeton on financial aid, I assume you're working the whole time."

"I sure did. Luckily for me, they paid the tour guides well."

"Do you know if Katrina worked a job like that?"

"I don't think she did, at least when I knew her." He looked at his watch again. "Cassie, I really need to—"

One more big question.

"You mentioned that things tapered out a few months after you got to England. Was there a reason for that? Are Cambridge and Oxford that far apart?"

He froze. For the first time in the interview, this jovial optimist frowned, his lips quivering.

"She stopped responding. And I haven't spoken to her or heard from her since. The Marshall program hosts reunions every year; she's never shown up for one."

He lowered his head as he finished the sentence. They may have only been friends, but Razi Dallas was an open book. Her disappearance had wounded him.

The door cracked open again. Iris was back.

CHAPTER 82

MARBLEHEAD, OHIO

J ack, we have a problem."

I'd just showered, replaced the bandages on both leg wounds, and dressed, when Chief Santini called.

"And what's that?" I asked, scratching the itch on my right calf that refused to go away. Overnight, the wound had become a bit infected, so even with the new bandage it stung at my touch.

"Your jail buddy? The hit man?"

"What about him?"

"He's heading our way."

"How do you know that?"

"A cleaning lady in a motel off I-90, east of the Indiana border, found a young woman cut to pieces, stuffed in a closet. A really bloody scene that had all the markings of our guy's handiwork."

"Does the motel have video?"

"We checked them. This guy avoided every camera. And he didn't park in their lot."

"So when you say east of the Indiana border, do you mean near Chicago?"

"Jack, I mean he's in Ohio."

I took a deep breath. Less than two hours away.

"Jesus. How the hell does he know where I am?"

"I'm guessing it's your phone."

"Right, which means he'll keep driving to Youngstown and end up at that locker down the hallway from you." We had left both my and Tori's phone with the chief in case they were being traced.

"And we're ready. But let's plan for the worst case."

"Which is?"

"That he's heading to Marblehead."

"Chief, that's not the worst case."

"Well, then what is?"

"That he's already here."

CHAPTER 83

MARBLEHEAD, OHIO

"Keep climbing, Arman. Keep climbing."

The Butcher shuddered as high-pitched, boyish voices whispered in his ear. On this perfect morning the view of Lake Erie from behind the white Marblehead Lighthouse was unleashing sounds and images from long ago.

The three boys had been tracing their small fingers along the stone walls of the medieval monastery nestled on the peninsula's edge, when they'd come across the thick wooden door. It didn't budge but was cracked open enough to allow them to slide their skinny bodies through.

Once inside, they tiptoed through the darkness and the musty air, past the clutter and the cobwebs, to a rickety, circular stairwell. Each wooden step creaked as he put his weight on it, the fifth one shaking as if about to break loose. He hesitated, peering up at his brothers, already at the top, ambient light framing their small heads like a dim, collective halo. Sensing his fear, they urged him to keep climbing.

After reaching the top, each boy found a gap in the brick wall where sun rays beamed through. Those gaps became their windows to the most wondrous view of their short lives. The clear blue waters of Armenia's Lake Sevan shimmered below them, small waves lapping up on golden beaches on the mainland shore while green- and white-tipped mountains loomed in the distance. The brothers, whose only view until that day had been the ground-floor dust and dirt of their war-torn town, sat motionless, in awe, for close to an hour. They chattered like birds, describing out loud the shapes of the clouds overhead, the curves and angles of the land as it stretched from shore to mountain peak, the colors they had never before seen. And they wondered aloud if this was what heaven looked like.

Less than a week later a bullet pierced the skull of the Butcher's oldest brother, killing him instantly. Weeks after that, his other brother stepped on a land mine. Ever since, when he remembered his brothers, the Butcher pictured that ancient monastery perched on the water's edge. The flimsy stairs. His brother's heads surrounded by light. Their eyes lined up with the gaps in the wall. The joyous chatter. The breathtaking view. Their heaven.

This morning there were no mountains in the distance, just low islands. It was not balmy but windy and cool. But the lighthouse, the water, the rocky point—so much was the same, it chilled him.

He'd ended up here because the old brick building where his targets had spent the night was less than a mile away. As he approached that building minutes before, a black SUV was idling in the parking lot. He drove past slowly, head facing forward, but his rearview mirror reflected a man sitting in the SUV's driver seat. Security of some sort. So he kept driving until he spotted the lighthouse, pulled over, and parked in its lot.

With at least one bodyguard posted outside, and with the targets armed with the weapons they'd secured at the old man's farm, a frontal assault on the inn would be too risky. Far better to attack once they were in transit. So he found the bench with the best view of the lighthouse and sat down.

He pushed the last joyous memory of his brothers aside, took out his phone, and reopened the app that was tracing his targets' every move.

CHAPTER 84

WASHINGTON, D.C.

R azi Dallas wasn't exaggerating: the Roosevelt School for Girls definitely educated the who's who of New York City.

Once back at the Republic offices, it had taken Cassie all of ten minutes to locate the school's yearbook from fifteen years ago. Over the years she'd used two websites to dig up old yearbooks, and they did the trick here as well.

But this yearbook stood out from any she'd researched before.

First was the school itself. The regal redbrick colonial building and its attached clock tower looked like the centerpiece of an elite college campus as opposed to a high school. Sitting at the water's edge at the southern tip of Manhattan—fittingly close to Wall Street—the school enjoyed equally stunning views of the Brooklyn Bridge, the Statue of Liberty, and the new World Trade Center.

Then came the students' names. Tessa Helmsley. Ashley Vanderbilt. Penelope Astor. Izzy Hearst. Heiresses to some of the nation's great fortunes. While all the girls in the yearbook wore the same uniform—blue skirt and white button-up shirt—the big names knew how to stand out. Designer handbags and sunglasses and expensive jewelry were on full display among the many cameo shots included in the yearbook's eighty pages, reminding her of Katrina's Oxford photo.

But nothing captured the rarefied air of the school more than its high number of foreign students, easy to spot because the photographs listed each student's city of origin. Olga Smirnova, Moscow. Ah Lang Huam,

Beijing. Fang Li, Guangzhou. Jia Chen, Shanghai. Irina Mazur, Warsaw. Nicoletta Rossi, Rome. No doubt the world's oligarchs ponied up to provide their daughters the best educational path to America's Ivy League.

Cassie opened the section for graduating seniors. Each senior entry included a photo, a summary of activities and accomplishments, and personal comments by the student. And at the side of each student's photo was a short, playful entry: "Most Likely to . . ." with the next words reflecting the consensus of the class.

As Cassie leafed through the pages to get to *R*, she recognized a few names that were already making good on their classmates' predictions: "Most Likely to Get Elected to Something" was now a well-respected second-term congresswoman from Virginia; "Most Likely to Lead Troops in War" was now a high-profile Chicago prosecutor; and "Most Likely to Star on Broadway" was a pop star.

And then she got to the name she was looking for.

Katrina K. Rivers, Brooklyn, NY

The photo displayed a skinnier, paler version of the somber young woman in the *Daily Princetonian*. No makeup. Straight brown hair. Large-rimmed round glasses. Expressionless face. She appeared intimidated by her elite surroundings. Out of place among the world's richest girls.

Most of the other students proudly listed multiple sports and activities, including high-society organizations and clubs beyond the school itself. Katrina listed only a few activities, all within the school.

Cross Country
RSG Coding Club
Model United Nations
Service Club

But the list of her honors and awards showed where her real talents lay.

Salutatorian
Summa cum laude
National Merit Finalist

The school's valedictorian must have focused on the humanities, because Katrina was listed as the winner of the school's Vanderbilt Prize for Outstanding Math and Science. And classmates recognized her scientific prowess, naming her "Most Likely to Invent Something That Will Change the World."

Cassie grinned. How prescient.

Each entry closed out with the senior's own comments. Most of the girls gushed about their friends and family, bragged about what college they'd be attending, or unleashed a burst of school spirit about "RSG" or some fancy club they were part of. A few included short poems or a favorite song lyric.

Not Katrina. She kept her comments short.

"Princeton, here I come" was the first statement, idle chatter similar to her classmates'.

But then came two revealing quotes.

"If you but knew the flames that burn in me which I attempt to beat down with my reason."

"Wrong does not cease to be wrong because the majority share in it."

Her entry closed out with three final words.

"Thank you, Dyadya."

CHAPTER 85

Two minutes after I drove onto the odd-looking orange ferryboat, its engine already humming, the ramp lifted behind me. A minute after that, the long, flat ferry pulled away from the dock, maneuvered around an anchored barge, then motored away from Marblehead. Just as we'd hoped, I was the last car to board.

"Nice work," Santini said over our three-way conference call. "You move fast when you need to."

"I move fast when I'm freaking out! Any sign of him at the ferry station?"

"Nope," the gruff undercover guy said, sitting on the VFW's patio to watch everything play out. "You timed it so no one could have gotten on if they'd wanted to."

"And no one tried?"

"Nope."

"Good."

Either the hit man was on his way to Youngstown or he was already in Marblehead. If the latter, it meant he was somehow tracking me, an alarming possibility we needed to ferret out right away. For several days the ferry had shuttled in and out on the half hour to a nearby island, so this was our best move.

"So what next?"

"I'll keep an eye out here," the undercover guy said.

"And you're sure there's no other way he can get to the island?" Santini asked.

"The other ferry only runs on weekends off-season," I said. "What do you think he'll do?"

"Hard to say. If he's there, my guess is he follows you over."

I agreed. "He lost valuable time in Wisconsin. And we're days into early voting, so his bosses must be losing patience."

My phone beeped with another incoming call. Cassie. I switched over.

"Jack, Katrina is Russian."

"Russian?" I laughed nervously. Just the mention of the country unleashed haunting memories.

"Well, not *from* Russia. But she has Russian roots—"

"Well, that's different," I said, relieved. "I'm English, with some German."

She ignored my joke.

"Yeah, but I'm talking recent. And she may have been supported by a Russian most of her life."

"And how the heck did you figure all that out?"

"First, she's from Brooklyn, and my guess is not the nice part."

"Millions of people are from Brooklyn." I really didn't want her to be Russian.

She ignored me again.

"Maybe so. But who else quotes Pushkin and Tolstoy in their high school yearbook?"

"Wait, you got her yearbook?"

"Oh, yeah. She went to the fanciest school in New York, studying with daughters of the world's wealthiest people. I tracked down the yearbook."

"And she quoted Pushkin and Tolstoy?"

"She sure did. Didn't you read them when you were eighteen?" she asked sarcastically.

"I hadn't heard of them at eighteen. I still haven't read them now."

"Exactly."

"So a Princeton and Oxford grad likes Russian literature. How do you know some Russian has been helping her?"

"Someone with serious money has been helping her for years. She started out in poverty. Then went to that ritzy high school, then

Princeton—and none of it on financial aid. A few years later, still a grad student, she wore the most expensive stuff you can buy."

"Good for her. So how do you know who helped her?"

"Because she thanked him."

"She did?"

"Yeah, in her high school yearbook. Right after the Pushkin and Tolstoy quotes, she wrote, 'Thank you, Dyadya.'"

"Sounds like a nickname. That could be a best friend or something. Maybe a boyfriend."

"Jack, it's not a nickname. Look it up."

I sighed, the back-and-forth exhausting me.

"Sounds like you already did."

"Yep. It means uncle."

She paused again.

"In Russian."

As the ferry chugged through choppy waters, I stepped out of my car and leaned up against the orange metal wall that encircled the boat. Ohio's northern shore offered a stark contrast: the old Marblehead Lighthouse in the foreground, the spiraling tracks of Cedar Point's roller coasters behind it to the left.

My goal had been to use the twenty-five-minute trip to research the best places to hole up on Kelleys Island, the ferry's destination. But Cassie's news shattered my focus. Even the cool breeze didn't bring it back.

My stomach churned. A secret I'd successfully buried deep for three years was clawing its way back out.

No one knew.

Not Mary Andres. Not Cassie. Not Alex Fischer or Bridget Turner. Not the chief.

None of them knew because I'd kept it hidden all that time.

And I didn't dare tell Tori.

I stared down, studying the water as it splashed up against the sides of the ferry.

The story that had made me an overnight sensation also involved a deal with the devil. And that devil's name was Oleg Kazarov.

Three years earlier I had let the authorities and the public believe that an American congressman was behind the Abacus vote-rigging scandal. And for many reasons that snake of a politician deserved the takedown I delivered. But he had not been the mastermind of the scheme; that distinction went to Oleg Kazarov, a Russian oil and gas oligarch. I'd figured it out late in the game, but to protect my family and myself, and because I wanted America to end the curse of gerrymandering, I hid that inconvenient fact from everyone. And it worked.

Kazarov had emerged again a year later. As I dug into the Dronetech scandal, I'd called out of desperation. He owed me, and he repaid that debt, protecting my team and helping me stymie the plot before it wreaked havoc on the country.

That was the last time we'd communicated. We were even, and that was that.

Two deep wails of a horn snapped my attention back to the present. Off of our left bow, an identical orange ferry plowed in the opposite direction, white water splashing up around it. Passengers from both boats waved at one another. And as we passed the halfway point, the contours and colors of Kelleys Island took shape ahead of us.

The last time I'd even thought about the Russian was months ago. An article in an energy journal had reported that, facing a bleak cancer prognosis, the mysterious oligarch had given up daily control of his oil and gas empire. While the article speculated about whether his vast operation could survive his demise, my glass-half-full response was that at least my secret would die with him.

But did Cassie's discovery mean Kazarov was orchestrating all this? He was the right age to be an uncle of Katrina's. The Russian was capable of anything, including the type of brutality we had been witnessing. And if our hunch was right, this scheme was all about gerrymandering—and no one understood the role of gerrymandering in American politics better than the Russian energy baron.

At the same time, there were lots of Russian oligarchs out there willing to cause trouble. And in our extensive conversations, not once had Kazarov discussed a member of his family, let alone one playing a central role in his operation.

Finally, how in the world would someone orchestrate all this from his deathbed?

The ferry's horn blared twice more, jolting me from my stewing. We passed the southern tip of Kelleys Island, the engine slowing as we plowed through the choppy waters parallel to a small beach, then a rocky hillside, then a series of modest homes. A larger marina, most of its docks empty, lay directly in front of us.

In theory, I had the option to communicate with Kazarov: his number was in my phone back in Youngstown. But if he was involved, doing so would only tip him off that we knew, putting us all in immediate danger.

And what would I do anyway? What would I say?

As the ferry pulled into the dock, I climbed back into my car and started the engine.

CHAPTER 86

WASHINGTON, D.C.

The call came from a 410 area code.

"Is this Cassie Knowles?" the voice asked loudly.

"It sure is. Councilman?"

"Please call me Razi."

"I appreciate your time this morning."

"Thank you. Sorry we got rushed at the end. I hope I was helpful."

"Very much so. I was ab—"

"I need to tell you something that might help more."

At her desk, she reached for a pen and a notepad, bottling up her breath to sound calm.

"Go for it."

"It's about . . . when Katrina disappeared. And why." His halting voice made him sound less sure of himself than he had this morning.

"It was shortly after you got to England, right?"

"Yes. She just stopped calling back. I was heartsick. I'd never told her, but I was convinced I was in love with her."

"You don't say!"

"That obvious, huh? Well, two days after she went dark, I hopped on a train and visited Oxford. I went to her dorm room and knocked on her door."

"So this would've been in late August or September?"

"Early September. A Sunday. I remember it like it was yesterday."

She wrote the details down.

"What happened when you got there?"

"She wasn't there. But I knew something was wrong as soon as her roommate opened the door. She looked so upset."

"Did she tell you what happened?"

"Katrina's mom and younger brother were killed. Back in Brooklyn."

Cassie gasped. She'd assumed something big had spurred Katrina's dramatic change, but not that big.

"Killed how?"

"Killed as in murdered. Even now, I can see her roommate shaking."

"So where did Katrina go?" Cassie asked, trying to stay focused.

"She'd already headed back to the States for the funeral."

"And you never heard from her after she got back?"

A quiet sigh came through the phone. "No. I think for security reasons she didn't stay on campus. When I checked with her roommate, she said she no longer lived with her but knew nothing else."

"Had she returned to school by then?"

"I think so, but I really don't know. I couldn't get a return call, then the number I'd been calling went dead. She never responded to emails after that. I did all I could to put her out of my mind. I met my wife two months later and never looked back."

"Good for you." She let a few beats pass before posing her next question.

"Razi, did Katrina ever mention an uncle to you?"

"An uncle? No. Her family never came up in our time together. I didn't even know she had a brother until the day he was murdered."

CHAPTER 87

PORT CLINTON, OHIO

The single-prop airplane jostled violently from the moment it lifted off the small runway, causing the Butcher to tighten his grip on the leather strap above the small cockpit door.

The turbulence only intensified as they climbed out over the lake. Unlike the mild bumps of larger jets, the bursts of wind lifted or dropped the small plane meters at a time. And the entire aircraft twisted left and right as though it were on a swivel.

"You gonna be okay, buddy?" the young pilot asked as he banked the plane so steeply that the Butcher faced the dark waters of the lake.

The Butcher cringed, worried one big gust might flip them upside down. "I'll be fine. I assume this is typical."

"Oh, yeah. These fall northeast winds always make for a fun ride. Cedar Point's got nothing on us."

Even as his stomach fluttered, the Butcher grinned at his good fortune. In most parts of the world, arranging a private flight—even one this short—involved days of planning. Bribes. Connections. But in Ohio it only required a single phone call, $110, and a fifteen-minute drive to the small airport.

His targets' last-minute ferry ride was an attempt to smoke him out, something he was not going to oblige. So he'd decided within minutes that a plane or a private boat offered his only options. But he wouldn't have guessed he'd find one so quickly.

The plane leveled out from the roll, placing the island square in the middle of the small windshield. The pilot pointed to a small radar monitor at the center of the flight's console. A dark green splotch with a bunch of tiny arrows took up the left third of the screen.

"A front's coming in from the west," the pilot said. "That might shut us down for the rest of today."

"I won't need a flight back."

"If it's bad enough, it might shut down the ferries, too."

The Butcher nodded, pleased to learn this useful detail. No ferry meant his targets had no way to escape.

CHAPTER 88

KELLEYS ISLAND, OHIO

nside the dockside restaurant, I downed the best perch sandwich yet as I waited for word on the assassin.

Outside, a storm was blowing our way. The abandoned docks rattled and squealed as wave after wave slapped against them before rolling into shore. The gray, billowy clouds in the distance and near-black horizon meant that the worst was on its way.

Only one more boat is getting out today, the chief texted me. My guy's getting on it.

So what's this do to our plan?

It may make you safer for the time being.

Funny. I feel more than ever like a sitting duck.

I understood the chief's point. But not knowing where the guy was was still turning my stomach.

No sign of him in Youngstown?

A few seconds passed.

Nope. But what's he going to do? Break into a
police station?

He broke into a jail, didn't he?

Fair.

A loud crash outside the window jolted me in my seat. On the restaurant's patio a round, wooden table with a closed umbrella sticking out of it had toppled over and was now rolling back and forth. A bunch of chairs also lay on their sides.

Your guy better have a hearty stomach. It's
getting nasty out here.

A few minutes passed without a response, then my phone rang.

Since he had just been texting, the fact that it was the chief was a bad sign.

CHAPTER 89

LONDON

Katrina had kept busy all day. And she'd purposely surrounded herself with other people.

But in the early evening, after completing his daily update, Drac stepped away from her office, leaving her alone at her desk.

With no distraction from the emptiness, she leaned forward, her head in her hand. As it did every year, the soreness started in her lungs and climbed to her throat while cold chills shook her limbs.

Eleven years ago.

To the day. Almost to the hour.

Two phone calls. First from Brooklyn. Then from Dyadya. Two short calls, delivering permanent news. The life she'd lived up to that point ended when she hung up. The new life she was hoping to live? Never even started.

She opened her top desk drawer and removed a framed photo, taken the day she'd left for England, the Brooklyn Bridge behind them. The snapshot of their final time together perfectly captured the dynamics of their small family.

Mother stood on the left, a fragile smile that mixed the pride she carried for Katrina with the worry that her only daughter was moving so far away for so long. Mother had devoted all she had to Katrina's success, which also meant she'd fretted over her endlessly, urging her not to forget where she'd come from, not to become like the rich girls from school, not to let Dyadya's largesse change her. To remain her idealistic self.

Dark-haired, bespectacled Katrina towered over her mother in the middle, mustering as playful an expression as she ever did back then—nervous to leave home but excited about the upcoming journey and her new life. The distance would be liberating.

And her even taller, bushy-haired brother, Mikhail, stood to the right, his white teeth gleaming through a wide-open smile as he flashed devil's horns with two fingers held over her head. He'd struggled through his childhood and teen years, getting in trouble often, always providing excuses, running with the wrong crowd. His recent tattoos, visible on his left biceps and knuckles, had greatly upset Mother. Still, he'd always kept Katrina laughing, warming her spirits.

Through it all, he'd found the joy in life. Knowing that, she'd always prayed he'd never seen the gun that had killed him.

Her phone rang.

"Katrina?"

She closed her eyes, steadying her breath.

"Dyadya, how are you?"

He always called on this day, around this time.

"I am well. But today is the day I ask how you are."

"I'm fine," she said with a choked voice. "We are proceeding well—"

"Katrina, you can mask it with others. Not me. How are you?"

She laid the photo on the desk and brought her hand up to her mouth. The emotion she'd kept buried all year finally burst out, large teardrops falling onto the mahogany top of her desk. Several fell on the picture frame itself.

"I will be fine. Tomorrow."

CHAPTER 90

KELLEYS ISLAND, OHIO

irport? What airport?" I asked.

The chief replied. "It's more like a strip. No tower or anything. Or terminal. It's on the east side of the island."

"How in the world—"

"There's a service out of Port Clinton that flies single-prop puddle jumpers back and forth. But outside of tourist season, few people use it."

"Let me guess. Except today."

"I'm afraid so. The local cops gave the company a call and they said one flight went out. They're on their way there now."

"Who? The flight?"

"The flight landed. The cops are heading to the airport."

"Jesus. It already landed?"

It was a small island. The airport couldn't be more than a few miles away. I pushed the plate of perch away, having instantly lost my appetite.

"Just a few minutes ago."

"Has anyone talked to the pilot?"

"He took off again right away to beat the storm. They're trying to reach him now."

"Next you're gonna tell me there was a limo waiting at the airport at the end of a long red carpet."

He ignored my sarcasm. "If it's him, he'd have to walk."

"So what do I do?"

"A cop is coming to get you now."

"Just one?"

"Yeah. The other two headed to the airport."

"So there're only three? And you're telling me to be calm?"

"Sharpe?" a voice boomed from behind me.

I wheeled around to see a barrel-chested guy in a black police uniform, tattooed biceps stretching his sleeves to the breaking point.

"We know the situation. Let's move."

"Your cop's here, Chief. But he may count as two all by himself."

I hung up and stuck my laptop in the small backpack I'd been lugging around, and we hustled out the door.

The ride lasted all of two minutes, and if the size and gruffness of Officer Eric Bosko lifted my confidence, the tiny Kelleys Island police headquarters sent it plunging back down. The one-story gray-stoned building looked like a police station on the streets of Disney World as opposed to a real town.

"Can you fit in there?" I joked as we jumped out of the car and sprinted through the door.

"You're funny," he said in a mocking tone, implying the opposite. "It may be small, but a tank couldn't knock this old jail over. It's as old as the lighthouse and built like a fortress."

He shut the door behind us, bolting three locks up the door's side. The front room was a typical if small lobby of a police station. Through an open door, I could see the iron bars of several cells in the other room— but instead of prisoners they held filing cabinets.

"I see what you mean: those will never escape."

He finally cracked a wry smile. "Sharpe, they told me you were a reporter, not a comedi—"

"Airport is clear," a woman's voice crackled over his radio. "Nothing here."

Officer Bosko tilted his chin down and to the left while activating the mike of his small radio. "Ten-four. Toth, any word along the roads?"

"Nothing. Woodford was clear. Monagan, too. Circling back to take a second look."

I had to speak up. "Officer—"

He glared at me for interrupting but listened.

"This guy won't do what you expect. I'd definitely check any indirect routes as well."

"We got this, Sharpe."

He tilted his chin down again.

"Check out Ward and Division, too."

"Ten-four. Heading to Ward now."

Bosko's eyes blazed with intensity. "Only two ways to get here from there, unless your friend's gonna traipse through deep woods or tiptoe along a bunch of rocks."

"My guess is that's exactly what he'll do."

As I spoke, he stepped into the other room while pulling a ring of keys from his pocket. He stuck one into a metal locker next to the first cell and opened it.

"Either way, if he makes it this far," he said, pulling a black pump-action shotgun out of the locker, "he'll be staring into the wrong end of this." He flipped the gun over, slid the action forward, and quickly filled the chamber with five shells.

CHAPTER 91

KELLEYS ISLAND, OHIO

Brother, what in the world are you doing out there?" With his portly midsection, ruddy face, and white beard, the man looked every bit the fishing boat captain.

The Butcher, his gray hoodie and jeans soaked all the way through, answered with alarm.

"Captain Rick, I need your help. My wife and kid are back at Marblehead. She needs medical attention. I came out on the ferry but now I'm stuck because of the storm. Can you make a trip back to the mainland?"

Captain Rick's beard and cheeks shook as he laughed out loud. "The ferry's canceled for a reason, friend. It's nasty out there. You're better off waiting. Come on in out of this mess."

The Butcher entered the small shack at the end of a long dock. From the bumpy vantage point of the small plane, he'd spotted a few large boats docked in the sparse marinas. So, after landing, he'd jogged the long way—along back roads, away from town, then along the rocky shoreline, then more back roads—to find this place.

"I know it's rough," the Butcher said, mimicking the frustration of a worried parent. "I wouldn't be asking if it wasn't urgent. My kid's eighteen months old. I'll pay extra. And folks in town said you're the only guy who can do it."

The captain laughed again. "What the hell, I can do it. It's a straight shot, just a rough one."

"Thank you," the Butcher said. "Let me get my stuff and I'll be right back."

CHAPTER 92

KELLEYS ISLAND, OHIO

S
o you really think this guy stabbed you in the leg?" Officer Bosko asked. "While you were both in a jail cell?"

Holed up as the other cops scoured the roads near the airport, I walked an entertained Bosko through my past few weeks, leaving out the underlying details of the plot.

"He enjoys using knives, so I assume it was him."

"I gotta hand it to the guy," the ex-Marine said, shotgun resting in his lap. "That's a slick move."

"I'm glad you're impressed."

"But what was the damn point?" he asked gruffly.

"That's what I've been asking myself."

He trained his gaze on the gun, brushing something off its barrel, then looked back at me.

"I mean, think about all he gave up, tactically, by walking into that jail cell. If he stabbed you, even more so, because an investigation would have delayed his release."

"I know. He lost days. And missed his chance to trap us when we visited the old man."

"Even worse, he let you get a good look at him and that battle scar."

"True."

"You only take risks like that for a major reward. So he must've gotten something out of his voluntary jail stay. Something he *only* could have gotten by doing exactly what he did."

He stood up, paced to the front door, and returned to his chair.

"And you have no idea how he knows where you are?"

"Well, *if* he's tracking me, it's either my phone, which is in Youngstown, or something on me."

"Sharpe, I hate to break it to you, but I wouldn't be holed up in here clutching a loaded Remington if I wasn't damn sure that was your man who chartered that plane. And that means he's *definitely* tracking you."

"Are you serious?"

"Deadly serious." Chest puffed out, he was in his Marine mode now. "How well did the doctors check that stab wound?"

"Thoroughly, as far as I could tell."

"Maybe the wound is how he's tracking you."

"Wait, you're saying he implanted something when he stabbed me? Wouldn't the doctors have found that?"

"You'd think so."

"And is there even technology that does that?"

"The military was testing it when I was still in Iraq, and that was years ago. Hell, I read a story the other day where a bunch of Swedes are implanting tiny microchips in themselves for all sorts of reasons—like paying for stuff or unlocking doors, for God's sake. If those are for sale commercially, could some high-priced hit man get his hands on military-grade tech that does that? Wouldn't surprise me at all."

It still sounded far-fetched, but I played along.

"That's a scary thought."

"Scary, but it also would explain everything that's happened since this guy arrived on the scene."

I nodded.

"I've got an idea. There's one way to check." He bounded into the other room before I could say a word.

I shifted in the chair, fearing that he had something surgical in mind. Right when the thigh was finally feeling better, too.

"Um, not sure if there's anything we can do about—"

"Sure there is." He stepped back through the door. "This should do the trick."

I was about to protest again when he held up a black and yellow device shaped like a cricket bat, the type of handheld metal detector cops used for large crowds.

"Okay. I can live with that."

His radio crackled, the woman's voice coming back on. "I ran into Elmer Saunders, who spotted a guy in a gray hoodie jogging east from the airport."

"East? Towards Barnum's Point?"

"Yep."

He glanced at me, then spoke into the radio again. "But that goes nowhere."

"I know," she radioed back. "I drove to the dead end and didn't see him. But there were some fresh tracks in the mud along the shore, heading southeast."

"That's him," I muttered. "This guy doesn't quit."

"Shit," Bosko said. "He can connect up to Point Road that way, and double back to town."

"I'm headed there now."

The male voice piped back in, talking quickly. "I'm down here already. On Lakeshore. But haven't seen a thing."

"Keep your eyes out. This guy's a pro."

Bosko pointed the wand at me.

"Drop those."

"Huh?"

"Drop your jeans."

He stepped toward me, wand in hand. Two short high-pitched beeps sounded from around its handle.

"You got some metal in your jacket?" He waved the wand near my midsection as the beeps picked up their pace.

"No, but I got a nice rod in my throwing arm." I angled my elbow out. The beeps ran together into an uninterrupted high-pitched tone as he brought the wand up to my forearm.

"That's some rod."

"It was some hit."

"Well, at least we know it's working. Now, where is that stab wound?"

Standing awkwardly in my boxers, jeans down to my knees, I pointed to the thick bandage on my left thigh.

He lowered the wand over the front of the bandage.

Nothing.

He moved it to the back of the leg, then around both sides.

Still nothing.

"Guess not." I wasn't surprised. "The doctor would have found it."

"Right. Up they go."

As I pulled my jeans back up, I winced as the lower-right pant leg tugged against the bandage of my other jail cell injury, the puncture in my right calf. The sharp pinch reminded me of the slow healing, the itching, the raised scab, and the infection, all from this odd injury that never went away.

"Before you put that thing away, let's check one other spot."

I sat down in the chair and removed my jeans entirely.

"Where?"

"There." I pointed to the smaller bandage over my right calf.

"That come in the jail, too?"

"Sure did," I said, angry at myself for not having thought of it earlier.

He lowered to one knee and positioned the wand close to the bandage.

Nothing.

I ripped off the bandage. This had to be it.

"Do it again."

"As long as you clean this thing after," he joked as he pushed the wand against the scab.

A series of soft beeps emanated from the device.

CHAPTER 93

WASHINGTON, D.C.

M a'am, it's quitting time. You'll need to call back Monday." The detective's Brooklyn accent couldn't have been thicker.

"I'm looking for information on two deaths that happened there eleven years ago," Cassie said, "but I can't find a thing in the papers."

"Monday, ma'am."

"It's five till four. And this is an emergency." Although it really wasn't, waiting the entire weekend would be torture.

A long sigh came through the phone. "What kind of deaths were they?"

"A mom and son. Murdered, I believe. Last name was Rivers. In the Brighton Beach area, likely in September. Survived by a daughter named Katrina."

"You said eleven years ago?"

"Yes."

"Okay. Give me a few."

He came back in ten minutes.

"Ma'am, I got nothing like that in my records. And if it happened like you said it did, it would be there. Have a nice weekend."

CHAPTER 94

KELLEYS ISLAND, OHIO

've got a medical kit in the back," Officer Bosko said, leaping to his feet. "I can dig the thing out."

Knowing I was being tracked like an animal, and that my own leg was the traitor, had sent goose bumps rising all over my skin. But Officer Bosko's enthusiasm to dig into my leg was giving me a cold sweat.

"Are you sure? That's like doing surgery."

"Hell, I dig fishhooks out around here a couple times a week in the summer. And the things I had to do in Iraq probably qualified me to be an ER doc."

In the end, there was no choice. Taking my silence as a yes, he jumped back into the other room and returned with a medical kit in his hand.

Then his radio crackled again.

"There's a guy walking this way from the docks." The male officer sounded amped up. "Gray hoodie."

Bosko dropped the kit on a chair and picked the rifle back up.

The grunts and quick breaths of a larger man running came through the radio. Then a loud yell: "PUT YOUR HANDS UP. DON'T MOVE."

The woman's voice joined in. "I'm right down the street. Wait up—"

"Wait for backup," Bosko ordered through his mike, pacing back and forth. "This man is dangerous."

"KEEP YOUR HANDS UP. DO NOT MOVE." A pause. "GOOD. NOW TURN AROUND."

"Wait for backup," Bosko warned again.

A thud and then a loud, guttural groan came through the radio. Then a second thud and another groan. We waited to hear the officer's voice again.

Nothing.

"MAN DOWN!" the other officer yelled through the radio. Her heavy breathing made it clear she was running. Three loud bangs followed.

"I've gotta get out there," Bosko said, undoing the locks.

"I'm coming, too."

"The hell you are. Stay in here and don't move."

He jumped out the doorway and slammed the door behind him.

With the door closed, no radio, and no Bosko, the station fell silent. Even the rain and wind outside were muffled by its thick stone walls.

Following Bosko's order, I twisted the first lock, the bolt clicking loudly into place. I reached for the second lock, then stopped, staring at the door for a few seconds.

Then I reconsidered.

These three young officers were in danger only because of me, and here I was cowering in a dry, quiet mini-fortress behind a locked door. What was I going to do? Wait all night? Pathetic.

And as long as I was holed up here, the hit man had all the time he needed to wipe out this small Kelleys Island police force, whose first concern was to help their fallen comrade. My sitting put was doing him a favor.

If this hit man was going to trace me, he should at least have to chase me. I ran across the room, threw the medical kit Officer Bosko had left behind into my backpack, and rushed out the door.

As the short drive in Bosko's car had made clear, the most common inhabitant of Kelleys Island was the golf cart.

So I charged out of police headquarters on the hunt for one, and three appeared in the first hundred feet. I hopped on a slick black vehicle with rugged tires—it was a cross between a golf cart and an ATV—found the keys in the ignition, and drove off.

With the drama taking place in the marina area, east of the police station, I drove west along a road that paralleled the shore. The wind and rain lashed my face as I drove, not because of the speed of the vehicle—with the accelerator floored it was still only going thirty miles per hour—but because the storm was blowing so fiercely in off the lake. The gusts and the crashing waves nearly drowned out the chugging of the motor beneath me, while the low, dark clouds made it feel like nightfall even though it was only 4:30.

After a few minutes the road curved to the right, around the far western edge of the island, then north, then slightly east. Out of the direct line of the wind, and desperate to know what was going on back at the harbor, I took out my cellphone.

Chief Santini picked up after two rings.

"Chief, he's on the island. He's got some kind of tracking device in my leg. And he may have taken an officer down alrea—"

"Jack, slow down! One thing at a time. Where the hell are you?"

"On a golf cart driving away from town."

"What? You're supposed to be in a police station."

"I was, until he showed up and started stabbing police officers. At least one is down and needs help. I figured going on the run might pull him away."

"You're a sitting duck out in the open," he said. "How can I help now?"

"Did your guy make it?"

"It was too rough. They abandoned that trip five minutes after pulling away from the dock."

"Damn. Then I need to be able to get in touch with the officer from before."

"Bosko?"

With no warning, the road dead-ended. I slammed on the brakes, skidding to a stop only feet from some large rocks.

"Shit."

"What's up? You okay?"

"The road ended. I'm turning around. And, yes, Bosko. Do you have his number?"

"Yep. He's the one I was talking to."

"Great. Text both of us so we can be in communication."

"Will do."

I swerved left on a new road, away from the shore. As I headed east, now sheltered on both sides, the wind died down even further.

> Officer, it's Chief Santini from Youngstown.
> Connecting you with Jack. He tells me you're
> in trouble.

A few seconds passed.

> Yes. Officer stabbed in gut. Bleeding bad. Fire
> chief on his way. Suspect gone. Sharpe, you
> still at HQ?

I slowed to ten miles per hour so I could text back.

> No. Figured running would give you some
> space. On golf cart.

A longer pause.

> You should NOT have ignored my order.
> Where the f are you?

> Circled island to west, now on north side.
> Approaching state park.

I had just passed a sign saying that the park's entrance was ahead.

> Avoid park. Take your next right. Then your
> second left a couple minutes after that. If he's
> following you, that keeps you ahead of him.

The right came up quickly, a 270-degree turn. The straightaway that followed gave me a moment to think through a plan. With an otherwise losing hand, the past twenty minutes—and the fact that he'd left the cops as I'd hoped—showed that I finally held one good card. How could I best play it?

> Guys, I need a boat right away.

The chief replied instantly. Jack, stop.
Bosko seconded. Not a chance.
Anticipating their protest, I had already typed two-thirds of my next message.

> No time to waste. Been boating Lake Erie my whole life. Need a boat in the next fifteen minutes. Call someone if you have to or I'll find one myself.

"Untie the stern before you jump on, sailor," a smoker's gravelly voice barked through the roaring wind.

Bosko had texted that the boat was called *Old Faithful*, but I'd spotted it before even seeing its name. In the ghostly harbor of empty docks and slumbering, tarpaulin-wrapped boats, its tall bridge was lit up like a Christmas tree, illuminating the smoke rising from its stern, the sign of an old engine warming up. And with its worn paint, angular lines, and squarish windows, it definitely matched its moniker of "old."

I quickly unwrapped the thick rope from the rear cleat and, backpack in hand, jumped over the back gunwale onto the wet deck. The boat thrust forward, pushing me back a few steps before I recovered my balance.

"Welcome aboard," the voice yelled.

I stepped forward as we accelerated, docks and boats now flying past us on both sides. *Old Faithful* shuddered from the burst of speed, her engine roaring like an old propeller plane on takeoff. I reached the metal ladder to the bridge, gripping its sides to stabilize myself, and yelled up.

"Captain Terry?"

Obscured by the bright lights above, his only visible features were that he was heavyset and bald. But Bosko's simple summary—"the best boat captain on Lake Erie"—was all I needed to know.

"Affirmative." Smoke curled from his lips.

"You were ready quick."

"I was told you needed help quick."

"I sure did. Thank you."

Old Faithful took a hard left as we left the safety of the harbor. The first big wave hit immediately, sending the bow vertical. The jolt upward pushed all my weight back, almost causing my wet grip on the ladder to come loose.

"Hold on down there," the captain yelled over the din of the engine. "There's some chop out here."

"You don't say," I managed.

The bow rolled back to even and then lunged forward, as if we were curling over the front of a waterfall. We then plunged down at a forty-five-degree angle before crashing into the front of the next wave, a loud boom shaking the boat as if we'd collided with a brick wall. Even though I braced with my arms, my chest slammed against the metal ladder, knocking most of the wind from my lungs. As a thick curtain of spray flew past and over us, the bow wrenched upward again, and I gripped the ladder to avoid falling backward.

"Can she get through this?" I yelled up to the bridge as we rolled forward and down again.

"If we can, she can," the skipper yelled back, laughing. "This old Ensign was designed for Navy specs. It can withstand a lot more than this, not to mention small-arms fire."

We crashed into the front of the next wave.

"Where to?"

"Marblehead, if possible."

"Coming right up."

CHAPTER 95

CLEVELAND

I t has been a long time."

Oleg Kazarov received the call as his steel-gray Gulfstream sat on the runway at Cleveland's Burke Lakefront Airport. He'd felt weak on the car ride over, but once back in his plane—nestled in the seat he always flew in, a private nurse by his side dispensing medicine when needed—he regained some strength. He planned to sleep as soon as they took off, but the first storm of the fall was interfering with those plans. High winds were forcing the pilots to wait for a hole in the cold front big enough to poke through. They were now into their second hour of delay.

Then the call came. From Brooklyn.

"It has been."

"How may I help you?" a guarded Kazarov asked as the plane rattled from a strong gust.

"You said to call if anyone ever inquired about the murders."

"I did. That was eleven years ago."

"Yes, well, an hour ago someone called."

CHAPTER 96

LAKE ERIE

W hat gives, brother?" the red-faced captain asked minutes after they'd hit the wild open water. "I waited for you, and I would've taken you either way."

"Keep going and stop talking," the Butcher said.

He'd debated whether to pull the Glock so early on the trip—he didn't want Captain Rick radioing in that they were leaving—but brandishing the weapon also risked resistance. However, the rage boiling up within had settled the debate in favor of aggression. Before the targets had run from their hideaway, he was within minutes of accomplishing his mission. Instead, he'd wasted precious time racing around the island's wet roads on a golf cart.

The Butcher had driven his share of boats over the years—on the French Riviera, the Gulf of Finland, the Dead Sea—although nothing this big, in weather this rough. But he'd always been a quick study, building radios, cleaning guns, and fixing cars after observing someone else doing so only once. He was confident he could fly a small plane if necessary.

So bracing himself with one arm, gripping the Glock in the other, the Butcher was far more focused on the skipper's actions than his words. Every adjustment to the throttle. The angle at which he was hitting the waves. The direction he was heading, marked by both the compass and the lights on the horizon flickering between waves. Even the way he stood and how he gripped the wheel. He studied every detail.

Every second that Captain Rick remained at the helm posed a risk. A proud skipper would not accept being a prisoner on his own ship for long. He'd radio or signal a cryptic message back to shore. Hit a wave in a way that would knock the Butcher off his feet. Flash his lights in Morse code. Something. There were too many options to cause trouble.

So, once comfortable that he'd learned the basics, the Butcher unsheathed his knife and thrust it below the captain's rib cage. Twisting it up, he impaled Captain Rick's heart, killing him instantly. He shoved the rotund body aside and manned the controls, but not before the boat had slipped well to the left.

The first wave slammed into the boat at a near-perfect right angle, rolling the craft violently and sending water crashing over the side gunwale. By the time it recovered, another wave hit the boat sideways with equal force, propelling even more water over the side. A disconcerting thud caused the Butcher to shoot a quick glance behind him: Captain Rick's bleeding body was sloshing back and forth across the back of the boat, slamming into its sides.

The next wave was smaller, giving the Butcher time to fling the wheel to the right. Just as Captain Rick had, he pushed the throttle forward, powering over the next wave. From there, he mimicked everything else that he'd observed. After a few more waves he found a rhythm to the rollicking water that allowed him to steady the ride.

At the top of each crest he eyed the most prominent light in the distance, slightly to his left, a point that Captain Rick had focused on as well. He'd assumed early on it was the lighthouse from the beginning of this endless day. The fact that his targets were heading its way confirmed that hunch.

CHAPTER 97

CLEVELAND

The turbulence was no rougher than on other flights Kazarov had taken over the years, flights which hadn't trifled him in the least. But in his weakened physical condition, he threw up twice before the Gulfstream reached its cruising altitude fifteen minutes after takeoff.

But even after his stomach settled down, his mind did not.

Kazarov made another call.

"It's me. Dyadya. Someone called the authorities about your mother's death today."

A long pause on the other end. Dumbfounded, as he had been.

"Did they know anything?"

"I don't believe so. But the call itself is worrisome, the timing even more so."

"Eleven years to the date."

"More importantly, right as our entire operation is unfolding. That call means someone is learning too much. Can you take care of this?"

"Of course. Who was it that called?"

CHAPTER 98

D on't tie that up."

Stern line in hand, I was hopping from *Old Faithful* onto the wet dock when Captain Terry growled his command from the bridge.

"Wait, you're going back out?"

"Yes, sir. If that *is* a commandeered boat, I'll run interference for you. *Old Faithful* is a beast at ramming speed."

A few minutes into our trip, Captain Terry had spotted another fishing boat leaving Kelleys Island, following the same course we had. But its captain had not radioed once and had struggled to keep a straight line in the rough waves, so we assumed it was the hit man. If nothing else, it reminded me that I had to get the tracker out of my leg.

For a moment, his ramming plan sounded like a good idea.

But then I gamed it out. If it worked, great. If not—and nothing had worked so far—I'd be right back on the run with no idea where he was, reliving a nightmare I'd already endured for days. Plus, I was tired of relying on and endangering others.

"Do me a favor instead, Captain?"

"What's that?"

"Watch him, but from a distance. Then let me know when and where he lands."

It was time to press my one advantage.

"Are you sure? *Old Faithful* could sink the son of a bitch."

"I'm sure. But I've got a plan."

"Whatever you say."

I gave him my phone number before he pulled away.

My first few strides along the wood planks of the dock were wobbly ones, as everything around me rocked up and down as if I were still riding waves. But with no time to waste and every leg muscle burning from my standing boat ride, I stumbled down the dock and back onto land as fast as I could manage. I passed the VFW hall to my left, crossed the street, and reached the inn two minutes later, and my room a minute after that.

I stepped out of my wet jeans and, placing a clean white towel under me, sat down on the edge of the bed. Between the wave surfing and the running and the cold and the water, my legs were numb from top to bottom. Now was as good a time as any to do it.

I opened the medical kit. Then, like a doctor scrubbing up for surgery, I laid every necessary implement in a row next to me—small scissors, tweezers, alcohol wipes, gauze, anesthetic gel, and bandages.

I flipped my right foot onto my left knee, exposing my right calf. Water had soaked all the way through my jeans, so my skin was white and fleshy, the wound soft, wet, and oozing with watery pus. I dabbed the gel over it to numb it even further.

My teeth chattered as I reached for the small, pointed scissors.

Then my phone vibrated.

> He went 200 yds further to a private dock.
> Smart move. 2 mins from docking.

> Gotcha. Thanks.

That left ten minutes at most to get out the door. Time to focus.

After putting a small towel in my mouth, I pinched the loose skin around the wound with my left hand and picked up the scissors with my right.

Bracing for the pain, adrenaline spiking, I bit into the towel as hard as I could.

It looked like a grain of rice.

While the stinging pain from the scraping had jolted my numb leg awake, most of the blood flowed after I tugged the tiny gray device from just below the surface, pulling it out from one end, careful not to squeeze too tight. I pressed a bandage against the fresh wound to stop the bleeding, then wiped it clean with alcohol, unleashing a new burst of pain. Then I pressed a new bandage against it, wrapping two pieces of medical tape around my whole calf to make sure it stayed on.

As my breathing steadied, I held up the pint-sized tracker with the tweezers. The damn little thing had inflicted so much damage.

The medical kit included a small plastic bottle of Tylenol, which I now emptied of its pills and replaced with the tracker. Knowing more pain was on its way, I washed four pills down with a glass of water. I pulled my wet jeans and tennis shoes back on, put the Tylenol bottle in my jacket pocket, and ran out the inn door and into the woods behind it.

Jimmy, the limestone crusher and campaign volunteer who suspected I was up to no good, had mentioned a helpful detail the night before.

CHAPTER 99

MARBLEHEAD, OHIO

A rare smile crinkled the Butcher's mouth as the tension in his muscles eased.

They'd hesitated, and he was catching up.

Finally. After too many days and a body count that was growing uncomfortably high—each killing heightened the risk of capture—he could end this maddening chase and leave America behind.

He checked his phone again as he pulled up to the dock. His targets, a kilometer away, still hadn't moved, huddled back at the inn. Feeling safe, the fools were trapping themselves.

Without tying up, he leapt from the boat and sprinted off the dock, climbed over a gate, and ran down two short blocks of residential streets before veering left on the main road. The large conveyor belt spanned across the road not far ahead, so the inn was close.

After passing under the conveyor belt and then by the ferry parking lot, he first saw the narrow top floor of the inn, ahead to the right, rising a story above the other buildings in town.

Only several hundred meters now.

He slowed to a jog, approaching the inn carefully, when he peeked down at his phone. The targets were on the move again, leaving the inn, heading to the right and farther away from the road. Trying to escape.

He sucked in a deep breath. Not this time. He remained as fast as he'd been back on the village soccer field and would not be outrun now.

He sprinted by the inn's dimly lit old stone wall before turning right, running through the parking lot. More good news. The vehicle that had been on guard in the morning was not there. The targets were unprotected.

He checked his phone again. They were dead ahead, making their way through the large trees that were now visible on the other side of the parking lot and behind the inn.

He activated his phone's flashlight function and followed them into the woods, jogging through mud and wet grass, between and around thick trunks. His screen showed him gaining ground on his slower-moving targets, which loosened his limbs even more.

They were so close he imagined he would hear them—rustling leaves, breaking branches, breathing heavily—if it weren't for the rain and the wind. He'd heard it so many times before, the sound of desperate escape, followed by the pathetic pleading for mercy that he knew to ignore.

Then, on his screen, the tracker shot suddenly forward. His targets were opening up more distance, running faster. Perhaps the woods had ended and they were on a firmer surface, no longer dodging trees or sloshing through the mud that was slowing him down.

A few meters away, the dark shadows of the trees appeared to end. He drew another deep breath, knowing his burst was coming. He lowered his phone and mustered every ounce of speed he could. He would hit the flat surface like a center forward on a breakaway.

As he drew even to the last tree, the surface hardened under his front foot—his right. Flat rock, he guessed, allowing him to plant himself firmly and lengthen his stride. His left foot landed on the same flat, hard surface, from which he pushed off with even more force and speed.

Adrenaline raced through him, pumping his heart rate. He would draw even soon. Then it would be over. The long, draining day. This tiresome mission.

The vision from the lighthouse had not been an omen after all.

He swung his right foot forward, stretching it horizontally, then lowered it to plant again on the hard ground.

But this time no hard surface came to meet it.

Nothing met it at all.

CHAPTER 100

MARBLEHEAD, OHIO

Back at the inn, in bed, I shivered for the first ten minutes, then lay still.

When Santini's undercover guy knocked on my door, I sent him away. When Santini, Cassie, and Tori called, I let the phone ring through. When they texted after the calls, I let the phone vibrate without picking it up.

I just lay there, on my back, staring up the white tiles of the high ceiling.

It wouldn't go away.

I'd heard more than my share of screams of pain. When an offensive lineman snapped his Achilles tendon like a rubber band. When my ex's epidural didn't kick in time. When a gunshot victim on a stretcher stared at what was left of his hand. Their loud, high-pitched screams captured the agony of raw physical pain.

But what I'd heard an hour ago had been different. Horribly different.

Another knock on the door, this one lighter than the first. Since I knew no one in town but Santini's guy, I got up. Even through the foggy peephole, Tori's blue eyes glimmered, lifting my mood instantly.

"What the hell are you doing here?" I asked as she walked through the door.

"I got fired from the Cincinnati campaign and, rather than sitting around feeling useless, I drove up here to help you."

I almost lectured her about needing to stay away for safety's sake—something Chief Santini had been stressing since Wisconsin—but held back. It was too good to see her.

"I'm impressed that you got fired as a volunteer."

"Let's just say I took too keen an interest in their voter file."

I laughed, trying to appear calm, but my heart was still hammering away.

Huddled behind a thick tree trunk, I'd witnessed it all. First, the dancing light from his phone went dark a few yards from the edge. Then the hit man, vaulting with a broad, elegant stride that bore all the agility and finesse of a top-flight athlete, catapulted himself out over the quarry. Visually, it ended instantly—the thin, dark figure disappearing into the blackness of the quarry below. But the spine-tingling, high-pitched shriek—the animalistic reflex at the precise moment when he'd discovered his fate—pierced through the wind and the rain and the rustling leaves every second that he plunged to the quarry floor eighty feet below.

And, like a ringing in your ears that wouldn't go away, that shriek still reverberated now.

"Jack, what did you kill in that bed?" Tori asked, pulling my attention back to the room, gesturing at the bloody towel on the back corner of the bed.

"Oh, that." I looked toward the mess, patting my right leg. "Just a little minor surgery."

I chuckled, trying to let the lighthearted conversation block out the shrill echo in my head. Tori suddenly felt like my oldest, most intimate friend.

"Let's go grab a bite across the street. The perch is amazing."

PART 3

CHAPTER 101

YOUNGSTOWN

W ho's behind it all?"

Mary Andres posed the question over the din of a crowded Sunday morning at a popular Youngstown deli.

"Those two women I wrote about in the draft. Natalie DesJardins and Katrina Rivers."

"I'm all for women's lib, Jack, but two thirty-somethings? Somebody's behind them."

"We're still digging into that. It may be a rich uncle of Katrina's." This was a stretch, but she needed something.

"A rich uncle?" Her gray eyes narrowed. "There's no *rich uncle* in the stuff you sent me."

"Because I don't know enough yet to write him in."

"Then we don't know enough yet to print the story."

I glanced over at Tori, who was sitting to my left. "See, I told you she was demand—"

"And why is he doing it?" Mary asked. "What's he after?"

"Who?"

"Your mysterious rich uncle?" She made it sound ridiculous.

"We don't know that yet, either. We've been too busy proving the scheme is happening to fig—"

"We *have* to know what he's after."

"How would we know? You get so much from flipping Congress for a decade, he could be after all sorts of things."

"But he's not. He, whoever he is, is after one thing. It's always about one thing, usually preceded by dollar signs."

Tori stayed quiet, her head swiveling back and forth, watching our tennis match.

"Well, when he grants me an interview, I'll be sure to ask."

Mary ignored the sarcasm. "You've got yourself a strong start here. But until we know—"

"Strong start?" I asked, exasperated. "Mary, to win hundreds of upcoming elections, someone is accessing databases housing the private information of millions of Americans. That's big enough by itself. But because the winning candidates will begin drawing congressional districts only months from now, this will usher in a sea change in American politics for a decade."

"I get it. But we still need to know—"

"C'mon, Mary." Heat rushed from my chest up my neck. "If you knew a fleet of planes were flying toward Pearl Harbor at four a.m. on December seventh, 1941, would you hold up the story because you didn't know they came from Japan?"

"If I'd known on *November* seventh, I would have." She flashed a know-it-all smirk. "Calm down, Jack. You need to fill a few holes, that's all."

She stood up from the booth. "Get to work. I'm going to budget this story for two weeks from today."

My whole head throbbed. "Two weeks? That's a long time—"

"But it's a *Sunday*. Fill in those blanks and we'll run it sooner." She walked away.

I sat in silence. "Well, that was fun."

A cat's smirk came across Tori's face. "It's about time someone bossed you around a little."

I dug my fork into the plate-sized pancake I'd forgotten about and chewed in silence.

"Jack?"

"Yes," I answered, my mouth full.

"When you said there'd be a sea change in politics, what did you mean? We've never talked about it that way."

"I was trying to sell her," I mumbled.

I was fuming. Two weeks was too far away, given that I'd barely survived the past week. And identifying this rich uncle from one lousy entry in a yearbook was a wild-goose chase. Cassie would've called if she had any more than that.

"Sure, but you meant it, right?"

"Of course." I dug my fork back into the pancake.

"How, specifically, would that sea change play out?"

I closed my eyes briefly. Exhaled slowly.

"The stakes are so high in Washington right now, but everything's at a stalemate. It's like a championship game that's all tied up. You flip the House from Republican to Democrat in a permanent way, we're talking about a flood of change for ten years. . . ."

The pounding in my temples subsided. My posture loosened. Talking it out was helping. We'd been so busy proving the precise method of the hack and running for our lives, we hadn't talked about the big picture since that rainy afternoon at my lake house.

"The president's agenda alone would turn things upside down," I added.

"Right. And is there anything specific she wants that this might be about?"

I gazed up, chewing on an especially large piece of pancake, a blueberry exploding in my mouth.

Tori kept prodding. "Let me ask it differently. What's the biggest thing that would change if she had a Democratic Congress?"

"The biggest? She's got a lot of standard liberal things she wants to do." I finished the bite, washing it down with a swig of orange juice. "So those might happen."

"Think about what Mary said. *One thing.* Something big. Something concrete."

"I'm the one who told her that once, by the way."

She raised her eyebrows. "Then it must be right."

I paused, replaying past interviews and discussions with the president in my head.

"If I had to name one thing . . ."

The issue that had gotten me fired from Republic was the same issue

Cassie had talked to the president about. And it was the same agenda item that Speaker Paxton and his big corporate donors were most determined to bury.

". . . I'd say it's her plan to take a battering ram to monopolies across corporate America."

I was talking casually, but my mind was racing. Although it was good politics, I had never taken the president's rhetoric entirely seriously. Given the split in Washington, it had never seemed plausible. The big-money donors were too strong, and the political lift too heavy.

But . . .

"If she had the support in the House to do that, for enough time to see it through, it would revolutionize the American econo—"

I stopped, biting down on a growing smile. Tori's eyes blazed as she realized where this was going.

I slapped my palm against the edge of the table, the silverware and glasses jingling.

"That's gotta be it."

CHAPTER 102

Forty planes total."

"For the whole weekend? Are you sure you got them all?" Cassie asked. She and Rachel were lying in bed as she answered the 10:00 p.m. Sunday-evening call. "That doesn't sound like very many."

"It's Aspen in September," said Axel, the cabdriver. "It gets a lot busier during ski season. I mean really frickin' busy."

His voice kept modulating, sounding high or drunk. Which didn't help her confidence in his research.

"You get all the tail numbers?"

"Yep. Got 'em all."

"And were you able—"

"Every. Last. One."

Definitely high.

"Thank you, Axel. And were you able to see which planes used the high-end car service?"

"Those dark SUVs?"

"Yes. The ones that take people to the ranch."

"I did my best on that. It's all marked down."

"Do you think you got them all?"

"Definitely." He coughed. "I mean, probably."

Cassie ran her fingers through her hair.

"Great. Go ahead and email through what you got."

As she was about to hang up, her phone beeped. It was Republic's news line. Chuck Massa had been calling all weekend to see what she'd gotten from Aspen. She finally had something good to report.

"Chuck, I told you I'd—"

"This isn't Chuck." A female voice with a British accent was doing the talking. One of the weekday morning show's producers.

"Ginger, shouldn't you be in bed?"

"We've got a major breaking story we need your help on."

"Tonight?"

Rachel looked up from her book, glaring at the phone.

"First thing in the morning. But you may want to do a little homework tonight."

"Okay. I can do it. Where am I going?"

"To Baltimore. We already got your Amtrak ticket."

"Baltimore? I was just—" She stopped short. They had to be related.

"Cassie? You there?"

"Yeah. All good. What's the story?"

"It's about that star council member up there, the Republican. You know, the one we always have on?"

Razi.

"Yeah. What about him?" She swallowed to suppress the lump in her throat. Bad news was coming.

"No one can find him."

CHAPTER 103

LONDON

G ood morning, temptress. I see you were thinking of me as well."
Katrina cringed, not in the mood for the Armenian's bile so early in the morning.

"Have you heard from the Butcher, Mr. Terzian?"

"I have not. But I rarely hear from him when he is on a mission. It is safer that way."

"He was updating us at least daily. But he has been silent since Friday."

A long pause. "Nothing?"

"No response at all."

"Well, he's either in the final stages of his mission and cannot communicate, or he's dead." He presented both options in a bloodless, monotone voice. "Do you need me to send someone else?"

"I don't. And please let me know if you hear from him. Thank you." She hung up the phone.

"Nothing." Fuming, she glared at Drac across the conference room table. "He's dead."

Drac stood motionless. "What next?"

"Election operations continue to move forward, correct?"

"Oh, yes. The model is working perfectly." He gestured up at a large monitor displaying an electronic map of the United States. Diagonal stripes overlaid districts where they were actively engaged. "We are well on our way to hitting our targets, without detection."

She glanced at the map. This part of the plan was in good shape. Natalie and Drac could handle whatever came up.

The threat was elsewhere. And the hired henchmen had proven incapable of dealing with it.

She stood up from the table.

"What next?" Drac asked.

"Please get me all the information on the girl."

CHAPTER 104

BALTIMORE

We told you guys," the council aide snapped through the six-inch opening in the door. "The police are handling this. We aren't saying a word from this office."

Minutes after airing a live update on Razi Dallas's disappearance, Cassie had knocked three times on the door of the councilman's city hall office. The six reporters behind her grumbled that she'd cut past them.

"Oh, you don't think we've tried that?" an icy voice asked from behind her. "They aren't letting anyone in."

But through the crack Cassie spotted Iris, the councilman's aide and punctuality cop.

"Iris! Iris! Remember me?"

Iris looked up, eyes red-rimmed. After a double take, she stood up.

"Let her in," she said to the kid at the door.

He opened it another foot, allowing Cassie to slide through.

"Hey, wait a second. We've been here for forty—" The door slammed shut, cutting off the rest of the guy's grousing.

"Let's go in here," Iris said, stepping into the councilman's office, a good sign that she, too, wanted to talk in private.

Photos of Dallas, his wife, and his two young boys—one of them Aiden's age—stared at them from all corners of the office in a way Cassie hadn't noticed the day before. A beautiful family now going through hell. Because of her.

"We're off the record," Cassie said as they sat down in two chairs facing each other. "Do you know anything more than what the police are saying?"

Iris crossed her arms. "Nothing. What do *you* know?"

"Why would I know anything?"

"Because he was distracted all day Friday about whatever you talked about."

"He was?" Cassie recalled the lost look in Razi Dallas's eyes as they'd discussed Katrina.

"He wasn't himself in meetings all morning. Then he insisted on calling you back."

Cassie pursed her lips before responding. "He remembered a detail l had asked for."

"Well, he didn't get any better after that call. He sat through an important lunch like a zombie." She paused. "What were you guys talking about?"

Cassie arched her back. She'd once been cross-examined in a defamation trial, and Iris's battery of accusatory comments and questions felt the same.

"I can't share much, Iris, and I want to find him as badly as you do," she said, leaning forward. "I might be able to help if you share any other details of what happened."

Iris blinked repeatedly, then took a deep breath.

"After lunch, Razi wanted me to dig up the contact information of a New York City councilwoman he'd met at a conference a few months back."

"New York? Any idea what district she represented?" Had to be Brooklyn.

"Brooklyn. He was calling about an old friend from there. They talked so long, I had to leave someone waiting for ten minutes—something we never do."

"Yeah. I noticed."

Iris's face softened slightly. "Then she called back an hour later. They had a much shorter call, after which he bounced back."

Cassie wrote down "Brooklyn call" on her notepad, then circled it. That must have been the trigger.

Iris looked straight at Cassie. "So do you know the friend?"

"I don't know her at all. But I came here yesterday to ask about her."

"It's a she?" Iris asked, her voice cracking as if a scandal was brewing.

"Yes, but it's not what you think. They went to Oxford together. They were close a long time ago but hadn't spoken in eleven years. And she was from Brooklyn."

"Well, however long ago it was, he looked like he'd seen a ghost."

Cassie nodded. A ghost indeed. The perfect description of the Kat Simmons she'd been tracking all over the country, and beyond.

"Can you get me the name of who he called in Brooklyn?" Cassie asked.

"Of course. I've got the card at my desk."

CHAPTER 105

YOUNGSTOWN

D id you write these notes with your toes, Jack? I can't read your chicken scratch."

Two years of reporter's notebooks took up most of the *Vindicator* conference room table. When I'd walked out the doors of Republic for the last time, I took them, thinking I'd write a book someday. I never imagined they'd be so helpful this quickly.

"It's called shorthand, Tori. You try taking notes while you're looking right at someone spewing a million words a min—"

"I wait tables, Jack. I do it every day."

"Okay, okay. Just keep handing me the ones with any reference to her, and I'll decipher the Sanskrit."

Janet Moore and I had had several lengthy conversations during the general election, and three more after she'd won. A stack of six notebooks with those interview notes sat in front of me, which I was now scanning through one page at a time.

The first two notebooks covered the campaign and her strategies to win it, and the fourth was all about a shutdown that she'd averted. Nothing on monopolies came up, so I set all three aside.

But conversations about her anti-monopoly agenda took up big chunks of the three remaining notebooks.

"Here's one more." Tori handed me one last notebook. "June 22" was scribbled on the front.

"The last conversation before I was fired. We talked about it extensively then."

I leafed through the pages slowly, the details of our off-the-record discussion coming back to me.

"She was especially concerned about how the newest technology companies were getting so powerful." I read one direct quote aloud: "'It's like they don't think antitrust rules apply to big tech. Mergers and acquisitions are being approved that never would've been allowed decades ago.'"

Tori typed my words on her laptop.

"Facebook buying Instagram and WhatsApp. Google grabbing search companies left and right, putting others out of business, then grabbing companies like YouTube and Waze."

"I didn't know they owned all those."

"I didn't either until she told me."

I read further.

"She never had notes when I interviewed her but knew the industries cold. Banks, airlines—consumer goods, too."

Tori typed it all in. "Yep, higher prices, more fees, lower wages, and nothing anyone can do about it."

I took out the previous notebook. The words "political power" were circled on the first page.

"She worried about how these large entities were accumulating political power, reinforcing their ability to stay at the top of the heap for good."

"Makes sense." Tori typed away.

Then came another list of industries, including agriculture. Soybeans. Beef. Corn. Chickens. "It's killing the family farm. . . . It looks like your dad picked the wrong industry. Dairy is one of the most impacted."

"Tell me about it. The poor guy worked his whole life on that farm but could never get ahead. He always said he felt squeezed by all sides, and it got worse every year."

"That's exactly what the president said."

"Well, don't tell her, but I'm pretty sure my dad voted for the other guy."

I read for another fifteen minutes, extracting everything we could from the interviews.

Tori looked up after typing the last note. "This is all good stuff, Jack, but the big money is on the side of the monopolies. Who would benefit from breaking them all up the way the president proposes?"

"According to the president, most economists, and Teddy Roosevelt? Everybody else."

"Yeah, but who would benefit enough to pull off this plot? Not some liberal do-gooder helping out the American consumer."

"Definitely not."

"Then who?"

"I guess anyone in the industries that are about to have their monopolies broken up. Except for the monopolies themselves, the smaller fry are sitting on gold mines and don't even know it. Their fortunes are about to skyrocket."

I recalled the president explaining that mobile phones and home modems all soared after the breakup of AT&T, opening the door to AOL and other tech first movers. And smaller internet companies and start-ups took off after Microsoft was forced to curb its monopolistic practices.

Tori's lips twisted into a grimace and she put her hand to her chin but said nothing.

"What?" I asked.

"I was thinking about my poor dad. If this plan happens, he's selling his farm at exactly the wrong time. Just his luck."

She was right. The poor guy hadn't caught a break since his final NBA rebound.

"True. But that's also the answer to your question. If whoever is buying the farm from him is buying others, too—"

"And it sounds like that's what's happening."

"—that's the kind of person that stands to reap a—"

I paused. We stared at each other for a few seconds.

"Oh my God, Jack. Whoever's behind this isn't *sitting* on gold mines—"

I finished her sentence for her.

"They're *buying* them."

"Sal Pavano here. How can I help you?"

"Hey, Sal, my name's Rex Chalmers. I'm an ag lawyer in Ohio. I understand you're in the dairy-farm-buying business."

Tori and I had spent fifteen minutes on the phone with Lute, talking through the out-of-the-blue offer for his farm.

"Sure, I've been picking up a few here or there."

Quick research had shown that Pavano was a partner at a high-flying New York corporate firm, the kind of firm only large companies can afford. And the website listed Pavano's specialty as international transactions, with most of his deals coming out of eastern Europe and the former Soviet Union.

"From what I hear, you've been picking up more than that, and for a pretty penny, too. You've made a lot of people happy here in flyover country."

Lute had described Sal's fancy Mercedes, manicured nails, and tailored suits, so I figured flattery would help.

"They can thank my client for that. Just call me the closer."

Referring to his client whetted my appetite, but it was too early to press. All of Lute's legal agreements were with a six-month-old Delaware corporation, conveniently shrouding the foreign buyer. His lawyer wouldn't want to say much.

"Well, I may have some takers here in Ohio."

"How big?"

Lute had given me a crash course on dairy lingo that would tempt a potential buyer.

"We've got a good number of family farms. Fifty to a hundred cows each. Some corporate outfits would also consider selling. A couple hundred each. Some more than that."

"Not bad. Do you represent them all?"

"I do."

In case he did any research, Rex Chalmers was a lawyer at a respected Cleveland law firm. "But they had a couple of major questions before we sit down."

"Fire away, Max."

"It's Rex."

"Yeah, yeah. Fire away."

"Word on the street is that you represent some big foreign company. My guys are red-blooded patriots. They're concerned about handing over our food supply to Russians, or the Chinese."

"I'm sorry, but I'm not at liberty to discuss my client."

"I don't need to know the details. Just assure me it's not a Russian or Chinese company. Those are deal killers."

He paused for long enough that I worried I'd blown the call.

"Nope. He's neither."

"Or any other country like that?"

"Look, Max—"

"Rex."

"Look, Rex. I can't say anything about the client. He insists on confidentiality. All of *your* clients will have to sign an ironclad nondisclosure agreement."

"Of course, but we'll never get to the damn agreement if they don't sell in the first place. And they're not gonna sell if there's a chance they're selling out our country's food supply to the enemy."

He paused for a few seconds, then sighed. "Listen, Rex. Last time I checked, our government was sending arms to Ukraine to fight the Russians, so tell your patriots they have nothing to worry about. I'll leave it at that."

"Okay." I wrote "Ukraine" down on my notepad.

"What's your second question?"

Although he didn't want to share information, this guy wanted a deal more.

"Why is your client interested? It's not like the dairy business is kicking butt right now. But these guys are proud farmers and want assurance that what they've built will remain as dairy farms."

Sal laughed. "They don't have to worry about that. My client built up his dairy empire from one small farm himself. He knows what it takes to succeed."

"Even competing against the big corporations that have squeezed clients like mine?"

"Oh, yes. He'll be fine. He has a plan."

"And why now?"

"Excuse me?"

"Why buy these farms now? Why such a hurry?"

Sal let loose a throaty laugh. "Listen, bud. I don't know why he's so eager. I just go out and close the deals."

CHAPTER 106

WASHINGTON, D.C.

Iris was wrong about one thing.

The politician whom Razi Dallas had called in New York was not a member of the New York City Council. She was the Brooklyn borough president—essentially the mayor of Brooklyn. And she called Cassie back almost immediately.

"I was heartbroken to read that the councilman has disappeared," Emerald Herrera said over the phone. "What a shining star he is."

"The whole city of Baltimore is in shock." Cassie paused before dropping the big news. "Madam Borough President, I suspect his call to you triggered whatever has happened."

Herrera gasped. "The call to me? About that old murder case?"

"I believe so. Off the record, I had discussed the case with him earlier in the day."

"But why would such an old case lead to his vanishing now?"

"That's what I'm trying to figure out. Can I ask what you and he discussed?"

"That was between him and myself." Her voice faded. Fearing bad press, the politician in her was clamming up fast.

"Madam Borough President, I'm not interested in exposing the conversation or even mentioning that he called you. Assuming he's even still alive, I'm trying to find him. This is part of a much bigger plot."

A few seconds passed by. "Let me get my notes." A scratchy sound blared through the receiver as Herrera put her phone down.

Minutes later she picked up again.

"Razi wanted to know about the double murder of a Sophia and Mikhail Rivers. From Brighton Beach. Eleven years ago."

Cassie wrote the names down.

"And?"

"Ms. Knowles, this is highly sensitive stuff."

Cassie tapped her pen against the desk. The secrecy was getting old.

"Yes, apparently so sensitive that someone leaked it after your call and now the councilman's gone." She let the words sink in. "Please help me find him."

"Okay. There was no file on the case. But I talked to a longtime Brooklyn detective I trust. He remembered the case a little and checked around quietly."

"Apparently not quietly enough."

"True. I will ask him who he talked to. . . . Anyway, the case information is buried somewhere within the FBI."

"Why's that?"

"This was not a standard double murder."

"It wasn't?"

"No. It was domestic violence."

"Domestic violence? Between who?"

"Sophia Rivers and her husband."

"Her husband? She was married?"

"Apparently. To some midlevel member of the Russian mob."

"That's why the FBI got involved."

"Exactly. It's a brutal gang that's haunted Brooklyn since the early nineties. Even now more than then. Apparently the Riverses had lived separately for years; he rose within the gang's ranks, came back and courted her, then killed her when she snubbed him."

"And he killed the son, too?"

"Officially, yes. But apparently not in reality."

"What do you mean?"

"The son stumbled across the scene and then killed the father. Husband and wife were found dead, and the son ran off."

"So he's still alive?"

"I guess you could call it that. But killing a Russian mobster ends your life as you know it. He's been in witness protection ever since, with the public story being that he was killed."

Before Cassie had time to process these words, there was a loud knock on her office door.

CHAPTER 107

YOUNGSTOWN

ack Sharpe?" said Thea Pappas. "Didn't you used to work for Republic News?"

I chuckled at my new favorite question. "Sure did. I'm back on the newspaper side now."

"Isn't that like jumping from a Porsche to a Pinto?" she asked, chuckling. "How may I help you?"

"We're writing about a string of acquisitions of regional banks across the country, and the *Bankers Journal* indicated that you recently sold Athenia."

"I did," she said, media savvy enough not to offer more.

"You rebuffed offers for years. What changed your mind?"

"Are we on the record?"

"Let's start on background, and you can decide if you want anything on the record after." A standard journalist trick to get people talking.

"Okay."

"Why did you sell this time?"

"What's that old saying: 'They made an offer I couldn't refuse'? Well, they pretty much did."

"But hadn't the big banks made rich offers in recent years?" According to one article, FirstAmerica had aggressively sought out Athenia.

"That's true."

"Well, what was the difference this time?"

"This buyer uses an entirely different model from the American banks. They want to build up Athenia's footprint instead of chopping it into pieces. Their plan was best for our workers, our customers, and the communities we serve."

"Interesting. Tell me more about the buyer."

"I can't say anything beyond what's been reported."

"*Bankers Journal* said it's some outfit from eastern Europe."

"Yep."

She was holding tight to the details like a kid clinging a toy, so I kept pushing.

"And that they've bought a bunch of similar-sized banks across the West and South."

"I read the same thing."

"Isn't that a strange fit? An eastern European bank in America?"

"My attitude is, if they built up a national banking empire from small towns across Romania and then eastern Europe, they'll do fine in Price and Ogden, Utah."

Finally, something new. Romania.

"Even against the big banks?"

"I don't know. But they're confident they're up to the challenge. I sure wasn't, so I'm pulling for them."

I ended the call.

"Same pattern as the others?" Tori asked from the other side of the table, uncapped black marker in hand.

"The same."

A foreign entity swooping into a monopolized American industry, buying up low-performing, modest-sized assets for a premium, oddly confident that their newly acquired enterprise would succeed despite years of struggle.

On an easel next to her, she wrote the word "Banking" across the top column, next to the words "Dairy," "Wheat," "Soy," "Search," and a few other industries we'd researched where large companies dominated.

"Eastern Europe?"

"Yes. But Romania specifically."

She filled the row below "Banking" with the "Romania/EE," alongside "Ukraine," "Kazakhstan," "China," and other listed countries.

"Bought in the past year like the others?"

"More like the last month."

She added a check mark below "Romania."

"Incredible." Hands behind my head, I leaned back in the swivel chair from which I'd been making calls for hours. "It's some type of cartel, gobbling up everything they can. At least we can tell Mary we know what's driving all this."

Tori snickered. "That, and that you were wrong."

"Wrong?"

"Yeah. Forget a sea change in politics. This would be a sea change to the entire U.S. economy."

CHAPTER 108

WASHINGTON, D.C.

With Republic anchor Chuck Massa knocking on her door all afternoon, Cassie set Brooklyn drama aside for a few hours to dig into the list of airplane tail numbers Axel had sent her.

She stumbled around the internet, hunting for websites that allowed her to track flights by their tail numbers. She found two.

From Axel's list, Cassie first examined the planes whose passengers had left the terminal in the dark-tinted SUVs. She also focused on the planes that had stayed only a few hours, likely for a single business meeting as opposed to a weekend of leisure.

The weekend visits had kicked off with three state government planes—New Mexico, Arizona, and Nevada—all arriving Friday afternoon, flying in from each state's capital, and returning that evening. Cassie guessed the passengers were those states' governors, continuing their discussions with the president on her public lands plan.

Another three planes had flown in from Newark, Austin, and Chicago, landing and leaving on Friday afternoon, Sunday morning, and Sunday afternoon. They belonged to high-end private charter companies, so there was no way to know who their passengers were.

More interesting were two planes that had arrived Saturday midmorning and were registered to a major pharmaceutical company and a gas company. Quick research revealed that both companies were lobbying hard for controversial legislation before Congress. She jotted the companies' names down; those meetings would make for the kind of damaging story her bosses craved.

Three other visitors also met that test. Separate airplanes arriving Saturday afternoon belonged to a Hollywood director, a Texas trial attorney, and a San Francisco tech billionaire. The Federal Election Commission's website showed that all three were major contributors to the president. Again, her bosses' dream story: donors secretly getting special access to the president.

Cassie tried to pinpoint where these planes had traveled before and after Aspen. But that was where the trail ended. Both websites indicated all three were on a Federal Aviation Administration's "blocked list," whatever that was. No information was available on their respective flight histories.

But the most intriguing flights had arrived Saturday around noon, within ten minutes of one another. F-ZABB, TC-AB2, and UR-B1B—with one exception, these were the only tail numbers on the entire list that didn't start with the letter *N*. Quick research found that the *F*, *TC*, and *UR* signified planes registered in France, Turkey, and Ukraine, with the French plane bearing the tail number of an official government plane. They had flown directly from Paris, Ankara, and Kiev.

Pay dirt.

Cassie could picture the breaking news chyrons already: the president of the United States meeting in secret with officials from those countries, together. Surely the president owed the American people more information on such a meeting.

The three foreign tail numbers gave her pause for another reason. A plane earlier on the list had also displayed a tail number that did not start with *N*. She'd skipped it over the first time because it didn't look like a presidential visit. The plane landed late on the Friday night—too late for a meeting—and didn't depart until Sunday afternoon. And Axel had not listed it as a plane that had used an SUV.

But now the odd tail number piqued her interest.

G-M1M.

Several keystrokes revealed that tail numbers beginning with *G* were registered in the United Kingdom. She tried to find where the plane had flown from, but it, too, was on the FAA's blocked list. No flight history was available.

She closed her laptop. She could ask Jack about the block list later. He knew about that sort of thing.

For now, the foreign planes, fancy donors, and corporations were more than enough to keep her bosses off her back.

CHAPTER 109

YOUNGSTOWN

Jack, why are you playing games when you've got a story to finish?" Mary Andres asked, stepping behind me as I sat at the *Vindicator*'s conference room table.

"This *is* work. I'm helping another reporter on important research."

"Right. Then what are those doing on there?"

She pointed at the hundreds of tiny airplanes dotting my computer screen.

"Like I said. Research."

Mary left the room grumbling.

Although my screen looked like a video game, I'd told the truth. Cassie had asked for my help.

A gift to the rich and famous to keep their travels private, the FAA "block list" was a relic. Taking advantage of new airplane communication systems, plane buffs had established their own private networks to track and share all flights online, and the FAA was powerless to shut them down. I'd casually poked around those sites for years, nosing into the travel patterns of everyone from Steven Spielberg to Michael Jordan.

Now, with Cassie's hard work, these hobbyists might unlock the president's secret Aspen list.

The first of Cassie's tail numbers belonged to a well-known Hollywood director, and the private website traced every mile of his Aspen jaunt. He'd taken off out of Hollywood Burbank, stopped in Palo Alto, then flown to Aspen. He took the same route home. Odds were he picked someone up on the way.

Similarly, the San Francisco tech billionaire had stopped in Missoula on the way to Aspen, returning there for the night before flying back to SFO the next morning. Given the highbrow nature of the gathering, he likely picked up the eccentric fracking mogul and only Democratic mega-donor who lived in Missoula.

And the Texas trial attorney, the single largest Democratic donor in the nation, had flown to and from Austin.

While these visits would make a good story, the other tail number Cassie had shared piqued my interest more.

G-M1M. A British plane.

The equipment was a two-year-old Gulfstream G650, the most expensive private plane in the sky. The fastest, too, flying just below the speed of sound.

G-M1M wasn't a government plane like the other foreign flights she'd mentioned but was registered to a private company named Windsor Castle PLC. No other information was available on that entity. Whatever it was, Brits couldn't donate to the president, so this wasn't a donor meeting like the others.

The plane had traveled a puzzling flight path. It hadn't departed from either of London's major airports, Heathrow or Gatwick, but from a small field outside London. And then it made a head-scratching stop in the United States before flying to Aspen.

Because Aspen's airport didn't provide customs service, any international private flight would first need to stop at another American airport that did. Most pilots would stop as close to the northern flight route as possible—somewhere like Bangor, Maine. Others might land in Denver, pass through customs there, then make the short hop over to Aspen.

But G-M1M had made a peculiar stop: Burke Lakefront Airport, the small airfield on a spit of land north of downtown Cleveland.

While Burke provided customs service, it was well south of the route from London to Aspen, adding unnecessary hours to the trip. And the lakefront airport was notorious for its wind and weather. Sure enough, the Gulfstream had landed at Burke last Friday afternoon, around the time the storm had blown through Marblehead and Kelleys Island. Cleveland would've faced the same rough weather shortly thereafter, with even gustier winds, which explained why the flight's departure from Burke was delayed for hours, into the early evening.

The flight home Sunday added another wrinkle. G-M1M stopped back through Cleveland, then flew to Trenton-Mercer Airport in New Jersey before leaving American airspace and crossing back over the North Atlantic.

Only one scenario explained the circuitous route and the decision to fly into an approaching storm: Burke Lakefront had been more than a customs stop. G-M1M picked up a passenger there, dropped that passenger back off in Cleveland on Sunday, then either picked up or dropped off another passenger in New Jersey before heading back to England.

As I zoomed in on that ultimate destination, Tori walked into the conference room holding a paper bag. Sitting down across the table, she slid my way a sandwich wrapped in foil.

"Turkey on wheat, melted Swiss."

"Thank you," I said, eyes fixed on my screen.

"What's wrong, Jack? You're sweating. And your neck's all red again like it was in Wisconsin."

"Nothing." I forced a smile. "Just getting this done for Cassie."

But, as always, she'd read me perfectly. My stomach was fluttering like it used to before big games.

G-M1M had flown to and from a small airport called Blackbushe, located about forty-five miles southeast of London, in a county called Hampshire. The Windsor Castle PLC name made more sense now, because the famous landmark sat less than twenty miles away from Blackbushe Airport.

And all of it felt familiar.

Three years ago, as I was chasing down the final pieces of the Abacus scandal, two goons nabbed me from a Bob Evans in rural Pennsylvania and loaded me onto the nicest airplane I'd ever seen, a black Gulfstream. Seven hours later, as we descended through ten thousand feet, London's sea of lights sparkled below. But then we banked east, and south. With the exception of the well-lit Windsor Castle, which was visible off the right wing, the ground grew largely dark before we landed at a small airfield in the English countryside.

If my sense of direction was right, that humble airfield had been where Blackbushe Airport was located on the map now facing me.

And after a short car ride from that airfield, we'd pulled up to Oleg Kazarov's estate.

CHAPTER 110

The man didn't even look twice. Which alerted Cassie that he didn't belong.

After updating an excited Chuck Massa and calling Jack about the FAA block list, Cassie had left work early to escape to the sculpture garden on the National Mall. A slow walk through the understated garden offered the perfect elixir for her long, tense days at Republic. And her early morning in Baltimore, followed by an afternoon assuaging her ornery bosses, had made today particularly long.

Along the garden's manicured trail of complexity and abstraction, Cassie's favorite stop was a spare work of bronze. While sculpted in the 1950s, it appeared prehistoric: the rough figure of a man, with scant definition and detail, leaning straight back on a horse. The two formed a mangy duo. The rider's stubby arms shot outward to his sides, while his short, malformed legs clung to the horse's shoulders. The horse's spindly legs splayed toward the ground in an unnaturally wide stance, its undersized head lifted skyward, its ribs protruding out of the dark bronze.

But for all of the figures' physical imperfection, the intensity of their stances—their ramrod-straight legs, their taut necks, the man's outspread arms, their parallel gazes straight up into the sky—packed more power than any piece of art she'd ever seen. She'd often stare at the horse and rider, joined in their moment of joy and liberation, for so long that she had to remind herself there were other pieces in the garden to visit.

And she wasn't the only one. Over her many visits, she'd seen people stroll casually by the other works that dotted the garden's walkway. Not this statue. It stopped visitors in their tracks.

Which was why one visitor's reaction this afternoon so jolted her.

As she and five others stood around the horse and rider, a gray-haired, iron-jawed man had emerged from around a corner. In a sheepskin bomber jacket and dark slacks, he approached the small gathering, passing only feet from her. He shot a quick glance at her and an even shorter one at the sculpture. He then took a few more steps, stopping in front of a far less striking piece.

Politely smiling at the others gathered around, she stepped in the direction from where the man had come. If he was there to observe the art, he wouldn't backtrack that way.

But that's exactly what he did. When she rounded a corner and looked back, the gray-haired man loped in the same direction she was going, passing the horse and rider for a second time without even a glimpse.

Cassie's heart skipped a beat and she walked faster. The man sped up, too.

As she reached the wide dirt path lining the edge of the mall, heavy footsteps closed quickly behind her.

"Are you Cassie Knowles?" the man asked in a thick Brooklyn accent.

"I am." She spoke in a guarded tone, keeping her distance. "And who are you?"

"Ernest Foley. New York PD."

Cassie caught her breath. "Let me guess. Out of a Brooklyn precinct?"

"Brooklyn headquarters, actually. I'm a senior detective there."

"You scared the hell out of me—"

"I noticed. Those statues ain't my cup of tea."

"How can I help you?"

He gestured his right arm forward, lightly touching her back, inviting her to walk in the same direction. The call with the borough president played back through Cassie's mind—the part about someone having leaked Razi Dallas's call within the police department.

"Are we being followed?"

"Not that I know of. But I'm more comfortable walking while talking as opposed to standing in place."

"Makes sense."

They walked toward the Washington Monument as he sidled up to her right.

"You made some calls about an old case in Brooklyn the last few days. I was asked about it twice this morning, and I wanted to get down here before you got yourself hurt."

A familiar chill crawled down her spine. Back at the *Globe*, days before busting two corrupt Boston officials, several cops had visited her, warning that she'd "get herself hurt." But their attempts at intimidation hadn't stopped her.

"I'm afraid a Baltimore council member is in trouble because of it."

"Yes, he is. Unfortunately, that call went somewhere else first before I could stop it. Why do you think I flew the shuttle down here?"

"It's that serious?"

"Oh, it's deadly serious, Ms. Knowles."

Another phrase they'd used back in Boston.

The red sandstone and multiple towers of the Smithsonian Castle emerged on the left, a landmark that caught the detective's fancy more than the sculptures.

"And why is that? If it went down the way the borough president explained it to me, why is it so sensitive eleven years later?"

"One guess."

"Because it did *not* go down that way?"

"Bingo."

"So the bureau president lied to me?"

"No. She was fed the company line. She doesn't know the real story. Almost no one does."

"Well, what's the real story? And why are people still lying about it now?"

"You have to promise me you won't repeat a word. The people caught up in that case are very dangerous."

"I'm sure. Russian mobsters aren't exactly thrilled when someone kills one of their own."

Detective Foley smiled faintly, shaking his head. "That's not exactly what happened."

"Isn't that why the case is buried with the FBI?"

"Oh, it's buried all right. And the mob is most certainly involved."

"Okay?"

"But it's the mob that did the killing."

"You mean killed Mrs. Rivers?"

"Both Mr. and Mrs. Rivers."

"Wait, the mob killed them both?"

"Yes."

"And Mikhail witnessed it?"

"No, he didn't."

"Then why did he disappear?"

"Because *he's* the one who did the killing. He was a young mobster at the time."

Cassie gasped, swallowing hard and turning his way. "He shot his own parents?"

"In cold blood."

"Awful."

"Truly. You should've seen the bodies."

"Did *you*?"

"Unfortunately, yes. I was a newer detective back then and had to process the scene."

She still didn't know what to make of him. Those Boston cops had never said a thing beyond their threats. Foley was far more forthcoming, but his monotone delivery was disconcerting.

"Was it some type of civil war? The borough president said the dad was in the mob, too."

"That's more of the company line. The poor guy had sobered up, built up a modest life selling insurance, and was simply trying to put his old marriage back together. He and Mrs. Rivers had communicated again for about a year before they were killed."

"Well, then why—"

He eyed her, grim-faced. "I have no clue why the son did it."

"And now where is he? Jail?"

"Free as a bird. He moved up the chain. Mikhail Rivers has a new name and runs the most lethal Russian gang in Brooklyn. If he was protected then, he's untouchable now."

"So the case was buried to protect him?"

"You got it. Some bad apples on the inside cleaned things up fast, building the false narrative you heard. Then they buried it all."

"Who else knows about the case?" Cassie wondered about Katrina in particular.

"Almost nobody. My partner and I only worked the case at the outset, enough to get a sense of what really went down. After it got pulled from us, we played dumb and didn't bring it up again. And then it disappeared, which is why your calls caught my attention."

They stopped at a crosswalk and waited for the pedestrian light to flash green. The Washington Monument and a wide circle of flapping American flags awaited them on the other side of the busy street.

"Did you know there was also a daughter?"

"Lovely Katrina? You couldn't miss her. Her photos were all over the house, far more than Mikhail's. But she was overseas when it all went down."

"Do you think she ever found out what really happened?"

"Unless her own brother admitted it to her, I doubt it. We never saw her."

"Not even at the funeral?"

"What funeral?" he said, smirking. "You don't have a funeral for a mob killing if you know what's good for you."

The pedestrian light flashed green.

"So what am I supposed to do with this information?" Cassie asked as she stepped off the curb.

"Absolutely nothing. No more calls. No more questions. Drop it all. Let's just hope they release this Baltimore guy."

Just talk, or more threats?

They reached the other side of the road. Home was to the left, so Cassie stopped walking. She looked right into Detective Foley's heavy-lidded eyes as the photos of the councilman's young family flashed in her head.

"He doesn't know anything. The poor guy just cared about the daughter."

"Then maybe he'll be okay. Killing a council member might bring more heat than if they just let him go."

CHAPTER 111

As we warned you last week, you should not have traveled."

Oleg Kazarov lay back in his hospital bed, motionless and miserable, his apron dark and damp with sweat. An IV tube was back in his shriveled arm. But this time the drugs flowing through it were battling a bacterial infection as opposed to the cancer. And the bald, bearded doctor—the chief of oncology at the clinic—stood over him like an angry school principal.

He hadn't felt this ill the entire duration of his treatment.

"I understand," he said weakly. "What can be done now?"

Bad luck had conspired against him from the trip's outset. The long flight delay in the storm. Heavy early turbulence. Recycled cabin air, altitude, and rough storms over Illinois not only had kept him from getting needed rest but wreaked havoc on his weakened condition. By the time the flight had descended, he was shaking uncontrollably from chills and vomiting. The flight delay had pushed his meeting back to the next day, so a medical van shuttled him directly from the tarmac to the hospital.

"You need to rest completely," the Cleveland doctor replied. "No phone calls. No reading. Don't even think about work. This is a deadly serious moment in your recovery."

"Okay." He closed his eyes, stifling a cough.

On the other hand, the trip had been a success. Against the advice of the local doctor, he'd attended the rescheduled Saturday-morning meeting. Within an hour, and with the help of one other guest, all his questions about the final plan had been answered. Then he returned to the hospital for an extra day of rest before flying home Sunday.

A vibration to his right stirred him. His phone was sitting on a small bedside table, the lit-up screen in his line of sight. It was Katrina calling.

He reached for it.

"What did I tell you, Mr. Kazarov? No phone calls. You must rest."

"I will not talk."

The doctor shook his head, exasperated.

He picked up the phone.

I can not talk now.

Ok, Dyadya. How was the trip?

Successful. Good information to report to the group.

Okay.

Will call in 15 minutes.

CHAPTER 112

YOUNGSTOWN

H eart racing, I consumed the Gulfstream's full flight history like a
teenage kid rifling through his older sister's diary. And even my
initial glance erased any doubts about whether G-M1M was Kazarov's plane.

"Jack!"

Eyes narrowed, Tori was again staring at me across the table.

"What?" I wiped my brow, and a few beads of sweat moistened the
back of my hand. "I guess I'm getting excited."

"Whatever. I wish you trusted me."

"Of course I do." And I did, with everything but this.

Early in its first year, the plane hadn't flown often, but when it did, it
traveled precisely where Oleg Kazarov would've gone. Summer flights to
and from St. Petersburg, landing at a small airport near the dacha where
he'd hosted me. Flights to and from western Siberia, where he ran a major
oil and gas operation. And a flight to a small airport in northwest Pennsylvania, down the road from the Titusville headquarters of Marcellus
Enterprises, Kazarov's well-disguised American fracking operation.

But the history revealed a lot more than who owned the plane.

Late the year before, the plane had flown to Aspen twice in three
months. Both flights went from Blackbushe to Aspen, with a quick customs stop in Denver. It took two minutes of searching online to discover
that these trips coincided with weekends when the president had escaped
to her ranch.

Then came the first flight to Cleveland, six months ago. The airplane stayed at Burke for two days, then flew home. Three weeks later the Gulfstream returned but departed back to England an hour after landing. Four weeks later came another flight, but like this past weekend, the plane went on to Aspen, flying back to Burke three hours after landing.

At first, Cleveland made no sense. Even if Kazarov was visiting his Titusville headquarters, landing in Cleveland added hours of driving.

So why Cleveland?

Then I remembered the reason I'd dismissed Kazarov's involvement in the first place. He was battling cancer, facing a bleak prognosis. I did a quick search, digging up that energy journal article from months back—the one detailing Kazarov's failing health. Unsurprising, it had been published weeks after the first flight to Cleveland.

That was it.

The world-renowned Cleveland Clinic had a separate unit that provided care to the world's most elite leaders—royals, dictators, and run-of-the-mill billionaires—when they battled illnesses. Oleg Kazarov must have joined their ranks, undergoing tests on the first trip, then returning for an extended stay weeks later.

I stared at the screen, eyeing the small blue line tracing across the ocean, from the letters BBS to the letters BKL.

I let out a deep breath, my neck and scalp prickling at the realization that Oleg Kazarov was in Cleveland right now.

Tori was still irritated, her mouth tightly pursed.

But the flight history didn't end with Cleveland. Around the time of the first Aspen meeting, and then following Kazarov's first Cleveland trip, the Gulfstream became even more active. It traveled to more far-flung destinations: Ukraine, Armenia, Georgia, Syria, and several long, multi-stop trips to China. There was a trip combining stops in Bishkek, the capital of Kyrgyzstan, and Almaty, the capital of Kazakhstan. The longest trip took the plane to remote Siberia, then on to a small airport sixty miles from Vladivostok in the Russian Far East, then straight over the Arctic back to London.

Two of the shortest trips were a one-day visit to Romania and a more recent flight to Portofino, Italy. A flurry of multi-stop flights followed Portofino, circling back to the same destinations as before.

I glanced up at the whiteboard with Cassie's handwriting on it, re-viewing the countries listed across the top.

Ukraine.

China.

Kazakhstan.

And Romania.

The words on the whiteboard and the Gulfstream's flights matched almost perfectly.

"What, Jack?" Tori asked as I scanned her chart.

I had to tell her something.

"Mary was wrong," I said quietly.

"How's that?"

"She said, 'Someone's leading it.'"

What a wise woman. She had been so close to the truth.

"And that's not true?"

"It's close. But it's not some*one*. It's *two* people."

"Who?"

"Katrina Rivers and her very sick Russian uncle. And they've been flying all over the world to get it done."

CHAPTER 113

C assie stared at the ceiling for hours. Even with Rachel asleep next to her and three melatonin gummies buried deep in her stomach, sleep eluded her.

She still couldn't decide if Detective Foley's purpose had been to help her or spook her. And the double murder he'd described had been horrific. But that was not what was keeping her up.

She couldn't get Katrina Rivers off her mind.

She trudged into the kitchen of their modest apartment, where she had charged her laptop overnight. She flipped it on and reviewed the folder of photos she'd compiled.

The old Katrina. The new Katrina. Blond or brunette. Glasses or contacts. Stretching tall or stooping low. Cassie would recognize her anywhere.

But for all her weeks of tracking her down, Cassie hadn't come close to understanding what made Katrina tick. As a young woman, she'd been as shy as could be. Then she'd grown into a confident, liberated beauty. Smart from the get-go, her idealism evolved into cunning, and worse. Technically skilled, she also demonstrated a sky-high emotional IQ that allowed her to size up her foes before running over them. And she traded in her dreary rags for showy riches.

Katrina Rivers was a contradiction. An enigma. A sphinx.

Until now.

Now Cassie understood her in a way that few could.

They shared something—as deep and searing a wound as a person could experience. They'd both been through the hell of losing their families.

A drunk-driving millionaire had plowed into Cassie's parents' station wagon when she was fourteen, killing them both. The accident and the ensuing trial sabotaged her middle-class childhood, upended her world-view, and shaped every aspect of her life since.

The soul-crushing loneliness, until she married Rachel.

The decades of financial stress.

And her lifelong zeal to take down big shots. The acquittal of her parents' well-connected killer had awakened her to the unjust advantages of America's elite and made countering that rigged system the cause of her life. Whenever she doubted her mission, the tattoo on her arm, embla-zoned with the time and date of the crash, reminded her to keep fighting.

Katrina's family, too, had been wiped away in minutes. Not even the dignity of a funeral. The fact that she was thousands of miles away at a fancy school must've made it all the more wrenching.

Cassie's first days living with her uncle had been awkward. But his quiet house in South Boston became her home, too, where she remained under his watch and wing until college. On his mailman's salary, he toiled to be the father figure she'd lost. He was her rock until she struck out on her own.

As shy as Katrina was, Cassie guessed that only one person had re-mained for her as well. Her yearbook made clear she already felt indebted to her *dyadya*. So he would've played a central role after the murders, when the trappings of wealth had surfaced, along with Katrina's darker traits.

Every day of the trial, Cassie had sat in the front row, scribbling notes, recording every detail of the accident. She'd never speak to her parents again, but she could at least relive their final moments, feel what they had felt, understand every action leading up to the crash. In the fog of grief, her fact-gathering obsession diluted the darkness that consumed her each night in the cold new bedroom.

But it also meant every twist of the trial, every moment of the crash, was chiseled in Cassie's memory. The fancy, bow-tied defense lawyer with the polished shoes and plaid suspenders making small talk with the judge. The fat bank CEO with the jowls and the pin-striped suit and the pudgy fingers clutching his wife's hand, even when his mistress had been injured in the crash. The photos of both cars, shredded like ripped tinfoil. As time passed, those details anchored whatever smidgeon of closure she ultimately found.

Now she imagined Katrina's plight.

Perhaps she, too, had coveted every detail of her family's deaths. The motivation for her father's visit, the cause of the escalation, the precise sequence of events. In Cassie's experience, at least, knowing everything was better than knowing nothing.

How would Katrina Rivers react if, eleven years later, she learned the truth? That her own brother had committed the crimes and was still alive. And that she'd never been told.

Cassie knew that it would unsettle her if even one detail of her own parents' death were to change: the street they were on, the make of the car that hit them. She'd have to piece it all back together. And if some crucial element was not as she'd believed—say, that the mistress had been driving and not the CEO—it would rattle her to her core.

Katrina learning the truth about her mother's murder would be more devastating than that.

Which presented an opportunity.

Cassie logged off Facebook, then back on. But not to her own page. Instead, she created a new profile. She filled in the most bare-bones profile information, choosing a random birthday making her twenty-four years old. It would all appear fake, but that was fine.

She didn't add a photo initially but then changed her mind. She uploaded Katrina's high school yearbook photo as the page's profile photo and changed the account name to "Katrina Rivers." And she altered the birthday, selecting the day eleven years earlier that Katrina's brother had killed her parents.

She opened the Facebook page of Kat Simmons. There she was, brimming with joy in front of that fountain near Seattle. So many posts, "likes," and comments dotted her page, including in recent days.

Surely, to keep that front going, she would be monitoring any messages sent to the fake account.

Cassie opened up Facebook's direct message function and typed a few words.

> Katrina, your brother killed your parents. And
> he is still alive today.

She hit "send."
Then one other jarring message occurred to her.

> And they've taken Razi Dallas to keep it
> secret.

CHAPTER 114

YOUNGSTOWN

Your friend stopped by. She was as nice as can be."

As they did every morning since her dad had come to, Tori and he had their morning check-in call. They'd been on the phone for a few minutes Tuesday morning when he mentioned the visit in passing. It sounded odd from the outset.

"What friend?"

"Tammy. You know, your old roommate. You'd mentioned her a bunch over the years."

Dad was right. Tammy Logan had been a roommate for her final two undergraduate years at Lawrence. She now lived near Green Bay, but they still kept up actively on social media to this day.

"Why didn't you call me?"

"We're talking now."

"I mean when she visited."

"It was just a short visit—"

As he answered, Tori opened her laptop and went to her direct messages. She scrolled through old messages, finding her last one to Tammy Logan. It was three months ago, wishing her a happy birthday.

"—and she said you asked her to check in on me, so there was no need to call. She brought me a whole care package and everything."

Tori typed below the birthday greeting: Hey there, Tammy.

"That's nice. And the cops let her in?" she asked her dad.

"Of course they did. An old family friend visiting? Why wouldn't they?"

Tori didn't want to alarm him, so she slowed the conversation.

"Dad, what did you guys talk about?"

"How my recovery was going. Her boys." Tammy had two sons. "The fun you guys used to have at school."

Her laptop sounded a quick beep as words appeared next to the pleasant face and dark brown hair of Tammy Logan. Tori! How are you?

"Anything else?" Tori asked her dad. "Did you talk about me?"

Good, she typed back to her friend. Where are you?

"Of course. She obviously wanted to know how you were and if we knew who had done this to me."

? Green Bay. Where else would I be?

"And what did you say?"

"Tori, slow down. I feel like I'm being cross-examined here. It was actually nice to have a visitor. Pretty one, too."

Pretty? Not something she'd expect her dad to say about Tammy.

Did you visit my dad today?

"Sorry, Dad, I just don't want to burden anyone else with our drama. What did you tell her?"

"That you and a reporter friend were in Youngstown trying to figure it all out."

Nausea gripped her stomach. She knew even before Tammy's message came back what her dad had done.

Your dad? No. Is something wrong?

CHAPTER 115

YOUNGSTOWN

'm really sorry, Jack."

We were at a diner down the street from the *Vindicator* when she told me the bad news.

"It's not your fault, Tori. Did your dad know what the woman looked like? Your friend, that is."

"Tammy? Yeah, he met her a few times at school. But that was a while ago."

"Can we look at her real quick?"

"Sure."

Tori hit a few keys on her computer, then turned it so we both saw the screen.

"There she is," she said, pointing to a picture of a mom and two young sons sitting in a park.

Tammy had brown hair that dropped past her shoulders and wore oversized glasses that took up much of the top half of her face.

"Whoever did this clearly went through your Facebook page. And to be safe, they would've assumed your dad had met her in person. So they must've chosen someone who Tammy bore some resemblance to."

"Right."

"Maybe Katrina Rivers herself. Or some new hired gun."

"True. So how do we figure it out?"

"I've got a way."

I logged back on to the website from the day before and typed the plane's tail number back in. My gut told me there'd be a new flight listed.

There were two.

I pushed the link to the first flight and a map opened up on my screen, a thin line tracing the Gulfstream's first journey. It had taken off from England early in the morning, crossed over the Atlantic and Canada, reentered the United States over Lake Michigan, and landed at an airport with the three-letter code MSN.

Dane County Regional Airport. Madison.

I looked up from my computer, rocking back and forth in my chair. "It's Katrina."

She'd landed so recently, I was surprised that another flight was even listed; maybe the pilots had dropped her off and flown home. So I clicked on the second link.

I was wrong.

The Gulfstream was at twenty-two thousand feet and climbing. Traveling east at 530 knots, it was back over Lake Michigan, about to cross Michigan's western shore.

And its path was clear.

Katrina Rivers was heading our way.

CHAPTER 116

OVER MICHIGAN

Even as the plane leveled out smoothly at thirty-nine thousand feet, Katrina's jaw stiffened.

The cabin monitor showed that they were east and north of Grand Rapids. Enough time to accomplish the worst task of her day.

In order to keep her alternative persona alive, Katrina spent fifteen minutes a day freshening up Kat Simmons's social media activity, spewing the type of facile drivel and insincerity she had spent her life avoiding. Adding a new post on Facebook and an occasional photo. Liking friends' photos or posts. Sharing an article. Sending or receiving direct messages. All mindless nonsense, but necessary.

There wasn't much activity from the day before. Her most recent photo of Mount Rainier had generated dozens of likes along with comments praising the picture. She responded: Not hard to make Mt. Rainier look good!!

A Senate staffer who surfed Facebook day and night had written a long response to her post about the upcoming elections. She wrote a two-sentence retort to keep him occupied. The more back-and-forth, the more real Kat appeared.

And she added a fresh post cheering on Speaker Paxton's recent tirade about the president's excessive spending. That would light things up for a few days, especially with any liberals left from her early Facebook years.

Three new messages appeared. Two came from Facebook friends whom she communicated with regularly. One was a lonely older women who lived vicariously through Kat's more exciting life. The other was a flirtatious twenty-something who still worked at the RNC. She replied to each.

Then there was a new "message request," sent from someone who was not currently a Facebook friend. Such requests appeared on a separate page and overwhelmingly contained spam, bots, and flirts from men trolling for women. Knowing that, Katrina rarely went to that page to accept new messages.

But the general message page helpfully included the first names of those who'd made requests. And the latest request came from someone named Katrina.

Curious, she clicked on the "message request" list to learn more.

CHAPTER 117

I-80, NEAR YOUNGSTOWN

B urke Lakefront?"

Billy Luna's voice blared through the car's speaker system. The longtime sports columnist for the *Cleveland Plain Dealer* was one of my better friends in journalism. We'd bonded through the decades over Cleveland sports, and he wielded an especially poisonous pen capturing all that misery. But now he was the only person I knew who could help quickly and who was street smart enough not to get himself killed.

"Yes, in fifteen minutes. Twenty at most."

I was racing west on I-80 at eighty-five miles per hour, Tori in the passenger seat. Having just passed the hulking skeleton of the old GM plant in Lordstown, we'd be there in fifty minutes if I didn't hit traffic. Not soon enough.

"I'm at the paper now, so I can get there on time. What am I looking for?"

After arriving at the *Vindicator*, I'd logged on to the website one last time. The Gulfstream's flight plan had been modified en route, rerouting to Burke instead of Youngstown.

"It's called a Gulfstream G650. Sleek plane, eight windows on each side. Its wings are extra-long and have outsized wingtips. Tail number will be G-M1M."

"That should do it."

"A tall woman. Long brown hair, likely dressed to the nines."

"Wow. Sounds nice. Is this some kind of long-distance stalking, Sharpe?" he asked, cackling.

Tori cringed.

"Uh, no, Billy. This is deadly serious."

"Chill, man. I get it. What do you need me to do?"

"See what car she gets into. Get the driver's license if possible."

"That's it? You want me to follow her?"

"Too dangerous. Plus, I'm pretty sure I know where she's going."

"Where's that?"

"The Clinic."

"Jack, I'm game to follow. I've got writer's block anyway."

CHAPTER 118

PRINCETON, NEW JERSEY

As Cassie cracked the door open, entered, and tiptoed up a few short stairs to the back, dozens of young eyes looked her way. Most gazed curiously from behind the curved desks that encircled the small auditorium. But one set of bleary eyes at the center of the room studied her longer, then widened.

Professor Miguel Mercurio knew exactly why she was there.

When Jack had informed her that the mystery plane with the British trail number had flown from Aspen to Trenton, New Jersey, she looked up a map of the Garden State. The small airport was only thirteen miles from the Princeton campus. If the professor had already met with the president several times, maybe he'd done so again.

His look of alarm confirmed Cassie's hunch.

She waited through the final minutes of the class as he lectured passionately about the growing monopolization of big tech. Like his book, his words were compelling, even if half the laptops in front of Cassie were logged on to Facebook or Instagram as he spoke. A bell rang and most of the kids rushed out the door Cassie had entered.

A few students lined up to talk to the professor as class let out, so Cassie waited behind them. After answering the last question, the professor hustled toward the door.

"Professor Mercurio, we need to talk."

"I've got to run to a meeting. I really don't have time." Blinking rapidly, he looked frazzled, his ease from their first meeting gone.

Cassie lunged forward four quick steps, maneuvering between him and the door.

"Professor, I need five minutes. I'll walk with you to your meeting."

"Okay, but I can't say much."

"You were in Aspen again this weekend, weren't you?" Cassie asked as they walked down the steps to the first floor.

"Now, how would you know that?"

"You landed Sunday evening at the Trenton airport on a private flight from Aspen."

He stopped abruptly, then glared at her.

"What the hell? Why are you—"

"Why are *you* flying to Aspen in mysterious planes? And why the secrecy? From what I can gather, you flew out Friday on a charter, then back on a fancy Gulfstream owned by some British guy."

"British? I wasn't with anyone British."

Even better. He had just conceded a lot.

"Well, a British-registered plane."

"I don't know what you're talking about." The catch in his voice underscored the lie.

"Listen, you already told me you've advised the president on economic policy, both during the campaign and after. The fact that you were doing so over the weekend should not be a state secret. In fact, it has enormous national implications."

Reaching the building's main entrance, he pushed open the thick wooden door, sighing as he let Cassie pass through.

"Look, are we off the record?"

"Sure."

"She wanted to talk through my recommendations one last time. You're right: What's the big deal in that?"

"Nothing. Except that she's doing it in secret."

"It definitely is hush-hush. But it's urgent that my ideas happen, so I play by the rules I'm given."

"And who else joined you out there? Who flew you back?"

"What do you mean?" The strain in his voice returned.

"Don't play coy. As I said, a plane flew you out from New Jersey Friday, and another flew you back Sunday. What British Gulfstream owner did you hitch a ride home with?"

"Listen, I really can't get into that."

"Why not?"

"He's a major recent benefactor to this place . . . to my work here. But he insists on anonymity. If his name got out, my funding would go belly-up. And it's not like there are a bunch of billionaires eager to bank-roll research on breaking up the monopolies that made them billionaires in the first place. In fact, some of the school's biggest donors have pulled funding because of my work."

"Did this benefactor attend the meeting with the president?"

The professor chuckled uncomfortably. "Someone of his means is not going to wait in the hallway, that's for sure."

Cassie's mind raced as they walked down an elegant bluestone walk-way between two manicured lawns. She'd pursued the Aspen story to keep her bosses happy, always treating it separately from Jack's story. But Jack's latest theory was that a foreign cartel was attempting to seize the vast economic opportunities that would arise from breaking up Ameri-ca's monopolies. And here some foreigner was flying to Aspen to meet with the president, accompanied by an antitrust expert whose work he was funding. Did it all connect up?

"Young lady, I appreciate your persistence, but I've got to run." Mer-curio loped away on a perpendicular walkway.

Cassie suddenly remembered Katrina's yearbook: Dyadya. Russian for Uncle.

"Professor?" she asked, jogging four quick steps to pass him before wheeling around to face him. "Your benefactor is Russian, isn't he?"

His eyes blazed as he heard the question, answering it without saying a word.

CHAPTER 119

I-80, NEAR AKRON

assie called when I was halfway across Portage County, forty-five minutes from Cleveland.

"Jack, you're not gonna believe this, but that plane from New Jersey may have belonged to Katrina's uncle. I think he met with the president over the weekend."

I cracked the car's window a few inches, claustrophobia setting in as Cassie edged closer to my Kazarov secret.

"What makes you say that?"

"Remember that Princeton professor? The one who wrote about monopolies I talked to? He was on the flight. He had been in Aspen with some anonymous benefactor, meeting with the president."

"How do you know that? And how does that have anything to do with Katrina?"

"I pushed him hard and he more or less gave away that the benefactor was Russian."

"Pushed him?"

"Yeah. I'm at Princeton now. I took the train up and confronted him in person after his class."

She was good. "Cassie, 'more or less gave away' sounds flimsy to me."

"Well, my gut says that's exactly who he was with. And you know what that means? That our two stories are tied together—and that the president is connected to the plot to rig these elections."

"That's a pretty wild theory. It will take a boatload of proof to convince my editors to print that. Did the professor tell you what they discussed?"

"Yeah. The president is really interested in the details of his work."

"What work?"

"His proposal to set hard industry limits on corporate concentration. Apparently they were reviewing the specifics at the meeting."

My mind shuddered. Kazarov was discussing with the president of the United States the exact policy that would result if his operation succeeded. But that begged the question: What the hell was the president doing?

"Cassie, she's always been passionate about this anti-monopoly stuff. I'm unemployed because of it."

"Jack, if I'm right, this means she's in on the plot that you guys have uncovered."

"And if you're wrong, she's merely consulting with an academic expert about a critical economic issue."

Cassie sighed through the phone, frustrated by my roadblocks.

"Jack, there's one other development."

"What's that?"

She filled me in on the Brooklyn detective's visit and how Katrina was under the wrong impression about her mother's death.

I shivered at her words. Kazarov was capable of terrible things, but why would he lie to his own niece about her mother's murder?

"Jack, I messaged her."

"You did *what*? What the hell did you tell her?"

"The truth. I figured it might shake her up—maybe throw a wrench in this whole plot."

I recalled the diverted flight path. The Gulfstream heading to Youngstown, then suddenly rerouting south to Cleveland. Katrina's urgency to nab us had been replaced by a higher priority.

Now that priority was clear.

"Cassie, I've got to go. I'll call you back."

After hanging up, I dug up the old number for Oleg Kazarov and sent him a text.

CHAPTER 120

CLEVELAND

S tay here. I will be an hour."

Katrina opened the rear passenger door of the black Mercedes SUV and planted her black stiletto on the wet sidewalk. She walked several yards through a light drizzle and entered the nondescript building on the busy street east of downtown Cleveland.

Minutes later the wide silver elevator door closed behind her, the first time she'd been alone since she read the message.

As the elevator lifted, she clenched her eyes shut and took a deep breath. Her entire body trembled.

The sender not only knew her real name but was taunting her by using it as a Facebook profile. But it was the yearbook photo itself that packed the most jarring punch. She hadn't seen it in years. How young she looked. How innocent. The pale skin, the thin gray lips, the inelegant way her hair was pulled back. All the long-buried emotions of her young life were now rushing back in a torrent.

She'd been so complicated at that vulnerable age. Confident in her intellect and committed to making the world a more just place after the poverty and hunger of her childhood. But too quiet to make friends or attract boys. Too shy to show people the passion that burned inside her. And always mortified by her doting mother, embracing her so tightly, she couldn't breathe.

She wasn't sufficiently self-aware back then to see it. But now she could. That yearbook photo captured perfectly the mix of emotions buffeting young Katrina Rivers.

And then she'd read the message.

> Katrina, your brother killed your parents. And
> he is still alive today.

Dizziness had swamped her as the horror of the worst ten minutes of her life returned.

The two phone calls.

First was the Brooklyn detective. Kozlov—a name she recalled to this day, along with every word he'd shared in the first-generation accent so common in Brighton Beach. He'd encouraged her to sit down, so she sat on the small futon in her Oxford dorm room. Then he explained that her father had forced his way into her mother's house, an argument had erupted into violence, and that he'd killed both her mother and Mikhail before taking his own life.

Beyond the sheer horror, overwhelming guilt besieged her that day and for years to come. Her mother and father, never legally divorced, had first spoken again that spring. And she'd been skeptical. But her mother assured her he'd become a different man—sober and modestly successful, loving and fun, as he'd been when they were teenagers in St. Petersburg.

Katrina had kept her doubts to herself. Her mother had been so lonely, which was why she'd spent most days of her life smothering Katrina. Maybe a reunion with her father would be a healthy thing, for both mother and daughter. So she said nothing. And now they were all dead.

She was still planted on the futon, in shock, when the second call had come through. Dyadya. He shared the same news but added the wrinkle that her father had had well-known mob ties. There'd be no funeral and no obituary in the local papers.

"This was an attempt to get at me, I'm afraid," he had warned her. "And they may try to get to you as well."

A ping sounded. Katrina opened her eyes as the elevator doors separated, then took a step forward.

"Excuse me." A gray-haired woman in blue nurse scrubs wheeled an empty cot into the elevator, the cot's front corner almost colliding with Katrina. The nurse pushed the button for the eighth floor.

Confused, Katrina looked up. They were only on the sixth floor. She was going to the twelfth.

Lips pursed, still shaking, she took three steps back to the rear corner of the elevator, positioning herself behind the nurse as they both faced forward. The elevator jumped a few inches, then continued its climb.

Dyadya had always been supportive from afar. He'd visit for a few weeks each year, and she and Mikhail would visit his St. Petersburg dacha for a week every summer. But Mother had insisted that be the extent of it—that, despite his generosity, they should not become too close. And she'd cautioned Katrina not to let his largesse spoil her.

But all that changed after the murders. Dyadya had kept a close watch on her. "We must keep you safe," he urged. Feeling vulnerable and scared, she acceded. Without family left, where else would she have turned?

Another ping. They stopped on the eighth floor, and the nurse pushed the cot out of the widening elevator doors as quickly as she'd wheeled it in. The doors closed and the elevator lifted again.

She mouthed the words to herself: *Katrina, your brother killed your parents. And he is still alive today.*

She'd stared at them for minutes. Although the plane's cabin was empty, the pilots could see her through a small cockpit monitor, so she hadn't moved.

The short, crisp sentences declared the news with authority. Not a word wasted. Not a doubt projected—neither about the earth-shattering claim nor about the sender's underlying assumption that Katrina didn't know.

And then she'd scanned the sender's profile page. Bare except for the photo and the birth date—the day of the murders. Again, a detail nobody else knew. That was when she knocked on the cockpit door and requested they divert to Cleveland instead of landing in Youngstown. The Youngstown reporter and Victoria Justice could wait.

She closed her eyes again.

If the words were true, it meant Dyadya had lied to her. On the phone call eleven years earlier and every day since, including the annual check-in call on the anniversary of the murders. It meant the entire trajectory of her life since the murders had been based on a lie.

A final ping sounded in her ear as the elevator came to a stop on the twelfth and top floor, the wing housing the hospital's most elite patients. A walk-through metal detector greeted her beyond the elevator doors, a beefy security guard sitting behind a desk to her right.

"Hey there, young lady." His salt-and-pepper eyebrows danced up and down with feigned flirtation. "Who's the lucky guy?"

She glowered back.

"I'm here to visit Oleg Kazarov. He's expecting me."

CHAPTER 121

CLEVELAND

Y ou weren't kidding, Jack," Billy Luna said with enthusiasm. "That was one vixen of a woman, and she sure travels in style."

"Did she go to the clinic?" I asked, ignoring his gawking.

"Close. She got out down the street from the Clinic and walked into some bland building. Then the Mercedes SUV she rode in parked a few blocks away."

We were now only fifteen minutes from the Cleveland Clinic's east side campus.

"It's probably an annex or something." No doubt they kept their foreign VIP wing unit disguised.

After hanging up, I turned to Tori. "It looks like she's visiting her uncle."

But I kept to myself what that meant.

CHAPTER 122

Welcome, Katyusha."

Dyadya's whispered greeting, using her childhood nickname, was so faint she had to bow forward to hear him.

Lying back in the propped-up bed, crisscrossed by a jumble of wires and tubes, he was in worse shape than he'd let on. A white blanket covered him up to his waist and a light blue smock covered the rest, up to his emaciated, wrinkled neck. Two thin white bands encircled his head, holding a translucent mask over his nose. A tube ran from the mask to a toaster-sized machine to his left. With each breath he took, a whoosh, followed by two light thumps, echoed from the machine.

But the most jarring sight of all were his eyes. Usually bright with fire, they were now a dull, smoky yellow, laced with spiderwebs of crimson red. Exhausted. Defeated.

She pulled a small chair close to his bedside, sat down, and placed her hand over his. His fingers felt as thin as pencils, his skin cold and flaky.

"Dyadya, you should not have made that trip. The doctor said you have a serious infection."

"They are confident I will recover, and it was too important to miss," he whispered. He swallowed, then took a breath, the sound magnified by another whoosh from the bedside device. "We now know the exact policy that will be implemented."

Focus on his eyes, Katrina told herself. *Stifle any satisfaction.*

As the syndicate partners acquired assets in anticipation of the new law, they needed to stay below the thresholds. But how big was too big? Thanks to Dyadya's trip, they would now know.

On the bed's other side, his thin, hairless left arm rose inches above the blanket, a spindly index finger pointing across the room. Another whoosh sounded as he drew a long breath.

"Over there. That file has all the information we will need."

A thin manila folder sat by itself on a mahogany desktop. The final ground rules. Two or three pages that would shape a decade of American economics, guiding the syndicate to billions.

She stood up, stepped to the desk to retrieve the file, then sat back in the chair. The hand that had previously touched his now gripped the file at her side. She leaned over the bed and looked directly into his eyes, her cheeks burning.

"Dyadya, why did you lie to me?"

The rhythm from the machine sped up for a few breaths. His veiny eyelids rolled slowly down, held for a moment, then lifted back up. He knew why she was there.

"Because I believed it was best."

"I have spent eleven years alone."

"Have I not been here for you all that time?"

"I have always been thankful. But Mikhail is my own brother."

"And he needed my help as well."

"Why?"

"Katrina, have I not helped you when you needed it?"

"But he killed his own mother. *My* mother."

His eyes swelled, revealing even more intense redness at their edges. The rhythmic breaths from the machine quickened.

"Is that what they have told you?" Another breath. "Mikhail found your father standing over her. So he killed him, then called for help."

Katrina stared at him blankly. He spoke firmly, but the words in the message had been so clear.

"Father was coming back into her life. *Our* lives. They were happy. *Mother* was happy. Why would he kill her?"

"He was their pawn. They wanted my money and I refused. Killing Sophia was their punishment."

"Then why keep Mikhail a secret all this time?"

"The less you knew, the better for you both. The fewer people who knew he was alive, the better."

Her head throbbed. Dyadya was saying what he needed to say, and she had no grounds to rebut it. But the message rung in her ear. Beyond its words, the sender knew the day of the deaths. And the tie to Razi Dallas. No one back home had known she'd had a relationship in England, let alone with whom. But the sender knew.

"So where is he now?"

He drew three short gasps without answering.

"Dyadya, where is he now?"

Another breath. "Brooklyn."

"What does he do there?"

One breath, then another, echoed by the machine. "He runs some businesses."

"What types of businesses?"

"A variety."

"And how is he safe?"

Four breaths followed. Deeper than any thus far. He did not like this question.

She was getting closer. When healthy, Dyadya hid every emotion. He lied without detection. Unlike most, he didn't sweat, alter his breathing pattern, change the tone of his voice, or look askance. But his weakened lungs and the oxygen machine were exposing him like a lie detector, flagging moments of dishonesty or unease.

"What do you mean?"

"If he is now running businesses in Brooklyn, how is he safe when he was not safe eleven years ago?"

Rage enveloped her, her arms and legs trembling.

Two deep breaths.

"We came to an arrangement."

It made no sense.

"I would like to talk to him."

"But, Katrina, it has been so long."

Whoosh. The machine echoed his discomfort. *Whoosh.*

"Yes, it has. Which is why I must talk to him."

He sighed, reaching for his phone. His spindly finger touched the screen several times, then he held the phone up. The screen displayed a number beginning with the digits 917—the only area code she'd known before setting foot on the Princeton campus.

Below it, the name "Mikhail" appeared. The brother she had thought was dead.

Her legs fell limp, forcing her to sit back in the small chair. Every emotion that had coursed through her on that futon eleven years ago surged back.

"Katrina? Is that really you? It has been so long." His voice was a deep baritone, much lower than before.

"It is."

She paused.

In the seconds it had taken her to dial, memories of a young Mikhail flashed in her head—details she had blocked out for eleven years and that the photo in her London drawer didn't capture. Unlike her, Mikhail had always run with the troublemakers, in school before being expelled and even more so on the streets. Three times in the year before she died, Mother had been forced to get him out of jail—for stealing, selling pills, and destroying an old man's jaw. The skulls tattooed to his knuckles had caused loud arguments with Mother; she'd been around the neighborhood long enough to know what they symbolized.

When Dyadya mentioned businesses, Katrina imagined the type of mayhem her brother, fully grown-up, was causing. She also recalled the second part of the message.

They've taken Razi Dallas to keep it a secret.

She had never said a word about Razi Dallas to anyone. Not to her mother, who would have worried. Not to her *dyadya*, who would have pushed him away. Not to Mikhail, whom she hadn't communicated with about such things. Only her Oxford roommate had known they'd been growing close.

How the sender had learned the name was a mystery. But it reinforced the message's credibility. The sender must have tracked Razi down. And, knowing Razi, he must have started asking questions back in Brooklyn.

"Please release him at once. He has nothing to do with any of this."

Dyadya took his most strained gasps yet, staring at her as she spoke.

The deep voice on the phone replied. "Katrina, I'm confused. Who are you talking about? *What* are you talking about?"

"Mikhail, I have no time to waste. Release him. He knows nothing. He is not a threat."

CHAPTER 123

CLEVELAND

Whoa, sir. Slow down!"

The security guard lifted his hand like a crossing guard as I raced out of the elevator, stopping me inches short of the metal detector. "Who ya visiting?"

"A patient named Oleg Kazarov."

"Say the name again?"

"Oleg Kazarov. He's Russian."

"Does he expect you?

"He does. My name is Jack Sharpe."

I spoke quickly, hoping to spark some urgency. Dominoes were falling quickly. The rerouting of the plane in mid-flight meant that Cassie's message had packed a punch.

But the guard didn't catch my cue, studying the list in front of him for a good twenty seconds. "Ah, there you are. Mr. Sharpe. He's in room 1206. Please sign the sheet."

I scribbled my name quickly. Directly above my signature, shaky cursive letters spelled out the name Kat Simmons, who'd signed in twenty-two minutes before. That was more than enough time.

"Is Kat still in there?" I asked casually, as if she and I were old friends.

"She must be. She hasn't signed out yet, has she?"

"Doesn't look like it."

"Trust me, I would've noticed if she'd walked by."

I stepped through the metal detector, which beeped immediately. Another damn delay.

"You have any metal on you?"

I stepped back through the machine, patted my pants pockets, which were empty, then reached into the pockets of my gray fleece jacket, where I found the culprits.

"Here you go." He placed my wallet and keys in a small plastic tray as I stepped through again.

Another beep stopped me.

"Must be something else," the guard said casually.

"Sir, I'm in a big hur—"

"Do you think I care about your damn hurry? We've got world-class clientele here, so this floor's gotta be secure."

I lifted my right hand in the air. "I have a steel rod in my arm. That's got to be it."

His face lit up. "Why didn't you say so? I've got one, too. Take a step forward."

He stepped around the desk holding the same wand as the Kelleys Island Police Department. He waved it up and down, front and back. Nothing beeped until he held it near my right arm.

"You're good to go, buddy. Here's your stuff."

I jogged down the hallway, jamming my keys and wallet back into my jacket pocket.

The first door I passed displayed the number 1200 in large numerals. The VIP rooms were far apart, so it took me seconds to reach the next door, 1201, again on the left. Jogging faster, I passed 1202 and 1203.

Farther ahead, two nurses scampered from right to left across the hallway.

I was closing in on 1205 when a hand shoved me in my lower back, pushing me to the right. A short man in a white lab coat tore past, then disappeared to the left where the nurses had gone. I arrived seconds later, cutting into the same doorway.

Room 1206.

A yell pierced through the cacophony of noises. "All set!"

The young nurse with a deep tan then whirled my way, holding up two white handles attached to inch-thick pads, spiral cords curling out of each. Defibrillator paddles.

The man who'd run past me ripped the paddles from her hands, kicked a small chair out of the way, and leaned over the bed from its left side. He plunged the paddles into the chest of the brittle, hairless man lying on the bed. Most of his features were lost in his sickly condition, but the Russian mogul's sharp, pointy nose was unmistakable.

"Clear!"

A high-pitched tone whistled throughout the room, followed by three quick beeps. The doctor's arms tensed before a low, violent thud sent the patient's gaunt upper body into a violent convulsion.

The nurse who'd passed the paddles to the doctor now noticed me. "You need to get out of here now."

"I'm an old friend." I said it loud enough so that he'd hear me if he could hear at all. But his eyes remained sealed. "Did you see where the woman went?"

That's when I noticed a different set of beeps, recurring so quickly they almost ran together.

"Clear!" the doctor yelled. The woman ignored me and whirled back toward the bed.

The high-pitched whistle returned, then three quick beeps, then the thud and the convulsion.

"How the hell is he in cardiac arrest?" the doctor asked. "That makes no sense."

"I have no idea," the nurse said back.

My phone vibrated as a text came through.

Billy Luna.

> She got back in the Mercedes. Should I follow her?

What was he going to do, barricade her from boarding her own plane? He'd get himself killed.

> No need.

"Clear!" the doctor yelled. Whistle, three beeps, thud.

The second set of beeps, the short staccato ones, now ran together even faster. Kazarov's heart was beating at breakneck speed.

"We're losing him!" the doctor shouted.

A second text came through.

Tori.

> Katrina got into a Mercedes and drove off. I'm
> right behind her.

"Clear!" Whistle, three beeps, thud.

The rapid-fire beeps ended, replaced by a sound I'd heard many times in movies and three times in person: the uninterrupted tone of a person whose heart had stopped.

CHAPTER 124

CLEVELAND

The danger was obvious. No doubt that was why Jack had called twice in five minutes.

But Tori also could not erase the image of her dad's purple, puffed-up eyelids or the bandages wrapped around the rest of his head. Clearly the woman in the Mercedes, Katrina or Kat or whatever her name was, had ordered that monster to cut her dad's ear off. And then she'd had the nerve to visit him this morning and pretend to be close to the family.

Watching her climb into the Mercedes SUV up close—tall and stylish and beautiful—sent Tori's pulse rocketing. A woman with everything, torturing an old dairy farmer. She couldn't let her get away.

Driving Jack's Escape, she followed the Mercedes along a crowded boulevard. They headed west toward the hodgepodge of old buildings and towers dotting downtown Cleveland, looking like the real-life version of Gotham City.

The practice from Madison was paying off. She kept her distance, never getting closer than three car lengths, but never getting caught at one of many red lights, either.

She didn't want Jack to talk her out of following. But she'd also need his help if she was going to stop Katrina. So she texted him again.

Meet me at the airport.

CHAPTER 125

Like an ice pick through yogurt, the needle had plunged smoothly into Dyadya's lifeless skin. In the car's back seat, Katrina shivered as she relived it.

"Ma'am."

The copilot, who doubled as her driver, was saying something, but his words were rendered inaudible by the echoes of Dyadya's labored breathing and Mikhail's baritone voice.

Amid a maelstrom of emotions, rage dominated.

No one, not even Dyadya, talked to her the way Mikhail had just done. Not for years, at least. As if she were still the naïve sister she'd been back in Brooklyn, laughing away his troublemaking because she didn't want to confront it. He had been a bullshit artist throughout his teenage years—the way he'd explained away the tattoos, or the missing money, or how he'd wrecked her car. Both mother and sister had seen through the lies then but let them go. And with his supposed death, like a time capsule, Katrina buried those less flattering memories deep within.

During the phone call, his voice was deeper than in those teenage days, but the cagey tone was the same. He was clearly lying about not knowing where Razi Dallas was. He was lying about Mother's death, echoing the fairy tale Dyadya had tried to sell. And he and Dyadya had lied about why they'd kept it a secret all that time. Mikhail's voice revealed the lies, while Dyadya's strained breathing confirmed them.

Eleven years of lying meant one thing.

"Excuse me, ma'am."

She glanced back at her phone.

> Katrina, your brother killed your parents. And
> he is still alive today.

Unlike her family members, the message bore all the trappings of truth. She had done the right thing.

"Ma'am."

"Yes."

"A car has been following us for five or six blocks."

She looked out the back window.

"Are you sure?"

"Yes. It's three cars behind us as we speak."

"The Ford Escape?"

"Yes."

"Did you see the driver?"

"A few lights ago. A skinny woman with black hair."

Victoria Justice.

Katrina glanced at the folder that lay under her right hand. Dyadya was dead, but that folder meant the cartel was very much alive. *Her* cartel now. And the one woman who had the power to end it all, whom they'd spent weeks trying to kill, now tailed only three car lengths behind them.

"Do you have a gun on you?"

"Of course."

CHAPTER 126

CLEVELAND

The SUV cut the corner at the last possible moment.

After the two cars in front drove on nonchalantly, Tori pumped the brakes and followed the Mercedes onto the side street, just as the SUV's back bumper disappeared around the next corner, tires squealing. Tori navigated a minefield of potholes before turning right at the same intersection. The new side street was considerably narrower and devoid of traffic—including the SUV. Small, single-story homes with tiny fenced-in yards followed one after the next, many posting "Beware of Dog" signs. Parked cars lined the little street, making the drive back to the boulevard a tight squeeze.

She sent Jack another text.

They turned off Euclid onto a side street.

She slowed halfway down the road. Four car lengths ahead, prominent amid a row of run-down, rusty beaters, the Mercedes SUV sat parallel parked next to a squat gray home with boarded-up windows and two-foot-high weeds.

As Tori closed to within a car length, she braked further, inching along to peer at the lifeless car. The engine was off and the thick head of the driver was gone, as was any sign of the woman in the back.

She pulled even, then shifted to neutral and lifted herself high in her seat to get the best view into the car. The dark leather seats were spotless with the exception of a manila folder on the far end of the back seat.

A deep, ferocious bark from behind jolted her almost to the ceiling. She whirled around.

The black barrel of a gun was pointing at the window. She spun away and threw her hands over the back of her head, hoping they'd slow or divert the bullet from her skull.

A deafening bang exploded in her ear, followed by the jingling of glass shards around her. She moved her hands around, searching for a head wound, but found nothing. A thick arm reached around her neck and wrenched her against the car door.

Then a cylinder pressed hard against her right temple. It was cold, meaning the gun hadn't fired; the blast must've been the sound of the gun shattering the window.

"Do not move or I pull the trigger," a gruff voice said in a foreign accent.

Quivering, she took a deep breath, relieved to be alive.

Strapped tightly to the back seat of the SUV, Tori could see trickles of blood accumulating on the white towel curled around the back of her neck and over her shoulders. The flying glass had clearly inflicted dozens of small lacerations. But it was the jagged shards from when the driver had pulled her against the broken window that had done much deeper damage. While she could make out the precise sting of the largest cuts, the collective effect was worse: the back of her head, neck, shoulders, and upper back felt like they were on fire.

The rapid drumbeat of her heart pounded in her ears as sharp, raspy breaths pumped out from her lungs.

Her eyes teared up, blurring her vision.

She thought of the picture of Ned a few weeks back. Tied up in the back seat. Bleeding. Terrorized. She imagined she looked the same.

The tall buildings of downtown Cleveland towered in front of them. Like Ned, she was running out of time.

She closed her eyes.

Focus.

Jack had remained calm at even the worst moments. What was it he'd said? "Make it hard for them." She needed to do that now. As scared as she was, she had to look strong.

She took a hard swallow to steady her breaths, then turned to her left.

"What are you doing?" Tori asked, narrowing her eyes to bring the woman next to her into focus.

"Excuse me?"

The way her legs were stretched out under the driver's seat, she looked to be about Tori's height, a rarity. Still, on a rugby field, she'd be an easy takedown. Too skinny, little muscle.

"You're Katrina, right?" Tori asked, muzzling her fear with a frigid tone.

"Yes," she said, facing her for the first time.

Katrina's striking appearance threw Tori off. Emerald eyes. Long, glossy brown hair. A thin, pretty nose. Her eyes were puffy, and dark eye shadow traced down the sides of her cheek; she'd been crying. The gleam from the mild welling made them even more arresting.

Tori fixed on the damp eyes. Something had upset this cold-blooded killer.

Then Tori remembered Cassie and Jack's conversation as they'd raced to Cleveland. Katrina's parents had been murdered. She'd been lied to by her uncle. Cassie had just messaged her the truth.

"Katrina," she said, "what are you doing?"

Katrina's wavy hair bobbed as the car bounced through a few potholes before stopping at a red light, their third in the last five minutes. They were entering downtown.

"Making you disappear."

Goose bumps rose along Tori's long arms. She quickly flexed to subdue them.

"Oh, I assumed that. But what are you doing beyond that?" Her voice cracked slightly, so she took a deep breath to shore it up. "We know all about your uncle, and your parents, and the lies you've been told since they were murdered. I'd be devastated, too. But doing more harm, piling up more bodies, won't fix any of that. And stealing elections won't fix it, either."

Katrina shuddered, her cheeks turning red.

"Don't you dare." She looked right at Tori. "You don't know me or what I've been through. And you don't understand what I'm doing now. I'm trying to make the world better."

"By killing and torturing people?"

"No one knows better than your father. So many people have had no chance at success because of the larger forces at work in this country. Our plan will—"

"You cut my dad's ear off! You almost killed him. Others have been murdered in cold blood. Look at my neck and all this blood. If your uncle has convinced you that all that violence is making the world better, he lied to you. Again."

Katrina ground her jaw, her temples flaring. They stopped at another light, seconds of silence passing.

"I have bad news for you," Tori said, piling on. "The story's getting out. Too many people already know about your plan. Newspapers. TV stations. It's over."

Katrina smirked as the Mercedes veered right, cutting through a cavern of skyscrapers toward the lake.

"Which is why it was so helpful that you offered yourself up to us. I don't plan on killing you right away. But we'll hold you long enough to keep your friend from running his story."

Tori shook her head. Her neck was numb now, while the tension in her muscles had eased. She was gaining confidence as Katrina appeared less certain of herself.

"My friend?" Tori asked.

"Yes. The reporter who's been helping you."

"Oh." As scared as she was, she forced out a chuckle. "He's the least of your worries. It's gone way beyond him. The message you got? That's another reporter. She also knows who you are, who your uncle is, and the whole plan, including how you got into the parties. Her station's one of those big monopolies you're so concerned about—and they know running the story crushes your plan and protects their business. They wouldn't even know my name and could care less what my friend thinks. They'll be running the story no matter what and no matter what you do to me."

Katrina shifted in her seat, doubt creeping across her face.

It was working. Tori drew another deep breath, slowing her whirring mind so she could remember the states where early voting was under way. The more details she piled on, the more credible her case.

"Ohio, Michigan, Wisconsin, Florida. They know exactly where it's happening, and exactly how you're meddling: targeting the sporadic voters, mislabeling the undecideds, eliminating some from the file completely. They know all of it, and nothing you do to me will change that."

Katrina said nothing, facing forward again.

"It's over."

CHAPTER 127

CLEVELAND

She came out of the fancy terminal down there," Billy Luna said, one hand pointing, the other on the wheel. "Number four."

"Let's get there quick." After having sent a number of texts, Tori had gone dark. Not a good sign. But from a distance, no planes had taken off. This was going to be close.

We'd wasted ten minutes searching for where she'd turned off, then hit every other red light on the drive downtown. Now we were racing along a long two-lane road squeezed between the highway and the lake. We sped by an old submarine, then past the small public airport terminal. Billy cornered quickly into the next driveway after that, for terminal four.

"Shit," he yelled out, slamming on the brakes, plunging my chest and shoulders violently into my seat belt. We stopped inches short of a tall metal gate blocking the driveway,

Billy reversed quickly to come within a foot of a small box with a speaker. There was a keypad as well as a large black button, but no instructions. Billy lowered his window and pushed the button.

A high-pitched man's voice came through the speaker. "May I help you?"

I leaned toward Billy's open window and hollered. "I'm with Windsor Castle LLC. We need to get to our Gulfstream right away. G-M1M. My boss, Katrina Rivers, left something back at the office, and she needs it before taking off."

Enough detail to convince them I was legit.

"Nice equipment." He giggled. "Both the plane and your boss. What'd you say the company was called?"

"Windsor Castle LLC. And we need to drive right to the plane."

Seconds passed.

A loud click was followed by the clanging of a chain as the fence rolled to the right.

Billy floored it, and a gate fifty yards in front of us rolled open as well. We hit the second entrance at twenty-five miles per hour.

Billy guffawed in celebration. "I can't believe they're letting us go right to—"

It started out as a low buzz, then grew loud, quickly, becoming a deep and violent roar—the unmistakable sound of a jet engine taking off. The intensity of it shook the car as we cleared the second gate and drove onto the edge of the tarmac, an array of prop planes and jets in front of us.

The gray Gulfstream shot above the private terminal's tall hangar, screaming from right to left at a steep angle. Despite its speed, the number on its tail was easy to read: G-M1M.

The roar faded as the plane banked right and ascended over the lake, two gray contrails spiraling behind.

"Shit," I mumbled, watching it disappear. If Tori was alive at all, she was undoubtedly inside.

"I'm sorry, Jack."

We sat in silence. As Billy turned the car around, I rang Tori, only to get voice mail. I sent her several texts.

No response.

I swallowed hard to stifle the nausea rising from my stomach up into my throat. Although I faced forward, the terminal building and the lake and the sky all blurred, replaced by a sharper image of Tori's blue eyes stunning me into silence in the booth back at Bad Apples.

"Hey, there's the car." Billy pointed to a row of cars in front of the hangar, a sleek black Mercedes SUV on the far left. He drove over and parked behind it.

A sticker on the rear windshield indicated it was some kind of elite rental service. The car was unlocked, its keys lying in the driver's seat, so we were able to inspect both the inside and outside. The seats were bare, and the floorboards and black leather upholstery initially appeared spotless, although indentations on both ends of the back seat made it clear both Katrina and Tori had been sitting back there.

Searching the front seat, Billy yelped.

"Shit! There's blood on the steering wheel."

He flipped his right hand in the air, a thin coat of red fluid on his second and third fingers.

"Just a little?" My lip quivered as I forced a smile. "This girl wouldn't go down without a fight."

But his find led me to examine the back seat more closely. And that's when I spotted them, initially masked by the dark leather. Speckles of blood were spattered across the top of the right side of the seat. Some tiny splotches, but some bigger drops, too.

Right where Tori's neck would have been.

CHAPTER 128

CLEVELAND

Jack, it happened again."

Cassie called as we were crossing and recrossing side streets halfway back to the Clinic, searching for my car. There were only a few places they could have nabbed her without being spotted.

"What happened?" I asked, staying mum on the drama we'd been through.

"They're censoring me. It's clearly coming from Corporate. Bridget Turner and Massa aren't even comfortable with it."

"But why would they cut your Aspen story? It's the president's scandal."

"Oh, they're running it all right. They're gonna make a huge deal out of it. The corporate lobbying. The meeting of foreign governments. And the big donors."

"There you go."

"But they refuse to mention the meeting with the professor or the Russian."

I shook my head, smirking. "Let me guess: too much monopoly talk?"

"They didn't say that, but of course."

"Awful."

"I feel sick about it. What should I do?"

I stewed, reliving my turbulent journey since July Fourth.

"I know it's frustrating, but it's a hell of a story either way. Just go with what they'll run. I've got the monopoly story covered. It'll get it out."

My phone buzzed with another call. The *Vindicator* line. I put Cassie on hold and bounced over.

"Jack, it's Mary."

"I'm on another call, Mary. Can I call you ba—"

"Jack, I got a call from Cleveland police. It's about that girl Tori you were working with."

With an empty Cleveland Browns stadium looming to our right and a long blue warehouse on our left, we sped to the end of the pier, then veered left. Two black-and-white squad cars and an all-black SUV, lights flashing, awaited us at the pier's other corner.

Once Billy stopped the car, I jumped out and sprinted to a burly cop with a crew cut standing in front of the SUV.

"Where is she, Officer?"

"A driver found her tied up inside that door over th—"

"Where is she?"

"Hey, buddy, chill, will ya? She's right over here."

He ushered me to the back of the SUV. As we got close, the back passenger's right door burst open.

"Jack!" Tori leapt up from the back seat, throwing her arms around me in a tight hug, her sinewy bicepses and forearms bracing my neck and back. As firm as her grip was, her entire body was shaking.

"Thank God you're alive. And not on that plane."

"You're telling me. And that's where I was headed until the last second."

She loosened her embrace.

"How'd you get them to let you go?"

She took a small step back, smiling as her misted blue eyes beamed.

"I told her Republic was a heartless, horrible place and could care less if either you or I were dead or alive. They'd run the story regardless."

I chuckled. "You never change, do you?"

Her eyes seemed to ask a question.

"From the moment we first met, you've done nothing but tell the absolute, unvarnished, and entire truth. That's the only reason we're about to save this election. And it just saved your life."

CHAPTER 129

WASHINGTON, D.C.

t's been too long, Jack. I'm sorry about what happened with Republic."

I sat up straight in the ornate chair, shoulders back, chest out.

"Thank you, Madam President. I prefer newspapers anyway."

"Me, too. Although I hate seeing them all get bought up and down-sized by those corporate raiders."

She knew me too well.

"Trust me, I feel the same way."

Days after Cleveland, Cassie and I were seated in the White House's Vermeil Room, in the same chairs where she'd taped her interview a month ago. We'd briefed the presidential press shop on our stories, and they'd agreed to have the president do a joint interview on background.

She looked over at Cassie, who was as gussied up as I'd ever seen. "Boy, your producers did a number on our last chat, didn't they."

"I'm sorry about that. It wasn't fair to you."

"Or you."

Cassie flashed a half smile. This president still knew how to charm.

For most of our hour, I pushed hard. But, as always, she had an answer for everything, including Kazarov.

"Whenever I met with Professor Mercurio about his research, his benefactor was there. I found it odd as well. At times uncomfortable. But the purpose of the meetings was always to talk about the professor's ideas. I've been very enthusiastic about his work, as you both know better than anyone."

I leaned forward. "Did it not strike you as inappropriate to have a Russian oligarch in your meetings?"

She clasped her hands. "The man was funding important research at Princeton. He had never given me a penny. He never asked for anything, and I never asked *him* for anything. He just listened and posed questions along the way."

My polite smile wavered. A couple years back, the Russian mogul had told me his modus operandi was to collect dirt on everyone, then use it to get what he wanted. So the president likely had had no choice but to meet with him. But the career prosecutor had carefully choreographed their meetings so she could account for them later. And with Kazarov now dead, there was no way to prove this or the true nature of their conversations.

As if reading my mind, the president lowered her eyes and sighed. "I just learned that he succumbed to the cancer he had fought so valiantly. I can only hope that someone else will step in to support the professor's important research."

I pulled us back on topic. "Madam President, did Mr. Kazarov ever imply that Congress would change hands so you could enact your reforms?"

She chose her words carefully.

"He was an optimist. He often asked hypothetical questions based on that assumption. I'm more of a realist—less hopeful that I'll have an opportunity to enact those policies. But I answered his hypotheticals nonetheless."

Tracks covered yet again.

After a few seconds of uncomfortable silence, she leaned forward, narrowing her turquoise eyes.

"Jack, you do know I'm correct on the policy, right? If we don't do something about the monopolies eating away at our economy, we won't only stifle our economy, we may lose our democracy."

It was a jarring pivot, as if she were asking for my help.

I chuckled nervously, raising both hands. "You don't have to convince me. I got fired trying to explain your plan to Republic's viewers."

Her left eyebrow arched as she grinned. "See? That proves my point perfectly."

"But that also makes clear that the big boys aren't ever going to let you make your case, let alone enact your ideas."

She stiffened.

"They'll keep trying to stop me—"

She paused, her right eyelid fluttering.

"—but politics is a crazy game. You never know what's going to happen."

An awkward silence followed as I studied her face. Had I just seen a harmless blink or a loaded wink?

She turned to Cassie. "Now, I understand you have questions about my little getaway in the mountains."

"I do, Madam President." Cassie spoke quickly, clearly nervous. "How can you defend the policy of keeping visitors to the ranch secret?"

The president rolled forward in her chair, eyes gleaming.

"Cassie, you know what? I can't."

Cassie did a double take.

"You can't?"

"No, I can't. Your interview request challenged me to examine what we've been doing. None of our excuses pass muster. So I will be making an announcement next week."

"Don't tell me—"

"Every Aspen visitor will be reported going forward."

"No exceptions?" Cassie asked.

"None. Whether I'm meeting with the Turkish foreign minister or a big donor, Americans are entitled to know it. And you're going to get the credit."

"Republic is?" Cassie asked.

"No," said the president, "you."

CHAPTER 130

YOUNGSTOWN

E ven with my head throbbing, I tempered my tone as best I could. I respected Mary too much to yell.

"The entire explanation of what drove the plot has been cut out. What the hell?"

We were back in the *Vindicator* conference room one day after my interview with the president and three days before my story was scheduled to top the front page of twenty-eight newspapers around the country.

She frowned. "I know. We had to edit that part out."

"But *you* were the one who pushed me to find that all out. I almost got myself killed answering your questions—which, by the way, were the right ones."

"I know."

Her dancing pupils gave her away.

"It wasn't your decision, was it?"

"It wasn't."

"Let me guess," I said, memories of my final days at Republic pouring back. "Corporate nixed it."

She nodded.

"How does Corporate even review content like this?"

"Jack, this isn't the old paper. You know that. They review everything these days."

"So what did they say?"

"They love the story. They know it will sell. And they're ready to run it big everywhere and promote it big, too. Jack, with your arrangement, you're gonna make a mint out of this."

I wiped my forehead as she continued.

"They just want the motivation behind the plot edited out. As well as any mention of the president's anti-monopoly policy."

I studied her sullen eyes. Unlike Bridget Turner at Republic, at least she openly disagreed with corporate's demand. My guess was she'd fought back and lost. And in this new corporate model, her own job always on the line, she could take it only so far.

"So any discussion of monopoly and corporate power is out?"

"I'm afraid so."

"I wonder if it has anything to do with all the local newspapers they've been buying across the Midwest."

"Try the entire country, Jack. They're expanding aggressively. They're precisely the type of operation the president is targeting, and your story draws attention to all that."

I let out a deep breath, moving on.

"Mary, without this, the story is incomplete."

"We can make it work, Jack."

"'We'? Don't lump us into this, Mary. Corporate can make anything work, because they don't care about the actual facts. But you and I are professional journalists. It wouldn't be the whole story. We'd be knowingly manipulating the truth. If that's 'making it work,' I'm not interested."

I peered through the conference room window behind her, past the desks and chairs of the hollowed-out *Vindicator* newsroom, at the far wall where the front pages of my Abacus scoop from three years ago were framed. Despite the fanfare, I'd knowingly left key facts out of that story, and it had haunted me ever since.

I wasn't going to let it happen again.

"You're right," she said, close to a whisper. "It's a perfect story as is, but they've made their decision. This paper and the others have offered to run it with those edits. But, Jack, remember, you're a freelance writer now. You own the story, and you have the last word on whether to sell it. Of course, you'll be giving away a nice payday and the type of scoop that would make you relevant again."

I stood and walked toward the conference room door, my limbs leaden with disgust. The pounding in my temples felt just as it did in early July, in Republic's studio. I could still hear the producer's panicked voice in my earpiece, yelling at me to stop talking about the president's plan. I'd ignored him and lost everything.

Now I was being censored again.

"Just let us know what you decide," Mary said, still in her chair.

The way she phrased it struck me.

What you decide.

One thing was wholly different from my last day at Republic.

This was my story. My decision. Not theirs.

I had been ducking the freelance label for a month. But in this age of corporate power and corporate media, it put me in the most powerful position possible: on my own.

Unlike Mary, and unlike Cassie, no agreements hung over my head. And I had little left to lose.

I controlled everything.

And unlike three years ago, I could stand on principle—on the integrity of the story. The whole truth or nothing at all. If they didn't want that, screw 'em.

"Oh, I've decided," I said as I stepped through the doorway. "You can tell Corporate I'm keeping my story."

Mary picked up her phone as I shut the door behind me.

I trudged through the empty newsroom, walked down the lobby, and stepped into the elevator.

As it descended, I began making a mental list of where else I might shop the story. No major national paper like the *Times* or the *Post* would deign to run a freelance story. I couldn't appear on the networks because of my non-compete. So I'd have to find a smaller independent paper with some level of national credibility. But there weren't many of those left, and they certainly wouldn't pay much.

Still, I'd have to try. The story had to get out.

The elevator opened on the ground floor. I walked out the building's back door and into the parking lot, still thinking. The most likely papers would be in states where meddling was also happening, offering a natural hook for the story. I'd check with Milwaukee. Or Detroit. Or Pittsburgh. Maybe the *Tampa Bay Times*.

As I approached my Escape, my phone rang.

Mary, one more time.

"Jack? Are you still here?"

"Not for long."

I took my keys out of my pocket.

"Turn around."

"Mary, I've made my decision."

"So have they. And you won. They still want the story. The whole thing."

CHAPTER 131

GENEVA-ON-THE-LAKE, OHIO

Rain poured across the lake for the third straight day.

But just after sunrise on this second Wednesday in November, the clouds were breaking up off to the west. As the sun rose, rays of light beamed down through the gaps, shooting diagonally from the clouds into the choppy water.

Sitting in Dad's old chair, I relaxed, rocking back and forth, savoring each sip of black coffee.

I hadn't written a story in a month. But the voter file scoop alone had generated enough revenue to keep me comfortable for the rest of the year. Running on the Sunday front page of newspapers across the country, the story had whipped up a nationwide frenzy, opening every network news cast that evening. Days of cable television discussion followed, focusing on the parties' voter files, their security, and the stunning attempt to meddle in American elections for the second time in four years. The president decried the plot, and both parties claimed they had located and shut down the backdoors that had been built into their voter files. Politicians of both parties on Capitol Hill demanded hearings, scheduling them for after the election.

In the story, I had leaned hard into the concentration of corporate power, which led to a second and equally robust national debate. Independent newspapers, politicians, and activists advocated that the president's plan move forward regardless of the plot and that Congress do something about the problem. And Professor Mercurio had taken his star turn, appearing on numerous national networks, inevitably hawking copies of his book, which shot to the top of the nonfiction bestseller lists.

But, like everything in American politics, the hype died down after a week. The plot foiled, the capital and its press corps soon moved on to the next topic du jour, and campaigns returned to the thirty-second ads and personal attacks that dominate the airwaves in the final months of an election year.

Poor Cassie. After a few weeks in the limelight, she, too, was back to covering the hamster wheel of Washington politics. At least her scoop had earned her credibility and better treatment at Republic—although they'd shut down her attempt to renegotiate her contract. She was stuck for another year.

For me, things had settled down just as quickly, except for the occasional paranoia that someone was following me.

Last night had been my first election night in years without an assignment, either on the air or in the newsroom. With no expectation of drama, I'd turned in early. Up at the crack of dawn as usual, I picked up some donuts and coffee at Dunkin' Donuts in town, where I also bought a *Cleveland Plain Dealer*—the pint-sized version of the paper I still wasn't used to but the new owner insisted on to save productions costs.

Back at the cabin, I sipped my coffee while glancing at the predictable main headline.

After Nasty Mid-Term, Speaker Paxton Nets Four House Seats

In the story, the president expressed disappointment about the outcome but committed to work with the Speaker. The truth was, the next two years promised nothing but rancor as she sought reelection, and her agenda would remain dormant the entire time. At the same time, it was not as strong an outcome as the Speaker would've hoped for. A ho-hum election indeed.

I was flipping the folded paper over to the bottom of the front page, when the phone rang. Tori calling from Appleton. She'd spent weeks in Waterloo, bored stiff as she helped her dad get back to full strength. And now she was hustling to earn her degree a semester early. After my story hit, word had gotten out of her digital wizardry, so she was fielding offers for top jobs across Washington.

While we talked every few days, it was around 6:00 her time. Earlier than she'd ever called.

"Jack, did you see the results from yesterday?"

"I was just looking at them. Sort of a mixed bag."

"Jack! Read the whole paper."

As she said the words, the headline at the bottom of the page caught my eye.

Ohio House Flips in Wake of Upsets

"Remember Kovak in Marblehead and Seitz in Cincinnati?" she asked.

"Of course," I said as I scanned the details of upsets all over the state.

"They both lost!"

I jolted up, knocking my cup off the chair's handle and onto the floor, splashing coffee everywhere, including on my sweatpants.

"Don't tell me this also hap—"

"You guessed it. There were similar upsets in about a dozen states around the country. Votes are still being counted in some close ones, but it looks like the majority may have flipped in at least eight to ten statehouses, maybe more."

"Did you look into where the losses happened?"

"Not completely, but a good many of them were right where you'd expect them."

My mind spun, digging for explanations.

"Jack, the paper here is attributing it to great recruiting by the Democrats and the party's advanced use of data. They're also speculating that the late focus on the monopoly issue and districting motivated far more Democrats than usual to show up and vote in those statehouse races."

I shook my head. That was the analysis the *Plain Dealer* story was presenting as well. The news was truly the same everywhere.

"Do you believe that, Jack?"

I looked up. The break in the clouds had now shifted halfway across the sky, a blanket of sunlight turning the water beneath it a stunning crystal blue.

"Jack?"

"Not for a second."

EPILOGUE

BROOKLYN

Michael Molotov rapped the fingers of his left hand against the table, watching as the dark skeletons tattooed above his knuckles danced up and down. He was sitting in the back room of the small restaurant, the morning office where he'd conducted breakfast meetings for ten years. Next to a bowl of porridge, a small plate sat to his right. Using his fingers, he lifted the thin blin from the top of the small stack, folded it, dipped it in a small bowl of honey, and took the first bite.

"Did you release him?" Molotov asked as he chewed.

"Yes. We dropped him off in one of Baltimore's worst neighborhoods," John Kozlov said. "Shaken and bruised, but healthy."

"And he knows we're watching?" Molotov asked.

"He does. He won't say a word. He's made enough enemies in Baltimore; the story we gave him should suffice."

Kozlov scratched his head, his thick gray hair hardly budging as he did. "I'm still confused by it all."

Molotov dipped the remaining half of the blin back into the honey.

"By what?"

"All of it. Taking the councilman and now releasing him. Flying me down to D.C. to talk to the reporter, telling her the truth about your parents. All the new travel."

"It was time to get on the inside of a much bigger enterprise."

"What do you mean? You're the king of Brooklyn. No one's been able to touch you for years."

Molotov stared straight ahead, ignoring the ex-detective's inanity.

"No man should convince a teenager to kill his own parents, whatever the reason. So it was long overdue anyway. But, looking forward, I am now positioned to exercise power far beyond Brooklyn."

"Is that why you flew to London a month ago?"

He nodded while downing his final bite, gesturing toward the television set. The chyron running below the talking heads summed up the day: "Speaker Gains House Seats."

"Indeed. Yesterday's elections were an overwhelming success. We're on our way."

ACKNOWLEDGMENTS

From my first email, in 2013, announcing that I had decided to write a novel, to publication of *The Voter File* in 2020, two people have read every chapter draft, every chapter revision, and every final draft, of all three books. And always wanted to read more. Mom and Dad, without your encouragement and support, none of these books would have happened.

At some point, I ventured out beyond my parents, learning from so many thoughtful critiques and perspectives along the way. Early readers were encouraging, while offering key insights on politics, writing, and journalism: Carson Miller. David Skolnick. Sherry Coolidge. Greg Landsman. Pete Metz. Jared Kamrass. My brothers, John and Doug, and my sister, Susie.

Then came countless other readers who provided support, encouragement, and perspective. Jennifer Granholm, Brendan Cull, Dennis Willard, Ted Strickland, Josh Galper, Jack Markell, JJ Balaban, Celinda Lake, Matt Waxman, Daniel Gotoff, Joe Rettof, David Betras, Greg Beswick, Colleen Lowry, Liz Shirey, Kevin Tighe, Tom Perez, Dick Rosenthal, Monica Detota, Jennie Berliant, Rachel Rossi, Sarah Celi, Laura McIntosh, Zack Space, Joe Fuld, Brian Wiles, Cindy Matthews, Scott Stern, Mallory McMaster, Daniel Tokaji, Debbie Bartling, Jerry Springer, Bill Bradley, Shawna Roberts, Taylor Myers, Andrea Canning. And many others.

Several pros weighed in at key moments early in my writing journey. Author Alex Berenson, a friend from college, pushed me to dive far more deeply into my characters than I initially had, critical advice as I developed Jack Sharpe and others. Later, another friend and writer, Daphne

Uviller, gave me needed direction, including introducing me to Alissa Davis, a passionate editor who provided first-rate guidance in finalizing the first two books. And Lauren Sharp was tremendously helpful in fine-tuning *The Wingman* into a strong sequel.

A number of people were instrumental in the development of *The Voter File*. A longtime friend, David Fierson, pushed me to aim higher with my books, for which I'll always be thankful. And I'm equally grateful to Theresa Park, who took David's suggestion and guided an unknown and still new writer through the crucial steps of *how* to aim higher.

Then came Mark Tavani, of G. P. Putnam's Sons, who saw the potential in my work, and intuited from one read the same spirited response I've been receiving at book clubs all these years. But Mark challenged me as well—to go bigger and bolder in my coming stories. To raise the stakes. To make things more difficult for Jack and his colleagues. It was Mark's challenge that sparked the idea that grew into *The Voter File*.

Mitch Hoffman of the Aaron Priest Agency also took me under his wing, and provided wise guidance that converted the initial vision of *The Voter File* into the final manuscript.

And in Mark's good hands, along with the vision and expertise of Ivan Held, Sally Kim, and Danielle Dieterich, the final story emerged. I also must thank everyone in sales, promotion, and the art department at G. P. Putnam's Sons for their support, especially designer Eric Fuentecilla.

Back home, I'm also indebted to the dozens of book clubs that welcomed me into homes, coffee shops, workplaces, churches, and synagogues to talk through both books. That was where I first experienced the magic of having strangers read, discuss, and actually enjoy something you've written. There's nothing quite like hearing insights about your work that you've never thought of, all while you're still questioning: "Did you really like the book?" And just as rewarding, these book clubs have served as a good reminder that even in our divided political world, people of all viewpoints can come together and discuss our deepest political challenges civilly. Somehow, when a book kicks off the conversation, and it's face-to-face, thoughtful conversations can follow without the rancor of cable news and social media.

The Cincinnati Mercantile Library, the Hamilton County Library, the Cuyahoga County Library, and numerous local bookstores around Ohio, also generously provided for a local, first-time author to begin his trek in writing.

Finally, I owe eternal thanks and love to my wife, Alana, and my sons, Jack (six) and Charlie (three), for their love and support along the way. The 6 a.m. chapter. The 10 p.m. chapter. The chapter during nap time. Scribbling notes at 2 a.m. after a middle-of the night dream fixed a problem in the plotline. Reading phrases out loud to make sure they made sense. Asking Alana for good name suggestions (Tori Justice being one), or to smile for a few seconds so I could describe her perfect smile for a critical moment in the plot.

Alana has supported me through all of it, even at the outset, fresh off our honeymoon, when I told her, out of the blue, that I thought I'd like to try my hand at fiction.

What a journey!